The
Alone
Alternative

Linda MacDonald

Matador
9 Priory Business Park,
Wistow Road, Kibworth Beauchamp,
Leicestershire. LE8 0RX
Tel: (+44) 116 279 2299
Fax: (+44) 116 279 2277
Email: books@troubador.co.uk
Web: www.troubador.co.uk/matador

ISBN 978 1783064 335

British Library Cataloguing in Publication Data.
A catalogue record for this book is available from the British Library.

Typeset in Aldine401 BT Roman by Troubador Publishing Ltd, Leicester, UK
Printed and bound in the UK by TJ International, Padstow, Cornwall

Matador is an imprint of Troubador Publishing Ltd

To Alain
a special friend through the dark days

Acknowledgements

As I contemplate the end of the *Lydia* series of novels, I find I am conscious of how the trilogy came into being; how the past shapes the future and how a moment of impulse set about a chain of events that led to the first book being written.

Brian Hurn has been tireless in his support for the whole project and I should like to thank him once again for critical comments on the early drafts and for subsequent editing. Grateful thanks also to Ingo Herrmann for insights and eagle-eyed editing of a later draft, and to Pat Hewitson, Rowena Pavlou and my sister-in-law Lindsey MacDonald who acted as Beta readers and plot advisers. I am indebted to Kit Domino for her professional editorial expertise on the final draft and for her patience in dealing with numerous questions. The team at Troubador has once again provided excellent service and support, especially Amy Cooke, Rachel Gregory and Rosie Grindrod.

I should also like to thank several people who have helped with research queries and other matters: Robert Bewley, Andrew MacDonald, Modjeh Shirazi, Tina Tapster and Helen Trebble. I am especially grateful to Rosemary England for assistance in conducting research in Broadclyst, and to the villagers who made me feel most welcome.

Author's Note

The University of Devon, Stancliffe University in London and North Kent College are fictional institutions at the time of writing. The characters are fictitious with the exception of Pam and Julian Beresford-Smith of the Parsonage, St Agnes, Isles of Scilly.

L.M.

Prologue

April 2011

The Deer Orchard, Broadclyst, Devon

'There is no easy way to say this, Ted,' says Felicity. 'But I'm leaving. I'm going to Italy. I'm selling the Retreat and we're taking over a restaurant in Siena.'

'We?'

'I'm going with Gianni. It's his parents' place. They're retiring. I know he's a few years younger than me, but these things happen. You must've known.'

He didn't.

Until this moment, it seemed to Edward to be a normal evening: supper eaten, dishwasher filled, animals settled. He was about to retire to his office to do some work on his latest paper about the archaeology of St Martin's, Isles of Scilly. Instead he sits down again at the kitchen table, lost for words; stunned. If she had said she was running away with Brad Pitt, he couldn't have been more surprised. Gianni … He'd been so focused on watching her every move with Rick Rissington, the gardener, he hadn't paid any attention to Gianni, the chef. And of course with him living in a flat above her restaurant … It is so obvious now she mentions it. What a complete idiot he has been.

Felicity is standing by the double hob, a safe distance in their enormous extended kitchen. 'I don't want a fuss, Ted. You can stay here. The Deer Orchard's all yours. I'll just take the proceeds from the Retreat, and my own money.'

'Very generous, I'm sure.'

'It's a fair deal, give or take. And Chris is coming with us.'

He registers pain. 'No.' His youngest son is only sixteen. 'Don't take Chris away from me too.'

'Yes, Ted. Not negotiable. He wants to go into either food production or catering so it will be perfect for him. His choice.'

'He knows? Before me?'

'Ted, don't kid yourself that you care. We've been drifting since Mummy died. It's not going to happen now.'

'I've tried.'

'You've never been interested in the restaurant; never wanted to be involved. Gianni's been there for me when you've been buried in your mazes and your research and what-not. And those years you were in London, he was a sounding board and a great support.'

'You never said you minded me being away.'

'You never gave me an opportunity to mind, if you remember.'

'I came back.'

'Too late.'

'So this is it? A fait accompli?'

'Pretty much.'

'There's nothing I can do or say that will make you change your mind?'

'I'll speak to the girls and James. Harriet will keep an eye on you for the time being. The divorce shouldn't be a problem, irretrievable breakdown and so forth. I'm sure you won't want to drag Gianni into it. But there's no rush. We can deal with that at a later date.'

She says all this in her usual commanding tone and Edward knows it isn't worth a fight. But it doesn't stop him from being shocked and a mix of emotions jostle as he tries to retain composure. He is angry with her for cheating on him, furious with himself for not noticing and above all, hurt, sad and confused. They have been married for thirty years, have four children, made a life and a home – the usual. They were happy until Felicity's inheritance, seven years ago. Seven years of trying to make it work against a tide of impossibility.

Now, seven wasted years.

1

March 2012

Fanclub

'You should contact Fanclub,' says daughter Harriet.

Fanclub! There's a name Edward hasn't heard in a while. He pauses by the stile at the bottom of the paddock, scanning the wide expanse of crop fields, a shimmering green and brown chequerboard in the early morning sunshine. Meg, the Border collie, is taking them both for a walk before they go their separate ways to work.

Harriet continues, 'You never properly explained why you lost touch with her anyway. Did you fall out? Is it irreparable? She may be able to give you some of her psychological advice to get you back on track.'

'And how exactly am I not "on track"?' Edward thinks he knows the answer, but wants to hear Harriet's opinion; to see how well his penultimate and now twenty-three year old offspring knows the workings of his midlife mind.

They climb the stile and set off down the narrow lane that borders the Molwings' land, Meg trotting ahead of them, stopping every minute or so to turn and check they are still following, diving into the grassy verge when she catches scent of something interesting. A mist is floating above the distant fields giving the landscape the appearance of a watercolour painting with the diffused and blended colours of wet on wet technique.

'Oh Dad, you lack purpose. Yes, you work and write like

you always did, you hop on a train to give the odd lecture around the country, but you go through the motions like a robot. You lack drive, your old ambition. You seem content to drift towards retirement. And then what? What's happened to dreams of that TV programme you were going to do about sustainability and the Isles of Scilly?'

'The idea was never taken up by Patrick's contact at the BBC.'

'But you could try to regenerate interest. It's not like you to give up. Write the book. It's even more valid now than it was five years ago. Even I'm starting to worry about food prices and whether there'll be enough for the next generation.'

'The book is a possibility, but it isn't only my idea. Patrick was part of it.'

'Then call him. Be proactive. You could produce the programme with an independent company and then approach the major networks. But it's not just your work that needs overhauling. You don't seem to enjoy yourself any more. It's nine months since Mum left and over a year since she said she was going. It's time you rediscovered the plot. You hardly ever go out. I mean, *"Out"* out. You're still young enough to live, even to love.'

'Harriet, please.'

'Even my old school friends thought you had charisma. And they used to say, "Your dad's quite good-looking, isn't he?" Of course, I couldn't see it myself. But there's no chance if you don't get yourself sorted and liven up. I know you used to listen to Fanclub. I know she used to try to help you when Mum was being difficult.'

'And much good that did.' This wasn't strictly true because even though Marianne's advice didn't save his marriage, it helped him to understand what was going on and to employ strategies that were less confrontational. For a second he hears her words from the *Taoist* philosophers, about flowing like water round a boulder, and his heart does that indefinable thing whenever he remembers.

'Once Mum sets her heart on something, she doesn't waver. I've learnt that. It wasn't your fault that she left.'

'I could have joined in with her schemes, shown more interest, been more supportive.'

'You have taught me that you have to be true to yourself. If you had joined in, it wouldn't have lasted and you would've been the one to feel resentful. You didn't have time to be more involved.'

'I should have stood up to her when she started doing things behind my back. At least I could have been part of the decision-making process, even if not the practical support.'

'Easy to say in hindsight. I think you would have ended up arguing more. And none of us suspected her and Gianni. I thought he fancied Rachel.'

'And I thought she fancied Rick. What with his reputation.'

'Rick's changed.' Harriet flushes slightly. 'The rumours are ancient history. Why not call Fanclub or send her an email?'

Despite the fact that Harriet is now a young woman, she still refers to Marianne as Fanclub, the nickname from a time when she and sister Rachel were silly teenagers and thought Marianne Hayward, erstwhile classmate of Edward when aged about ten, had once had a crush on him.

'It's complicated.'

This is an understatement. Since Felicity left, he often thinks about Marianne. Five years of regretting his decision to break contact after three years of midweek lodging with her and her husband in Beckenham. This was when he was in charge of the archaeology department at Stancliffe University in London; when he was still climbing rungs and still ambitious. But he does not know how to undo it, especially after so long. They should have remained friends.

He has her old address, email, landline, mobile, any one of which might open the door again. But he can't intrude because his life has changed, because he is lonely, because he misses her. There is still her husband, Johnny. They had been unquestionably happy. Edward was a potential spanner. His existence had been a complication to Marianne, albeit subtly, and her warm and loving relationship with Johnny had become impossible for him to observe, especially as his own marriage was slipping into the mire.

And he can't bear to hurt her again.

'In any case, I *am* going out. I'm seeing Jessica on Wednesday evening.'

'Jessica Hennessy? The witch?'

'I detect disapproval.'

Harriet gives him one of her role-reversal sideways stares. Since Felicity left, it often seems that she is playing the parent and him the child. She has become quite a nag. In some ways he hopes she will find a husband soon and settle down in separate accommodation. But she appears to play the field, never staying with a boyfriend for more than a few months. At the moment he isn't aware of anyone in her life. He thinks she probably frightens them away with her acerbic nature. She isn't bad-looking, just a little scary with her dyed black hair, pale complexion and several piercings in her ears. At least she ditched the one in her nose when she took up teaching. If she leaves the Deer Orchard, he will be even more alone.

He offers some justification. 'Jessica makes a good stew. And it's not a date. But it is *"Out"*. She wants to know about planning permissions for a wind turbine. Not as big as ours, of course. That was your mum's extravagant madness. But Jessica suggested having a chat over a meal, and I said it would be my treat because of all the food she brings me when you are at your evening class—'

'It's a date, Dad. That's how she will see it. You really have no idea how women think.'

'I'll make my position clear, if required.' This is easier said than executed, but Harriet doesn't need to know that.

It is early spring and an exceptionally warm one. Such a beautiful time in Broadclyst and a poignant time for Edward. It was Felicity's favourite time, her seed-sowing time. He walks briskly in thoughtful silence with Harriet tagging along like she did as a child, finding it hard to keep up.

He thinks about what she said, about living and loving, and about Marianne. He is bereft of intimate female company. Perhaps this is why he has accepted Jessica's suggestion for a meal instead of merely talking through the issues over the phone. But Jessica isn't Marianne and he hasn't considered her as a romantic prospect. Indeed, he hasn't contemplated that anyone might want to start a relationship with a fifty-five year old man, scarred down his cheek and on his hand, wrist and chest from a mugging attack some eight years earlier; separated but not yet divorced and with a twenty-something daughter still in tow. He has more than enough baggage to sink a relationship before it has a chance to gather momentum. Marianne is different because she knows him. He has lived with her, albeit platonically and part-time. They know at least some of each other's ways and foibles. And she knew him when he was ten years younger. He remembers her once saying to him that scars can be quite attractive on good-looking men. But the problem with Marianne is that she is happily married.

Marianne …

How wonderful it would be to hear her voice again, her laugh again. She might hate him for leaving as he did. She might not forgive him. Not this time. Not like after the Taryn incident. And that took a while. Much may have changed in the five years since he's seen her. They are both drifting into

5

the late summer of their lives: the September, the chill of the approaching autumn, the nuts and berries on the trees.

'*Season of mists and mellow fruitfulness,*' he thinks. *It could be bountiful. A last chance to gather provisions before the winter cold sets in.*

He could phone her – assuming she is at the same number. But that would be such an intrusion, such a shock after all this time. An email would give her the choice of whether or not to reply, but might still be unwelcome. He wonders whether she is on Twitter or Facebook. He is on neither, averse to social-networking since his first forays with Friends Reunited. Once bitten … And he can't see the point of spending so much time idly talking about nothing in particular. He is too busy with work.

Yet it might be a door to Marianne again; to friendship again. He would settle for that now. And Twitter is less intrusive than email. He can imagine her tweeting. She likes to converse in pithy one-liners, linking to a blog, perhaps. She loved to write. He wonders if she ever finished her novel. He has been advised by his publisher to set up a Twitter account to use as a marketing tool to help spread the word about his books and guest lectures, but he has never got round to it.

After the walk, he lets the three buff Orpington hens out of their palatial night-time accommodation in the paddock, collects a couple of eggs and loads the dishwasher.

'Let me know if you can find Marianne Hayward on Twitter,' he says to Harriet before she leaves for work. It's a move in a direction that he never thought he would make. It is words that set his heart beating like the wings of a yellowhammer.

6

2

March 2012

Beckenham, Kent

Johnny

Through the window Marianne sees police uniforms: a man and a woman coming down the path to the door. It is late afternoon and she is wearing a blue dress patterned with pink roses, and a pink cardigan. Johnny likes this dress. Says it is his favourite; says it makes her look young – sure to bring a smile now she is fifty-four. He will be home soon, won't he? They will be able to have a cosy Sunday night in front of the TV after they've eaten the roasted free-range organic chicken. He has been away since the previous morning, walking part of the Jurassic coast in Dorset, as he often does. He will be hungry.

Police? Why? An anxious tremor. The bell rings and she opens the door, knowing straight away; knowing it isn't daughter Holly because they were speaking on the phone only minutes earlier. And it isn't her parents because they are already dead; her dad the year before, and her mum the year before that. If it was her brother Louis, the message would come via his wife or grown-up children. Even the one remaining tabby cat is on the rug in front of the electric fire. So it has to be Johnny.

A silent scream; a prickling of the skin.

The police follow her inside, suggest she sits down, say that they have bad news. It is the woman who speaks, small of stature, hard face, brassy blonde hair screwed into a tight bun below her hat.

Marianne perches on the edge of an armchair, her stomach already churning, her throat tightening, preparing for the worst.

They say it was a massive heart attack and by the time Johnny was found, all attempts at resuscitation failed. She looks at them with unbelieving eyes. It can't be true. Not Johnny who is fit and healthy and an expert on diet. But somewhere she remembers him saying that his family didn't make old bones. His parents died when Holly was small, when in their fifties. And there have been years of him drinking too much when he was young, and again when they had their crisis.

And that was a year ago. She can still hear the sound of her anguish after the police had gone. It has been a year of numbness and tears and waking up wondering how she could face another day without him. At first it was as if a cannon ball was lodged underneath her ribcage and she went through the motions of day-to-day existence, her spirit disconnected on another plane. She stayed off work only long enough to deal with practical issues.

'Take more time,' said the Principal.

But she didn't want more time, she wanted distraction. She was claustrophobic in the house, staring at the walls all day. Going back to work was the best thing. No time to brood when there's teaching to be done.

And she worked as she had always worked: efficiently. She was still at North Kent Sixth-Form College on the edge of Beckenham, still teaching psychology. There, she had the support of friends and colleagues and files of well-prepared resources, and although her students mentioned that she had lost something of her humour, she delivered the lessons with professional skill. She coped.

Coped. Such a loaded word. Coped … managed … survived. But it wasn't life. She didn't live. And at the end of most days, after the students had left, she worked on at the college until the premises officer came jangling his keys a few minutes before six. The longer she stayed away from home, the longer she could pretend that everything was as it always had been and that Johnny would be waiting for her, supper started, an evening of togetherness in prospect. Then she came back to Beechview Close and to emptiness and memories. She closed her door on the world, collapsing into self-pity and grief, tears flowing. She willed herself to prepare food and then had to force herself to eat it.

Sometimes she sat at the kitchen table looking at the empty chair, Johnny's chair, and the vacant space which she frequently laid because she wasn't thinking. And she would tell this vacant space about her day, talking out loud as if to Johnny, hearing his answers, his advice, knowing him so well. Occasionally she even had a heated discussion on an educational matter about which she knew they would have divergent opinions, imagining his attempts to convince with rational, logical, research-based arguments: *Mari, periods of exposition should not exceed fifteen to twenty minutes for sixteen to eighteen year olds. You know they have limited concentration span.* She always argued that if the exposition was interactive, with plenty of student input, this rule could be broken.

At other times she would sit in his place instead of hers, looking at the emptiness of her chair and wondering how he would have managed if the positions had been reversed. And when she couldn't stand it any longer, she took her meal into the living room and collapsed into the armchair in front of the television: Johnny's chair. It was easier sitting in it than staring at it, empty. And she would watch some mid-evening mindless rubbish on the TV, and hear his voice, castigating. He had been like that over some of her reading choices too. At the time, his intellectual snobbery infuriated her but now she would give anything to have him cast a disapproving glance at one of her paperbacks. She used to hide them under the sofa or behind cushions – like Lydia Languish in *The Rivals*.

Lydia …

As always when she thinks of Lydia, she remembers Edward … Edward Harvey. If he were here, still lodging, she would at least be less lonely during the working week. But he isn't here and it is no use wishing. In any case, if he had still been lodging when it happened, he might have left due to matters of propriety: a married man alone with a grieving widow. His wife probably would have objected.

After he left, the past few years battered her with one personal tragedy after another like a ten-pin bowl let rip among skittles. Her mother broke her hip in a fall and, disinclined to bear the pain and the rehabilitation, gave up the will to carry on. Her father's pleas were unable to bring back the light to her eyes and she faded away, weeks after the operation. Afterwards he told Marianne that he suspected the beginnings of dementia; that Daphine knew the future was an ever-darkening tunnel towards confusion. And Daphine had always been full of anecdote and conversation. To lose her mind had been one of her greatest fears. Perhaps she saw the hip problem as a way out before the inevitable decline.

And after she died, her father was grief-stricken. Marianne and Johnny suggested he came down to live with them. With Holly gone and Edward no longer lodging, there was plenty of space.

Her father said, 'I don't know anyone in Beckenham and I'm too old to start again. I love Cumbria and Allonby and the sea. The community will keep an eye on me.'

But as often happens with men, he was a lost soul and a year later, he had a fatal stroke. Marianne had been stoical, knowing that her father was cast adrift without his lifetime anchor.

So in many ways she was stronger for these difficulties, but those who knew her well detected brittleness in her emotional responses that had not been there before. Losing Johnny almost took her over the edge. She was unprepared. You don't expect to say goodbye to someone in the morning and then find they don't come home, that you never see them again, never hear their voice, or feel their touch or see their smile.

He was close to Lulworth Cove when it happened, such a beautiful spot, high on the edge of the cliff. She wondered if he had time or capability to shout to anyone who might have been sightseeing. He hadn't used his phone. If it had happened closer to home, things could have been done.

She tormented herself with alternative outcomes. Had he been aware of something wrong during the preceding weeks? She doesn't remember him mentioning any unfamiliar pains. If only he'd been to the doctor for a check-up. Thinking back, he had been stressed at work, a colleague unable to control classes, complaints from parents. *'She called my son stupid. He is not stupid. Naughty sometimes, but not stupid.'* A misplaced word and a heap of trouble. Johnny was a diplomat – he saw both sides and tried to diffuse the situation. It played on his mind.

And there was the never-ending string of new initiatives from the senior management team in preparation for a looming Ofsted inspection. Document upon document, sheet upon sheet, to read and attempt to implement. Every time Ofsted came the goalposts moved. She knew what it was like. What had once been *Good* was now *Satisfactory*. To achieve *Outstanding* seemed almost impossible. Even thinking about it brought her out in a sweat. She wondered how much sickness, how many deaths, were directly or indirectly the result of Ofsted inspections. As if teaching wasn't stressful enough. But Johnny hadn't looked ill. A bit tired, perhaps, but not so ill as to have a fatal heart attack. Marianne picked over the possibilities, trying to find an explanation, analysing the minutiae like she always did about everything. She tried to rationalise, but it wouldn't change the outcome. He wasn't coming home.

She hadn't said all the things you would like to say to someone if you knew they were going to die. She hadn't told him enough of her love, her gratitude, her delight in sharing her adult life with him. So the guilt set in and she tells him now, hoping he can hear; that he knows. She isn't sure; she has uncertain faith.

She and Holly had visited the spot in the summer holidays. They agreed that it was a most beautiful place for it to happen with the horseshoe cove below and Durdle Door not far beyond. It had been his favourite walk, monitoring the annual changes to the geology as the tide battered and encroached and reclaimed. They came down from the cliff top and threw white lilies in the foaming blue sea. They sat on rocks and stared out into the Channel. They wept and then laughed, sharing memories of the handsome Johnny with his sweet smile and luxuriant hair.

Her friends said she would come to appreciate the fact that it was quick and that watching someone suffer was never preferable. She knew they were right, but it wasn't something she wanted to be told.

She hasn't reached that stage, even yet, one year on. The little quirks are what she misses most, the things she knew so well. He was a creature of habit, was Johnny.

She went to identify the body.

The body. Not *his* body.

No longer Johnny. No longer a laughing animated soul. She had looked around, expecting him to be at her shoulder, wanting to feel his presence; something to help her through the next few weeks. But she felt nothing. It was as if she were surrounded by a vacuum. Indeed, she was puzzled to feel less of a presence than when he was at work or away. Perhaps that in itself should have been significant.

She was too shocked to cry much during the first few days. She operated like an automaton, following instructions, accepting help, busy making arrangements, keeping strong for Holly who was more resilient than expected.

Jeff Grimwade from work had been attentive, but she was uncomfortable in spending too much time with him or letting him see her complete vulnerability. She knew he liked her, maybe even fancied her, but she didn't want him to hold out any hope that she might one day feel the same.

She wished it had been Edward. If Edward had still been at Beechview Close, he would have been the supporting rock she needed. After three years of living with them midweek, he had seen her at her worst when she was ill. He had seen her underwear on the washing line and her just-risen face, devoid of make-up. She had nothing to hide from him. With Jeff, she had to tidy up before he arrived, not because she was trying to impress him, but because she didn't want him gossiping to their colleagues that she was in a complete mess.

She often wonders what Edward is doing now. Whether he and Felicity are properly reconciled and living the Good Life as a harmonious team. She never thought to tell him about Johnny, deducing that as it had been his decision to break contact, it would be inappropriate to intrude again, and unfair to invade his life at such an emotional time. It would have been like blackmailing him to get in touch, knowing he couldn't ignore her in grief.

Lydia ... The name still haunts her as it always did.

After she and Holly had been to Lulworth Cove, she had a strong, almost insistent feeling that she should do something with the novel she had written about meeting Lydia. It was as if Johnny was telling her to dust off the pages and make things happen. He gave good advice, did Johnny. She listened. She called an independent publishing company and set the wheels in motion. There was much editing and then copy-editing before she was satisfied. She bought in some outside help. After the typesetting, there were the proofs to check. She hasn't wasted the year. Not at a professional level. But her heart and soul have existed, not thrived, and only now, soon after the anniversary, has she decided it is time to stop the crying and move on.

3

Jessica

Two weeks after Felicity departed for Italy, Edward arrives home from work and wonders what he is going to eat. It's not as if he can't cook, but mostly he doesn't. For virtually all of the past seven years, he has been fed when in Broadclyst with Felicity's and Gianni's restaurant menu experiments or leftovers. When he came home after a busy day at the university, or returned late at night from a visiting lecture, there was nearly always something waiting in the fridge or in the oven. He may not have had his own choices catered for, but the food was interesting, varied and effortless, often with an accompanying sauce or jus or reduction that dazzled his taste buds. At most he had to turn on the microwave to have a hot meal, or at worst put together a sandwich from the mini delicatessen in their enormous fridge. And he did the shopping only under sufferance when Felicity was dealing with some animal crisis.

When he lodged with Marianne, it was a similar picture: either she or Johnny would cook and all he had to do was turn up, eat and look appreciative, even if it was one of Marianne's disasters.

So it is with some helplessness that he has been operating these past fourteen days since Felicity left, especially on the nights when Harriet is late or out and he is left to his own devices.

While he is looking in the fridge and contemplating that an aubergine and some mince might make moussaka – but he can't remember how and Felicity has taken all the cookery books – there is a knock at the door. Imagine the delight of the hungry archaeologist when he spies his nearest neighbour Jessica Hennessy, holding a casserole dish covered with a blue checked tea towel.

'It's just as easy cooking for two as one,' she says. 'I know how busy you are. I know Harriet goes to her evening class on Thursdays. I thought you might like some Lancashire hotpot.'

'I certainly do like,' says Edward, beaming gratefully. 'An answer to a prayer.' It does not cross his mind that in order to know about Harriet's manoeuvres Jessica has acquired a somewhat intimate knowledge of his family circumstances, especially considering she is a person on whom he has hardly bestowed more than a nod and a greeting since she moved to the village a few years earlier.

The hotpot was delicious. Edward left the washed dish on her doorstep with a message of thanks and since then, most term-time Thursdays, he finds a pie or a stew in one of the outbuildings and a Post-it note of instructions through the letterbox. Occasionally she calls with something when he is at home but he rarely invites her in. Considering his experience in dealing with the wiles of women at work, it is surprising he doesn't suspect her of ulterior motives. He hasn't yet internalised his new status of 'available man' and is unaware that the barrier that has protected him for thirty years has now been removed. Of course, vixen Taryn found a way through the barrier, but it was his choice at the time: his one and only transgression. He could have said no on the grounds of unavailability – as he subsequently did.

So now he finds himself in a pickle. He says it is a meeting about sustainable energy devices and planning regulations. Harriet says it is a date. Either way he is taking a woman to a restaurant for the first time in quite a while and he is distinctly anxious.

Jessica is one of two women in the village whom Harriet refers to as The Witches of Broadclyst. The other is Felicity's friend Olivia, now ex-wife of Alexander, since he finally came clean about his dalliance with one of the women working at

Killerton House and is now exiled to Silverton, where he lives with his mistress in her small wisteria-covered cottage. Jessica and Olivia frequent the local eateries where they are known to bitch about their exes, and any single woman who might bar the way to them finding a replacement.

Jessica is his closest neighbour, about fifty yards further down the lane in the direction of the village. Logic would suggest he pick her up on the way to the restaurant, but he considered this might make it look more like a date and told her that he had to collect some chicken feed first and would meet her there.

The Retreat is Felicity's old restaurant, a white-painted building located by the main road and known for its relaxed bistro style and cosmopolitan food. It is currently being run by a middle-aged couple from Hampshire. The Knotts have carried on Felicity's tradition of catering for dietary requirements, but they no longer put the ingredients on the menus as she did, preferring customers to state their preferences and tolerances when they make their booking.

Edward is shown to a table in the window by Kylie, his son James's former girlfriend. She is now in her mid twenties and has developed her communication skills sufficiently to be 'Front of House'. Indeed, she is very smartly dressed in a black tailored suit, far removed from the days when she waitressed for Felicity and had to be constantly reminded about too much flesh on display. She is now married to a local apple producer with whom she works in between shifts at the restaurant.

The window table is conspicuous to passers-by but Edward decides not to make a fuss, aware of the adage that it is the people tucked away in corners that attract the most attention. He orders a glass of apple juice while he waits and catches up on emails and text messages via his mobile.

Jessica is ten minutes late, by which time he is wondering –

and hoping – that she is not going to turn up. When she arrives she appears flustered. He notes the effort she has made with her appearance: freshly coiffed, fashionably short, golden-blonde hair, a smart cocktail dress and high heels. But this is not unusual as both the witches take trouble over their grooming. 'High maintenance', he calls it. He's not a fan. She is reasonably attractive, about ten years younger than him, hat-rack thin with cartoon curves and slightly popping eyes. He wonders, slightly curious, about silicone implants and an over-active thyroid. Harriet is convinced by the former. 'You can tell by the unnatural bounce,' she said. Edward had tried surreptitiously to see what she meant.

'Olivia gave me a lift and she was late,' says Jessica. 'I could have walked, but not in these heels. Forgive me if I just nip to the Ladies to powder my nose.'

She seems pleasant enough. To refer to her as a witch is perhaps unfair, as to him she has so far been very thoughtful. She is a widow, her husband having fallen down the stairs and broken his neck. He ran a private pest control business from a large shed shoehorned into their small back garden and Felicity had once used him to deal with some troublesome moles.

At the funeral, an unfamiliar twenty-something redhead had turned up in dark glasses, crying copious amounts of tears. Jessica had apparently stared at her coldly, knowingly. Villagers looked on, perhaps hoping for some drama to gossip about in the post office. But Jessica turned away, shed some tears of her own and was comforted by friends. Olivia whittled out of her that the redhead had been the husband's secretary in his former job in Exeter. She told Felicity that she suspected an affair – past or even ongoing. Felicity said to Edward, 'I wonder if Jessica knew about her before Ray died? According to Olivia, he was often drunk and violent. Rotten on three accounts; a complete bastard. She's better off without him.'

After the appearance of the redhead at the funeral, and the murmurings that dead-husband Ray sometimes used Jessica as a punch bag, there was talk that his death might not have been an accident after all. Village gossip. Tittle-tattle. But no one raised concerns at the inquest. Jessica's was all bug-eyed innocence and the verdict was 'misadventure'.

Edward and Jessica attract stares from a local family who are between courses. It is the first time he has been seen out in the village with another woman and there will be talk. As he has no ulterior motives, he isn't particularly bothered.

Over tomato bruschetta starters, they chat convivially enough about village matters and the economic crisis, leading into renewable energy, wind turbines, solar panels and Broadclyst's planning regulations which are unusual in that they require permission from the Killerton Estate in addition to the local council.

'This has saved me much Googling and many phone calls. I'm exceedingly grateful,' says Jessica, flashing her bright white teeth.

'Felicity did virtually all the paperwork for us,' says Edward, remembering her going behind his back to gain permissions without any thought to gauge his opinion.

Then over main courses of pasta – he with seafood, she with ragout – Jessica tells Edward about her life in Exeter before she and her husband moved to Broadclyst. Apparently she had worked in the office where he had been one of the partners of a major pest control company in the city. 'Once we married, Ray decided to branch out on his own. He said he didn't want a working wife and that he had money enough for both of us. His parents had recently died and left him their house. All he wanted was a tidy home, meals on the table and guests entertained. If anything didn't meet his exacting standards, he used to hit me.'

Edward shakes his head, shocked. Hearing it directly from the victim is surprisingly powerful. He is at a loss what to say that would adequately describe his abhorrence.

Jessica continues, 'When the neighbours started asking questions about the noise, he said we must move to somewhere detached. That's how we came to be here. I thought it would be a fresh start, but it didn't change anything. Olivia used to say I should leave, but by then, what would I do? I had become attached to the lifestyle.' She has a thick fringe under which she peers as she jabs her fork into her pasta and twirls it with skill.

Edward makes sympathetic noises. He has never hit a woman and even when Felicity was at her worst, he never imagined turning violent. He doesn't like to ask about the other woman at the funeral.

'It's lovely to be taken out by a man again,' Jessica says. 'And to find we have so much in common.' She touches her neck with a glossy crimson nail.

Edward is reminded of the events that led to his unfortunate night with Taryn. *Taken out?* Is that what she thinks this is? Perhaps Harriet is right. 'It's the least I can do after all the food you bring me.' He wonders where her interpretation of the event might lead, and if he should take steps to quell her obvious interest.

'I never went to university,' she says, suddenly, out of the blue.

Edward says, 'University isn't for everyone.'

'It would have been for me,' she says, bitterly. 'I had the potential to do so much more. Then I married a fool and it's too late now.'

'It is never too late for education,' says Edward. 'What would you like to do?'

'I'd like to show them that I won't be trampled on.'

'Who's "them"?' says Edward.

Jessica gives a weird little laugh and throws back her head. 'All of them at school who barred the way. The teachers who said I wasn't good enough, my dad for being discouraging, my husband who used my lack of a degree to wield his superiority and say that I was dim.'

Edward is uncomfortable with this turn in the conversation. If this is what *'Out'* out is going to be like, he would rather stay in. But no sooner is he wondering how to lighten the mood when she grins, laughs again, says, 'Don't mind me,' and normality is resumed.

Later, when he drives her back to her house on his way back to his, and she invites him in for coffee, he considers a range of excuses.

She adds, 'We're both free. Both mature adults. We can do what we please.' She drops her hand on his knee for a fleeting second.

It is dark and he can't see her expression. But he knows what this means. Interesting that underneath her quiet exterior, she is bold enough to take the initiative. She is quite sexy if you like lipstick and hairspray. In half an hour or so, after a few courteous preliminaries, he could be as colleague Conrad Vaughan might say, enjoying some action between the sheets. But despite so much abstinence, and although his one night stand with Taryn has given him confidence that it is possible to enjoy another body without any emotional connection, he does not fancy Jessica. Nor does he want any complications in a community where word is likely to spread.

'I can be discreet,' she says, as if reading his thoughts. 'Only Olivia knows I like you. She already thinks we have something going.'

If this is meant to reassure him, it does the opposite. 'Does she indeed?'

'I denied it, of course. But she knows I visit you with meals sometimes.'

Edward hasn't considered that anyone else might be party to Jessica's meals on *heels* service. If he wasn't already disinclined to take up her offer, this knowledge would be sufficient for him to banish any thoughts of intimate progression.

He cannot believe she should think him interested as even on the rare days when he does invite her in, he discourages her from staying long, always saying he has essays to mark or a paper to complete. It was somewhat against his better judgement to accept the invitation to join her for a meal at the Retreat.

'It's all a bit soon since Felicity,' he says at last, trying to be kind, to let her down gently, when in fact he knows there is no necessary spark to take the relationship onto a long-term romantic plane. And given her demonstrations of insecurity, anything less would be unwise. Little does he know that this act of kindness is to cause him trouble further down the line.

4

Alone

In the Beckenham cul-de-sac of Beechview Close, with its family-sized semis and mostly two-car occupants, Marianne hears the Saturday morning silence of singledom and switches on Radio 4 while she eats her toast. Despite the frequency with which Johnny went on walking trips at weekends, these are the times when she most notices she is alone. She misses the getting up together, the convivial breakfasting and sharing of plans.

When Holly left for uni, it had been difficult, but not desperate. Empty-nesting was a challenge exacerbated by Marianne's concurrent onset of peri-menopause and a rush of midlife worries. Her self-esteem was battered from erroneously thinking Johnny was having an affair with one of his colleagues. Her hormones were volatile and she obsessed like a teenager. When she reminisces about that time, she can't believe her insecurity and jealousy. It could have wrecked their otherwise stable marriage.

Now Holly is flat-sharing in Guildford, aged twenty-eight, fiercely single and working as a solicitor in a small firm. Since Johnny died, Marianne sometimes feels Holly is the one taking charge, constantly suggesting that her mother move to a smaller property. Marianne has resisted. 'I'm not doing anything for at least a year,' she told her, taking her own oft-given advice that any major trauma should not be followed too soon by other significant lifestyle changes such as job or home or relationship. But now that year is over she must consider her options.

She doesn't need to rattle around a three-bedroom house with a generous back garden. Much as she loves her outdoor space with fruit trees, vegetables and herbacious borders, thoughts about downshifting to a flat are beginning to merit consideration. She could even help Holly onto the property ladder with the proceeds. And if she does take early retirement – a persistent thought since her writing has taken a more structured direction – she could move anywhere in the country, back up to Cumbria, or even down to Guildford to be near her daughter. But Holly may not stay there, so she would then have given up her Beckenham life for nothing. She finds new friendships take time to mature. They are like trees, accumulating the annual rings of stability as the years go by. She may not have that time. It would be risky.

She feeds her cat and herself and contemplates the day. It is still unseasonally warm and sunny and there are so many things she would have suggested if Johnny had still been alive. It is even warm enough for a spring picnic, but a picnic for one has a lonely echo.

She wonders if being alone is her future. Fifty-five is an awkward age to think about romancing again, an age when people may or may not consider it is worth the effort. She thinks of all those she has known who have lost a husband in midlife. Most remain unmarried; most certainly live alone. And those who took a second chance sometimes had regrets after rushing in, snatching an opportunity, fearful of waiting and watching the years slip by. The womaniser, the secret drinker, the compulsive gambler, sometimes all three: a job lot of aggravation, a second chance into an abyss far worse than being on their own.

Although she's decided it's time to move on, she doesn't know where to start. Her book, *Lydia,* is now being printed and there is nothing she can do but wait. It has taken several years in its completion, juggling writing with her working week, a labour of love, of need, rather than a commercial enterprise. But once it was finished, she always wanted others to share.

First she sent sample chapters and the required synopsis to a few publishers. They sent them back, sometimes with a standard letter, sometimes with personal words of encouragement. She became used to identifying the sound of the returning envelope as it flopped onto the mat. It was the sound of dashed hopes and shattered dreams. After a while she gave up and concentrated on writing a sequel. It was Edward who first suggested self-publishing. But he said it at a time when such a thing was still viewed with suspicion. Only in very recent years has the industry gathered respectability and momentum.

She is anxious about the extent to which people will think it is autobiographical. Mostly it isn't, but the stories of the bullying at the fictional Oakleigh House preparatory school in Cumbria are inspired by her own experiences at Brocklebank Hall.

Inspired. That is the crux of it. Inspired. Not an exact one to one correspondence between actual events and those that lurk on the pages of *Lydia,* but there is a real Adam in the shape of Edward Harvey: *the only boy in the class whom she remembers never being horrible to her.* And there were actual teachers with some of the traits of her fictional ones and tiresome bullies who morphed into Barnaby Sproat and his gang.

She developed the idea for the book soon after finding Edward on Friends Reunited at the end of 2001, but she didn't tell him until after the first few chapters were written, until she realised it had the makings of a novel. The childhood story of Adam belonged to him, just as that of Maya was hers. Of course, his story was from her perspective and as such might be far from the truth. But there may have been something in the narrative that touched a nerve, and she needed his support and approval in order to be comfortable in completing it in case it was published. As to the crush that she had on him, she'd never confessed. No point in alarming him when there was no need. Maya had to have a crush on Adam to create a plot with sufficient romantic interest to drive the fiction forward. So she told him that.

Edward Harvey … the real *Lydia*, where is he now? When he left Beechview Close for the last time, he said to her, 'Do something with *Lydia*, it deserves to be read.'

Marianne blocks the thought, easier now with the passage of time and more pressing losses along the way. She hasn't written in her journal since he left, frightened of what she might reveal, not least unto herself.

Since Johnny died, Marianne realises how she has neglected many of her oldest friends and failed to cultivate new ones. Grief sapped much of her energy. If she retires at the end of the academic year, in addition to writing she might at last have time for other pursuits and for developing her support system.

Social networking has once again been her saviour and she is now a prolific tweeter. It is a useful platform from which to inform the world about her writing. Each time she tweets, she runs her words through a personal filter: *What if it is read by one of my students? What if it is read by the Principal of the college?* And if it passes both tests, it is let loose in the Twitterverse.

When she started tweeting, she wondered if Edward was registered. There were a few Edward Harveys, mostly anonymous eggs, none with profile information that looked like they could be him. Not that she would tweet him directly or even follow him, but she would be interested to know what he was doing, that he was still alive, still okay. After what happened to Johnny, nothing was certain. And the thought of him had made her pause and stare into empty space as she remembered the dark-haired boy in the classroom at Brocklebank Hall; the boy with the soft brown eyes and the razor-sharp brain; the boy she had never forgotten. Then she snapped back to the present. *Too busy to tweet,* she thought of him at the time. *Always busy* …

She hasn't looked since.

5

Tweeting Lydia

The morning after the meeting with Jessica, Harriet gives Edward a disapproving look as they roam the huge kitchen, making their own breakfasts as they habitually do before leaving for work. 'Anything to report?' she asks. 'Did the witch put a spell on you?'

Harriet teaches science at a secondary school in Exeter. She leaves early to catch up with preparation before the queues form in the photocopying room. Edward has more flexibility, but generally prefers to be off soon after her so he can keep track of the rest of his archaeology department at the University of Devon. When he returned from his three years in London, he observed some unwelcome and sloppy time-keeping practices from two of the senior members of staff. He knows they are disillusioned with the modern trends in university education and are treading water until they can retire.

'I told her it was all too soon since your mum,' says Edward, multitasking cereal, toast and tea.

'So she *was* under the impression it was a date. Told you! And now you've said that, she'll think if she hangs around long enough, you'll become interested. Anyway, enough of her, I have news too.' Harriet sits down with her cereal and waves a spoon at him, an excited expression on her face. 'I've found a person called Marianne Hayward on Twitter. She's a psychology teacher in Beckenham and has a book called *Lydia* on the verges of publication. It's got to be Fanclub.'

Edward's half-dead emotions begin to pulse.

Harriet continues, 'She's using a picture of the book cover as her avatar. It's got purple rhododendrons on it.'

Rhododendrons ... They were the most prevalent flowers at Brocklebank Hall; a panoply of lilac and magenta blooms lining the driveway and the playground in summer. And a book called *Lydia,* named after him; after the character he played in their prep school production of *The Rivals*: Lydia Languish, niece of Mrs Malaprop and lover of Captain Absolute. His memory stirs and for a moment his thoughts skip back to that time when he was eleven and involved in one of the most exciting, if scary, things he had ever done.

'I should never think of giving my heart to a man because he could swim!'

Even now, all these years later, he can remember some of the more entertaining or dramatic lines. Three boys had taken female roles so wearing a dress hadn't been too much of an ordeal, though the material did feel unpleasantly tickly against his skin and the back zip presented difficulties – something that later helped him to understand Felicity's need for assistance after parties. Thankfully the experience had not enticed him into dressing up in women's clothes after that.

If they had been a year or two older, being wooed by another boy might have been embarrassing. As it was, he was able to ham it up, exaggeration that perfectly suited Sheridan's melodrama.

'I am so astonished! And so terrified! And so overjoyed!'

He had been nervous about remembering the lines and acting appropriately, but had enjoyed the opportunity to escape his normally quiet demeanour and be an exhibitionist. Even now it is the performance aspect of his lecturing role that gives him the greatest satisfaction. He has an enduring memory of caked-on make-up – almost impossible to get off with the cold cream that bore a distinctive and almost pharmaceutical smell, unlike anything he had come across either before or since. Marianne had been the only true girl in the play: Lucy, Lydia's maid.

'Will you tweet her?' says Harriet, bringing him back to the present.

'I might,' says Edward.

When Marianne found him on Friends Reunited, she referred to him jokingly as Lydia. And it was their reuniting that had inspired her to write a novel of the same name. He is curious to read it in its entirety and hurt she hasn't told him. He wonders if she has found a publisher, or at last decided to publish independently – something he suggested once or twice while he was lodging. She let him read the bits that were based on their childhood at prep school and his memory had been stirred by the facts – the bad times and good times, the bullying and camaraderie. And he was amused by the fiction – at least what she said was fiction. Even if she didn't have a crush on him then, she possibly developed one later, although she never said. And so did he; more than a crush.

All day he is unusually distracted. It takes something significant to remove his focus from his working life. It happened once before when scheming hussy Taryn seduced him. Now, in between lectures and meetings, all he can think about is Marianne. He remembers her shiny hair, her vivid green eyes, the way she teased him sometimes for taking her too seriously or literally.

At lunchtime he walks the landscaped grounds, full of trees in early blossom, and muses on what to do. To do nothing is not an option. He will send her a tweet and see if and how she responds. Tweeting is impersonal. She can ignore it if she chooses. She might still be mad with him. And there is still the question of her husband, Johnny. If Edward couldn't stand it then, what difference now? But age and the loss of Felicity have changed him and he yearns for her friendship again.

As soon as he arrives home at the Deer Orchard, he lets Meg into the paddock, checks the hens and then disappears into his upstairs office to look for *Lydia* on Amazon. His heart races as he reads the blurb; the blurb about Adam and Maya and their re-acquaintance via Friends Reunited. In a few weeks it will be published.

He can't resist Twitter any longer. He sets up an account. After a few attempts, he becomes *@Edward_Harvey1*. He adds *Archaeologist* to the profile and will add a picture later, but probably not a photograph of himself. For now he is content to be an egg. He types Marianne Hayward into the search box. There are several. He looks at the avatars, the accompanying photos, and soon he spies the cover of her book that Harriet mentioned. She is *@marihay1*. He sighs and realises he has been holding his breath.

Mari. It's what Johnny calls her. And after a while she let him too.

Her profile is as Harriet said: *Teacher of psychology, married with daughter, living in Beckenham, almost author.* Her tweets, as far as he can see, are about the forthcoming book with a few random ones about environmental matters, health issues, food and science.

He decides it is time to be bold.

@marihay1 Have seen your book on the web. Am very much looking forward to reading it.

He clicks on the Tweet button and then takes Meg for a walk, his mind waltzing with possibilities.

He heads towards the village. A curtain moves as he passes Jessica's house, but he is travelling down a different road in his head and barely notices.

31

Until this single word string on Twitter, he has not been in touch with Marianne for five years. He was the one who decided that when he left Stancliffe, he would break all contact. Indeed, there has been no communication between them since then. But that was the way he said it must be. No phone calls, no emails; nothing. This was for his benefit. He needed to forget her completely. He was so stressed by weekend rows with Felicity and by living in two locations, he wasn't thinking straight. At the time, it was the only way he could see himself devoting the necessary energy to trying to save his marriage.

Needless to say, Marianne wasn't pleased.

He returned to his old job at the University of Devon, outside Exeter – a job that in the intervening three years had been filled by three other members of the department on a rotational basis. It was an unsatisfactory arrangement, each trying to outdo the other, implementing initiatives which were then unimplemented the following year; each hoping to impress sufficiently to be awarded the job on a permanent basis. In the absence of a better solution, and with the certainty that in time Edward would want to return, Dick Fieldbrace, the Dean of Studies, believed this was the best thing to do. He had been proven correct.

Now Edward still retains Honorary Visiting Professor status at Stancliffe, and returns each October to do a short series of weekly lectures with the final year students. He also supervises a PhD candidate. And when he makes these visits, he often thinks how nice it would be to have a sleepover at Beechview Close instead of making the round trip in a day, or staying over in a characterless hotel. His efforts to banish Marianne from his mind have always been unsuccessful and even more so in the past six months. She appears when he least expects it, sometimes during a television documentary when he can almost hear her making some point or other as she was wont to do.

His efforts to repair his marriage were zealous and focused for a time. He showed interest in the livestock, even donning a bee suit and making explorations into the hive to collect honey, ending up badly stung for his efforts. He drove lambs to market, milked goats and did a few stints of selling at the farmers' markets during the abundant weeks of autumn when they had enough produce to cover more than one location. And all the while he looked to Felicity for approval, for appreciation, desperately hoping that she would welcome him once more into a night-time embrace.

She didn't.

'It's about time,' was all she said when he confronted her about his efforts to be involved with her business.

And on the rare occasions she accepted his amorous advances in bed, their union was soulless and unsatisfactory. Neither mentioned love any more and Edward, who believed he still loved her when he resigned from Stancliffe, now found his feelings ebbing away with rapidity.

After Felicity admitted her affair with Gianni and packed her bags, there was no reason to feel guilty about Marianne so she popped up even more in his thoughts, often wearing fewer clothes and engaging him in some pleasurable distraction. His fantasies are now much more graphic than they were when he was in touch with her. It is as if she has taken on the status of a fictional character, permitting free rein for his imagination. With his rediscovery of her on Twitter, he is non-plussed, embarrassed even. It may be difficult putting these images back in the box.

He has only been home from his walk for five minutes, and is contemplating supper options, when there is a knock at the door.

It is Jessica, this time carrying half a meat pie. 'Thanks for last night. It took me out of myself.'

Edward suddenly has an image of two Jessicas, one a little more transparent, like a case shed by a marine creature.

'I hope we can do it again,' she says. 'As friends,' she adds. 'My treat next time.'

'Yes, indeed,' says Edward, hoping to leave it at that. He smells her perfume wafting through the door on the breeze, cloying, overdone, inappropriate for the delivery of a pie; likewise the heels on which she struggled through the gravel.

'Shall we say same time next week?' she says.

'I'm rather busy next week,' says Edward, hastily.

'Two weeks' time, then? I can do Thursday.'

He is taken aback by the speed with which she is operating. 'I'll have to check my diary. I may be away, lecturing. Not sure.' He tries not to sound enthusiastic, hoping she will take the hint and preparing her for disappointment when he discovers he has an important meeting or a talk to give to the Chipping Camden History Society, or some such organisation. 'I'll let you know.'

Jessica frowns, hands him the pie without a word and delicately picks her way back down the gravel path.

He expects Conrad would tell him to keep the option open. But he isn't Conrad and there must be more suitable women than Jessica. Since Felicity left, it has crossed his mind once or twice that he may never have sex again. He counts the months. It was infrequent for several years. He blamed her hormones, she blamed her hormones. Conrad said this was normal and that women are biologically programmed only to want sex during fertile years. Edward didn't believe this was a universal truth, though it might explain why older men seek younger women. Yet since the discovery of Felicity's liaison with Gianni, this theory seems irrelevant. His pride is wounded.

Harriet is out at her Italian evening class. She joined as soon as Felicity said she was leaving. Said she would go to visit them in Italy and that it would be good to know some of the language. Edward hasn't yet heard much evidence of progress, but then Harriet has always been reluctant to display any intellectual prowess. So Edward retires to his upstairs office, alone with his thoughts and Jessica's pie. In truth, he's never been a fan of pastry, but in such gastronomically scarce times, he puts his aversion to one side.

In between writing his latest paper and munching mouthfuls, he keeps checking his interactions on Twitter, but there is no sign of Marianne although she is tweeting in his timeline. As he is only following one person, he is bound to see everything she writes for general public view.

Very dry for the time of year. Looks like we're heading for a drought.
A warning that we should make provisions when the rain comes.
We are an 'after the horse has bolted' society. Everything in hindsight. #drought
Those without water meters need to be reminded to turn off their taps.
Leaks must be fixed, waste reduced, water stored.
Is there justification for water expenditure on golf courses or for other leisure pursuits?

Typical Marianne.
She must know he is watching.

It is late the following evening, Friday, before she replies.

@Edward_Harvey1 How do I know it's you?
@Marihay1 Archaeologist?
@Edward_Harvey1 Not an infrequent occupation on Twitter.

@Marihay1 Lydia Languish.
@Edward_Harvey1 Ah ... ok, I believe you. Your support will be appreciated – as always.

Again, the pulsing heart.

If he was expecting her to show delight, this is a disappointment. If a tweet could look cool, this is as cold as an underground cave. No exclamation marks and no emoticons. He wonders what she is thinking and why she has taken three days to respond. She is skilled in giving nothing away.

@marihay1 Of course I am biased but I see you have quite a following.
@Edward_Harvey1 It would seem so.
@marihay1 I hope all is well with you.
@Edward_Harvey1 Pass.

His stomach registers alarm for the first time since Felicity made her grand announcement. So much could have happened to her in the intervening years. He had lost two parents. They were of an age when this was not unexpected. He hopes Holly is okay and that Mari and Johnny are well. That is another problem with fifty-something. No sooner has one dealt with the illnesses of parents, but one's own health starts misbehaving too. He is still relatively robust, but his wrist is stiff from when it broke during the mugging of September 2003 and he believes the stresses of the past few years have taken their toll in that he no longer feels as vital as he once was. He isn't exactly ill, but he finds it increasingly difficult to say he is well. He wouldn't be surprised if he is depressed, but not sufficiently so to take medication. In any case, if he is depressed, it will be reactive depression, a consequence of life events over which he has had little control. No medication will solve the problems and he isn't attracted to being on the receiving end of therapy despite several times thinking of retraining as a counsellor. When he was lodging with Marianne and Johnny, she had been his counsellor of a sort.

@marihay1 Please follow back so I can send DM.

Harriet had explained to him about DMs and neither he nor Marianne is likely to divulge personal information for the world of Twitter to see. You can only send a direct message if a person is following you. All Edward can do is wait.

Another day passes. Another day when he has difficulty focusing on his work.

In the evening, he knows she is on her computer because she continues to tweet about the drought that is now causing serious water shortages across the country. He will wait another day or two. He will be patient. He knows she is curious by nature and that her apparently unforgiving heart is a protection mechanism against the hurts she suffered as a child when at school, and also since. She forgave him once before; a far greater hurt in that he made a dreadful mistake and let her down. Surely this time there are mitigating circumstances. Inside her protective igloo, she is all warmth and compassion.

And he knows she cared.

He hopes she will thaw if he gives it time.

6

Past Blast

Two weeks after Johnny's funeral, Marianne comes back from work, dumps her bag in the hall, flings off her coat and is sitting in the living room in an almost catatonic trance, numb and red eyed, when the doorbell rings.

Standing on the threshold is a tiny woman, muffled up to her ears against the March winds in a high-neck red padded coat and with a matching woolly hat.

The woman says, 'I didn't phone, but I had to come to see you. I've only just heard. I'm so sorry.'

Marianne blinks, wondering who … then recognises the low dusky voice and the eyes. 'Taryn!'

After that it is all reflex actions. She doesn't have the energy to engage her brain and analyse the pros and cons of possible responses. It is seven years since she has seen her, yet many times she has wanted to pick up the phone. Since Edward left, their falling out has become less relevant and time has healed. She leads the way into the living room and collapses onto the sofa.

Taryn unwraps herself, revealing a still-toned body in jeans and an emerald green sweater. She shakes a canvas bag at Marianne. 'I bet you aren't eating properly. I've brought some pasta sauce, and a bag of fusilli. It can be rustled up in ten minutes – or if you'd rather, you can keep it till tomorrow.'

Marianne starts to cry again at this simple act of practical kindness.

Taryn comes over to the sofa and puts her arm around her erstwhile friend. 'I don't generally do hugs, but this is an exception.'

★

Since then, their friendship has resumed almost as if the missing years had not existed. They play tennis, like old times, although not so frequently or energetically. And without Johnny's disapproving presence, Taryn spends more time at Beechview Close than she ever did before.

They talked about their rift, each recognising that they had learned much from what had happened. Taryn's life had transformed. She had sought more therapy, ditched her old *femme fatale* habits and formed an enduring relationship with Neil, Head of History at the school in which she still teaches English. He has calmed her down. She is no longer a loose cannon in the company of other people's husbands. She and Neil continue to live in separate accommodation, but are acknowledged as a couple in all but residence.

'He'll do anything for a piece of cake,' said Taryn when telling Marianne about their commitment. 'Indeed, it is my opinion, many times confirmed, that one of the best ways of dealing with men is to give them cake.'

Once again it is to Taryn that Marianne turns in the face of an Edward dilemma. It is Saturday afternoon and they are in one of the many coffee shops in Beckenham's High Street, sitting at a table at the back, away from the huge windows that deny privacy. Even though it is March, the temperatures this year are more like those expected in June. Both women wear long summer dresses with sandals, Taryn in jade, baring spray-bronzed arms and Marianne in a blue ethnic print with plain blue cardigan.

'Edward has been in touch via Twitter,' says Marianne.

'Edward Harvey?' says Taryn. 'Your long-lost crush? My dalliance? Our downfall?' As ever, Taryn speaks her thoughts, generally not one for tact and diplomacy.

'The very same. He started following me a few days ago.

And I probably shouldn't be telling you.'

'Of course you should be telling me. This is wonderful news – isn't it? Time you were distracted. And you don't need to worry about me.' Nowadays her dark brown hair is in a neat bob with fringe and it barely moves despite the flamboyance of her gestures.

'I wasn't.' She believes Taryn is no threat any more, not only because Edward was never particularly interested in her, but because she is now safely domesticated in the clutches of Neil.

'He wants me to follow him back so he can send me a direct message. I'm not sure whether I should. Direct messages will likely lead to personal revelations.'

'Aren't you curious to know about his life? If he's no longer with Felicity, just think.'

'And if he is?'

'He's the one choosing contact. You could have him as a friend again. You always claimed that was all you wanted.'

'I never told him about Johnny, so it's unlikely that he knows.'

'If you don't message him, you'll be forever in the dark. I can't believe you would want that. Surely it is worth taking a chance?'

'I've never forgotten him,' says Marianne. 'I never forgot him between the ages of eleven and forty-five, so it was hardly likely I'd forget him over the past five years.'

'I know,' says Taryn. 'Finding him changed your life. He will always be part of your psyche. You have to respond.'

Marianne is thoughtful. The business of her separation from Edward is a confused muddle. Without Johnny, there is no safety-net, no power-assisted emotional brakes, and she suspects it wouldn't take much to push her feelings beyond the bounds of propriety. If Edward and Felicity are still together, she may be the one who can't stand it if they resume contact; she may be the one who will need to run away. But Taryn is correct in that an even more unsatisfactory option would be to remain ignorant of what has befallen him in the intervening years.

When they part, Marianne drives home to do some more preliminary marketing of her book. After the madness of proof checking, she has been as lost as a parent sending a child on a first holiday with the school, worrying about what may befall it and whether the transformation upon return will be as expected.

This Twitter business from Edward has unsettled her. It is all she can think about. She submits the dilemma to an in-depth 'Mari-analysis', a term coined by Edward when he was staying with them to describe her extraordinary powers of endless scrutiny. He claimed he had never known anyone to dissect a problem like she did. It was as if she placed all the components on a cloth-covered bench, sorting them into categories and re-arranging them to see what fit best with what. She was adept in identifying which elements to discard and which to keep, assigning imaginary points to possible outcomes. Her logic ensured a workable solution. So long as the problem wasn't hers, in which case the bench had no cloth to highlight the pieces and all ended up in a jumble of indecision.

When dealing with her own issues, she occasionally resorts to the Runes. These were introduced to her by a woman from work who knew her fascination for astrology and other forms of fortune-telling. *A little bag of psychologists* is how she thinks of them. Designed to connect questioners to their Higher Selves; to what they already know but are unable to see because conscious thought obscures the view.

She sits on the floor in her living room, quietly contemplating her dilemma, with the red velvet bag containing the twenty-five runes clasped between her hands. She dips her hand into the bag and feels the flat stones slipping through her fingers. *To message or not?* she asks. *Do I open the door; forgive the hurt?* She draws out a stone that seems to stick to her fingers. It is blank: the Unknowable. This is the rune that calls for taking a chance with what we can't yet see. It highlights our fears of being abandoned. It is a test of faith, pointing to self-change.

The meaning is unambiguous. She knows exactly what it is telling her to do. She always knew.

7

Reawakening

And all that fills the hearts of friends,
When first they feel, with secret pain,
Their lives thenceforth have separate ends,
And never shall be one again.

Henry Wadsworth Longfellow

When he tells her he has to leave, her eyes fill with tears. They are in her kitchen, sitting at the table; it is morning, after breakfast, just before leaving for work.

He says, 'I am too involved with you and I cannot bear being so close and yet not close enough.'

Then he almost cries. Almost, but not quite, because he is an expert in not crying, learned from prep school days.

And then he tells her that he needs to sever all contact; to forget her in order to focus on his marriage.

'No phone calls?' she says.

'No.'

'Not even an email?'

'That's how it all started. It will be easier for both of us in the end.'

'You truly believe that?'

'I know that. And so do you.'

She walks away.

For the remaining weeks of his term, she hardly speaks to him. Then on his final morning she comes to his room, her daughter's room, where he is gathering the last of his belongings and zipping up his case. First she hovers in the doorway.

'I'm so sorry you're leaving us and even sorrier that you don't want to keep in touch.'

'I'm sorry too. But you do understand … don't you?' He sits down on the bed and gestures for her to come in and sit next to him.

She closes the door. It is Friday. Her day off since she went part-time at the college. Her husband Johnny has gone to work at his school. They are alone.

Edward dares to put his arm around her shoulder and she leans towards him, allowing herself to be hugged. She sniffs and he notices her eyes are wet.

She says, 'Yes, I understand. But it's so harsh. We've done nothing wrong.'

He wants to tell her that his heart is breaking; that without his weekly visits to Beechview Close, his world will darken. Their time together forms a montage in his brain: the suppers and breakfasts, the debates with Johnny, the gentle flirting with Marianne, meaning nothing, meaning everything; the laughter – oh how she made him laugh with her off-the-wall zaniness, the randomness of her thoughts, her original take on events. And she has looked after him in a way that Felicity seems to have forgotten how to do. She is a feather pillow on which to lay his troubled soul. But she isn't free to love him back in the way he wants and even if she were, he isn't free either.

He has a wife, and a marriage to save, and there is no chance of that while he works most of the week in London and no chance while he spends so much time thinking about Marianne.

He dares to kiss her hair, so lightly she may not notice. It would be easy – knowing he is going – to kiss her on the mouth. But it wouldn't be fair. Instead he wraps her in both his arms, and she hugs him back, hugging in a way they never have before. It is okay to hug like this if you are about to say goodbye forever. There they stay for an age until she starts to cry audibly and he too has to choke back tears.

'I'll miss you beyond words,' she says.

44

Beyond words.
He has never forgotten her face: the hurt, the tears …

It was July 2007 when he left. Almost five years ago. And it is three days since their brief exchange of tweets. He cannot bear this waiting; this wondering if she will give him a chance to make amends. Now he has found her, it consumes his waking moments and his dreams. On Monday morning, before going down to breakfast, he tries again.

@marihay1 Please.

It is a simple enough request. She will understand the weight of emotion behind the word; she who bestows meaning on the quantity of exclamation marks in emails – even when they signify nothing.

Downstairs, he catches sight of Rick in the greenhouse. Rick is the gardener, among other things. Tall and lean, wild hair, early forties and a reputation in the locality as long as one of his organic leeks. If Felicity was going to have an affair, it would surely have been with Rick. That's what Edward thought and that is why when Rick and Felicity were together by the beehives or in the greenhouse he watched them closely, searching for signs of intimacy beyond the weekly gardening schedule. That is why he never bothered to keep an eye on Gianni the chef; never noticed what was going on in the upstairs flat of the restaurant after the clientele were gone and the plates were cleared. He naively thought this was when the menus were concocted; never dreamed one of the courses involved a shag with his wife.

Now Rick has become a confidant of Edward's. They rarely used to speak before; hardly a word. But since Felicity left, Edward is often on his own in the evenings or at weekends and

Rick sometimes drops in for a cup of tea before he goes back home. At first they talked about Felicity.

'Can't understand why she would want to leave all this,' said Rick, reassuringly. 'She's bonkers. You and the kids; so much to lose. Must be her age.'

And Edward agreed, unable to face the thought that he might be partly to blame.

Now, they talk about what to do with the garden. Mostly it is Rick who makes suggestions and Edward who concurs. Felicity was the one with the botanical brain but Edward is keen to maintain production and keep the household supplied with fresh and nutritious organic vegetables. Rick continues to sell the excess produce at the farmers' markets, but on Edward's behalf. It pays his wages. He comes and goes during the daytime, letting Meg into the garden while he plants or harvests, digs or waters.

It is a smoothly operating arrangement, but in recent weeks Edward has been thinking about the future. Although it is great having home-grown produce, he believes this could be achieved on a much smaller scale. After breakfast, he grabs his car keys, locks the door and heads for the greenhouse.

Rick looks up from his thinning and potting on of various seedlings.

'I'm thinking we should turn some of the vegetable plots back to grass,' says Edward. 'Lower maintenance.'

'Trying to make me redundant,' says Rick.

'No chance of that just yet, but I have to plan ahead. I may not always be here,' he adds. 'We could scale back on the quantity we send to market. We'll talk some more at the weekend, see what you think.'

At work he wonders if there are savings to be made in the department. Cutbacks in funding mean constant pressure to tighten belts and avoid waste. The photocopying bill is huge and he considers that some of the packs they produce for students could either be recycled or purchased by individuals if required. While he was away in London, his colleagues had become profligate with resources and so much ended in the scrap box or recycling bin. Their bad habits have been hard to eradicate.

In the evening, Harriet confronts him in the hallway as soon as he walks through the front door.

'Rick says you're planning to reduce his hours.'

Edward reaches down to pat Meg who is delighted that he is home and is anticipating a walk. 'I said we need to talk about downsizing but nothing's been decided.'

'It's the profits from the surplus that pay a large part of Rick's wages.'

'This isn't about money, Harriet. It's about whether it is practical to continue on this scale – especially as I may want to move somewhere smaller eventually. In the meantime I fancied a return to more grass.'

'It will need to be mown.'

Edward had forgotten about that. 'I will pay Rick to mow it then.'

'Not very cost-effective compared with the vegetables. I don't think you've thought this through.'

He hadn't. 'I'll give it some more consideration. But now I would like a cup of tea.'

They move through to the kitchen and Harriet switches on the kettle. She says, 'Any contact with Fanclub yet?'

Edward flushes. 'I've said hello and she said hello back, but she hasn't followed me yet so no personal details have been exchanged.'

Harriet narrows her kohl-rimmed eyes and gives him a searching stare.

If Marianne responds, he wonders how quickly he should

tell her about Felicity. Might it frighten her off if she knew he was effectively single? Might she wonder at his intentions? But how can he omit this most major happening in his life?

Later in the evening, he finds the longed-for tweet. Even before he reads the words, he pictures her face; the face that she had five years ago.

@Edward_Harvey1 Curiosity has made me follow you back.

He contemplates what this means; the tone of voice. She wrote it only twelve minutes earlier. He wonders if she is still there; still sitting at her computer in the upstairs spare room. He sends a direct message, away from the prying eyes of other Twitter users. He decides to deliver the most shocking information first.

@marihay1 Felicity has run off to Italy with Gianni the chef.

He knows that this will bring a gasp. She cannot be emotionally immune to the news. Then he alerts her to the DM by tweeting in her timeline.

He waits. Harriet told him there is often a delay in a direct message showing up on Twitter, but they can sometimes be accessed more quickly via email.

@Edward_Harvey1 Sorry to hear.

She is still there. Good. Perhaps they can converse. He must write quickly before she moves away from the computer. And he must be careful about every word he uses.

@marihay1 Am glad that you have completed Lydia, but more importantly, how are you?

@Edward_Harvey1 Truth or lie?

@marihay1 Are you still cross with me?

@Edward_Harvey1 Cross? Such a little word for what I felt at the time.

@marihay1 I had no choice. I was too involved.

@Edward_Harvey1 And now because Felicity has run off, you think it ok to be 'involved' again irrespective of my feelings?

Ah, the first sign of her flashing green eyes. *She is cross!* He understands why she might think this, but he has considered her feelings and he can't help himself. He is a ship adrift on an ocean tide and surely they can resume a distant e-contact as they had when she first found him on Friends Reunited? Surely if they don't meet, then their emotions will be kept in check?

@marihay1 I miss you.

Perhaps this is risky. But it is truth, from the heart. Silence. Silence for a day, then two. But she doesn't unfollow him. And he knows she is out there, tweeting away about *Lydia*.

At work, in between lectures and meetings, all he can think about is Marianne. And when the weekend comes, his usual focus on his writing is constantly interrupted by her image. Their current contact has the fragility of an old dried leaf with ragged edges and holes and broken veins. He can't stand the thought of it being crushed into dust. By Saturday afternoon, his agitation at her silence becomes unbearable and he sends another DM at a time when he knows she is tweeting.

@marihay1 Nothing, in essence, has changed.

What he is trying to say is that his feelings are still the same, although whether that admission will help or hinder his cause, he isn't sure. He wants her to know that he still cares, still wishes she were his friend.

@Edward_Harvey1 Everything has changed.
@marihay1 How so?
@Edward_Harvey1 To tell you would be to open up a gate that it may not be wise to open.
@marihay1 Was I wrong to leave you?
@Edward_Harvey1 You may have been wrong to break all contact. Took time to get used to absence. Do not want to go through again.
@marihay1 I promise not to leave you again.
@Edward_Harvey1 No one can ever make such a promise.
@marihay1 As far as it is reasonable or possible to promise.
@Edward_Harvey1 I am more vulnerable now so less inclined to take risks.
@marihay1 Explain.
@Edward_Harvey1 Five years is a long time at our age. The petals begin to fall.
@marihay1 Shakespeare wrote, 'To me, dear friend, you never shall be old.'
@Edward_Harvey1 Romantic clap-trap. You're a man.

He could see her smiling as she wrote this. This was the old Marianne again.

@marihay1 Indeed!
@Edward_Harvey1 And I am a woman of a certain age.
@marihay1 'Love looks not with the eyes, but with the mind.'
@Edward_Harvey1 'Lysander riddles very prettily.'
@marihay1 Touché.
@Edward_Harvey1 Johnny died last year.

The smile that was beginning to dance in his heart as the exchange grew more flirtatious, disappears to be replaced with a sensation of panic and a sharp intake of breath. *Bloody hell; not Johnny!*

He sits back, immobilised, thoughts pinging and snapping like a severed power cable spouting flames as it blows against wires in a gale force wind. Johnny: this was something he hadn't foreseen. Johnny had become something of a friend during the years Edward lodged with them at Beechview Close. And he was the husband of the woman he loved. Yes, in her absence, and since he had been alone, his feelings for her had flourished unchallenged. And now, suddenly and unexpectedly it is legitimate, he can love out loud and shout to the world. He can tell her what he has never told her about his twice-broken heart.

No he can't. What is he thinking? Johnny. Dead. Several minutes pass while he collects himself. The computer screen darkens before his eyes, shutting off into sleep mode. He clicks it back to life.

@marihay1 When?

No answer. She has gone. He checks her Twitter feed. Nothing.

He imagines her rushing away from her computer, taking refuge with tissues, grief still fresh enough to burst forth when memories are stirred. She and Johnny were close, finding a way through the midlife mire of uncertainty and empty nest, to a comfortable, enviable companionability with a touch of added sparkle that few seem to manage.

He decides a tweet would be inappropriate in the circumstances. He reaches for the phone and dials her old number. There is no response. He lets it ring and ring. *Still no answering machine!*

He uses her old email address.

To: Marianne Hayward
From: Edward Harvey
Date: 17th March 2012, 14.41
Subject: Condolences

Dear Marianne,

Am stunned. Words cannot begin to tell you how shocked and sorry I am. Johnny was such a fine person. And your marriage was strong. You must be devastated. Learned a lot from him about geology, but also about women. Helped me to understand Felicity better, even though not possible to save our relationship.

What happened? Wish I'd been there for you. Would have liked to pay respects too – but understand why you didn't contact me. Can be there now if you will let me into your life again, as a friend. Please mail me and tell me more. Or even better, call me.

love, as ever,

Edward

Then he goes for a long walk with Meg, up through the village and across the main road to the patch of grass where two imposing Holm oaks stand sentinel to the road leading to the Red Lion pub and the church. Sheep graze in a small field on the other side of the wall and Edward stops to watch them, noting the roundness of their bellies, remembering his own forays into lambing when Felicity needed help.

The churchyard is accessed via two lych gates with gnarled old yew trees on either side. Daffodils are beginning to show among the ancient lichen-covered headstones and Edward thinks of William Wordsworth and Cumbria, and his own parents, now both dead, their ashes scattered on the lower slopes of Helvellyn.

The church is of impressive size for a village, with huge arches of stained glass windows and a mighty Somerset tower rising high. He opens the door, aware of the chill and the silence and the history. His footsteps echo as he goes to sit on one of the old wooden pews at the back, glancing at the carvings and the tombs, Meg at his feet. He doesn't come here often but when he does, he is overwhelmed by things beyond his understanding and he feels small and insignificant and alone.

For a while he reflects, conscious that this is his first visit here since Felicity departed. So many things have changed. His vibrant family has fragmented, the animals have all but gone, and now his contemporaries are dying. He must reassess and decide what he wants from the next few years. Harriet is right. He has been drifting and purposeless. He says a silent prayer for Johnny, for the safety of his own children and asks for guidance in his dealings with Marianne.

❦

8

The Uncertain Age

The almost flirtatious tweet exchange caused Marianne to flush, but when she told him about Johnny, her mood changed, knowing she would have to explain.

Oh Johnny, dear Johnny, I miss you so. She started to cry again.

She heard the phone ringing and knew it would be Edward. But she wasn't ready to speak. Not then; not yet. She had been struggling all week to absorb the fact that Felicity had gone and that he was free.

Free.

And so was she. There were implications; an altered dynamic. That was why she had taken so long to tell him about Johnny. In the same way as hearing about Felicity had affected the boundaries from her perspective, so too would this knowledge about Johnny affect Edward.

Attainability causes some to retreat.

She goes down to the kitchen to wash the dishes before returning to check if he responded to the news via the internet. It is with relief that she reads his email. It prompts her into action. While his tweets and even his direct messages had a distant and casual feel, the email seems a sincere attempt to re-engage at a level they shared many years ago. If she ignores it, she will be treading on a bright orange spark winking at her from the darkness in the depths of her heart. It will forever close that chapter of her life.

Residual feelings for her former classmate and lodger stir like desert seeds when the rains come. Quickly they spring into life, each contact from him like water droplets softening the tough coatings, providing the stimulus for the roots and shoots to grow. But she is frightened of caring again.

It wasn't that she had loved him in a dangerous sexual sense, but her feelings were strong. She likened them to a crush not dissimilar from the one she had on him at school. And after three years of lodging, he had become almost part of the family. She came to care deeply for him as a friend. For her it wasn't complicated, it was compartmentalised. Johnny was romantic love and sex; Edward was platonic love and friendship. She was careful not to let it get out of hand and Edward stuck to his word and kept his distance, both physically and emotionally. This was why it was such a shock when he said he had to leave. She hadn't understood the depth of his involvement.

To: Edward Harvey
From: Marianne Hayward
Date: 17th March 2012, 15.37
Subject: Re: Condolences

Dear Edward,
This has been the worst year of my life. It was so unexpected – a massive heart attack near Lulworth Cove. One day he was here and the next he was gone. I went into shock, onto autopilot, somehow muddling through the arrangements and the funeral. Holly was the strong one. She said that having had to deal with Dylan's death enabled her to cope in a way she wouldn't have expected. But Johnny was her dad and she was very shaken. As soon as she saw I was coping, she let go and grieved. Since you left, life has been hard. First my mum died, then Dad, then Johnny. I have been numb for such a long time, but with the anniversary and the coming of spring,

I have resolved to try to snap out of it. As you have seen, I am at the point of publishing Lydia – which is why I've been building a Twitter following. In some ways it has been my saviour. Work also keeps me occupied, but doing both has left me even more exhausted and depleted.

I am yearning to do something different with the rest of my life. After what happened to Johnny, I don't want to leave it too late and am considering early retirement from teaching.

love,

Marianne

She has dropped her guard and she relaxes. *Love Marianne* …

To: Marianne Hayward
From: Edward Harvey
Date: 17th March 2012, 21.54
Subject: Re: Condolences

Dear Marianne,

Thank you for replying with details. Am also shocked and so very, very sorry.

Glad you have Lydia to distract you. Looking forward to reading it!

Think early retirement is a great idea. The teaching life is physically and mentally demanding. I have been treading water since coming back here. Harriet tells me I need a new challenge too. Hope to discuss further!

Do keep in touch.

love,

Edward

During the next Monday at college, Marianne goes to see the Principal to talk about her future. Malcolm Prowse has something of the American bald eagle about him, a sharp hooked nose and pale staring eyes, a ruffle of white hair on the horizontal plane from ear to ear. She suspects he will be relieved to be able to replace her expensive experience with cheap young blood. The college is undergoing a budget squeeze.

It is therefore no surprise to find he is receptive and understanding, appreciating both her personal circumstances and her desire to invest more time in her writing. He alludes to her financial situation and she confirms that the benefits she received from Johnny's death help to compensate for her years of part-time working and an actuarially reduced pension. He runs through the timeframe of what needs to happen, tells her to speak to Angela, the woman in charge of personnel. She says nothing yet to her friends and colleagues.

Back home, she is eager to mail Edward to tell him about setting the retirement wheels in motion. Before doing so, she checks Twitter and finds another DM from him.

@marihay1 Why don't you come to stay for a weekend? Would love you to see Deer Orchard.

She is taken aback by the speed at which this offer has been made. *So unlike Edward to be rash.* But she smiles to herself. It would be wonderful to see his home, yet she is frightened of the implications.

@Edward_Harvey1 That's very forward of you!

She replies to several other book-related tweets and is about to go to make supper when an email informs her of another DM.

@marihay1 We could catch up properly.
@Edward_Harvey1 When you were here, there was always Johnny.
@marihay1 Harriet will act as chaperone!
@Edward_Harvey1 Do I need a chaperone?
@marihay1 Alternatively, I could come up to London and meet you for lunch in town.

She does not reply. She is at a loss as to what to do.

First, she must deal with Johnny.

She goes upstairs and finds a box in the bottom of the bedroom wardrobe. It contains all Johnny's remaining personal effects and her throat catches at the sight of his glasses and wallet, still in the plastic bag the hospital put them in when he died. She takes the items out and lays them on the bed, stroking each one, trying to recapture the man to whom they belonged. There is something so sad about these pitiful reminders of a life. But what to do with them? She is not yet ready to dispose of them and she replaces them in the bag. Perhaps if and when she moves she will find courage.

She has kept a shirt of his to wear when she is at her lowest, but it no longer holds his scent. It is pale blue, the colour that suited him so well. And she remembers him wearing it in summer with jeans, with the sleeves rolled up and his tanned forearms on display. She puts it in the laundry basket to wash for the charity shop.

Next, in the spare bedroom, two boxes of folders full of his lesson notes and photocopies. She remembers him telling her about the Burgess Shale; he was a walking encyclopaedia of all things geological and geographical. She makes a start on sifting through them in case there are any gems of information that might be useful in her writing. The plastic wallets and some of the empty binders can be recycled. She will bin the rest. If she is going to move to a smaller place, she will need to downsize the clutter. If she tackles even one folder per evening, the job will eventually be completed. And if she's going to retire, soon there will be all her psychology stuff to accommodate.

His slightly spidery handwriting catches her attention, pages and pages of notes that had been amended and re-amended. She is drawn to his loopy I's and continental 7's which she copied when she was a teenager, when she fancied him from across the playground at the grammar school, watching his every move, his languid walk, the way he and his friends leaned on the wall outside the boys' cloakroom, scanning the girls, eyeing up the talent, perhaps even looking for love.

All the while her thoughts flicker back to Edward: to what Johnny would think, to whether he would approve if anything were to develop, to what Taryn said, to possibilities that are comfortable as fantasies, but frightening as realities, not least because she is not as young as she was.

These days she is aware of dull nagging pains when she climbs hesitantly out of bed, no doubt the beginnings of arthritis. She used to hear her older colleagues complaining about aches and pains. Now she knows what they were talking about. Every morning she carefully tests her joints before doing anything quickly. Her lower back needs coaxing out of a supine position. Her dodgy knee, from when she fell over on some wet cherry blossom and bashed it on the pavement, requires constant care and strapping when she plays tennis or partakes in other sustained activity.

She eats plenty of fish and takes Evening Primrose and Vitamin D capsules. And even when she's not playing tennis, she exercises to Lilia Kopylova's *Latinatone* exercise video, bought in the early years of *Strictly,* when ballroom dancing became fashionable again. So she could be in worse shape. She is still relatively slim and toned, but she is not like she was five years ago.

It was different when she had Johnny; growing older together, one day's face indistinguishable from the last. Ups and downs; tired after a working day or refreshed at the end of summer; the pinched features and shadows after a bout of illness versus the glow and bloom of health. Together they had watched it all and behind the slowly ageing skin and hollows of time, they could still see the face of twenty-three, or even further back, the face of seventeen. She knew he saw it too because he told her and she was buffeted by the knowledge against the invisibility of age.

If forty-five was the certain age, fifty-five is the age of uncertainty. Without Johnny, she peers in the mirror and sees the woman of fifty-five, the woman that ten years ago was a vibrant flower by comparison. This woman that stares back could easily transform into the pensioner with the shopping trolley and the shuffling gait. Without make-up and unsmiling, she looks tired, the whites of her eyes less bright than once they were. But her hair still shines when the sun catches it; a coppery dark brown, still on her shoulders with a modern graduated cut at the front.

What will Edward think of her now? She knows that some middle-aged men want women at least ten years younger. That's what it says in the Personal columns. *Man, 55 seeks woman, 35 to 48.* Marianne thinks they have a nerve, unless they are Richard Gere or Clint Eastwood. And a large age difference surely has its downsides, especially when one partner retires and has to wait several years for the other to share the freedoms. By then, a difference in physical capabilities may be preventative of mutual wing-spreading and pursuing the bucket list.

But if no men ask for women of the same age, what option

is there for women, other than to go out with older men? She thinks about Charles and Camilla. Not enough recognition was given by the media to his choice; his choice of a mature woman of comparable age.

Woman, 55, widow … Even the word 'widow' has connotations of age and decrepitude attached to it. She most definitely wasn't a 'merry' one at the moment.

She consideres what Taryn said. With Felicity vamoosed, Edward will likely be looking for someone else. Many men are not good on their own. They want someone for domestic purposes and sex. A housekeeper and a prostitute rolled into one. He will have younger options. She knows he will. An old jealousy stirs: a jealousy associated with other women, with potential rivals, whoever they may be. She is confused. Now there are different possibilities for her and Edward – possibilities that were once taboo – she feels second best, as in the days of her teenage years when the Brocklebank bullying had taken its toll. Her self-esteem has ebbed away again; ebbed away for the third time in her life: adolescence, menopause, widow. Why would Edward be interested in starting a relationship with a creaking wreck? Of course he might be creaking too. She hasn't thought of that. She doesn't think she'd mind; not with Edward.

Oh, the analysis! She doesn't have the energy any more.

Perhaps it will be wiser to let the dogs sleep.

9

The Uncertain Life

When a be-suited Edward returns from work on Tuesday evening after a difficult departmental meeting, he hopes Marianne has responded to his invitation. He is still unused to her reappearance in his life and when he remembers, he dares to feel excited. Another email from her would be encouraging; but he is an expert in restraint, in delaying gratification. He doesn't like using his phone for checking emails or Twitter and there is much he needs to do before settling down with his computer.

First, he changes into jeans and a sweatshirt and roams the gardens of the Deer Orchard, checking the boundary fences out of old habit when the place was alive with animals. Only three buff Orpington hens remain, the fourth or fifth incarnation of Helen, Amy and Sarah. They have sole use of the multi-storey chicken coop built by Rick, and he wonders if they feel as lost as he does in a space that's suitable to accommodate families rather than individuals.

Felicity's sheepdog, Meg, now eight years old, doesn't count as livestock. She is a trusting ally. He takes her shopping, where she waits patiently in the car, eyes anxious until she sees him again. He is thankful Felicity didn't want to take her to Italy. After Clint and Gryke died, months apart, aged twelve, one lost without the other, Meg – hitherto on the periphery attending to important sheep-related matters – crept into the vacant space of family pet. And after Felicity left, it was as if she felt rejected too, moping around with flattened ears, her once metronomic tail hanging low and still. Together he and Meg regrouped, learning new domestic routines, man and dog, the oldest and most faithful of partnerships. Meg could read his mind, sneaking up to put her black and white nose on his knee when he sat staring into space, wondering what had gone so horribly wrong with his marriage.

Tonight he takes her to the Three Tuns pub in Silverton, a thatched establishment with low, beamed ceilings. It is his colleague Conrad Vaughan's home territory and they have arranged to get together for a bite to eat and an after-hours drink away from academia where they can have an off-record discussion about a couple of the earlier meeting's agenda items. Two issues are causing division of opinion in the department, specifically who is going to teach taster sessions to visiting sixth formers at the Open Day in July and the proposed hosting of an archaeology conference at the university in 2014.

They sit in a corner of the pub at a rectangular wooden table in the window, Meg snoozing across Edward's feet determined that he won't go anywhere without her knowing. Conrad is drinking beer as he isn't driving, while Edward plays safe with apple juice.

They debate work strategies over lasagne, Edward seeking the diplomatic route while Conrad pushes him towards a more autocratic solution.

Edward's return to the role as Head of Department five years earlier wasn't as straightforward as he expected. Firstly, there was animosity from the senior staff who had been rotating Heads of Department and secondly, ambitious newcomers didn't welcome his previously unrivalled reputation. Even now, two of the young guns poached from Exeter remain uncooperative, seizing every opportunity to disagree, to stir, to gain allies for their schemes. Conrad, ever loyal, keeps him up to date on what's being said behind his back and of whom he should beware. It is tiresome and he wonders for how much longer he will have the will to fight.

After the meal, business concluded, he tells Conrad about Jessica.

'And you turned her down, I'll bet,' says Conrad, taking a long slow drink from his pint. His ponytail has been replaced by a grizzled mat that is kept in check by his current girlfriend, an ex student from the 1990s who has returned to work in the department as a research assistant. Conrad and his wife Sandra are still not officially separated or even living apart, but continue to do their own thing by mutual agreement.

'You remember Marianne from a few years back?' says Edward.

'I certainly do. "Fanclub" – of the undisclosed dimensions.'

'Harriet found her on Twitter and we've exchanged a few tweets and a couple of emails. It transpires her husband died last year.'

'Ho-ho,' says Conrad, matter-of-factly. 'Say no more.'

'So even if I was interested in Jessica – which I'm not – I think it best to steer clear of complications with anyone else. At least until I see if and how things develop with Marianne.'

'Two merry widows in pursuit. When you've selected, send the other one in my direction. I have a spare slot on Fridays.'

When Edward returns home, he finds a curiously brief email from Marianne, completely ignoring the suggestion that she pay him a visit.

To: Edward Harvey
From: Marianne Hayward
Date: 20th March 2012, 17.54
Subject: Catching up

Dear Edward,
You have said nothing about the whereabouts of your children.
love,
Marianne

To: Marianne Hayward
From: Edward Harvey
Date: 20th March 2012, 22.42
Subject: Re: Catching up

Dear Marianne,
James is still with Kate. Both have completed PhDs and are currently working on the effects of wind turbines on marine and bird life. They are based in Cumbria (Maryport) and researching the Robin Rigg wind farm in the Solway – but the job involves other installations around the UK, so they keep moving.
Rachel is in London, a copywriter for an advertising agency, a slave to deadlines. Christopher is learning to be a chef with Felicity in Italy. Harriet is a biology teacher at her old school in Exeter, still living at home, and looking after me.
What about Holly?
love,
Edward

To: Edward Harvey
From: Marianne Hayward
Date: 20th March 2012, 23.07
Subject: Re: Catching up

Dear Edward,
Holly is flat-sharing in Guildford, working as a solicitor,
still single.
Marianne

Another short response. It is impossible to gauge her tone.
Over the next two evening there are more emails and more
tentative disclosures about dismal topics such as the illnesses
and deaths of both sets of parents, the state of flux of their
respective lives and whether the current property market
makes it an unwise time to downshift. When it seems there
are no more life events to catch up on, Edward decides to be
brave.

To: Marianne Hayward
From: Edward Harvey
Date: 22nd March 2012, 20.41
Subject: Re: Catching up

Have you given my invitation any further thought?
Edward

Harriet would probably tell him this was rash, but he knows
Marianne will be cautious and unlikely to take any chances
unless she is sure his original offer was serious.

He is about to take Meg for her last walk when the house
phone rings and as soon as he hears the voice, he remembers.
With all this distraction, he has completely forgotten about his

second and thus far provisional meeting with Jessica which was suggested for this very evening.

'I'm sorry. I completely forgot to let you know. Been extremely busy with work.'

'I'm at the Retreat now. I've been waiting for the best part of an hour, feeling like a lemon.'

'I'm sorry, Jessica, but we hadn't confirmed.'

'I assumed, as I hadn't heard from you, that we were on. I thought better of you, Edward.' This is Olivia's tone. Or Felicity in a bad mood.

'I'm sorry,' says Edward again. And he is genuinely sorry that she has misunderstood. He had intended to make an excuse.

There is a silence during which he can hear her breathing. He shifts his weight onto the other foot, unsure of what to say next.

'It's not too late,' she says.

'I've already eaten, I'm afraid.'

'A drink, then?'

My God, she is persistent. 'I'm sorry, Jessica. But I have work to do for tomorrow,' he lies.

She is terse. 'I could have made other plans. My evening is wasted.' Then a sudden switch of mood. 'Make it up to me. How about tomorrow, or Saturday?'

Edward panics. This is the response of a woman who is a little too desperate. He is alarmed. 'Jessica, much as I enjoyed our previous meal together, as I said afterwards, I'm not quite ready for what I think you have in mind. I have a lot on at present and I can't afford any emotional distraction.'

There is another long pause.

Another switch of mood, this time she is businesslike. 'When you provisionally agreed to meeting me again, I supposed … Never mind, I'm having a party on the twenty-eighth of April.

Put it in your diary. Summer will be on the way and you'll have had more time to sort out your life. I'd very much like to see you there. It will be a relaxed atmosphere. Mostly locals.'

'Okay,' says Edward, deducing that this is the quickest way to save face and get her off the phone.

Afterwards Harriet says, 'I told you she's weird.'

'It wasn't weird, exactly. Something I couldn't quite identify.'

'You can't possibly go to her party.'

'There'll be other people from the village there. I don't want to cut myself off from the community. Assuming I'm free, I think I should show face.'

'Then you need to assume she will throw herself at you.'

10

Panic

Edward's second invitation to stay at the Deer Orchard sends Marianne into analysis overdrive, not because she doesn't want to see him, but because she is frightened of becoming more involved while still unclear about his intentions, or indeed her own. Felicity's disappearance changes the order from his perspective and she is so crushed by loss that she balks at risking the potential for further hurt. He is a very different person from Johnny and she is not like Felicity. It could be a disaster.

Taryn says over the phone, 'You'll never discover his intentions if you don't meet. He probably doesn't know what they are after five years. And you don't know either. You have to give it a chance.'

Marianne is very familiar with the midweek version of Edward. She knows him as a tidy, suit-wearing individual who likes ironed shirts – which he does himself – and polished shoes. He shaves and showers every morning and appears for breakfast pressed, clean and coordinated with a well-tied tie. He is more soap than aftershave, but now and then she caught a hint of something expensive wafting in his wake through Beechview Close, usually after Christmas and on days when he was meeting university big-wigs or lecturing in some other institution.

She knows he rises at the same time each day, always the first one up. He likes fruit, cereal and toast for breakfast, or a bacon sandwich if time permits. He will also eat eggs of any persuasion if anyone else is having the same, and he drinks decaf tea at all times, saying he has no need for any extra stimulation. He was livelier and more talkative than she or Johnny and as Radio 4 was usually on in the background, he often picked up on current affairs and tried to engage one of them in conversation.

In the evenings he reappeared slightly more dishevelled but still conservative, respectable, hair more wind-blown ruffled, the beginnings of an evening shadow. And he liked to collapse in a chair and read the paper he had bought at the station, or listen to the news. She and Johnny shared evening cooking duties depending upon their school and college commitments. If they were both out, Edward brought something microwavable for all of them to eat when they returned home, if they wanted.

Most evenings, after supper was cleared and the dishes were done, often by Edward, they each had their own routine for working and preparation. Edward would disappear to his room, tapping away on his laptop, occasionally reappearing if there was a programme on television that they had all said they wanted to watch. *University Challenge* was a particular favourite and all three of them were extremely competitive when it came to answering questions. Thankfully their specialist areas were mostly different so they each had an opportunity to shine. And very occasionally Edward would go with Johnny across to the Jolly Woodman for a pint and a chat. According to Johnny, this was usually about politics or the environment. He had only once gone out with Marianne alone since they had walked in the park after the mugging incident, months before he came to lodge with them. And she can only remember a couple of times when the three of them went out to the pub together.

Taryn says, 'What is there not to like? Predictability may not be the most exciting trait, but the variety he lacks in routine behaviour is more than compensated for by variety in action and thought. You know he's always off doing something interesting work-wise. You'd never be bored.'

But Marianne hardly knows the weekend Edward at all. A glimpse of him in photographs where he seemed to favour jeans and a casual style, and the few days after he came out of hospital when he stayed with them to recover before Johnny drove him part way to Devon to meet up with Felicity. Then it had been jeans with an open-neck shirt or sweater. The weekend Edward is most probably sartorially acceptable, but one can never be sure with academics. She remembers Tweedy Tom from when she was at college who dressed like one of the hunting set, and Derek Yard who wore red jumpers (her mother had warned her not to trust such men), and Alan Cooper who had a taste for slacks and V-necks, even though he was only twenty at the time.

She doesn't know if Edward gets up early when he's off work, or if he likes to laze in bed. He is so lively in the mornings she has always suspected him of being a lark. And she is an owl, so straight away their body rhythms are incompatible. Not serious if neither is an extreme version of their bird, but in some cases it can be grounds for divorce.

Taryn says, 'If dating agencies took biorhythms into account, the human race might miss out on some of its most exciting unions. In any case, if you're taking early retirement, you will be more adaptable.'

The more Taryn tries to convince, the more Marianne resists until she has no arguments left other than a natural pessimism borne out of the previous few difficult years, and a dented self-esteem from having become even more invisible than she was when she hit midlife and menopause. She has lost her bounce, her sense of humour, her enthusiasm. Perhaps meeting Edward would reinvigorate and inspire.

She reflects on their last meeting; the day he left. *That hug!* She blushes at the thought. A hug that betrayed emotions as deep as the Grand Canyon, as turbulent as the Inga rapids on the Congo. *Oh, to see him again …* To be able to share thoughts and feelings without the shackles of their previous interactions. It could be sublime; it could be a new life adventure, new hope and new joys. Or it could be a disappointment far worse than the one she feared before she first met him. Yes, their parting betrayed passion; the potential for passion. But that was five years ago. He will have changed. She has changed. She feels dull: a monochrome shadow of her former self, lacking verve and wit and all the things she believed captured his interest before.

If he wanted only to be friends and if she were to fall in love, or vice versa, imagine the pain for either or both of them. She believed she couldn't take any more; that her heart was held together by the weakest glue. And even if they did start a relationship, what if they didn't gel when it came to romance or sex or simple day-to-day living?

It is with these doubts in mind that she sends an email that again ignores his invitation.

To: Edward Harvey
From: Marianne Hayward
Date: 22nd March 2012, 21.22
Subject: Re: Catching up

Dear Edward,
Remember I wrote to you once about my reservations about tagging and tracking animals? I've come across a report on the net that says it is probable that radio tracking kills some of the animals because of the effects of electromagnetic radiation. There is no scientific proof

of this, but an increasing amount of evidence is stacking up suggesting that though the negative health effects of such devices have yet to be proven, we are surrounding ourselves with ever increasing problems.
love,
Mari

He will be astute enough to realise her deliberate omission is a need for more time to adjust to his reappearance.

11

More Invitations

Mari.

How casually we often write a word, how carefully the recipient might read it. Edward read and re-read this word as if he was expecting the letters to give him clues as to her current feelings. Mari: a resumption of intimacy and friendship, or a mistake? Yet no mention of the invitation. The content was the old Marianne; the Marianne that liked to expose him to whatever thought was on her mind on any particular day. He took it as a compliment that she believed him to be a worthy beneficiary of her musings. And it was true that he appreciated receiving an email that contained more than just an update on health, family, work and weather. But sometimes at the end of a long day, he preferred not to have to think; to deal with facts rather than theories.

Before he has time to contemplate a suitable reply, he receives an email from Patrick Shrubsole, Dean of Humanities and Social Sciences at Stancliffe university and famed for his dynamic presentation on a couple of Channel 4 series of archaeological flavour.

To: Edward Harvey
From: Patrick Shrubsole
Date: 22nd March 2012, 21.25
Subject: Our Fragile Earth

Edward,
Remember the idea we had about the Isles of Scilly as a

model for sustainability across the globe? Time for it to be revived! 2012 is the year of planetary realisation. Weather-related catastrophes everywhere – never mind the debt crisis. The current drought and the reported state of groundwater reserves suggest we may be in for some food shortages later in the year, or in 2013.
Suffice to say, wheels are in motion again. There's a belief that because of soaring prices, the TV viewing public will see the relevance. I have an interested contact at an independent production company that specialises in this type of documentary. If we go ahead with them, it will be their responsibility to negotiate with the major networks.
Ideally we need to meet. Do a bit of brainstorming. Fancy a trip to London? I see you're not due to lecture here again until October. Next Friday morning would be good for me.
Cheers,
Patrick

Much of Edward's recent professional life has been wrapped up with the Isles of Scilly. In 2002 he discovered the original Troy Town maze on St Agnes. This led to a book about labyrinth mazes and participation in an exhibition with lectures at the British Museum. Soon after, he completed a lecture tour round the islands and was subsequently invited to excavate there every summer with his Stancliffe students. During these visits they had made considerable progress in uncovering burial sites, leading to further material for talks and papers. Since leaving Stancliffe, there were proposals in place for his Devon uni students to explore the now-flooded expanse between Tresco and Bryher, possibly in 2013.

The idea Patrick refers to concerns a conversation in

September of 2003, immediately before Edward was attacked, when they had been supping beer and idly discussing how the ravages on Scilly in the 1800s could be used as a model to predict what might happen to the UK as a whole – and even the world – if population and economic growth were allowed to continue unchecked. More recent practices of sustainability on the islands could also be used to shape a potential future for the UK. Their discussion had led to a proposal to the BBC regarding a documentary series. Much interest was expressed at the time, but after a few initial meetings, the plans had been abandoned. It was this idea to which Harriet referred during their walk a couple of weeks earlier when she said that it was time he pursued one of his academic interests with the zeal of old.

How coincidental that the machinery has started to whirr again even before he has had a chance to decide what to do.

The historical records suggest that in the early 1800s, the Isles of Scilly were thriving. Potatoes and fish were abundant and there was no problem with hunger. Then in 1825 there was a drought from May to September and the famine began. In those days, the law of primogeniture did not apply on the islands and ever decreasing portions of land were shared between offspring to a point where they were unsustainable in feeding a family.

In 1834, the new Lord Proprietor of the islands, Augustus Smith, re-allocated the land so each farmer had enough to be economically viable. This then succeeded to the eldest son while other children had to find employment elsewhere on the islands, or relocate to the mainland. It was a harsh solution which split families and caused much heartache, but the prosperity that ensued was justification for such drastic action and the islands have continued to operate in a similar fashion.

The email from Patrick excites Edward's professional juices.

He has already done a considerable amount of work on the project so would not be starting cold. It is also a new challenge and a doorway into television; a launch-pad for disseminating his books to a wider audience. He calls Patrick and arranges a meeting at Stancliffe. Then in an unusual fit of spontaneity, he emails Marianne.

To: Marianne Hayward
From: Edward Harvey
Date: 22nd March 2012, 22.43
Subject: Beechview Hotel

Dear Mari,
Am making an unexpected visit to London next Friday 30th – to meet Patrick Shrubsole to discuss that old idea about Scilly and sustainability. Apparently he has resurrected the original proposal and a production company is interested. The weather conditions we have been experiencing make it ever more relevant.
I know this is short notice, and a sudden escalation of our tentative reunion via email. No pressure, but it would be great to see you. I remember once asking you if I could stay overnight when I had a meeting with Patrick. I promise you don't need a chaperone!
Alternatively, if you are still not working on Fridays, we could meet in town for a bite to eat before I return home.
Hope you are okay.
love,
Edward

Faint heart, as they say. It's a chance he has to take, battering on the steely panels of her defences. She can be so stubborn. He knows how reluctant she is to shift from an opinion that is deeply held; how long it takes her to forgive. Once it didn't seem to matter so much, but since he turned fifty, he senses an acceleration of time, of limits, of the sand over half way through the fragile curvaceous glass.

To: Edward Harvey
From: Marianne Hayward
Date: 22nd March 2012, 23.01
Subject: Re: Beechview Hotel

Dear Edward,
Okay. You can stay. I presume we're talking next Thursday night? Send me your travel plans and I'll pick you up from the Junction.
Mari

Edward breathes a happy sigh and then is vaguely aware of a crunching on the gravel outside below the window. The security light flashes on. He stops to listen. Nothing. He looks out of the window and there is only the eerie semi-circular glow of light surrounding the back entrance. Perhaps it was a fox or a badger. They are always setting off the lights although they don't usually crunch the gravel. Maybe it was a rare visit from a deer, but it is a long way from the woods behind Killerton. If it was anything untoward, Meg would bark, but he decides he will sleep better if he takes a look downstairs.

On the mat by the back door is a white envelope with his name on the front. Inside is an invitation to Jessica's party. On the back, in childlike script, she has written: *Sorry I was a bit crabby on the phone. I do understand why you don't want to rush things. Look forward to seeing you soon. Jessica.*

Edward mutters a few expletives, replaces the card in the envelope and tosses it onto the kitchen table.

When he goes to bed, he dismisses any thought of Jessica and snuggles under the duvet with his Marianne fantasy, a ray of hope, the beginnings of a new dance, of infinite possibilities.

12

Meeting Lydia Again

If I should meet thee
After long years,
How should I greet thee?
With silence and tears.

Lord Byron

Marianne stops her hatchback in the small car park on the other side of the tracks to the main entrance of Beckenham Junction station, behind a bar which was once called the Lazy Toad, and near Waitrose supermarket. It is dark and chilly and her muscles are tense. She sits motionless, gripping the steering wheel, anticipation growing, emotions wildly falling over each other in their attempt to make themselves visible.

Her decision to have him stay was an act of subconscious winning over conscious. She knew he needed a quick response so he could make plans. There was no time to prevaricate, to weigh up the pros and cons of him staying versus her meeting him in town. And to do neither, to ignore both of his suggestions, was not an option if she wanted their friendship to be re-established.

Her eyes are misty in the lamplight. She is almost as overcome as she was some nine years ago when sleet was in the air, when she was due to meet him in town at a lecture he was giving to the Antiquarian Society, when the trains and then tube let her down and she had returned home to Johnny with a cold red nose and unshed tears.

When she did finally meet him at the British Museum a year later, she had been so overwhelmed, so excited, because in live human form he impacted beyond expectations in a way she never could have imagined. Her worst fears were that he would have ballooned beyond recognition into bloated and jowly caricature, shattering her childhood dream and obliterating the thrill of their innocent emailing. And if not that, then he might be aloof and academic to the point of weirdness; a pompous geek. It had been with a mixture of relief and disbelief that neither of these fears was realised. In fact he was in good shape, warm and approachable with distant traces of a Cumbrian twang in his accent. She remembers thinking, *my God, he says 'graph' with a short 'a',* and even though she says it with a long 'a', this made him seem more grounded.

They had chatted in the museum café and thirty-four years had evaporated and she was once more Marianne aged ten, gazing in adoration at her first crush. If it were possible to have a similarly innocent adult crush, then this is what she experienced when after their meeting, she walked to the tube station with a spring in her step and a smile on her face. This would be the beginning of an enduring friendship, she had thought. And so it seemed for a few weeks until her image of him as a person without human frailties was dashed by the discovery of his one night stand with Taryn.

She jumps. How long has she been drifting? Probably only seconds. A train is snaking stealthily into the station. She gets out of the car, smoothes her hair and walks to the wire-mesh fence that borders the pathway from the platform. *What will he think of me? What will I think of him? Have we changed too much in these past five unkind years?*

A moment's anxiety lest he isn't there among the throng of evening commuters, carrying their bags and newspapers, eagerly rushing home. But soon she spies him through the fence, striding towards her, black overcoat, briefcase, overnight bag, eyes crinkling when he sees her, unmistakably Edward. He weaves round the fence and comes back to her, drops his case and bag at her feet and neither hesitates. Their hug is long and tight and slow. He kisses her cheek and she is almost crying: for him, for Johnny, for her parents, for a rich life now gone, and a hope, a promise, a glimpse of something special in the future.

She stands back, unsure where to begin. There is so much to say, so much catching up to do. Yet her throat tightens with emotion and she is speechless.

He grasps both of her hands and looks her in the eye. 'It is so very wonderful to see you again.'

'And I you. Sorry,' she sniffs, and takes a tissue from her coat pocket.

He hugs her again. 'Oh Mari … Where do we start?'

She brushes away the tears. She cries so easily these days. 'With trivialities and practicalities. Have you had a good journey? Are you ready to eat?'

They get into the car and head back to Beechview Close, making small talk about how things have and have not changed in Beckenham. Waiting at the Junction traffic lights, the four corners are not perceptibly different from five years ago: the shoe repairer and key cutter with the flower stall nearby; the O'Neill's pub, its outside seating adorned with blue umbrellas; the estate agency; the village green surrounded by London plane trees and dotted with old-fashioned street lamps; the sandstone building that looks as if it should be a bank, now a Thai restaurant. But here and there the old has been demolished to make way for the new, each empty space like a missing tooth, soon cosmetically replaced with a block of flats or offices. Marianne is aware that Edward is looking at her, his eyes searching through the channels to her soul. She unblocks her defences, relieved to be in the company of someone who knows her so well.

In Beechview Close, she shows him up to his old room, Holly's room, still the same furniture and girly colour scheme.

'Just like old times,' he says.

Just like old times, but strangely intimate; no husband or daughter keeping watch.

She leaves him to sort his things and goes downstairs. Her oven clock is already pinging; time for the vegetables. In a dream she puts water on to boil, prepares some carrots and opens a pack of frozen peas. By the time Edward comes down, she is placing a steaming rectangular oven dish on a cork mat in the centre of the table in the dining room.

'We're having Mrs Tapster's Haddock Cheese Casserole,' says Marianne. 'I have rediscovered the recipe in a collection I used at college. It's from the mother of a friend, written out with the detail necessary for an eighteen year old who could barely roast a chicken – in my case. And I know you like fish, and I didn't want to give you the same old things we used to eat; as if I haven't moved on .Which I haven't, much, culinary-wise. But I intend to. Soon. Oh gosh, I'm rambling …'

'Ramble away,' says Edward, sitting down. 'This is lovely and your rambling means I can eat. Tell me about *Lydia*.' He digs the offered spoon into the cheese and breadcrumb crust.

'Due out at the beginning of May and currently with the printer. Launch lined up at the college and a signing at Beckenham Bookshop. Nothing too fancy, but it's a start.'

'I knew you could do it,' he says.

His hair is greyer than it was but still with more dark colour than she expected. And his brown eyes are sad. But overall, he looks well and rested. The commuting took its toll, especially after the trauma of the attack. His scars are now but faint silver lines on his cheek and wrist. And he has retained a relatively youthful physique. She notices his hands on the cutlery, strong and well-defined. Her mother would have approved. Her mother had a thing about men and their hands. *'You don't want pudgy sausages touching you; or damp and sweaty; or limp.'*

Marianne says, 'I hope there's no fallout from the people we knew at Brocklebank Hall.'

'It is fiction,' says Edward.

'But inspired by fact. In some cases, at least.'

'Isn't most literature, to a lesser or greater extent?'

'I wonder what my parents would have thought. The bullying, and so forth. They would know at least some of it was true. Perhaps that's why I have waited until they are gone. Not consciously, though.'

'After my parents died,' says Edward, 'I found myself taking on their roles; doing things that they had done, almost without thinking about it. I used to leave it to them to keep in touch with the more distant cousins and to remind us all about birthdays.'

'I've started baking,' says Marianne. 'As you know, I never used to do more than the odd loaf. Of course, it's trendy at the moment, but it's as if I am the guardian of the family recipes, the ones that have been handed down from the great-grandparents. I do flapjacks, crumpets, gingerbread, drop scones, sponges. And a Twitter contact has led to banana bread and chocolate brownies.' She remembers what Taryn said about men and cakes. These new skills might come in handy.

'We started going to the cenotaph in Exeter for Remembrance Sunday a couple of years before Felicity left.'

'It might be age,' says Marianne. 'Many things start to become relevant once you reach fifty.'

Edward agrees. 'Checking the pension pot and worrying about getting sick.'

After supper, together they wash and dry the dishes, as they did during his lodging days, on the days when Johnny was at a meeting at school or playing badminton.

'And still you haven't a dishwasher,' says Edward.

'Even less reason now, with just me.'

Once settled in the living room with a cup of decaf tea and a piece of cake, Edward takes a deep breath and says, 'We can't avoid talking about what happened. Shall we get it over with?'

Marianne uncrosses her legs.

'I'm sorry I left you. It was the worst decision; my last attempt to save my marriage. I was becoming more comfortable here with you than at home, but it was difficult seeing you happy with Johnny. It highlighted the gulf between Felicity and me. When Conrad from work said, "marriage is always like that once the menopause hits," I looked at you two and knew it didn't have to be true. I couldn't believe my contentment could disappear because of her inheritance. I was sure it must be salvageable if I could find the formula. I remembered you mentioning to me once about compromise. I thought I'd give it a try. I knew my work–home balance was out of kilter. I knew my inability to involve myself in her enterprises annoyed her.' Edward pauses to take a bite of cake.

'Feigning interest wouldn't have worked long term,' says Marianne.

'She resented my taking the job in London – even though at the time she seemed to relish telling her friends that I was now "Professor Ted". That's what she started to call me – but always with an edge to her voice. Being here was a distraction. It meant we never addressed the problems – not that it would have made any difference as I later found out. Once I decided to go back home, the thought of living away from you seemed unbearable. I foolishly thought it would be easier if I didn't see you at all.'

'We could have written or talked on the phone.'

'But don't you see how impossible that would have been?'

Marianne didn't. She saw it only from her own perspective and remembers the sense of abandonment. 'I thought we were friends who would support each other for ever.'

'That is a very idealised view of friendship. The partner must always take priority – as he or she does when you first set out on the path. Friends take a back seat. They may not like it, but it comes with the territory.'

Marianne recalls how insular she and Johnny were during the early years and how Taryn had been marginalised. She knows he wants her to say she forgives him; that it doesn't matter. But it did. She struggles with her thoughts. She needs to know how he sees the future; to be sure she won't be abandoned again should he meet someone else.

Edward continues, 'At the time I thought I was doing what was right; honouring my marriage. What I didn't recognise was that Felicity had already betrayed me and didn't deserve such honour. By the time I realised this, it was too late.'

'And are you still in touch with her?'

'Only via the children, or occasionally when a letter arrives for her that needs attention. Even then, we don't talk as such. I don't want to know about her new life and if she wants to know about me, I expect she would ask the kids.'

'Will you divorce?'

'That was the original plan, but neither of us has made any move yet. Both too busy; both avoiding the unpleasantness of it all. Given that she was the one to leave, I suppose I'm waiting for her to do what she must.'

Marianne changes the subject and they talk for a while about the children, gradually relaxing into the way it always was when they had a chance to chat. Edward says how much he misses Christopher.

'It was too sudden. With the others, I got used to them

going away during term time and returning during the holidays. Chris was here and then gone. I haven't seen him since. I phone him quite often and he sends me the odd text.'

'Will he come to visit, eventually?'

'I hope so but Felicity seems to have a powerful influence over him.'

'So what's it like being back at Devon uni?' asks Marianne.

'Those who have been HoD in my absence are still disgruntled and uncooperative, even after all this time. This encourages the new staff who don't know me so well to be similarly awkward.'

'When I was acting HoD, covering a maternity leave, I went on a course in leadership run by a man with a most captivating anecdotal style. Two of the most useful things I ever learned about managing people were "Think amoeba" and "Think geese". Dealing with teachers – or possibly any group of underlings – is like trying to persuade amoeba to cross a road. A few go in the direction you want while others slip and slide and do their own thing. It taught me patience and acceptance. Not everyone was going to think like me. I had to find their strengths and try to develop them. But you know this.'

'And the geese?'

'If geese see a member of the skein lagging behind, they do one of two things. If it's sick and can't keep up, they send another goose to support it until it's better. If it's just being lazy, they honk at it.'

'In that case, I need to do more honking. It's not my preferred way, but I can do it if required.'

At night, Marianne pictures Edward alone in the guest room and fantasises that he is restless, unable to stop thinking about her. She imagines him knocking on her door, asking to talk some more, getting into bed with her because it's cold, and holding her close. She so misses that human warmth since Johnny died, the comforting heat from skin against skin, the reassuring rustle of the duvet as he stretched beneath its feathery softness, waking to the breathing of another soul, the monosyllabic murmurings as the day unfolded. She wonders if Edward misses Felicity in the same way. Or perhaps it's the sex he misses most. She dismisses the thought. The fantasy Edward likes cuddles as much as she does – because still she cannot go beyond the bounds of propriety.

Next morning, when they have breakfasted and she drives him back to Beckenham Junction, he says, 'Now will you agree to come to the Deer Orchard for a few days? Perhaps while we're both on holiday over the next couple of weeks. Bearing in mind we will have the added bonus of a chaperone in the form of Harriet – although it is plainly evident we don't need one.'

'Yes,' says Marianne. 'Of course I will.'

13

Sustainability

'Good to see you again, Ted,' says Patrick, shaking him by the hand, slapping his shoulder, proffering a chair and then picking up the phone to summon tea from one of his minions. He is brisk of manner with a sharp and almost aristocratic air. He wears a dark blue suit and tie, his hair noticeably thinner, his long fair forelock wispier than when Edward last saw him the previous October. He has also acquired some metal rimmed glasses over which he peers. They are in Patrick's office on the third floor of the main Stancliffe building. Plants line windowsills and books cover almost all of two walls. Edward takes a seat at a large round black wooden table, a sheaf of papers in front of him.

'We cannot continue to cling on to our comfortable middle-class lifestyles,' says Patrick, sitting down opposite and opening a file. 'We cannot persist with this obsession for growth. The idea of infinite growth is a delusion. And we can no longer afford to avoid the population debate. It is almost ten years since we said it may not be long before there will be no turning back. If we don't aim for a sustainable population now, more radical measures may be required in the future.'

Edward has noticed that Patrick rarely starts with any small talk but launches straight into business mode. There is an ex Mrs Shrubsole and no children so it is difficult to ask questions about family.

Patrick continues, 'If we don't act, the population will naturally adjust through starvation and war. But imagine what an unhappy Earth it will be. Carl Safina says that if everyone had a US standard of living, we would need two and a half Earths for sufficient supplies. Given that we are depleting forests and fish stocks, and rapidly encroaching upon land suitable for crop production, more people means either everyone getting poorer, or the poor getting considerably poorer.'

They are interrupted by tea being brought in by a thin-faced young woman in a narrow red skirt and white blouse. 'One decaf and one ginger,' she says.

Edward's attention slips momentarily and he starts thinking about Marianne and the shine in her eyes when she met him at the station, the touch of her cheek against his, the familiar scent of her and the hug that stirred his sleeping passions …

Patrick is speaking again. 'The key issues as I see it are resource depletion and climate change, both exacerbated by an increase in population; the upshot being land degradation, loss of biodiversity and stress on water supplies. Some experts believe unless something is done, we will need two or even three times the amount of water, food and energy by the end of this century.'

'But world population growth is decelerating,' says Edward, forcing himself to engage. 'And in the West, ageing is the main reason for the increase.'

'It may be the main reason, but it will probably level off in time unless someone discovers how to reverse the ageing process. The birth rate can't be overlooked. Governments are reluctant to grasp this particular nettle because any sudden and significant fall could lead to a different crisis in that there wouldn't be enough young to support the old.'

'And the relentlessness of the urban sprawl,' says Edward. 'All this talk of the need for more affordable housing, yet no mention of an equal need to curb the size of the population.'

'Ludicrous,' says Patrick. 'Of course I want everyone to have a home. But we are being greedy. We want two homes; even three. We want spare bedrooms, offices, en-suites; more yardage per person than ever before. And we are less inclined to share. We have become too used to our own space – probably made worse by social networking. Without the social support of Twitter and Facebook, I suspect more people would cohabit to combat loneliness.'

'That's an interesting theory,' says Edward. 'Perhaps the premise of another paper.'

'Something for the psychology or sociology lot to examine,' Patrick says, laughing. 'We have more serious matters in mind.'

'If we overbuild our way out of trouble, we could end up with an economic housing disaster on our hands when the population readjusts,' says Edward.

'Even if you reduce fertility,' says Patrick, 'this does not guarantee a reduction in consumption – China being a case in point. While the natural world has a constantly shifting population in line with available resources, modern mankind tries to outmanoeuvre. But we can't do it for ever. Consumerism has to stop eventually.'

'So are we saying a pincer approach is needed: reduce population and consumerism?' says Edward.

'Sustainability is very difficult on a large scale. However, this is the message we need to put across. The notion of everyone aspiring to live like those in the West has to be debunked, and we in the West need to change our ways. More sustainable and frugal living must become the fashion, the norm, rather than the domain of eco-warriors from the hippy generation and the cranks. You and I and people like us need to abandon our cars, our labour-saving devices.'

Edward thinks about the dishwasher and the endless arguments it caused when their son James first jumped on the eco-bandwagon. He says, 'In the short term at least, I don't see people giving up their washing machines. In many households, both partners work.'

'It would solve unemployment in a jiffy if women went back to their traditional role in the home.'

'Controversial and retrograde,' says Edward, imagining what Felicity or Marianne would say at the very suggestion. No wonder Mrs Shrubsole escaped.

'There may be no choice in the future,' says Patrick.

'Today's women are as likely to press for the men to stay at home. Modern working practices mean that physical differences are less relevant.'

'Transport is a more urgent problem,' says Patrick. 'Car usage will have to be cut dramatically.'

'But have you thought about the practicalities of getting from A to B? Our world is structured with A and B often being a considerable distance from each other. And those of us who live in the country often have poor public transport options.'

'It can't happen overnight. There will need to be a slow reversal of geographical mobility. Many young people are already choosing to stay at home when they go to uni. They can't afford to leave. Some go and then come back: boomerang kids like your Harriet. In this respect the change has already begun. Once families re-cluster, travelling will be reduced. It will take another generation, but it will happen if we encourage it. We need to advocate the attractiveness of working near the family home instead of promoting commuting and endless hours in traffic jams or sitting on trains. Grandparents, aunts and great-aunts – the extended family – were once the babysitters. Like meerkats.'

'Like many Asian families,' says Edward.

'I also see a return of the horse,' says Patrick.

'Not for a long time, surely?'

'In the cities it will just be a question of expanding Boris's bike scheme or making it safe and practical to use Segways. But, out in the sticks where you are, could one not run a horse hire business on the same lines?'

'Are you serious?'

'Semi-serious. I don't see it as likely in the short term, but it will only take an enterprising person who is willing to take risks. A pony-and-trap taxi service, perhaps.'

Edward is cautious. 'People may give up their cars or even turn garages into stables, but it will take years to develop fully. Not enough horses for a start, or the necessary supporting workforce.'

'Could easily expand numbers within our native pony breeds. And Kwik-Fit and such like could retrain their mechanics to become farriers and grooms, perhaps through broadening the NVQ offer in further education establishments.'

'A pretty thought,' says Edward.

'But not as crazy as it sounds,' says Patrick, slapping the table, his eyes bright with enthusiasm. 'These are the ideas that we need to plant in people's minds and it is the radical proposals that will get the media talking. Someone somewhere will take a chance and start the ball rolling. Trams came back. Remember the scepticism at first? Now, every city wants one.'

Already Edward's mind is whirring away. 'Lateral thinking. I take your point.'

'Anyway … to business. Flying Owl is the name of the production company who are interested in our idea. They believe if we don't develop it now, someone else will and that would be a lost opportunity. Programme-wise we are thinking of a three-parter. Firstly, lay out the problem, scare the shit out of everyone, make them sit up and take notice.'

'Research would suggest if we scare them too much, they

will be turned off,' says Edward. 'Stephen Emmott believes people are more likely to shift their behaviour if they are nudged rather than pushed.'

'Okay, so we scare them a bit – but tell them if we do x y and z, everything will be hunky-dory. I'd also like to include a world view. This is a problem that will affect all of us sooner or later and there's little point in one country reining back if others don't do the same.' Patrick's slightly arrogant, supremely confident public school manner is perfect for the academic on television.

'This is going to be extremely unpopular. What government is going to implement draconian strategies? Indeed, what are those strategies going to be?'

'We present the demographic history of Scilly, examine their current sustainable living practices and then extrapolate to mainland UK,' says Patrick. 'We discussed some of the options when the idea first came to light, if you remember. St Agnes is a perfect example. Being a tiny island, it's easy for people to see why it must operate sustainably. For our idea to be acceptable to Joe Public, we have to start at the micro level: village level, or in the case of towns and cities, where population is very dense, this may mean operating at the street level or possibly on the principle of the square mile. Projects need to be community based and micro-managed.'

'Which is the exact opposite of the way the modern world works,' says Edward.

'So we advocate slow introduction of a new philosophy. This will mean using incentives to encourage all people to have small families. It's already happening in parts of the world. The government will need to be brave but also fair.' Patrick shifts forwards in his seat, placing elbows on the table and forming a firm arch with his thin fingers. 'And it isn't about right-wing politics. We have to convince everyone that unless people of all persuasions buy into these policies, we're doomed. Doomed as a country and ultimately doomed as a planet.'

Edward feels momentary guilt at the size of his own family.

'We don't let wild animal populations burgeon out of control if there's no natural predation,' continues Patrick. 'Deer in Scotland, for example. Some advocate the re-introduction of wolves, but that's another debate. And there have been some unsavoury suggestions in fiction. Have you read P. D. James's *The Children of Men*? Set in 2021 in a world where no babies have been born since 1995. People are not allowed to become old and infirm because there are not enough young to look after them, never mind the financial constraints. Steps are taken. The elderly are shipped out to sea in a ceremony called a Quietus. The plug is pulled as it were: an enforced drowning. Seems a horrifying prospect to most of us, living as we are at a time when life is preserved no matter what. And I don't see much changing by 2021, but one day it will. One day we will look back on current western attitudes to death with amazement and incredulity.'

'I must read it,' says Edward, thinking that his own parents would have gladly joined in a Quietus when their lives became unfulfilling and their pain unbearable.

'Changing gardening habits is where we could have most impact in the short term,' says Patrick. 'Already we are seeing people being encouraged to grow their own vegetables. This needs to be rolled out at a wider level. Chelsea Flower Show may be a place to start. Or Hampton Court. Try to get sponsorship for a sustainable garden. Of course, people have played with this notion before, but we need it to be the norm to have carrots in the front garden and salad veg instead of bedding plants.'

'Which is very much what my wife did at the Deer Orchard. We turned lawns and flowers over to vegetable production.'

'Splendid!' says Patrick. 'Perhaps we should pop round and do a spot of filming.'

'You better make it quick, then,' says Edward. 'I've instructed our gardener to reinstate some of the lawns.' Perhaps this is another reason to delay Rick's makeover for at least a few months. He hopes he hasn't already ordered the turf.

'And most people with gardens could have a couple of hens,' continues Patrick. 'But we need programmes about how to look after them.'

'Animal husbandry replacing cooking programmes,' says Edward. *'MasterSmallholder; The Great British Hen or Bee Keeper.'*

'Excellent idea. It's wartime thinking again. We don't need to re-invent the wheel completely.'

'Indeed,' says Edward, at last joining in with a similar level of enthusiasm and wondering how many more clichés Patrick is going to toss before him. 'There have been several "Living in the Past" series, but we need to show how it can be done in the future. Different episodes tackling different produce: vegetables and poultry being basic; fruit and animals for those with more space and ambition. There are one or two institutions one hears about doing something like this. In prisons, for example, because it gives the inmates something worthwhile to do; helps to rehabilitate. Working on the land is therapeutic.'

Patrick says, 'How about an education initiative? A pack of materials that can be purchased: seeds, basic instructions and resources for lessons. There have been forays before – particularly in the primary sector. We need to get schoolchildren involved. It's their future. If they jump on board, teachers will sign up to it, and by default, parents will be dragged along. This needs to be all schools, secondary as well as primary, and country-wide. We need an educational specialist.'

'And I know just the person,' says Edward, thinking rapidly.

'I have a friend who has worked in education all her life. She is trained in secondary and currently teaching psychology in a college. She's probably taking early retirement at the end of the year because she has a novel about to be published. She's interested in all of these issues.'

'Would she be able to design an educational resource pack? Ready to go when the programmes are aired?'

'Would she be paid?'

'Ideally, we need government funding, or sponsorship, to have maximum impact. There may be an environmental group that would like to be involved. It might be that Flying Owl will oversee it. Leave that side of things to me. Ask her and let me know. If she's interested we need to talk or email to discuss details. Soon. From you I need script outlines for the programmes and ultimately chapter outlines for the book. We'll be missing a financial opportunity if we don't have a book. It will probably be a Flying Owl publication too. And we'll plan a filming trip to Scilly after the school holidays.'

Patrick shows Edward a more detailed draft of his initial proposal and they begin to fine-tune the detail on which the scripts will be based. Afterwards they go for lunch at a nearby pub, all the while continuing to brainstorm ideas from the sensible to the bizarre.

On the train back to Devon, Edward can't wait to contact Marianne. The night before, he had been shocked by her vulnerability; as if being without Johnny had diminished the force of her physical presence. She looked tired and deflated, yet as he became used to her five years older self, as she dismantled her barriers and let him through, he caught glimpses of the woman she was, the woman he loved, and he felt an overwhelming desire to take care of her.

He considers emailing, but he wants to hear her voice

again. Also he can be more persuasive by phone. He calls her from his mobile.

She seems pleased to hear from him and they exchange a few thoughts about their reunion.

'You cheered me up,' she says. 'For a few hours, I felt like a normal person again.'

She seems enthusiastic about creating educational resources and says she will mail Patrick. Now all he has to do is pick the right time to speak to her regarding fixing a date for her to visit the Deer Orchard. With the school holidays just starting, it will have to be soon.

He settles back in his seat and watches the green fields scudding by. How quickly his life has changed from one of desolation to one of hope.

14

Lessons in Taryn, Part 1

After Edward's call Marianne is buzzing and cannot keep still. She flits around the house searching for books that may stimulate her creativity. She uses Google to find information about schools that already weave environmental practices into the curriculum. She has always considered ideas to be her forte as a teacher and as she is retiring at the end of summer, it will be fantastic to have another education-related project to work on, especially one that is outside the classroom and self-contained. It will complement her writing perfectly.

However, this is assuming Patrick Shrubsole thinks her capable of what he has in mind. She sends an exploratory email to him, expressing interest in what he and Edward have discussed.

Her working life has followed a similar path for the past two decades and revolves around Monday to Thursday at North Kent College on the edge of Beckenham. As is typical of teaching, the workload does not remain confined to timetabled slots, but spreads beside and beyond, rather like an oversized person in public transport seating. She continues to work late after the finish of the day, either at the college or at home, and marking and preparation take up most of her day off on Fridays. Since Johnny died it seems she rarely puts the job to rest and at night while the world sleeps, her brain continues to whirr, planning new strategies for discipline, or new methods of teaching a particular topic, or reflecting on any unpleasant incidents and considering their resolution. She is often awake before dawn and unable to sleep again because of the masses of information ready to spill from her brain in preparation for the next day.

Publishing a book on top of all this is almost stretching her energy reserves beyond their limits, but it is something she feels compelled to do and her weekends and late evenings have been absorbed with this for several months. Johnny dying and her reaching fifty-five have focused her mind on the future. Whatever time is left, she needs to pursue her writing dream and if there is a freelance option with Patrick Shrubsole to add to her reduced pension, so much the better.

Now she has met Edward again and found all the old *frissant* of attraction still there, she can't help but wonder where their relationship might lead. But although quite open about his feelings when he stopped lodging with them, and although their reunion was warm and affectionate, his words as he left are bothering her: '*added bonus of a chaperone … plainly evident we don't need one*'. She isn't sure whether he feels the same as before. Perhaps the freedom to be able to take things forward has reduced her appeal. And she is five years older; a battered shadow of her former self.

She needs Taryn for consultation purposes and arranges a game of tennis for Sunday morning. Then, with spring weather continuing and sunshine showing up the smears on the windows and the dust in the hard-to-reach crevices, she decides to be extravagant and order a total spring clean from a local firm. If she is going to sell the house, there is much to do.

Since Johnny died, she has engaged a couple of Beckenham services to help with plumbing and IT support. She found them via Twitter and the amazing #BeckBromFL community who are keen to advertise their businesses or to recommend others. And the previous summer, she hired a gardener. She had hoped for someone like Edward's Rick, but ended up with a bearded ex-hippy called Terry. In his favour, he is an advocate of organics and permaculture and she has been fascinated listening to him extolling the virtues of crop rotation and old-fashioned composting methods. She instructed him to start growing vegetables in patches between the flowers and she has noticed that the remains of the winter crop are looking untidy. *Time to give him a ring and talk about summer salads, carrots, potatoes and courgettes.* A few peas and beans will help with nitrogen fixation for the following year, but if she isn't going to stay much longer at the house, is it worth all the effort? She wonders if Beckenham – and specifically Beechview Close – is ready for tolerating vegetables in the front garden.

She recommended Terry to the Pines, who live two doors away. Fiona and David. They kept an eye on the cat whenever she and Johnny went away and will no doubt do the same when she visits Edward. David Pine is a surveyor and Fiona runs an upmarket dress hire business in West Wickham. Since *Strictly* introduced the Argentine Tango a few years earlier, they go dancing on Wednesday nights in London and on Saturdays in Croydon. Marianne sees them going out to their car, all slinky satin frocked and shiny suited, a flower in her hair and liberal amounts of gel in his. They are sprayed to a South American bronze and look the part, but whether their skill matches their flashiness, Marianne doesn't know. A few months after Johnny died, they tried to persuade her to join them. 'So many single men of a certain age,' trilled Fiona.

'And all obsessive tango dancers,' said Marianne. 'I couldn't be so committed.'

She thought she didn't want a man any more. Not if it required hassle and tango dancing to get one. Now Edward is back on the scene, she's not so sure.

Tennis on Sunday is less warm than the previous few weeks

and there is talk of cooler conditions and rain to come. Marianne is so concerned about the drought, she is quietly pleased at the prospect.

She has been neglecting her fitness regime during the past couple of weeks and she loses the set of tennis without putting up much of a fight.

'You're out of condition, girl,' says Taryn, ignoring a tanned and muscular tennis coach who is trying to catch her eye.

Afterwards, they return to Taryn's pristine flat in Coppercone Lane, still with its *trompe l'oeil* on the living room wall: two pillars with a cottage garden beyond. Since Neil became a part-time cohabitant, she has removed to the bedroom the nude silhouette of her torso.

In response to Marianne's gushing about the visit from Edward, Taryn says, 'Seems to me that the old embers are stirring back to life on both sides.'

Marianne tells her about the chaperone comment.

'He's just being careful after your earlier reticence to visit.'

'Stirring is one thing, doing anything about it is a different matter.'

'You are both effectively single people now. Free to bend with the wind. Why not?'

'You told me once that you were tired of starting again with men,' says Marianne.

'Imagine that! But I did, in the end. With Neil. We're settled as a couple now. The fact we don't live together is immaterial.'

'I don't know if I have the energy or inclination to go down that path at my age. There's so much to learn about a new person. I know we get on as friends, but making a life with someone as a partner is different. We are set in our ways.'

'Isn't friendship the most important building block? Especially at our age.'

'He's extremely work-focused and more typically male role-orientated than Johnny was.'

'You have been spoilt with Johnny, but Edward has attributes you admire – or so you have led me to believe. People do change depending upon their circumstances, age and who they're with. You would find him a tad more difficult than Johnny and he would find you easier than Felicity – the post-inheritance Felicity.'

'There's so much I don't know about him. I only had a snapshot of him during his working week. He didn't have to make domestic decisions when he was with us and I'm of the view that Felicity ran that side of things at the Deer Orchard. I'm not keen on becoming a domestic drudge.'

'Indeed not,' says Taryn. 'But Edward is a thoughtful soul, and even knowing what you know is still a huge advantage compared with starting afresh with someone you've just met. And in the difficult areas, all you have to do is apply some psychology: appreciation and cake.'

'What about sex?'

Taryn hesitates and raises an eyebrow. 'Sex is a useful if extravagant reward for domestic help.'

'I didn't mean that,' says Marianne, flushing. 'I mean sex as in whether or not we are compatible. It was important to me when Johnny was alive. But post-menopause, I discovered he had to make more effort to interest me. Once I was interested, it wasn't too much different from before. But without those initiating stimuli, I could take it or leave it. Johnny understood and cooperated. That's after years of honing our communication skills.'

'I'm sure Edward is very much able to become your initiating stimulus.'

'But the thought of learning another person's foibles … One is less flexible as one gets older.'

'Flexible as in bendy, or flexible as in adaptable?'

'Honestly, Taryn! Adaptable.'

'Edward is very accommodating, if I remember. Quick to take the hint and eager to please.'

'You were both younger then; it was an exceptional circumstance. And I'd rather not think about you and him.'

'I could give you undercover details.'

Marianne blushes again. 'Taryn! Then I would miss being surprised – should I decide and should he be interested. In any case this conversation is ridiculous.'

'You know it isn't. I know the thought has crossed your mind.'

'Crossed but not loitered.'

'All you need is a strategy.'

'Your strategy didn't work so well with him.'

'Because I broke all my own rules. Because, for the first time, I cared. The best way is to act as you would if you didn't care, even if you do. Many men run away if they are chased. Consider how many of your married friends are committed to their Grand Passion. Often as not it is Mr Steady Reliable who signed the register. Could that be because they genuinely weren't interested in him at the start? That they gave out vibes that meant he had to work hard and do some serious wooing?'

Marianne remembers how duplicitous Taryn was; how she trailed Edward to the British Museum, lured him to a local bar, charmed him over glasses of wine, took him home and seduced him. But afterwards, all further attempts at chasing him had failed. 'Felicity chased Edward. He told me. It worked for her.'

'He's older now. Probably persuadable to be less single-minded about his work. More relationship-orientated. Take the lead from birds,' says Taryn. 'Flap a few feathers; show him you're there, then walk smartly in the opposite direction. Respond positively, but never initiate.'

'When Edward and I started emailing, it was nearly always me who initiated and he nearly always responded.'

'That's got to stop,' says Taryn. 'Turn it on its head. Roughly seven to one, him to you initiating contact by whatever method.'

'But he's a chasee, not a chaser.'

'If he wants you, he'll chase – so long as you give him the signals that it might be worthwhile. It was he who sought you out this time; tweeted you first. And remember how he chased you when you discovered about us; when you stopped mailing him? He's definitely got chaser potential.'

'But why would he want me? Middle-aged men want sweet young things. You talk about biology. That's their biology.'

'Edward is more cerebral than that. It's a generalisation and not a universal law. In any case, it's different when you've already an attachment – which you two did, in a way.'

'Severed, though.'

'You have to regain your old confidence. If it's not there naturally, pretend. Don't tell him you're insecure and worried about being a woman of fifty-five. That's not going to attract him. Remember Rule 1, you have to love yourself.'

'When I was married and safe, it was easier to do all those things.'

'And he loved you for it. You weren't a threat. He lowered his guard.'

'It's safe to love what you can't have.'

'Exactly, but that doesn't mean he can't love you when you're available.'

'I'm five years older.'

Taryn closes her eyes and grits her teeth. 'So you keep saying, but Edward's not fickle.'

Marianne is silenced.

'Rule 2 is not to make unsolicited advances. Do not touch

him, unless he touches you first. And even then, be sparing. Even touches on the arm should be rationed and best done in public than in private. Ditto compliments. Give, only when you have received. And don't become a Mother Hen. If you do too much for a man, they become unmotivated towards you. Make them think they have to do more to please you.'

'This seems a very unfair strategy.'

'I have observed relationship rituals all my life; I've read all the books and added a few thoughts of my own. An element of meanness is what promotes desire. You see it all the time in the animal world. We liberated women have forgotten how to play the game.'

'I don't like games,' says Marianne.

'Everything we do to attract men is a game. You don't go out wearing a sack, therefore you're playing a game of a sort. Make-up, high heels – and cake. All games.'

Marianne isn't sure. She is not like Taryn, and Edward is not typical of men. Yet some of it makes sense. The problem is, she is not good at playing it cool.

'Rule 3 is to keep him guessing where you are. Don't always be available when he phones. Every few texts or emails, delay your reply.'

'That seems so calculating.'

'Remember how you feel when someone does that to you? It fires the spark, the necessary passion. And Rule 4 is not to mention the relationship – where it's going or the future. Take your lead from him. Keep busy doing other things until he makes a commitment.'

'Might have a long wait,' says Marianne.

'Can you hear yourself? You are countering all my suggestions with a negative response. If you want to give it a chance, you must change your mindset and open the door to your heart.'

15

Life of Edward

Meanwhile, when Harriet picks up the returning Edward from Exeter station on Friday evening, she grills him about the visit. He knows what she's after, but as they walk back to her car, he explains in detail about Patrick's proposals.

'Dad! That's great news but tell me about Fanclub. Is she still attractive? Do you fancy her? Are you in with a chance? Does she have step-mum potential?'

'You may meet her soon. You can judge for yourself.'

Now every time they pass in the house, Harriet gives him a look, inviting information which he is disinclined to share, not least because having found the old attraction hasn't dimmed, this has created the complexity he had feared. When Marianne was unobtainable he could indulge his fantasies; now he has met her again, now she is effectively free, his more colourful imaginings seem somewhat disrespectful. He is faced with pleasant distraction on the one hand, but decisions and some discomfiture on the other. He is unsure of what he wants and much will depend on how she responds to his home territory, if and when she deigns to pay him the promised visit.

He is aware he has rediscovered his energy and resumes a state of busyness that was once the norm. His filing system for work-related items is exemplary and within seconds of being back in the house, he roots out the drafts that he wrote in 2004 in preparation for the TV documentary and the book that never happened. He will need to add some of the latest research findings and projections, but little has changed in environmental terms bar the urgency with which some of the ideas need to be implemented. He wonders if government ministers from around the world will carry on prevaricating and clasping tightly to their techno-driven lifestyles while low lying island nations are engulfed by rising seas, food shortages become a fact of modern life and civil unrest returns to the West.

This TV series is long overdue and if it is accompanied by a book and real educational change in the classroom, the three-pronged approach should ensure notice is taken. Too often these ideas are floated in one-off documentaries pitched at the thinking population, most of whom are already converted to the message.

It won't take long to update the script and chapter outlines. He places the drafts by the computer, intending to make a start after he has had something to eat. By the end of the weekend he should have the information required by Patrick.

It is with hopefulness that he takes Meg for her last long walk of the day, striding through the paddock with acute awareness of leaves and blossom and mellowness in the air that is so rare at this time of year. A twinge in his lower back as he climbs over the stile reminds him that he is no longer thirty-five, but nothing dampens his mood. He has found Marianne and he doesn't intend to lose her again.

On Sunday evening, Olivia pays him a visit. Since her break-up with Alexander, and Felicity's defection to Italy, she is somewhat at a loose end and continues to turn up at the Deer Orchard on a pretext of using the kiln to fire her pots, or to barter bottles of wine for home-grown vegetables – as she has been doing for the past few years. Edward deduces she is lonely and it is only because he is lonely too that he tolerates her company, but only in small doses. He can't stand the woman and is relieved that she now spends more time with Jessica.

After placing her latest selection of ghastly ceramics in the kiln, Edward invites her in for a cup of tea. He is feeling charitable since his productive visit to London and more inclined to spread his good fortune.

Olivia is always overdressed and today she is tightly encased in a cream suit, her gold jewellery shimmering and gleaming at her neck, wrists and ears. She is still all teeth and hair; the latter a stiff nest of vibrant red, most definitely not its natural colour any more.

They sit at the breakfast bar. Edward doesn't want her to be too comfortable and outstay her welcome and he knows she finds it difficult perching on a stool because she has sciatica.

He has barely placed the mugs of tea on the work surface when she launches.

'Darling Edward, I am so pleased to hear about you and Jessica.'

He is taken aback. 'You are mistaken, Olivia. We were talking Killerton planning issues.'

'Yes, dear, but she said that you told her it was too soon since Felicity.'

'I did, and it is.'

'Give it time. You would be good together.'

Edward hesitates to tell Olivia the truth; that he isn't interested, especially not since Marianne re-emerged. He doubts that she would keep the knowledge to herself, and he doesn't want to hurt Jessica's feelings. It was so much simpler when you were a teenager with fewer scruples and could tell a friend to pass on such unwelcome news without anyone feeling awkward. Not that he ever did, because he was always buried in a book, but he saw it happening with classmates and with his children when they were younger.

Yet he is curious about Jessica, especially as she seems so desperate. 'How well do you know her? Before Broadclyst?'

'Not at all,' says Olivia. 'Why do you ask?'

'I was wondering about her background, from where she came originally.'

'She rarely mentions her family. Her parents are now both dead, I believe. That is one of the reasons she has money – an only child like Felicity. She was married to someone else before Ray. I don't know what happened. It wasn't for very long. She was young. Probably an impulse. She did say she needed to make a complete break with the past. I don't think she'd been happy for a long time. That was why she moved to Exeter – from somewhere in Yorkshire, I think. And then she met Ray. Another mistake, by all accounts. Absolute brute. Probably did her a favour when he died.'

'Married twice already,' says Edward.

'But she's older and wiser now. She deserves someone nice.'

Edward recognises the strong hint and gives a weak smile. Felicity used to tell him about Olivia's matchmaking of single villagers. He suspects he and Jessica have become one of her projects.

To: Edward Harvey
From: Marianne Hayward
Date: 2nd April 2012, 19.01
Subject: Patrick

Dear Edward,
Mailed Patrick and we have since talked on the phone. He's very charming, isn't he!? (Have just discovered that one of these !? is called an interrobang. US term,

of course. Sounds faintly untoward to me!)
He's asked me to generate a list of ideas that could be used in a resource pack. Perhaps create some detailed samples and a lesson plan or two. Then he suggested the three of us meet for a discussion – and if he likes what I come up with, I will be working with someone called Gillian Fylde from Flying Owl to bring it into production.
love,
Mari

Charming? Patrick? A pang of annoyance or even jealousy.

To: Marianne Hayward
From: Edward Harvey
Date: 2nd April 2012, 20.33
Subject: Re: Patrick

Dear Mari,
I understand punctuation purists frown upon the interrobang but can see purpose in email and on Twitter in that it perfectly conveys both surprise and uncertainty.
Glad you have had fruitful discussion with Patrick. Let me know if I can be of any help.
love,
Edward

To: Edward Harvey
From: Marianne Hayward
Date: 2nd April 2012, 20.46
Subject: Re: Patrick

Dear Edward,

Apparently the interrobang can be written either way round. (!? or ?!) I wonder, though, if the editing arm of the publishing world will feel its usage should have a consistent format in the work in which it appears? I don't use it consistently – sometimes one way seems more appropriate than the other.

Perhaps I could run through my list of thoughts with you when they are finalised? Or indeed, do a little brainstorming next time we meet.

love,

Marianne

To: Marianne Hayward
From: Edward Harvey
Date: 2nd April 2012, 20.55
Subject: Re: Patrick

That being the case, how about fixing a date for your visit to see us?
Edward

Seconds after he clicks *Send*, his landline rings. It is her, at last receptive to his invitation and because it is the school holidays, she is not restricted to the weekends.

'How about Tuesday, after Easter?' she asks. 'I could stay until Friday. That would give two full days for you to show me round.'

'Excellent,' he says. *And only a week away … only a week away* … This sudden turn of events sets his heart racing.

He checks his emails again before he goes to bed. There is one from Patrick: *Your Marianne sounds delightful. Looking forward to seeing what she produces …*

Again the pang of annoyance. *Delightful … Charming …*

But Marianne is coming to stay. Where will he take her? What will they do? He retires to bed with happy thoughts of untold promise.

16

Broadclyst

If Marianne's previous meeting with Edward was emotionally charged, this forthcoming one registers as high on the excitability scale as an impending earthquake of magnitude that might shake the ground along the San Andreas fault. She sits on the First Great Western train heading for Exeter St David's, daydreaming out of the window like a teenager. She finds it impossible to concentrate on her paperback, so many other real-life twists and turns to contemplate, some of which she knows must yet be confined to her imagination.

Edward meets her at the station entrance: a hug, a kiss on the cheek and only eyes for each other as they walk across the zebra crossing to the car park opposite.

'So much lost time to catch up on,' says Edward, opening the passenger door to his silver Volvo.

'Two meetings in less than two weeks,' says Marianne, trying to get in gracefully. She remembers watching Princess Diana once, sitting first, then both legs together.

'I can't believe you're finally here,' says Edward.

'How was Easter?'

'Uneventful. I hoped – even expected – that at least one of the other children would appear, but all I received was a phone call from James, an email from Christopher in Italy and a text from Rachel. Harriet and I ended up staring rather morosely at each other over a roast duck, wishing we had gone out instead.'

'Holly is the same,' says Marianne. 'It's what it's like when twenty-somethings are making their own lives away from the nest.'

In the car they talk about Patrick and the work each has been doing in preparation for meeting him. This easily fills the time on the five-mile journey along the country roads to Broadclyst.

'I've brought a draft of ideas if you wouldn't mind looking over them for me,' says Marianne. 'I'm not used to this way of working so you can perhaps tell me if I'm on the right track.'

When they near the village, she goes silent and absorbs her surroundings. As a newcomer to Broadclyst, she sees through a visitor's eyes, noticing the minutiae that Edward has probably taken for granted for over twenty years. She has always had an interest in town and country planning and as Edward drives her to his home on a circuitous tour, she comments on the character of the village and how the old and the new appear side by side as if they have been thrown up into the air and come to land in a random pattern.

Modern red-brick houses line one side of a street opposite ancient cottages with thatched roofs, some lime-washed or white-painted, some bearing the yellow-ochre trademark of the properties leased by the National Trust. A bungalow appears between two semis; a modern detached at the end of a row of ancient cottages.

'What an unusual place,' she says. 'I've often wondered what it would be like to live in a thatched cottage. But they usually have a lot of exposed beams.'

'Is that not good?'

'Bad Feng Shui, apparently. Exposed beams bring oppressive Chi. They are considered a poisoned arrow. It depends how they are placed in relation to the layout of the room. If they run in the same direction as the marital bed and between partners, it is said to cause unease and poor communication.'

'We have exposed beams at the Deer Orchard. And Felicity did move our bed when we had the room done after her mother died.'

'Probably coincidence,' says Marianne.

'I'll move it back, just in case,' says Edward.

Quickly she loses her sense of direction as narrow roads twist and turn every which way, bordering homes of different shapes and sizes, some detached and some in clusters. But in the centre, there are modern developments with broader roads, tiled sections, pavements and a townie feel. She muses that somewhere in the village, or on the outskirts, there will be a type of home for every possible requirement. But its identity is unclear. Or perhaps that is its identity: a village for all, unique by virtue of its connection with the Killerton Estate and its yellow-ochre properties.

She is captivated by the bus shelter with its own moss-covered thatched roof and rustic bench. And green spaces are plentiful, not least a large expanse with goalposts at one side and a children's playground at the other, and a field of sheep in front of the church.

The landscape without is gently undulating. Fields are smallish and hedge-bordered, mostly containing crops, the occasional one under plough. Trees are abundant.

The Deer Orchard is off one of the lanes on the eastern edge of the village, accessed through open wrought-iron gates onto a gravel drive which sweeps all around the property. A blue Peugeot and a green van are parked at the side of the house next to a new-looking double garage. Edward draws alongside. The house is long with numerous low extensions. It is lime-washed white with a grey-tiled roof.

The front of the house overlooks a narrow rose bed interspersed with shrubs and behind which is a perimeter wall. Edward says that generally they use the back door, which faces the vegetable plots, a small lawn with a sundial in the centre, the paddock, the orchard and fields beyond.

'Are there deer?' asks Marianne.

'In the forest behind Killerton. And presumably the property acquired its name from deer being around – perhaps when the village was smaller and quieter. I can't remember seeing one close to the house. In any case, we made the orchard fences high enough to deter any that might be passing by, so the name is something of an anomaly.'

A tall and rangy man with long brown hair and hollow cheeks is digging next to the greenhouse.

'That must be Rick,' says Marianne. *'Mr Versatile.'*

'Knowing him, he'll chat you up if you give him the chance, though come to think of it, I haven't heard much gossip about him for a while.'

'Probably because Felicity was your supplier of village news.'

'Indeed.'

'He is rather nice-looking if you like "wild".' She thinks better of adding that she does like wild, that Johnny looked wild, that Rick is not too dissimilar from the younger Johnny. Instead, she says, 'But too young for me.'

Edward gives her a searching look but she maintains an inscrutable expression.

The house is cosier than Marianne imagined, despite the beams. From the outside it has the ancient sprawl of a farmhouse and outbuildings, but inside the rooms are modern and fresh with tasteful furnishings and a light and airy atmosphere. It is clear that Felicity had been upgrading and updating before she left.

Harriet greets them effusively. 'Been dying to meet you. Felt left out when Rachel and James met you after Dad's mishap.'

So this is the feisty one. Marianne notes the Gothic black hair and the pale complexion with dark eye make-up, toned down from earlier teenage photos since she started teaching. She is dressed simply enough in jeans and a loose black tunic that might double as a dress.

'I was going to take you out for dinner tonight,' says Edward, 'but as Harriet said she'd cook before she meets her friend, I thought we should take up her offer and go out tomorrow night instead. I've booked a table at the Retreat so you can see where Felicity ran her empire. I'll cook on Wednesday, just to prove I can. I still have the Catherine Waldegrave adaptation you gave me when you were doing a *Delia* by email years ago. Do you remember? When the Japanese from Okayama uni came to visit and Felicity had an evening class? Lunches we can grab on the hoof depending upon where we happen to be.'

So organised, thinks Marianne.

'We're not having anything flash,' says Harriet. 'Just so you know. I don't do flash. I'm not like Mum. But I wanted to have a chance to talk to you properly before Dad spirits you away.'

After Marianne is settled in the unfussy cream-painted guest room upstairs – next to Edward's and apparently belonging to James before he left home – Harriet cooks very tasty paella over which they chat about teaching and how it encroaches on social life during term time.

'My old schoolfriends are off clubbing and I'm having a cocoa and an early night,' says Harriet.

Marianne remembers well how in her young working life she was always saying 'no' to invitations from her non-teacher friends. No wonder teachers often end up in relationships with people from work. Or on their own.

Afterwards, she accompanies Edward for a walk with Meg round the orchard and the paddock. He takes her hand to help her onto the stile that leads into a narrow lane and she feels a tremor at his touch and dares to anticipate something more.

Although he catches her eye, it is with nothing more than friendliness and all the while she is wondering if and how they will ever slip from this to greater intimacy.

'There is something I haven't told you yet,' says Marianne. 'I'm back in touch with Taryn. It was after Johnny's funeral. She came to see me and brought me pasta. I didn't have the energy to object. Nothing mattered any more. And with you gone too, our falling-out had lost its significance. She's been a great support.'

'I'm glad,' says Edward. 'I never wanted to be the cause of your rift.'

They talk about how Taryn has changed and the difficulties she has faced in starting a new committed relationship in later life. Neither mentions their own situation.

After the walk, Edward drives them both about half a mile outside the village to the New Inn, a white building set off the road at the side of a large car park. Inside they sit next to each other under a picture of an owl and near to an open log fire. They talk more about their missing years, their losses and their children, and tentatively dip into their hopes for their futures, downshifting at work, both focusing more on writing than teaching.

'I believe it's useful to reassess one's life every seven years,' says Edward. 'Every ten years is the obvious time: the big zero. But I think that's too wide a gap. And five years is too short.'

'So by your reckoning, fifty-six is the next one. We're almost there.'

'You have already decided to retire. Perhaps I should too.' And he looks at her intently as if trying to elicit approval.

They talk about the pros and cons; the desire to try something different before it is too late.

'My publishing agent would like me to focus more on writing,' says Edward. 'He believes if I had more books, it would be easier to generate interest in the existing ones. And if I gave up full-time lecturing, I would have more time for promotion and marketing. But I worry about being bored, becoming too insular.'

'You could maintain contact with UD – adopt a visiting role as you have at Stancliffe. And if you keep giving your talks around the country, you'll be promoting your books as well as avoiding boredom.'

'It's worth considering,' says Edward. 'And I do need a break from the in-fighting and the annual merry-go-round of education.'

They steer clear of mentioning relationships.

For another time, thinks Marianne. She doesn't want to break the spell.

At night in bed she reflects, wishing he were with her, but apprehensive of all that is involved in getting to know another body. And when she remembers how old she is and the bits that are not as toned as they were and the odd bulge and the shadows, she thinks perhaps it is better to stay covered and keep her fantasies than to have him disappointed, forever dashing the dream. Perhaps he's having second thoughts anyway – always assuming he had first thoughts. Even the flirting from the lodging days has stopped, not only from him, but from her too. Before, this thing between them couldn't and wouldn't go any further and now it can, they are clearly both afraid.

'Don't touch first,' said Taryn. So she doesn't. And nor does he, except when helping her negotiate country hazards. She thinks perhaps Taryn is wrong, but it's early days and she doesn't want to take a chance.

And then she goes to sleep and dreams of Johnny.

The following morning, Marianne finds herself alone in the

kitchen. A note on the table says Edward has taken Meg for a short walk and that she should help herself to tea or coffee. He will be back soon and will cook breakfast if she wants to join him for something more substantial than cereal and toast.

Edward cooking breakfast, that's novel, she thinks. *Only he could make a note sound like a work memo.* She remembers the notes he used to leave when he was lodging with them; notes when she had gone to work early and he had been the last to leave the house. They were always detailed and courteous. And he always signed them simply 'Edward'. Never any indication of the desire that he later revealed.

Johnny used to leave romantic messages, sometimes in surprising places like the fridge or on the kettle or on her dressing table mirror. It's hard to stop making comparisons.

She pours some orange juice and helps herself to cereal. At Beechview Close, she or Johnny made breakfast. She has no recollection of Edward making more than a cup of tea in the mornings.

Sitting at the table by the French windows that lead onto the patio, she looks around the vast kitchen and imagines what his life must have been like with four children, three dogs, goats, hens, a cat, a rabbit, some sheep and a wife, all clamouring for attention in addition to his high-powered and demanding job, not forgetting all the extra lectures and visits. No wonder he is organised.

She muses that the bare hooks that line the walls and ceiling must once have been adorned with Felicity's cooking equipment. There is something sad about their emptiness, a reminder of loss. She admires the impressive size of the space, even covets the idea of a central work station, but counting how many extra minutes it would take to cook a meal, walking backwards and forwards from one side to the other, she prefers her own bijou culinary space. She supposes it would keep a person fit. But it isn't a kitchen for retirement and later. He had hinted as much in the pub.

Harriet disturbs her reverie. She has secured her hair on top of her head with a bulldog clip. A long fringe hides one of her eyes. She wears no make-up and is looking tired.

'I'm so glad you've come to see us,' she says, turning on the kettle and coming over to sit at the table. 'Dad's been drifting since Mum left. He's like a lost soul. I think he's in shock. It wasn't as if they were getting on, or anything, just that Mum was another presence and I think he expected her to be here always. She filled the house with her business and her friends. Now it's so empty.'

'It's a beautiful place. So different from where I am. A proper Escape.'

'When you live in a place all your life, you take it for granted,' says Harriet. 'I would like to be in a small cosy flat with no garden, no damned chickens and no responsibilities.'

'Do you have plans?'

Harriet pauses and looks as if she might be about to confide. Then her expression lightens. 'Currently saving. I'm here until I know Dad's all right. This TV series should get him motivated again. It's been on the cards for years, but this time it's for real. I hope he doesn't let the opportunity pass. It's something he's always wanted to do.'

'He's asked me to be involved. He and Patrick think my experience in education might be useful in helping them to launch some kind of initiative in schools.'

'That's great,' says Harriet. 'More reason for it to happen this time.'

Marianne wonders about the ambiguity of this statement, but decides not to probe.

Harriet continues, 'I was sorry to hear about your husband. How's Holly?'

'Holly is living in Guildford, working for a firm of solicitors and not in a steady relationship.' She experiences a momentary twinge of consicence. She hasn't told Holly about Edward; merely said she was going to visit a friend.

'So you're on your own in a house too. Not that Dad's exactly on his own yet.'

Marianne wonders where this is leading. 'I'm not about to take over your caretaking duties re your dad, if that's what you're thinking. He and I hadn't spoken for a long time, until recently.'

Harriet blushes. 'He never told me why you lost touch. I've had to make up my own story. Perhaps I romanticised it more than I should.'

'There has never been anything untoward between me and your father.' Marianne is alarmed lest Felicity should have defected because of suspicion.

'No, no! I wasn't implying. I know. He's too principled – and I think he still loved Mum a bit despite everything. But I know he liked you very much and we – that's Rachel and me – thought you had a crush on him – when you were kids. I deduced emotional involvement of a sort.'

'Harriet, I'm uncomfortable having this conversation with you when I've never had it with your father. A lot has happened since he was lodging with us. We're both changed by our personal tragedies. Both wounded and trying to re-establish our place in the world; find a way forward.'

'Perhaps you could help each other?'

'Perhaps. But it's too soon. I'm here as a friend; because it's easier to talk face to face than on the phone or by email or on Twitter. And I wanted to see your home. Your dad thought it would do me good to get away from my surroundings. I haven't been anywhere since my husband died.'

When Edward returns with Meg, he announces that after breakfast he is taking Marianne to see Clyston Mill.

'And after, we'll go up to Killerton. We might have some lunch at the Stables.'

'Fetch me some flour from the shop, please,' says Harriet.

More organising! Marianne asks Harriet if she will be joining them on either trip.

'No thanks. Dad banging on about watermills and Killerton – had enough of that when we were kids.'

'It's always nice to have an expert guide,' says Marianne. 'I remember the father of one of my best schoolfriends driving us round Newcastle, back and forth over the Tyne, giving us a history lesson. I appreciated it afterwards.'

'I will remember to be concise and not to "bang on",' says Edward.

After a cooked breakfast, they step outside into a dry but cloudy morning, the temperatures much lower than they were, and more as one might expect in a normal April. Marianne is wearing jeans which she realises are the most suitable attire for dealing with all the walking and the country lanes. She is relieved to see that her deepest fears about Edward's casual style have not been realised as he too is in jeans, a blue chunky jumper and black windproof jacket.

Edward shows Marianne around his territory as the male bower bird displays its nest to prospective females: shiny stones, twigs, scavenged oddments from the material world, some coloured leaves. Or specifically: Broadclyst church surrounded on all sides by yew trees standing as sentries, alternate ones with their tops lopped off, and Clyston Mill, accessed down a sloping field at the bottom end of the churchyard.

Afterwards they head for Killerton House, parking in a large tree-filled area surrounded by a high red-brick wall. They have a light lunch in the Stables café, where Marianne has the best carrot and coriander soup she has ever tasted with a hunk of bread apparently made with flour from the mill. Then they visit the gardens before dropping in at the shop to pick up flour for Harriet. As promised, Edward keeps his local history lessons short and Marianne finds she is the one asking questions, wanting to know more.

By supper time she is walked-out but contented. It is the first time in over a year that she has been on a day out and not been constantly aware of missing Johnny. All the while Edward has been a perfect gentleman, opening doors, insisting on paying for everything, no attempts to ravish her down a country lane.

She is slightly disappointed that he didn't try. Not anything heavy. But something. If he had, she's not sure how she would have responded. She is still uncertain, still grieving Johnny, still bothered by whisperings of guilt. Yet she wants to feel desirable and desired. How complex the workings of the female heart. She is reminded of Taryn's comment that she should flap a few feathers. Maybe later.

She showers, puts on a velour robe and then lies on her bed in the guest room, recharging her batteries before changing for dinner at the Retreat. Edward is out again with Meg. She wonders how he has the energy and drifts into a light doze, waking with a start when he knocks to say they will be leaving in half an hour. He doesn't come into the room.

She dresses simply in a patterned frock with a cardigan.

Later, in the restaurant, Marianne sits opposite Edward and is aware of attracting stares from a family on the other side of the room.

'Friends of Felicity's,' says Edward. 'She knew everyone and there is bound to be curiosity and speculation.'

'And I wonder what you will tell them, should they ask,' says Marianne, with a twinkle in her eye.

'What is there to tell?' says Edward, searchingly. 'A special friend from long ago?' He looks at her wistfully, giving nothing away.

During their starters of scallops with bacon and salad, Edward says, 'Do you think you might marry again one day?'

Marianne knows she must answer with care. She must remember Taryn's rules and seem open, but not too eager. 'If the right man came along, perhaps. But I doubt I would go looking. And I'm not sure about marriage.'

A silence falls between them. The air dances with unspoken thoughts. They exchange a long and lingering glance, a smile, an intake of breath. Then the moment passes and they resume eating and discussing book marketing strategies.

During the main course Marianne says, 'Please don't feel you have to entertain me all the time or show me everything that Broadclyst has to offer. I've brought a novel. I'm happy reading or even helping in the garden if you have work to be done.'

Edward looks relieved. 'I could do with catching up on emails, and tomorrow we must talk through your ideas for Patrick.'

Next morning, Edward comes in from his early morning walk with Meg, eagerly anticipating the day. In his head he is twenty-two again, when romance first entered his life with Felicity; when he was temporarily distracted from archaeology and discovered a new challenging adventure involving trying to understand a woman and the mental and physical pleasures this could bring. He had never transgressed in the physical sense before or since the Taryn incident and even the contemplation of embarking on a similar path with Marianne, although exciting, is causing him moments of trepidation, not least because he is unsure how to proceed.

He is acutely conscious of Marianne's vulnerability, of her

deep attachment to Johnny and uncertainty about the future. He has had much more time to become emotionally detached from Felicity whereas Marianne's love for Johnny will never die. Even if he knew what to do, he doesn't want to push too much or too soon. He thinks he wants to take things further; he hopes she wants what he wants; he wishes she might give him signals and that he will notice if and when she does.

Marianne is waiting for him at the breakfast bar, drinking tea and reading her book.

'I slept in,' she says. 'All this fresh air and exercise. I'm not as fit as I was.'

He registers a white bra strap peeping out from the loose neckline of the top she is wearing.

'I've had breakfast,' she says. 'Harriet's looking after me very well.'

Edward prepares cereal for himself and sits opposite her.

'You've hardly changed in the last five years,' she says.

'Nor you,' he says, meaning it, because underneath the tiredness and strain he can still find the vibrant woman from ten years ago.

'I wasn't looking for compliments – I know I'm not as I was.'

'You look fine to me,' he says.

'That's the nicest thing anyone's said to me for such a long time.'

He knows she means since Johnny died and he reaches for her hand across the worktop. Their eyes meet and he gives her hand a squeeze, remembering the last time he did the same, a few months after starting to lodge with them. It is one of those movie-moments when time really does stand still.

Before either of them can wonder what might happen next, they are interrupted by Harriet, coming through the back door with a carrier bag. Edward hurriedly releases Marianne's hand.

'Met the Coven in the shop,' says Harriet, unpacking a few groceries.

'The Coven,' explains Edward, 'is two women who lunch: a friend of Flick's, whose ghastly pots are in the kiln, and another Broadclyst women with a husband who fell down the stairs and died.'

'How sad,' says Marianne.

'I think he was pushed,' says Harriet.

Edward gives her a warning glance of the type he used to give her when she was a child.

'And they fancy Dad something rotten,' adds Harriet. 'Especially now Mum's left, and especially Jessica who Dad made the mistake of taking out.'

'So you keep saying,' says Edward.

'Taking out?' says Marianne.

'It wasn't like that at all,' says Edward. 'We merely had dinner together because she wanted my advice.' He notices Marianne frown and sit back in her chair.

'Taking out,' says Harriet. She always was provocative.

'It was only when I went out with her and saw how she reacted, that I could be sure she had ulterior motives.'

'So naive,' says Harriet.

'Typical man,' says Marianne. 'They don't seem to recognise when a woman is interested.'

Edward wonders about the layers of meaning that might be identified in this comment if he were to subject it to analysis.

'So your turning up has put the cat among the pigeons – so to speak,' says Harriet, grinning at Marianne. 'Olivia asked who you are. Said she'd seen you out driving a couple of times and that you had been spotted in the Retreat and the New Inn. Nosy cow probably following Dad's every move.'

'And what did you say?' says Edward, suddenly alarmed.

'I told them you were Dad's new girlfriend,' says Harriet, with a glint in her eye.

'You did what?' Edward flushes ever so slightly. He turns to Marianne. 'I apologise for my daughter.'

Harriet says, 'They're so smug and self-satisfied. Jessica always gives the impression that you're both an item in waiting. She's convinced you're interested in her because of that date.'

'It was nothing. There was nothing to tell. It wasn't a proper date,' says Edward. 'She asked me to meet to discuss a planning issue.'

'It was a date.'

'She wants a wind turbine.'

'It was a date,' says Harriet. 'You've been out of the game for too long, Dad. You're not safe let loose. Anyway, this should get her off your case.'

'How old?' asks Marianne.

'Mid forties, I should think,' says Edward. 'But I'm not good on women's ages.' He thinks he detects a sigh from Marianne; a resigned expression. 'She's invited me to a party at the end of April. I've already said I'd go. Harriet says I'm sending the wrong signals.' He looks at Marianne for support.

'I'm afraid so,' says Marianne.

'If I said no, she would think I was being antisocial. I do need to get out of the house. I'm not a recluse.'

'She'll be all over you,' says Harriet. 'A few glasses of wine and who knows what—'

Edwards remembers the wine and the 'who knows what' with Taryn. Before then, he trusted himself. 'So what do you suggest?' Again, he looks to Marianne for help. 'I'm not interested in her, but I don't want to cut myself off from the village. The community is important, especially now.'

'You could make your position clear,' says Marianne.

'I thought I had. I keep dropping hints. Being too blunt can be hurtful. And I do feel sorry for her since her husband died.' As soon as he said it, he hoped Marianne wouldn't think this also applied to her.

'Her husband used to beat her up, so Mum used to say.'

'Harriet! That's enough!'

'Why not invite Marianne to stay again? Take her with you to the party as a foil. You'd love to go, wouldn't you? And a perfect opportunity to pretend you're going out together. Make it look a bit more permanent. That way, Jessica saves face.'

'I doubt Marianne would wish to be put in such a position.' Edward's mind is already somersaulting at the implications.

There is a pause during which glances are exchanged by all three.

'Oh, I don't know,' says Marianne.

'It would mean coming back for another weekend in two weeks' time.'

'If you're happy to have me, it might be rather fun. It's been a long time since I was involved in theatricals. It would be like *The Rivals* all over again. Lydia and Lucy reprised.'

'Sorted,' says Harriet.

'I'm not wearing a frock,' says Edward, joining in, beginning to see the potential.

17

Lessons in Taryn, Part 2

Back in Beckenham, Marianne is all over the place with anticipation of what might befall at the party. Here is an opportunity to move things on to a different level if they both want it.

They may both test the water.

She knows that he broke contact with her because of his feelings. He has told her as much and she has no reason to doubt him. But that was then and this is now. It was five years ago. They are older now; she is older now; and it is one thing having feelings that can't be acted on and quite another to be able to give them free rein. Yet his attentiveness during her visit might give reason for hope but for the fact that decorum was maintained throughout.

Edward wouldn't have asked her to stay again if he didn't still like her. *Like* … She contemplates the word, repeating it to herself, wondering if it is enough to sustain a more intimate relationship at this time of life.

Like: *prefer, choose or wish; to be fond of.* She hates that word: *fond.* Like pond: *a small watery expanse for fowl and fish. Insignificant compared with a lake and generally unworthy of mapping.* She wants to be loved to madness like Hardy's Eustacia Vye. A lake of love, not a fond pond.

Her pulse quickens at the memory of him at Beechview Close all those years ago. He had become one of the family, no real threat to her and Johnny because they were as solid as they ever had been. But she had quietly and privately loved Edward just a little, never allowing it to get out of hand, blocking all sexual thoughts. It hadn't been difficult at the time but now, a year since she had felt the touch of a man, the kiss of a man, the soft-focus eyes of desire, the urgent power …

Now she is carried away, and then some. She is hot and flustered.

Practicalities. What will she wear? Harriet said a little black dress. Taryn said if she's going down the black route, she must slap on the make-up. Black is less forgiving when over fifty, but not so much of a problem at night. Taryn said with a little black dress and made up to the tens, she might blow him away like Julia Robert's Vivien did with the Edward in *Pretty Woman*.

'I forgot he was called Edward,' said Marianne. This was on the phone, soon after she returned when she was bursting to tell someone and in need of reassurance, affirmation and advice.

'Is there a stool you can sit on to create the same effect?' said Taryn.

'In the kitchen. What's weird is that in all the time he stayed with us, I don't think he ever saw me properly dressed up for a night out. It was always midweek, you see.'

'All the more impact,' said Taryn.

And then there is Jessica; a ten years younger Jessica. Harriet said he took her on a date. He denied it. Whom does she believe? Perhaps he was interested in Jessica until he took her out. Doubts flicker, a twinge of jealousy reminiscent of the time when Charmaine, the Cow-Charmaine, befriended Johnny. She doesn't want to go there again – too old for that. He may not be enamoured by Jessica, but there will be others who may catch his eye; younger others who will be attracted by his status and financial security. If *younger* is what Edward wants, then there is nothing she can do except retreat again, get over him again. She knows how to do it. Six months and the worst of the pain will pass. Twelve months and she will be able to move on.

And so far this is just pretend romance. The real thing might never be; might never come to pass. Perhaps all he wants is a decoy from the witch.

She makes a noise like a duck and laughs at herself. She thought the mad-woman phase was lost and gone with the passing of menopause, the settling of the hormones to a new, less excitable level. Clearly not. The sleeping dragon of passion has raised itself from the floor of the cave.

She invites Taryn for a home-cooked Chinese meal.

Over sweet and sour chicken, prawn fried rice and beef in oyster sauce, Marianne says, 'It's very difficult starting an intimate relationship from two hundred miles away.'

'Time is of the essence,' says Taryn. 'With the witches of Broadclyst circling and flexing their claws, you must leave him in no doubt about the best pursuit option. This party is your chance, and Harriet has given you the excuse. You must make everyone believe that you're the chosen one, not this Jessica. And then there's afterwards.'

'I was worrying about afterwards,' says Marianne. 'It could be awkward.'

'Afterwards, you must seduce him,' says Taryn. 'While the alcohol is coursing through his veins, and while his sexuality has been awoken, you must carry it through to the bedroom.'

'Won't that seem a little forward? Especially after everything you've said. Doesn't that break all your rules?'

'When you live two hundred miles away, you have to remember about boats and not missing them. You go back to the rules afterwards.'

'He doesn't drink more than a glass or two of wine these days. He told me. Since that time he was attacked, he said he likes to keep his wits about him.'

'I'm sure there is enough of a spark between you two already. Wits or no, it won't take much to rekindle his flame.'

'What about my flame?'

'I can tell you're interested. You're alive again for the first time in a year. Take your chance to test the water in a "no-pressure" kind of way. Play the girlfriend role until morning. And then … Then back off. Let him wonder; let him chase. Even if men don't think they like chasing, they become more enthusiastic and excited if they have to. You know this but when you were younger and you liked someone, you were too much of a pushover.'

'It worked with Johnny.'

'A fact which never ceases to amaze me.'

'And what if Edward doesn't chase? You said yourself that he's naive when it comes to dating rules.'

'He's an intelligent man. He will learn fast. In any case it's biologically programmed. He won't be engaging his brain, just his dick.'

'Taryn!'

'Your Mr Perfect is just as much fuelled by primal needs as the next man. Give or take. I know.'

'I don't wish to be reminded,' says Marianne, recognising a tremor from the past; the betrayal, the double betrayal, forgiven but not forgotten.

'You need to be unpredictable and funny – which you are, naturally. Create a little resistance, tease him and challenge him. You can do all these things, and you must appear confident, even if you're not. It's important you believe me,' says Taryn. 'When you're in Broadclyst, you're on your own. The best you can hope for from me is the odd text. Call it distance learning. You need my support now while I'm available. Jessica has her buddy Olivia to engineer on her behalf.'

'And the pies,' says Marianne. 'I can't compete with pies.'

'Edward doesn't like pies,' says Taryn.

'How do you know?'

'He told me – when I was complimenting him on his flat stomach. And you do a mean Chinese,' she adds, licking her lips, waving a delicate hand at the three separate dishes of delights on the table. 'However, I also know he likes pasta. On the two occasions I met him it was pasta that he chose when eating at the museum. And I can teach you a thing or two about that – though your Tagliatelle Cavalli hits the mark already. All you need to do is learn to make your own with eggs and 00 flour. You need a machine; a rolling pin is too much like hard work.'

Marianne dares to imagine Edward kissing her ever so gently, taking his time. For a few seconds she is filled with a childlike glow of hope and excitement. Then she remembers Johnny.

'I feel guilty having those kinds of thoughts for another man,' she says.

'I expect that's normal,' says Taryn. 'And if you were ten years younger and had time to wallow in your guilt, or seek therapy, or wait until you felt an even more respectable amount of time had passed, then I would say fine, wait. But you're fifty-five. You're a woman. The closer you get to sixty, the less attractive the prospect, in real terms. I know that's harsh; I know there are plenty of celebs out there flaunting it in their sixties, but the truth is that we can just about get away with the sex-bomb thing now, at a push, and in two or three years we risk looking foolish. Do you happen to have a basque?'

'I do, but there is no way I'm confronting Edward in a basque. He will run a mile. Far too overt.'

'But they do hold you in, while still maintaining sexy.'

'Are you saying I need holding in?'

'Not much, but we of the certain age all have a less streamlined silhouette than we used to. And those shapewear undergarments may prevent the VPL, but if you have to get out of them in a hurry, it's not pretty.'

'I wouldn't wish to deceive. Imagine the shock. Like wearing one of those super-stuffed bras before you have your first unclad encounter with Mr Gorgeous. And I would hate to be confronted by a man in a corset.'

'Or with a sock down his pants,' says Taryn. 'You're probably right. Stockings and suspenders it will have to be.'

'Does it have to?'

'Have you ever seen anyone looking sexy parading around a bedroom in a pair of tights?'

'I'm not sure I shall be doing any parading. I'm not ready to go that far.'

'But it's as well to be prepared, just in case. You will feel sexier in stockings. It will help you to play your role at the party.'

After Taryn has gone, Marianne makes a list of things to take on her next visit to the Deer Orchard. She surveys herself in her full-length mirror from as many angles as she can. She knows she has kept in reasonable shape – give or take an ounce or two of the dreaded spreading in the middle – but the prospect of romance makes her hypercritical.

Oh bother this getting older! Bother the constant pushing of the inevitable tides, the pressure to re-invent, to present a package of artificiality to the world. Why can't we, as a society, embrace age and all its physical imperfections? Why can't we celebrate its wisdom? There must be some compensation for the creaking and the aching and the shock of the mirror.

Perhaps an existing relationship removes the age problem. Remembering people when young has the effect of being able to iron out the lines and look beyond the grey. That is how it is for her with Edward. But is it the same for him?

She plays a few delicious scenarios in her head and then takes a deep breath, goes to her office in the spare bedroom and tries to distract herself with some work for college.

18

Other Women

'You haven't said anything to James and Rachel about Marianne, I hope,' says Edward to Harriet.

'You keep telling me there's nothing to say. But after the party, I'm hoping for developments.'

It is still the university holidays but Edward goes to his office to catch up on paperwork. Gemma Saborey, the archaeology department's administrator, is pleased to see him. She is Edward's BlackBerry in human form and she monitors his appointments at home or away with patient efficiency and more personal attention than is necessary in her professional position.

She started out in the university at much the same time as Edward and has refused all offers of promotion, saying that she prefers the job she knows. Conrad tells Edward she is in love with him and that is why she stays. Edward is always careful not to lead her on; more so since Felicity left and Gemma began visiting the hairdresser's and wearing perfume every day, none of which alters the fact that she is angular and awkward, prim and pathologically precise.

Over the years he has gleaned something of her home life, looking after an ailing mother for many years and now somewhat at a loose end with little social life. He gathers that she follows *The Archers* passionately and has been known to write to the producers suggesting storylines. In the 1980s she became obsessed with some US actor – he can't remember whom. She apparently went on holiday to Florida and hunted him down to a bar he was known to frequent. When she returned home, she told Edward that she met and talked to him and that he had bought her a drink and said he would write to her. It didn't make any sense and Edward deduced she was something of a fantasist. Since then Conrad has always believed her to be unstable.

She inhabits the office next to Edward's, accessible through a door between his rows of bookshelves, as well as from the outside concourse. Visitors are encouraged to see Edward via Gemma and she acts like a filter system, rejecting those whom she sees as tiresome. When Edward is alone, the door between their offices is left open, principally so he can shout through to her to provide him with any information he requires.

Over the weekend he has printed off some articles from which he thinks Marianne will draw inspiration for her presentation to Patrick: two primary schools with gardening on the curriculum and a secondary school with the environment as part of its pastoral programme. He takes an acknowledgement slip from a drawer in his desk, scribbles on it: *Thought you might find these of interest, love Edward x.* Then on a piece of scrap paper he writes Marianne's name and address before taking the pile through to Gemma.

'Would you send this lot off first class, please, and then if you could get hold of Patrick Shrubsole for me.'

He returns to his desk and momentarily thinks of being at Beechview Close again, alone in the living room with Marianne. He wonders if he should have made a romantic gesture during her visit to see him. He is so used to treating her as a friend, he doesn't know where to start in moving the demarcation line.

After speaking with Patrick about June being a good time for the three of them to get together, he phones Marianne to confirm the date, asks Gemma to log details in his diary and then meets Dick Fieldbrace about the two awkward members of staff with the time-keeping issues. He is back in his office for a mid-morning cup of tea when Gemma appears in the doorway. Usually she phones through details of visitors she thinks he may want to speak to, but today she closes the door behind her, indicative of an intrusion he might rather not have.

'There's a Jessica Hennessy here to see you,' she says, the ruffles on her high-neck blouse stiffening with disapproval. 'Says she's a friend of yours.'

Edward frowns. 'What does she want?'

'She says it's important she speaks to you; that you will want to see her.' It is clear from Gemma's brisk manner and sharp expression that she does not approve.

'You'd better show her in. But tell her I'm busy; that I only have a minute before an appointment.'

Gemma retreats backwards through the door and almost before being invited, Jessica breezes in, all tarted up and clearly fresh from the hairdresser. She is wearing a bright turquoise mac, impossibly high heels and is carrying bags from two up-market boutiques.

'I wanted to see where you worked,' she says. 'And I thought it was time I paid you a visit.' She eyes one of the easy chairs and sinks into it, dropping the bags to the side and kicking off her shoes. 'My feet are killing me. Heels can be such a drag. What price we pay for glamour.'

Edward wonders how she came to be passing when the university is not exactly on the direct bus route from Exeter to Broadclyst.

'Given that it is the holidays, how did you know I was here?'

'I recognised your car in the car park.'

He bristles. 'Did Gemma not tell you I'm very busy?'

Jessica looks startled by his tone. 'I didn't mean to intrude.

It's just that now we are getting to know each other better … And I wanted to check something with you. Olivia tells me she saw you out with a woman a couple times last week and that Harriet said she was your girlfriend.'

'So?'

'I assumed that can't be right. You told me you weren't ready. I took that to mean that you might be ready in time. Ready for us, perhaps?'

Edward is beginning to realise that Harriet is correct when she says that some women make all kinds of assumptions and are inclined to put their own interpretations on events with the flimsiest of evidence.

'And maybe I will be ready for a relationship in time,' he says, thinking of Marianne, 'but I'm at a transitional period in my life and I don't know how I will feel in the future.'

'Oh, so it's not serious, then. I can still hope, can I?'

Edward marvels at her persistence but he is at a loss for the right thing to say. It is one thing for Harriet to say Marianne is his girlfriend, quite another for him to lie. 'Felicity and I are not yet officially divorced. There are many things to address. The person Olivia saw is someone I've known for a long time.'

'I see,' says Jessica. 'An old friend; a shoulder to cry on. Not someone important.'

Before Edward has a chance to decide how to respond to this, his buzzer rings. It is Gemma giving him the excuse he needs of a fictional caller on the line.

'If you'll excuse me, Jessica, there's a call I have to take.'

Still she sits there. He covers the mouthpiece, stands up and looks at her. Eventually she takes the hint, puts on her shoes, gathers her bags, then leaves.

For the rest of the day Edward is impatient and unusually short-tempered. His attempts to deal with the backlog of paperwork are less productive than intended and he snaps at Gemma when she calls him during a second meeting with Dick Fieldbrace.

This is all because of Jessica. Intrusions at work are beyond the pale. He realises he's been too gentle with her and that she has chosen to misinterpret his signals.

He knocks on Conrad's office door and finds him feverishly tapping away on his computer keyboard. For all that Conrad gives off an air of being laid back, he is one of the most hardworking in the department and has a prolific list of publications to his name – even more so since he starting night-time liaisons with his research assistant.

Edward tells of his dilemma, first regarding Jessica and then about Marianne, the party and the pretend girlfriend plan.

Conrad sits back in his swivel chair with his hands behind his head. 'Used to think your life was so straightforward when I first knew you. Jess needs to be told; Marianne sounds like she needs a good seeing to.'

'I don't want to presume anything with Marianne. She's still grieving.'

'Given that she lives so far away, I'd take the chance. Couple of glasses of wine and there you go.'

Edward thinks perhaps Conrad is not the best person to advise him about Marianne. It can take a long time to recover from the loss of a loved spouse. Some never do; never want to move on. He would hate her to think he was being opportunistic.

But Conrad is probably right about Jessica.

On his way home, he stops the car on the road outside Jessica's house. It is of modern build, red brick, one of a kind, set back off the lane behind a five-barred gate and surrounded by tiled paving interspersed with shrubs.

She answers the door quickly and greets him effusively.

'Might we have a word,' says Edward, as if to one of his colleagues.

He refuses the offer of going into the house. 'I'm not staying, Jessica, but I want to clear up any further misunderstandings.'

Her face falls.

'I don't want people to misconstrue our relationship when there isn't one,' he says. 'We hardly know each other and I thought I had made it clear.'

'You made it clear you need time.'

He carries on regardless. 'I'd like to ask you if it's okay to bring my friend Marianne to your party. She will be staying here during that weekend.'

Jessica hesitates and folds her arms. 'As your girlfriend?'

'My relationship with Marianne is private,' says Edward.

Jessica looks at her feet and screws up her mouth. 'Oh, well, yes, if that's the only way you'll be able to come, I suppose so. Hang on a minute.' She disappears for a few seconds and returns with a tin. 'I forgot to give you this earlier. Don't want it to waste. Eat hot or cold.'

'I think perhaps you shouldn't be giving me all this food.'

'Think nothing of it, I like to cook.'

'Well, thank you – but no more, please. I feel guilty.'

Back at the Deer Orchard, he finds Harriet chatting to Rick in the greenhouse.

'Glad I've seen you,' he says to Rick. 'Forget reinstating the lawn. Let's keep things going as they are for another year. Might want to do some filming.'

Harriet follows Edward back to the house. 'Rick'll be dead pleased. He thought he was going to be out of a job.'

'It's a stay of execution, not a complete U-turn.'

'Either way, it's great.'

He tells Harriet about Jessica, taking a pie of some description from the tin and cutting a small slice.

Harriet says, 'Did you actually specify that you weren't interested in her, that you never would be, even with time?'

'Not exactly.'

'You're hopeless, Dad. Women like that need to be told in words of one syllable. You have to be blunt; saves aggro in the long run. Is that one of her concoctions? Should you be eating it?'

'Why not?'

'Husband, stairs, broken neck.'

He takes another bite. 'She makes damned good pies, though.'

'A woman scorned.'

He looks at the pie, then at Harriet, and eats it all the same.

19

The Party

Marianne arrives at the Deer Orchard the evening before the party and spends the following day relaxing with Edward at Sidmouth on the coast, strolling along the promenade while admiring the spectacular sandstone cliffs on either side of the bay. *Not a place for walking underneath,* she thinks, commenting on a deep fissure a few feet back from the edge. Edward tells her of a recent news item about the rocks giving way and burying a woman.

They are still catching up on their lost years, sharing more in-depth worries about their children and the future.

'I always believed Johnny and I would make the next step together,' says Marianne, 'be it retiring to the sea, returning to Cumbria or moving into a smaller house. What happened to him is a reminder of the pointlessness of planning too far ahead and the importance of *"Now"*.'

She notices the age demographic in the town is mostly that of the silver haired, often with crepe bandages, sticks or mobility scooters aiding their perambulations. A man who looks like an old rock star walks in front of them: straggly grey hair, wiry limbs, saggy faded denims and a cowboy hat. A woman with long, blonde crinkly hair, limps at his side, a patchwork skirt, a denim jacket, black suede boots. Marianne thinks they would have been A-list glam in their youth. Briefly she wonders where she will be in ten years' time. If this is a spyglass to her future: Sidmouth prom.

Edward says, 'Would you consider moving away from Beckenham?'

'If there were a good enough reason, I might be tempted,' and she gives him one of her coy glances.

Then they both fall silent, lost in thought.

They lunch on crab sandwiches in The Mocha restaurant and then drive up to the cliff tops for a cup of tea in the Clocktower café, all the while maintaining barriers of propriety and leaving Marianne wondering how in the evening, they will accomplish the transition from friendly conviviality to something evoking at least an impression of passion.

Back at the Deer Orchard, she takes a bath and goes through the old ritual she practised as a prelude to a special night out with Johnny. It isn't that she has any firm plans about the outcome of the evening – no matter what Taryn may have said – but she knows it will be easier to play sexy if she feels sexy, and that it is what lies under her dress that will govern her state of mind. She would like to feel that should the circumstance arise, she is prepared. She does not want a Bridget Jones big-knickers moment. And she's been neglecting herself. There is much to do with a razor, a pumice stone and an exfoliating mitt. By the time she emerges in a kimono-style satin robe and with her freshly washed hair in a towel, she is glowing. She will moisturise in the bedroom.

She passes Harriet on the landing, already changed into black leggings with a short black dress over the top. Her hair is bunched and twisted, gelled and sculpted and has something of an Ascot hat about it.

'When you're dressed,' says Harriet, 'how about I help you with your hair? I have tongs. We could do the sexy tousled look.'

Marianne laughs. 'I'm too old for sexy and tousled. But I'm willing to give it a try.'

'Don't underestimate yourself. You're not *Old*-old yet. I keep telling Dad fifty-five is the new forty-five, and some would even say forty. It's a new life-beginning time, not a pointer to the scrapyard.'

'Sometimes you remind me of me,' says Marianne. 'The confident half of me that's been buried for a year.'

After Marianne has slapped on some body lotion, donned stockings and some matching black underwear, added the little black dress and then some night-time make-up with smoky eyes, she wraps the kimono over the top and knocks on Harriet's door before entering.

The room still has the air of a student's, with arty posters on the walls and files and folders heaped on shelves and on a desk. Childhood trinkets and a teddy bear sit on shelves and the windowsill evoking memories of a more distant time.

'I feel I should apologise for this,' Harriet says, waving her arm in an arc.

'Holly's is the same,' says Marianne, aware of the familiar nostalgic maternal tug in her heart.

'It's time I moved on. Keep thinking there's no point in making myself comfortable here when I could be gone at any moment.'

'Is this why you're so keen to match-make your father?'

'Ah! I've not been very subtle, have I?'

'About as unsubtle as it's possible to be.' Marianne sits on a chair offered by Harriet and unwraps her half-dry hair.

Harriet takes a comb and gently teases out the tangles. 'Only if it's you. Not that Jessica cow. She's a strange woman. Blows hot and cold. Dad hasn't seen much of the other side to her because she's usually all over him. But when she sees me, sometimes she's full of smiles and sometimes it's like she doesn't know me. Even Mum said she was moody, but excused it on the grounds that her husband was a nightmare. You're nice. You and Dad understand each other. You'd be good for him. You *are* good for him.' Harriet stares at Marianne's reflection in the mirror.

'I'm honoured – but both of us have had a rough time. We may not want to start again.'

'Is that true of you? Is friendship all you want?'

Marianne wonders. This is such a direct and honest question. But despite discussions with Taryn, she isn't sure. One minute her wild side says life's so short, take a chance; then the guilt sets in, even though she knows that Johnny was too selfless to want her to compromise her happiness.

'I think sex is important to men,' continues Harriet. 'Even old ones like Dad. Although I don't like to think about it.'

'You've just said we're not old.'

'Whoops! I mean relative to the young. I find it sad thinking of him being all alone for the rest of his life. Mum was difficult for years. He was very patient, considering. I can't stay forever and it'd be good if he had company – at least some of the time. But the right company. You're a known quantity. He could get together with someone fresh and who knows what might happen in a year or two.'

'No one ever knows what's going to happen in a year or two.'

And that's the other problem, thinks Marianne. If they did take a chance, what if it didn't work? Think of the disappointment; all the hassle of readjustment for nothing.

But she's getting ahead of herself. There is as yet no Relationship.

Harriet produces her tongs. 'I hope you trust me. I do know what I'm doing. And it is in my interests that you look fabulous. At least more fabulous than Jessica – which wouldn't be difficult. I'd be happy to have you for a step-mum. Especially as my own has gone AWOL with an oversexed gigolo.'

Marianne can't help but laugh. 'Oh Harriet, love, it's so sweet of you. This, everything. But you hardly know me. I don't know where this is going. I agreed to this plan of yours

147

because it sounded fun. And I like your dad very much. I always have. I know he's a good man. But a relationship is many steps along a path we haven't yet begun to tread.'

Ten minutes later, Harriet stands back and surveys Marianne with a critical eye. 'You look brill and I'm sure Dad will think so. That Jessica witch won't stand a chance. Can't wait to see her face. Do you want to make a dramatic entrance downstairs, or would you rather Dad found you?'

Marianne remembers what Taryn said about Julia Roberts in *Pretty Woman*. 'How about I sit on a stool in the kitchen, then it will be relaxed? He won't feel obliged to say anything. If I make an entrance, he may be embarrassed.'

Soon she is unwrapped from the kimono and drinking a cup of tea by the breakfast bar. Eventually Edward emerges from the study upstairs. When she hears footsteps, she turns to look over her shoulder.

'Ta-rah!' says Harriet, arms outstretched.

'Very nice,' says Edward, in the tone of someone who finds compliments difficult to give. If he is blown away, Marianne isn't sure. What is certain is that when he joins her for a cup of tea, he can't take his eyes off her.

Inside Jessica's house it is open plan with a wooden central staircase leading down into the living area. Marianne shivers, visualising the husband tripping and tumbling; bruising contact on each of the step edges before crashing to the floor in a crumpled heap. He wouldn't have stood a chance against the laminate floor.

'Darling,' says Jessica to Edward, pointedly kissing him on both cheeks before he can step back. 'So this is your new friend?' Her eyes scan.

Marianne's initial impression is of a moderately attractive and younger woman who has been generous with the blusher,

148

highlighter and bright red lipstick and is exposing cleavage adorned with a sparkly necklace.

Jessica extends a hand to Marianne and gives her a tight smile.

Coats are taken upstairs by a young man in a bow tie, while a woman in a plain black skirt and blouse offers drinks from a tray.

Not short of a bob or two, thinks Marianne.

'Edward, do be a dear and introduce Marianne to some of our friends and neighbours.'

Already the room is filling with an assortment of people, mostly of a certain age, some with a teenage child or two in tow.

The music is eighties New Romantics, Adam Ant and then Duran Duran. Marianne is a seventies girl and not a fan, although she tolerates Ultravox and The Cure. Edward told her he missed the pop scene across both decades, his nose buried in archaeology books while his peers grew their hair long and dabbled in drugs. He favours classical music and opera but not to the point where they form a major part of his life.

Harriet goes to talk to a young couple with identical beaked noses. Marianne at first assumes they must be siblings but Edward says they are married.

'More evidence for the theory that those sharing similar physical characteristics gravitate towards each other,' says Marianne, knowing Edward enjoys hearing snippets of psychology. 'A subconscious strategy to increase the probability of one's own genes appearing in the phenotype of any offspring.'

'Felicity and I look nothing like each other,' says Edward.

'Perhaps not at first glance, but there is research to suggest that the similarity may be found in less obvious features such as the length of bones – like those in the arm or fingers.'

'I'm not convinced.'

Over a period of about an hour, Edward introduces Marianne to Olivia, Lyn Wade from the post office, one of the women from the Killerton shop whom she remembers from the day they went to look round the gardens, and two couples who live next door to each other in the newer houses in the centre of the village. She thinks they are an unlikely bunch of friends but no doubt this is typical in a village. They all shower her with questions and she sees it as a good opportunity to promote her book.

Two waitresses circulate with a seemingly endless supply of varied canapés from the kitchen, while the young man who took their coats looks after a table of drinks.

Each time Marianne and Edward move on to the next person or group, she has a sense that she is being discussed in their wake; that their relationship is under scrutiny. In a village where Felicity was such a pivotal figure, she can imagine the difficulty in gaining acceptance. It is as if she is staring through a window, looking on a life in the future should things develop between them. These are some of the challenges she will face; this is a trial run. If she doesn't like what she sees, she can scurry back to Beckenham and remain there.

Marianne doesn't want Edward to think she is the type to be clingy. She says, 'Don't feel you have to stay with me all evening. I'll mingle and then I'll be back.' She touches his arm before she goes, feeling his eyes following her towards the other side of the huge lower ground living space towards the dining table and the man with the drinks.

She asks for half a glass of white wine with added sparkling water. She needs both courage and a clear head.

Nearby, she finds Lyn Wade again and the woman from the Killerton shop whose name she can't remember. Lyn has typical postmistress credentials: bespectacled, earnest, small, mouselike. They chat convivially about village life compared with that of suburban London.

Marianne wonders if there's a Mr Wade, but doesn't like to ask. She has noticed women out-numbering men by about four to one and wonders if this is a village trend or peculiar to the friends and acquaintances of Jessica. Either way, it suggests Edward will likely be in demand from the unattached.

Harriet is talking to the beaky couple again and as Marianne passes, she turns away from them to whisper, 'Girlfriend behaviour.'

'Message received,' says Marianne. 'I'm working up to it.' She wafts her almost empty glass.

The Coven is in conversation nearby, standing side by side, surveying the thirty or so guests, pointing surreptitiously, gossiping. Behind them is a tall wooden stand with a cage on top, covered with a thick Paisley-patterned scarf. Marianne wonders what lies underneath.

'Lovely party,' she says to Jessica. 'Thank you for inviting me.'

'Ah, Marianne, what a delight to meet you,' says Olivia. 'Ted's kept you very quiet. How long have you known each other?'

'Since school days.' She omits the bit about the thirty-three year gap in their communication, and also the fact that even when they were at school their association didn't extend much beyond a shared classroom. The only times they spoke to each other were during *The Rivals* and a paired appearance on the Sweeping rota.

If Olivia is thrown out of her stride by this, she doesn't show it.

'You're not the Marianne that Ted lodged with some years ago?'

'I am.'

'I thought *that* Marianne had a husband.'

'I did. He died just over a year ago.'

'Oh, I'm sorry. And you and Ted have been dating since when?'

'Possibly something for "Ted" to divulge if he so wishes.' Marianne is rattled inside, but maintains composure. There is distinct hostility in their eyes. *'There are daggers in men's smiles,'* she thinks.

'Ted says you've written a novel.'

'I have. It will be out next week. I tried to get a book signing at one of your Exeter bookshops, but their current policy is that unless local or with proven track record, they are only interested if you have something else to offer – like a talk.'

'And you're not exactly Michael Palin or J. K. Rowling,' says Olivia, exposing a mouth full of enormous teeth.

Marianne is taken aback at the bitchiness of the comment.

'And Ted will have told you about Jess, of course,' continues Olivia. 'I expect he mentioned that they've been out to dinner.'

If this was another comment designed to unsettle Marianne, then it has the desired effect. *How dare they!* This is the red rag that motivates her to take matters into her own hands.

'He's lovely, isn't he?' adds Jessica. 'Such a gentleman: so kind, so talented.'

Marianne doubts that this overdone woman could ever turn his head, but you never know. Stranger things have happened. She excuses herself without answering.

She finds Edward talking to Rick about the garden and is about to interrupt when Harriet appears by her side and says, 'I think my being here is cramping Dad's style. There's nowhere to hide. So I'm going to leave soon. It's all a bit staid for me anyhow. See if you can get him to dance; make you look more like a couple.'

'I'll do my best,' says Marianne. She takes a deep breath and another gulp from her glass which she then places on the mantelpiece. Now is the time for the acting skills.

She goes over to Edwad and links his arm, ignores his initial look of surprise, beams at Rick and says, 'Might I drag him away for a dance. They're playing one of my favourite old songs.'

Edward appears happy to be dragged and they join three other couples on the floor, smooching to 'Bridge over Troubled Water'.

'This makes me sad,' says Marianne, placing her hands on his shoulders. 'But you are my bridge.'

She knows it is risky.

'Likewise,' says Edward, clasping her waist hesitantly.

Marianne relaxes.

'Olivia and Jess have just given me a grilling. I don't think they believe we're serious. Assuming you want to throw them off your trail, this is the time to show them. So …' It was time for the teacher tone. She knows he responds well to that. Felicity and Taryn both used it to good effect. He told her once. Once a long time ago when they walked in the park in Beckenham, when the rhododendrons were in glorious magenta bloom and they both thought about Brocklebank Hall at the same time and said it out loud and laughed at the synchronicity. For a moment they held each other's eyes and lost themselves in a soul-searching gaze that exposed feelings beyond the ordinary and led to Edward's decision to leave.

Of course, he may no longer feel the same; no longer more than friendship.

'So … Hold me with conviction. And move in a little closer. If your hand just happens to stray a little, I won't slap you down. Don't be shy. Remember Lydia. This needs an Oscar performance.'

She wraps herself more tightly to him, her head against his

neck, closing her eyes, caressing his back and being transported to the last time she danced with Johnny. She is being carried away by the lyrics. 'And in a moment we are going to kiss,' she mumbles, like an instruction manual.

He doesn't flinch.

She starts with his cheek, the arching scar, tracing the line down to his mouth. The contact brings tears to her eyes. Confused emotions, memories of Johnny, but also a powerful resurgence of the feelings she has long suppressed for Edward. She catches sight of Olivia watching them. She closes her eyes and goes for it like a movie star, a sudden intimacy that has never been theirs in all their years of knowing each other.

Edward responds and she muses that if this is acting, then he is extremely good. But then she knows he is from the time when he played a starring role as Lydia. She must be the one to stop first. She doesn't want to, but nor does she want to cause an uncomfortable moment.

She meets his gaze and winks at him; an ambiguous wink that he can take any way he chooses.

His hands have moved back up to her waist.

'Bottom,' she commands.

'I don't wish to take advantage.'

'These women will have been reading bodice rippers, anything less than full-blown sex is going to seem very tame to them.' She moves her body against his, aware of his aftershave, of mounting desire, of wanting more.

'You look so beautiful tonight,' he says.

'Hey, steady on! Not so much Lydia as Captain Absolute. I could get used to this.'

'But you do.'

'Why, thank you, sir. All down to Harriet and the subdued lighting.'

Edward looks into her eyes, and the voices and the music

fade into the background. She leans against his heart, knowing there must be something more before the clock strikes twelve. Taryn is right that this is the perfect excuse to take things at least a little further with an easy escape route and no loss of face.

On the way back down the road to the Deer Orchard, with only a torch to light the way, Marianne links arms with Edward and allows him to guide her. Neither is drunk, but she is a little light-headed, buoyed by atmosphere and flirtatious intimacy.

'It's been such fun,' she says. 'For a while I felt the old *me* resurfacing, the *me* that has been lost for over a year.'

'You seem to have recovered something of your spark,' says Edward. 'I'm so glad you came. It's been one of those evenings I don't want to end. Except I haven't the stamina I used to have.'

The scrunch of shoes on gravel as they turn into the driveway and the calls from an owl in a tree on the Molwings' land are the only sounds in the windless night.

'It doesn't have to end just yet,' says Marianne. 'If you don't want it to.'

'Are you saying what I think you're saying?'

'We could stay in character a little longer. If you like, don't you think? While the mood is with us. At least until the pumpkin hour.'

'I like,' says Edward. 'I like very much.'

'It's good to be hugged again.'

'Ah, hugs. Is that what you mean? Not that I'm averse.'

'I'm not sure what I mean,' says Marianne. 'One step at a time; see how it goes.' And she isn't sure, but like him, she doesn't want the evening to end.

'Only if you want to,' he says. 'It's been such a long time.'

20

The Night

It is after midnight when Edward opens the back door of the Deer Orchard. Marianne follows him inside and he takes her hand. They share another kiss in the kitchen and creep around like teenagers, making tea, trying hard not to disturb Harriet, giggling quietly; shushing each other, patting Meg who is excited by their late night entry, hopeful for a walk, circling with a wagging tail, nails clicking on the floor tiles.

Edward is going with the flow, as Marianne told him once that he should when Felicity started on her enterprises. He is trying not to overthink the situation or guess what might lie behind or beyond what has gone before. He is glad he hasn't had too much to drink, but is sufficiently relaxed not to be overawed by the situation; a situation that might paralyse him in the cold light of a sober morning.

They remove their shoes and pad silently upstairs, Edward trying to guide her on a zigzag path that avoids the creaky floorboards. Marianne goes to the guest room, then the bathroom, coming out, closing the guest room door and then tiptoeing into Edward's room, where he has taken their mugs of tea. She closes the door. If Harriet is listening from her room on the other side of the landing, she will have heard both bedroom doors close and assume they have parted. She is unlikely to hear them talking, but they whisper all the same.

In Edward's bedroom with the lights low, they lie on the bed, propped up on pillows, drinking tea, reflecting on the evening. Edward has removed his jacket to a hanger. He is as yet unsure exactly what Marianne has in mind.

'So it's a hug you want,' he says, after a while, replacing his mug on the bedside table.

'I haven't been hugged for so long,' says Marianne. 'I know men sometimes don't see the point of hugs, but if they could only realise that it is in their interests; that they get their pay-back in other ways, though not always at the same time.'

'Is that so?' he says, and puts both arms around her. She snuggles into his shoulder.

'When we were kids,' she says. 'Teenagers. We had a code for our dealings with boys, as all kids do, but I believe our code was unique. We used to call it, "going to Carlisle and back". It came about because one of us had a boyfriend visiting from East Grinstead, and in the evening when we were all together, we asked her what they'd been doing during the day. She said they'd been to Carlisle and back – with the parents of course. But we teased her with lots of nudge-nudge, wink-wink innuendo, and somehow it stuck. We developed it as a code with places along the Carlisle road being significant.'

'There aren't many places along the Carlisle road from where you lived.'

'There are enough: Moota, Bothel, Mealsgate, Thursby, Dalston. You can add complexity by including Aspatria, Wigton and several others which are accessed from the road. I travelled along there many times – by car of course. I wasn't that type of girl.'

'So where have we been so far on this night of nights?' he asks, amused.

'Not very far at all. Papcastle, I should say. Hardly out of town. Some close dancing, kissing, hand-holding; that sort of thing. Not serious stuff.'

'And do we have Bothel or even Thursby in mind?' he asks,

careful to gauge her response before he proceeds, frightened of disrupting the momentum that has brought them this far. He wonders that when she said the night didn't have to end, perhaps all she means is that they talk and at most share a kiss or two.

'There has never been anyone since Johnny,' says Marianne. 'Thirty-odd years. Even going to Papcastle with you feels new and different.'

'There's no need to be anxious; it is just me, after all,' says Edward, trying to sound cool and collected when in fact his own thoughts are very much the same.

'This evening has stirred parts of me I thought were dead.'

'Moota,' he says, thoughtfully. 'That's about five miles from where you lived. A prisoner of war camp,' he remembers. 'But there was nothing much there in terms of domestic settlement. I don't think it counted as even a hamlet.'

Marianne says, 'Blindcrake is the nearest village, a mile or so away. There was a quarry. Moota Quarry. In the sixties and seventies there was a motel. Like the one on *Crossroads*. The Moota Motel. There was a restaurant open to the public and a frozen food centre. The restaurant eventually became a venue for functions. They held Young Farmers' dances every week. I went sometimes with my friends.'

'But you were never a young farmer.'

'I know. Odd, isn't it?'

He imagines her aged seventeen, dressed as a milkmaid like Tess of the D'Urbervilles, in a white pinafore with frills. The look would have suited her. He shifts position because he is getting cramp in his arm.

She says, 'And now it's a garden centre. What made you think of Moota?'

Time stills and he kisses her hair and then her neck and strokes her shoulder, his hand slips lower and he feels the change of texture, the softness. He removes his hand quickly. 'I'm sorry.'

'Don't be. Moota's allowed.'

She replaces his hand, gives him permission and she shifts too so she is leaning over him. She kisses him on the mouth like she did at the party.

He feels the gentle weight and muses that all that is between his hand and her skin is the material of her dress and the satin of her bra.

'We are just playing after all, aren't we?' she asks.

'Are we?'

'We haven't been on a proper date yet.'

'You mean "*Out*" out?' he says, thinking of Harriet.

She laughs. 'We haven't talked about a relationship – or indeed anything else. I don't know what I want – if I'm ready. All I do know is that I'm very happy lying on your bed, being close to you.'

'And I,' he says, kissing her again, running his hand down her back, smoothing the folds of her dress down to her knees. He stops abruptly. 'What do we have here? Are you wearing suspenders?'

'I am,' she says.

'Hussy,' he says. 'And all the while I thought you were so sweet and innocent.'

'Looks can be deceptive. I can play hussy,' she says, kissing him back.

What a delicious prospect, he thinks. There is more to this woman than meets the eye. It is enough to know. No wonder Johnny was a happy man.

'But not tonight,' she adds. 'It is too soon. I don't want either of us to get carried away by this moment and have regrets. We could get hurt. We need to know what we both want. And I'm so sleepy now. All that sea air and walking in Sidmouth has caught up with me.'

He knows she is right. 'Stay a while.'

Like a cat, she flops across him, snuggling into his chest. 'I'll leave you before morning. We don't want to set a bad example to Harriet.'

'Role-reversal,' says Edward.

'And if you would undo the top of my zip – to save hassle later,' she says.

She doesn't move and he struggles to pull it about half way down her back, remembering Lydia, the pink chiffon meringue and his own need, long ago, to ask the same question.

Soon she is breathing deeply with the abandonment of sleep. He dare not move, but relishes her presence on his bed, so long empty of another body, and even longer, another soul with which to share.

Stay with me a while my dear Mari, my enchanting joy, till the dawn breaks across the Broadclyst fields and the warming sun drives all sadness from my heart. Stay with me and leave your presence as the tide leaves ripples on the sand so when you go, you will be forever here where I might lie beside your essence and remember …

It isn't like him to feel poetic.

Then he drifts off to sleep and when he wakes she is gone.

21

Cause to Pause

When Marianne comes downstairs late the following morning, she is tired and achy but it is as if she is enveloped in a fluffy cloud. She is sixteen again, basking in an afterglow that says *you had a successful night, last night, your best laid plans succeeded.* It is the feeling of having been asked to dance by the good-looking guy you've been fancying for ages; the joy when nothing else matters for those precious hours before the doubt sets in; before *what next, will he call, will he ask me out?*

Harriet is sitting by the breakfast bar.

'Morning,' says Marianne, bright and breezy as if it is just another morning and not an earth-shatteringly significant one. She is devoid of make-up and has loosely plaited most of her hair over one shoulder, the rest flopping over her face in a youthful and casual style.

'Fancy a trip to get some croissants?' Harriet looks pleading.

Marianne knows this look. It is a look born out of anxiety from having met each other on the upstairs landing at four in the morning when Harriet was sneaking upstairs to her room and Marianne was tiptoeing from Edward's, next door to the guest room. It is difficult to say who has the moral high ground. Both were fully clothed bar shoes, so neither could claim to have previously been in their own bed. Marianne hopes Harriet didn't notice the sagging shoulders of her dress betraying the half-opened zip.

'Dad's out with Meg. He said we'd have breakfast when you appeared.' Harriet slips off the stool and fetches a short black coat and her bag.

'Okay,' says Marianne.

Harriet leaves Edward a note and as soon as both doors shut on the Peugeot, she says, 'Please don't tell Dad you saw me last night.'

Marianne considers the situation carefully and speaks in a light and non-judgemental tone. 'We thought you were already home. I can only assume you have a very good reason for not wanting your dad to know where you were or, presumably, whom you were with.'

Harriet is twenty-three and doesn't have the freedom to do what she pleases in secret like her siblings. Marianne empathises.

'I have good reason,' says Harriet. 'Nothing Dad could say to me would make any difference. And he has had enough to worry about.'

'So he would worry, if he knew?'

'He would, but there is no need. Really. Please trust me, Marianne. I'll tell him when the time is right.'

'Is he married?'

'No. But in a village it's hard to keep things quiet – and when you don't know where things are going … I don't want unnecessary aggro. Please don't ask me to tell you any more. Perhaps you feel the same in your situation?'

Marianne considers how she and Edward had intended to keep their shared bedroom experience from Harriet, despite Harriet being on side. The implications of telling Edward might be more detrimental than not telling.

'I won't tell your dad about you, provided you don't let him know that you know I was in his room.'

'I thought, but I wasn't sure,' says Harriet.

'We were drinking tea and talking.'

'Yes, yes. You don't have to explain to me.' She giggles.

Marianne joins in and the tension is broken. 'Where are we going for these croissants?'

'First stop, post office, but if they've run out, there's the Stables café at Killerton. And we need more milk.'

The post office doubles as a general store and is a yellow-ochre building with a steep slate roof, set beside the main road that runs through the village, not far away from the church. There are zigzag lines outside because of the Pelican crossing, and double yellows beyond. Harriet turns down a side road that leads behind the shop to a small car park bursting with cars. Some vehicles wait with drivers inside.

'Milk and croissants?' says Marianne, leaping out. 'You stay here in case you need to move.'

The shop is tiny and L-shaped: two small aisles of grocery products and an off-shoot housing the post office section. There are several people jostling around the till by the door, mostly buying papers and croissants. Music plays in the form of Tom Jones singing 'It's Not Unusual'. Marianne worms her way through the crush to find what she needs and then joins the queue. She is startled by a voice behind her. It is Olivia.

'My dear, did you have a good time last night? It looked as though you did.'

'We had a lovely time, thank you.'

'Nice to see Ted out socialising again. He's been a tad reclusive since Felicity left. But don't get too fond of him, will you? Wouldn't like to see you hurt.'

Marianne adopts a cooler tone. 'We are aware of our respective circumstances.'

'Ted's on the rebound,' whispers Olivia, undeterred, checking over her shoulder that there is as yet no one behind her. 'It's only nine months since Flick left. Still early days. Ted was devastated. They were so perfect together. The whole village was aghast. Since she left, he and Jess have become – shall we say, close.' Olivia glances again over her shoulder.

'Nothing's happened as such. They have an understanding. He told her it was too soon.'

'Yes, he told me what he said.'

'She's younger, dear. And we both know what men are like. Even the Teds of this world. You can never be more than a fling, a stepping stone. Jessica's of his type, of his social world. You may be too, dear, for all I know, but you're not Felicity. Sorry to be blunt, dear, but you're not.'

Marianne's stomach sinks and her throat contracts. The fluffy cloud disperses as mist into a sun-drenched morning.

'What exactly do you mean?'

'It would be impolite of me to be specific other than to say Felicity was a dynamo, a superwoman. She did a lot for the village. And it was she who left him, not the other way round. He's bruised. I expect he needs reassurance.'

Once again the Brocklebank ghosts see hope of a return. They leap to attention, grinning at her discomfort. Barnaby Sproat, *Who'd want to play with a weed like you?'* But she isn't going to be bullied any more, no matter what she feels inside. This time she won't show her hurt. Instead, she rises in height and thinks of what Taryn would say.

'It is impolite of you to speculate on the nature of our relationship and to judge me,' says Marianne, with little attempt to lower her voice. 'You know nothing of me, or the past that Edward and I have shared. And it is none of your business. Don't presume that I want any more than Edward does. You could say I'm on the rebound too.' She is surprised at the strength of her reaction. She remembers when she was similarly bold on the Greenwich Pier, when she confronted the Cow-Charmaine about the amount of time she was spending with Johnny.

Olivia takes a step back. 'I was only saying; preparing you. I don't mean to upset you.'

The other customers have silenced.

'No? I think that's exactly your intention.' Marianne turns away from Olivia and shuffles forward in the queue, breathing quickly.

Olivia stalks out of the shop and the chatter resumes.

Marianne feels herself flushing as she waits to be served.

Lyn Wade gives her a warm smile and whispers, 'Don't take any notice. She was Felicity's friend.'

But once outside, Marianne's shoulders drop and all she can hear are Olivia's words – *you're not Felicity.* Olivia is right; she isn't Felicity and truth hurts.

By the time she has walked round the corner to Harriet's car, her mood has changed from joyful to downcast; two seasons in a matter of minutes. There is now good reason to carry out Taryn's instructions to play hard to get.

'I take it all went to plan last night?' says Harriet.

'It did,' says Marianne. But her eyes are smarting and she doesn't elaborate.

'I do approve.'

'There's nothing much to approve. Jessica thinks we're an item. Job done.'

'And *are* you?' says Harriet.

'Last night was last night,' says Marianne. 'I'm not sure where we go from here.'

When they return, Edward is out feeding the hens and Marianne's knees do that weakness thing when she sees him. Her stomach lurches, remembering the closeness of the night before. This hasn't happened to her since she first went out with Johnny. It is reminiscent of teenage years and the unexpected encounter with the love-interest of the time. It is indefinable, indescribable ...

He strides over to greet her while Harriet goes straight into the house.

A touch on her shoulder, the broadest smile, the kindest eyes. 'Thank you for last night,' he says. 'It was the most perfect evening.'

'It was,' says Marianne, wishing it hadn't been tainted by Olivia.

They go inside, unspoken thoughts hanging in the air.

Harriet is laying the breakfast table and she looks at one and then the other. 'What time did you two get back then?' A parental tone which Marianne is beginning to recognise as similar to the one Holly has been adopting since Johnny died. 'How was the performance? Were you convincing? Did the Coven see? Will Jessica leave Dad alone now, do you think?'

'Oscar-worthy,' says Edward, going to unload the dishwasher.

'I think we managed to set tongues wagging,' says Marianne.

'Ordinarily, I wouldn't want details, but I'm rather curious to know what you did after I left.'

'We did enough for them to be in no doubt,' says Marianne, thinking that Harriet is trying hard to keep her side of the bargain. 'Enough to dissuade Jessica from her pursuit, at least for the time being.'

Over breakfast the subject is changed and Harriet tells Marianne more about her job and they all discuss the current state of education.

Afterwards, Harriet disappears upstairs. 'You left me,' says Edward.

'Easier to start the day from a normal perspective.' Marianne decides to play it cool; Taryn's words are loud and clear in her head. She is no longer sure what he wants, how much he wants, how much of the night was acting. She isn't sure that she wants to know, in case he was. Acting. In which case it would be another thorn to spoil her dreaming.

They talk some more about Patrick's proposals, then go

down the road for a late lunch at the New Inn. Edward orders lasagne and Marianne a ham salad with chips.

'I have enjoyed your being here very much,' he says, while they wait in the small restaurant area beyond the bar. 'I would like to think we can do it again sometime.'

'Which part of "it" were you thinking about?' says Marianne, speculating that it might be what happened after the party and thinking, *typical man*.

'All of "it".'

'There is a lot for both of us to think about,' says Marianne. 'But I've had a lovely time. My head is trying to assimilate all that has happened. I'm a little confused about my feelings; your feelings.'

'I understand.'

She thinks he could say more at this point. If he was sure. But she doesn't push.

They chat about less sensitive matters: about her hopes for the book, plans for retirement; his eagerness to progress with the TV project and wishes that it may lead to more work in the media. Too soon it is time to head back to the Deer Orchard, collect her things and be taken to catch the late afternoon train from Exeter to Paddington.

She begins to descend the stairs with her bags when she catches part of a conversation Edward is having with Harriet in the hallway below.

Edward is saying, '… no one can ever replace your mother.'

When they see her, Harriet immediately ushers her through to the kitchen while Edward takes her bags to the car. 'I wish you weren't going so soon, Marianne. May I have hopes for you and Dad? Will you come again?'

Marianne would love to tell her *yes,* but she doesn't want to make false promises. 'When you're young things move so fast. At our age, we need to take it slowly.'

'Not necessarily,' says Harriet. 'When you get old, you can't afford to hang about.'

Marianne laughs and hugs her, thanks her; tells her to take care, knowing Harriet will understand the allusion.

The drive to the station with Edward is mostly quiet. There is so much to say, yet both seem unwilling to start a conversation that may have to end abruptly. Marianne peers absently out of the window, watching the spring unfold along the verges and in the fields, commenting on the appearance of lambs and leaves and celandines.

On the platform they hug and he kisses her cheek. She boards the train, finds a seat, waves and wonders if he is going to stand there until the train departs. She finds her book, settles in her seat, organises her water bottle and still he is there, catching her eye. She is embarrassed, she waves again, and as the train pulls out of the station, she chokes back tears and is alarmed by the power of her emotional response.

22

Bridled Joy

There's life in the old dog yet, thinks Edward, bounding over the stile at the bottom of the paddock, Meg leading the way down the narrow lane, her black and white tail held high. Then he feels that twinge in his back again and stops bounding.

It is early Sunday evening and he has returned from dropping off Marianne at Exeter St David's station. It is a pity her stay has been so brief but she has to be at college the following morning and he knows that she will have much to catch up on, having spent a weekend away.

His senses are heightened and he notices the features of spring with the same wonderment and joy as during his first few years at the Deer Orchard. Trees are awakening, blossom is bursting, birds are singing and the one remaining hive in the orchard is showing small signs of activity, although the recent cold and wet weather seems to be deterring the usual level of buzz.

Generally not one for jumping to conclusions or counting unhatched chickens, even he is surprised to find his thoughts wandering down the provisional paths of an as yet uncharted future. He can visualise himself and Marianne having passionate sex on a rug in front of a cosy fire in some fictional dwelling place. Her response to the 'hussy' comment has excited him. But he cannot quite see how either of them will make such a dramatic transition from their current lives. There are no signposts to show the way and there are hazards round every bend. He doesn't want to lose the Deer Orchard, yet it is an uncompromisingly excessive space for a couple approaching retirement unless they are, as Felicity was but Marianne isn't, inclined towards self-sufficiency.

He and Marianne are likely both to be writing into their dotage. Also, giving the odd lecture in his case, and talks or book signings in hers. They would need space and peace with minimalist garden responsibilities – although his concerns for the future of produce availability suggest it would be unwise to sacrifice a garden altogether. He doesn't fancy moving to London, although it is a useful hub from which to radiate if travelling to lecturing or book-related venues. It is also an excellent source of cultural entertainment, and he likes to think of having more time to spend visiting exhibitions and theatrical performances once his working life slows to permit more time for leisure. In his mind he is accompanied on these excursions by Marianne and he relishes the idea of being able to converse on the merits of a Turner or a Matisse, or an installation at Tate Modern, or an exhibition at the British Museum of artefacts from China or the Middle East.

He wonders if Marianne would move to Broadclyst. When he probed, she said that if there was a good enough reason to leave Beckenham, she might consider it. But she didn't say what that reason might be; whether it might be connected with having a relationship with him. Her life and her friends are mostly in Beckenham and it would be a challenge to start afresh, particularly when retired. He remembers a conversation at Beechview Close when Johnny was alive, and the three of them speculated about a return to Cumbria. Marianne said it was colder than the south-east and not well served by convenient hospitals at a time of life when such might figure more on the calendar. And Broadclyst is not as well located as London should her writing career take off.

All this assumes Marianne wants a committed relationship with him. This is the crux.

And then what? Living together? Marriage? Bloody hell, he's not yet divorced. Or maybe something more long distance, overnight stays at each other's homes and a looser partnership? He finds the logistics difficult to contemplate.

She was pretty convincing during the party and afterwards on the bed. But her slight coolness after breakfast and over lunch had not gone unnoticed. He replays conversations, trying to fathom the meaning behind the meaning as she once told him was the key to understanding women.

Although she had only been at the Deer Orchard for two days, Edward notices her absence as he noticed Felicity's when she went to Italy. But differently so. When Felicity went, he was angry. Now he is filled with a sense of loss.

Later, she calls him from home to say she is back safely and to thank him again for a lovely weekend. She says, *'Do keep in touch,'* as one says to an intermittent friend and not one with whom one is conducting a relationship.

He says, 'Of course I will.' How could he do anything otherwise?

On Monday after work, Jessica appears with a casserole dish.

'A lamb stew,' she says. 'I saw Harriet wasn't at home.'

Edward is beginning to be annoyed that Jessica seems to know so much about the comings and goings at the Deer Orchard, yet it is hardly surprising when he and Harriet have to pass her house every time they make a car journey through Broadclyst.

'I said no more food, Jessica.'

'But I know you didn't *mean* it,' she says, giggling flirtatiously. 'You were being polite. It would be a shame to waste it. It needs to be eaten. I haven't any more space in my freezer.' And she hands him the dish.

'This must be the last time,' he says, sternly. 'Thank you.'

He is about to close the door but she hovers on the step. 'So, how serious is it between you and this Marianne woman?'

Edward is taken aback at the directness of the question. How can he get out of this one without lying? He considers his options rapidly while taking the stew into the kitchen. Much to his surprise, Jessica follows him inside and sits on one of the stools by the breakfast bar.

'It's early days,' he says.

'Does she know about us?' she says, sharply.

'There is no "us".'

'I thought we had an understanding of a sort. That you needed time. Now I find you all over Marianne at the party, *my* party, you can understand why I might be disappointed, even offended. Hearing the news from Harriet the other week was rather a shock.'

She sounds angry and Edward begins to think he is going mad. 'Jessica, I thought I had made my position clear when I dropped by. I asked if it was okay to bring a friend. I'm sorry if it was inappropriate.'

Jessica pauses. 'You keep telling me you're not ready. I assumed when you said *friend*, you meant "friend". It was Harriet who said she was your girlfriend, and that's exactly what it looked like at the party. You never made it clear to me. I was under the impression that we would have some fun as soon as you were sufficiently ready.'

Given the lack of fun he has so far had in Jessica's company, he thinks this is highly unlikely. He remembers the touch of her hand on his leg, the invitation to come into her house after they had been to the restaurant. There was no ambiguity about what she had in mind.

'Marianne and I have known each other a long time. We're already starting from a different level.' Again, he is obtuse in order to avoid lying.

'Olivia says her husband died. So she's on the rebound too. She was acting a little desperate.'

Edward marvels that Jessica can see this trait in another and yet not in herself. He walks back towards the open door and holds it.

Jessica remains seated. 'Do you see her as a long-term prospect?'

'Who knows what the future holds for any of us, Jessica?'

'Do be careful, Ted. Rebound relationships have a poor track record. And so do long-distance ones. With her in London and you here, it could be lonely. Whereas I'm a stone's throw.'

'Jessica, you know as well as I that new relationships at our age are uncertain animals. We both bring baggage; half a lifetime of baggage.' He means himself and Marianne, baggage-wise, but he doesn't see the ambiguity until the words are out.

'So I can still hope, can I?' Jessica laughs and slides off the stool. 'Don't answer that, I'm teasing.'

And then she leaves without further word.

He knows Harriet would say he should tell it to her straight, but although able to tell colleagues and subordinates exactly what he thinks and feels, when it comes to women and personal relationships, he has always struggled, a fact which Felicity made known soon after their relationship began to go downhill.

Afterwards, he decides he needs some clarification from Marianne. She said she wasn't ready – almost the same thing he said to Jessica after their meal at the Retreat. He hopes she isn't stringing him along; giving false hope. His 'not ready' to Jessica was a polite 'not interested', but what of Marianne's? It has only been a year since Johnny died. He opts for sending a direct message via Twitter, and over the next two days they have the following somewhat impersonal interaction.

@marihay1 When you say you're not ready, do you mean 'not

*ready yet', or do you mean 'not interested but trying to let you
down lightly'?*

@Edward_Harvey1 Certainly not the latter.

@marihay1 Would you like to elaborate?

*@Edward_Harvey1 I think we should take our time; not do
anything hasty.*

@marihay1 Am I still allowed to visit you, and you me?

@Edward_Harvey1 Of course.

He is relieved, but puzzled. And he is not sure what to do
next.

23

Unsettled

Catapulted back into the working week, Marianne has little time for brooding, not least because she hears her printed books have arrived at the publisher's and she is eagerly awaiting her requested copies which will be delivered when she is at home on Friday. She is still smarting from Olivia's remarks in Broadclyst Post Office and is all at sea, emotionally tossed on the frothing foam of a high spring tide.

When she left Edward in the middle of Saturday night and returned to the guest room, she had lain spread-eagled on her back suffused with optimism: hoping, wishing, wondering; almost sure that this was the beginning of a new and exciting phase of her life. It was like when she finished college and peered into the crystal ball of an unknown future full of expectation and promise. But the gods can be cruel, dashing her dreams before the next nightfall. *You're not Felicity ... Felicity was a dynamo.*

She may be ten years older than when her own marriage hit choppy waters, but she hasn't yet learnt how to harness the brain chatter of uncertainty and her dilemma has been subjected to extreme levels of scrutiny. She concludes that she and Edward could have a most enjoyable fling, but she is convinced that this would end in tears and pain for at least one of them. She doesn't believe she could stand any more hurt or loss until she heals from the miseries of the past few years, nor does she want to cause him any further suffering.

Commitment and a future together is a pleasant prospect in

some ways, but she fears she is creating a fairytale illusion in her mind. Being fifty-something and both with previous relationships that worked well over at least two decades, the idea of starting again feels like embarking on a mountain climb. In truth, she is not sure how it can be achieved, or indeed whether it would work.

Taryn phones, wanting details. Marianne doesn't wish to disclose anything too intimate in case Taryn experienced something similar. She wants her night with Edward to be unique. It is never easy thinking about your man with another. She and Johnny were always very cagey about past conquests. It was taken for granted that each had a previous sexual history and that in Johnny's case it was more substantial. The less said on the subject, the better.

'I didn't ask *you* for details. It wouldn't be fair on Edward.'

'He's nice, isn't he? I mean, you couldn't complain,' Taryn fishes.

'I didn't follow your instructions to the letter. We went some way down the path – enough for now.'

'What an opportunity missed,' says Taryn. 'You could have relieved all your frustrations and tested your compatibility. But I suppose it wouldn't be easy for you. Tell me, are you remembering to go back to the rules?'

'I have no difficulty following them when it is unlikely that he would want to be with me permanently.'

'Evidence?'

'I'm not Felicity.'

'For goodness sakes! I can see we need to have a serious chat.'

'Not now, Taryn. I need to think first.'

After Taryn, Marianne is cooking supper when the phone rings again. She turns the heat down, hoping it is Edward, but by the time she gets to it, it has stopped.

Curious, she thinks, but not to the point of concern. Probably an automated system malfunctioning, or one of those dreadful overseas callers that tell you your computer has a zillion viruses and that they can sort them out for a fee – before extracting credit card details and emptying your current account.

But later in the evening the phone rings again and this time when she answers it, she is met with silence. She hangs on, waiting. The caller doesn't hang up. After about twenty seconds, she places the phone by the side of the cradle and carries on watching TV. Ten minutes later, when she checks, the caller has gone. She tries 1471, but as expected, the number has been withheld.

It is a while since she has been bothered by nuisance calls. She remembers when she was flat sharing, soon after college, she was phoned by a man who said he was from the Thigh High Boot Company. She thought it might be a friend of her brother's, playing a practical joke, as had happened once before. So she talked to him, asked why he was calling and how he had obtained her number. She even laughed and said, 'Do you know my brother?' This seemed to unsettle him and she was suspicious. Then the heavy breathing started and she realised what a fool she had been.

She checks her Twitter feed, interactions and messages. The brief bout of direct messaging from Edward since her return has exhausted itself and following Taryn's rules, she is not going to be the one to start another thread, send an email or pick up the phone. If he wants contact, it is up to him to initiate. The old order of her initiating has ceased.

A few hours later, she is dragged from the deepest sleep by the phone again. She thinks about not answering it, but she has never been able to ignore a ringing phone. *It could be an emergency.* Once again there is silence. She says, 'Hello,' once.

No answer. She replaces the phone. It rings again. Still silence. She hangs up and checks her watch. It's two-thirty and she has college in the morning. Who would be calling in the middle of the night? She goes to the loo, fetches some water and dials 1471. Again, the number has been withheld. She returns to bed, tries to sleep but can't. Anxious thoughts pervade: *Who could it be? Someone with a grudge or a random nuisance caller?* What seemed merely an inconvenience during the day, now takes on a more sinister tone. Her imagination will not be stilled and she lies awake for hours.

On Friday, late morning, a courier brings a hundred and twenty copies of *Lydia* in six boxes which the driver stacks up in her hallway.

Lydia – the novel that would never have been written but for Edward Harvey's presence in her class at Brocklebank Hall.

She rips off the tape from the top box, revealing four covers awash with purple rhododendrons, *Lydia* in silver type across the top, her own name in white across the bottom. She takes one from the box, anxious to see if it looks good, that the type is clear, the pages aligned correctly. Her initial flick through it is reassuring, but she is frightened of reading it and being reminded of the risks she has taken in baring her soul of the autobiographical components in the book.

On the dedication page it says simply *'To Johnny'*, and the suppressed grief returns briefly and she wishes he were here to share her achievement. She knows she should be delighted, that receiving the first printed copies of a book is supposed to be one of the joys of an author's life, like having a child. She looks upon the open box and waits for the euphoria to build and burst out of her like the showering sparkles of a Roman candle.

Nothing.

Without anyone to share it, she is empty and alone.

After composing herself, she takes a copy, writes a message on the title page and packages it up in a recycled padded bag. Then she drives to Beckenham Post Office.

When she returns, she breaks one of Taryn's rules and sends Edward an email.

24

Lydia

To: Edward Harvey
From: Marianne Hayward
Date: 4th May 2012, 14.34
Subject: Lydia

Dear Edward,

Have sent you a copy of Lydia – though please don't feel any obligation to read it. I'm not as excited as I expected to be. Feel strangely depressed.

Forgive me for borrowing a few ideas from our early interactions in cyberspace. There is no intention to plagiarise our communications, but a few of our shared thoughts were useful in reflecting on the happenings at Brocklebank – or Oakleigh House in the case of Adam and Maya. And then there was that IQ question which you answered so originally, it seemed a pity not to use it. Mostly, Maya and Adam as adults have different stories from ours – apart from them being married and their respective jobs. I think psychology and archaeology complement each other in that it is easy to imagine each subject being of curiosity to the other person, without being so interesting that they would wish to do it themselves. I am never bored listening to your archaeological tales and I know you are fascinated by human behaviour.

Yes, the children are essentially us, give or take, but as I

told you before, I had to spice up the emotional side
otherwise there wouldn't be a plot with sufficient
interest to hook the reader.
First book signing at Beckenham Books next Thursday!
love,
Mari

Edward is disappointed by the neutral tone of the email. The
reference to their shared interests is encouraging, but no more
than one would expect from a friend. She is giving nothing
away about her current state of mind regarding the status of
their relationship.

To: Marianne Hayward
From: Edward Harvey
Date: 4th May 2012, 18.51
Subject: Re: Lydia

Dear Mari,
Looking forward to reading it.
Don't be surprised at feeling down. Was the same after
my PhD. Expected to feel relief and joy, but felt flat and
unmotivated. It was as if completing it was reaching the
top of the mountain and gaining the award was like
coming back to the bottom. The pleasure of the journey
was behind me and all I could see ahead was the
beginning of another climb.
Hope your signing goes well.
love,
Edward x

To: Edward Harvey
From: Marianne Hayward
Date: 4th May 2012, 20.03
Subject: Re: Lydia

Dear Edward.
Mr Psychologist!!
x

To: Marianne Hayward
From: Edward Harvey
Date: 4th May 2012, 22.42
Subject: Re: Lydia

Sorry!
Encroaching on your territory!
Edward

The following morning *Lydia* arrives on the mat. He gathers it up with the assorted envelopes and junk mail and takes it through to the table in the kitchen.

He thinks the cover is on the girly-side, but it is attractive and the book has weight and quality about it. Inside, she has written: *To dear Edward, the real Lydia and my inspiration. Lots of love, Mari x*

Something for future generations to wonder about. Or even current generations. He considers his position in academia to be assured but if he were younger or embarking on a new career, he is not sure how being hailed as Mari's muse would be viewed. He imagines the headlines if the book became a best seller: *Archaeology World Rocked: Edward Harvey exposed as Lydia.*

He laughs to himself at the thought.

Unsure exactly what to expect between the covers, he is slightly wary in case he cannot find anything to like about it. It may not be good for relations if he were to be anything less than complimentary. He mails her to say it has arrived then considers delaying reading it with diversionary excuses of archaeological tomes and unfinished novels. But curiosity gets the better of him. After all, he has previously read drafts of the schooldays chapters – and they were absorbing and well crafted, not that he can remember much of the detail.

That night, in bed, he puts aside a half-finished thriller and opens *Lydia*.

As he reads, the action from the classroom and the playground captures his interest and takes him back to a life that now seems long ago. It is difficult to be detached when some of the happenings are so close to how he remembers.

He wonders about Adam and Maya and whether or not they will have some type of affair. Marianne has always said she had to 'spice up' the reality, but how much spice will there be? She has never said and he has never asked. It doesn't concern him as much as it might have done if Felicity had still been at home, not so much for his sake, but hers. Although Felicity had never given any indication that she was bothered by Marianne's existence, this might have been because of her own white-coated Mediterranean distraction. In view of the recent turn of events, he is attracted by the prospect of spice, the more the better, though he doesn't think Marianne has written *that* kind of novel.

He sleeps fitfully, waking more than usual, uneasy, but unable to attribute any cause other than the absence of Marianne. It is only a week since the party. How long ago it seems since she was lying on his bed, relaxed and happy, making exploratory noises about some kind of future association with him. A week is a long time in relationship terms. He wonders if he should be doing anything to hurry things along.

Next morning after a rare lie in, Harriet says over breakfast, 'I've downloaded Marianne's book onto my Kindle. Can't wait to read it.'

'Yes, she sent me a copy yesterday.'

'Sneaky! Weren't you going to tell me?'

'Not until I finished it and deemed it suitable.'

Harriet snorts. 'I am twenty-three, not twelve. Please let me see.'

Edward goes upstairs and fetches it from his bedside table. He hands it to Harriet, imploring her with a stern look not to say anything that will make him uncomfortable.

'Lots of love,' she says, with a tilt of her head and a raised eyebrow.

'I wouldn't read anything into it.'

'And a kiss,' she teases.

'Like signing a card,' he says. 'People don't expect you to take it literally.'

'More intimate than "Best wishes", though.'

'We moved beyond "Best wishes" a long time ago.'

'So?'

'So, what?'

'What's the latest since she went back to Beckenham?'

'No latest; she needs time to think. I'm giving her space. No pressure.'

He is saved from further cross-examination by the clanking sound of garden implements.

Harriet scrapes back her chair. 'Is that Rick? I need to speak to him about herbs.' And she dashes from the table leaving Edward relieved not to have to elaborate.

On Monday morning at work, much proceeds normally in the

way of a meeting, a lecture and a tutorial, but an encounter by the tea urn after lunch takes him by surprise.

Billy-Jo Lawrie is American and a senior lecturer specialising in forensic archaeology. She arrived while he was at Stancliffe, was the last of the three rotating Heads of Department and the most unwelcoming when he returned. Her generally hostile presence is made more bearable by her undoubted attractiveness. She is in her mid forties but looks younger, possibly due to cosmetic procedures which she seems to undergo each time she returns to the States. Her hair is long and blonde and as straight as fibre-optic filaments. Conrad says she wears extensions, but it's hard to be sure. Her curves are pronounced and possibly enhanced, her teeth are too even to be natural and remind him of piano keys. The overall impression is that of a mature Barbie. If you had to guess her profession, you would not say academic archaeologist but perhaps an actress or former model. She is far from his perfect woman, but he can't help but look at her and be curious.

After making a comment about the shabby quality of a pile of essays she has received from the third years, she says, 'We haven't made the best of starts, have we?'

He thinks *'starts'* is an understatement considering she has been a colleague for five years, all the while looking to disagree with his initiatives.

'I understand the difficulty, given your former position and mine,' says Edward, cautiously.

'I was determined to be right and to be awkward, but now I know you better, I think you're a real nice guy and I've been a bitch. I'm sorry.'

'Apology accepted,' says Edward.

'I didn't realise about your wife and such until recently. That's tough. I have an ex- husband in Chicago. He left me for a younger woman, so you could say we have something in common. Perhaps we can start again on the right foot? Fancy a drink sometime?'

Edward is taken aback by the speed with which matters have progressed from 'war zone' to being propositioned. Assuming that's what it is. Or perhaps she is merely being friendly and professional. He wonders who told her about Felicity and if that is what has sparked the change of demeanour. He also wonders what Harriet would say.

He searches for clues in the body language. She is standing in what might be interpreted as a seductive pose and has remained close to him while they made their coffee and tea.

'I'll bear it in mind,' he says, opting for a safe response that takes account of either of her intentions.

Seeming satisfied, she sashays down the corridor with, he believes, an extra amount of wiggle.

Conrad had tried to attract her attention earlier in the year, but the research assistant got wind and put a stop to it. She said, 'I am not going to be one of a harem, Conrad. If you want me, you ditch the old habits.' And Conrad, who had previously taken out any woman he fancied since he and his wife came to an arrangement to lead separate lives, capitulated with this request and vowed to be monogamous for the first time since his wedding day. But Edward thinks that what Conrad says and what Conrad does may not necessarily be the same thing. It is only a couple of weeks since he was hinting that he would be happy to take on Marianne or Jessica, whichever one Edward rejected.

Perhaps it is Conrad who pushed Billy-Jo in Edward's direction. And despite not being his type, he knows, because of Taryn, that this doesn't necessarily preclude enjoyment in the sexual sense.

Now he is available, it seems there are women everywhere, all vying for his attention. A small part of him wonders what it would be like to play the field, to have half a dozen Taryns. But if indeed that was an aberration when he wasn't thinking straight, even though he is now essentially a free agent, he doesn't want an emotionless affair and the risks that might be involved disease-wise, or otherwise.

And the biggest reason of all: Marianne.

After three nights and fifty pages of *Lydia*, Edward finds himself fascinated by how the story is unfolding and how both similar and yet dissimilar are the adults in the book from their real selves.

Harriet says, 'Can't put Marianne's book down. Have you started it yet? Was that really what life was like at Oakleigh House – I mean Brocklebank Hall? Were there bullies as bad as Ollie Root and his gang? Poor you; poor Marianne. Were you sad, like Adam? I feel so sorry for Maya. And that teacher, Mr Rawton! Did he really lash out like that? He wouldn't get away with it nowadays.'

'There was a teacher called Mr Wallis who was very like Marianne's creation. And Ollie Root is probably based on Barnaby Sproat. Yes, it was like that.'

'Tell Marianne I love the book so far. I've texted Rachel to download it.'

'Have you said anything to Rachel about Marianne being here?'

'I may have said something since the party. Only that she came to stay. No details. Is that a problem?'

'She may not be as eager as you to promote the idea of us having a relationship. She's still very upset about Mum. I think she believes Mum will come home and all will be as before. Because Rachel's away, it creates a different concept of time.'

He and his eldest daughter share a special bond which came under strain when Felicity left. Rachel had said, *'I know Mum has been difficult, but you used to be happy. Can't you lure her back?'* He remembers replying, *'Gianni is the last straw,'* and thinking that his particular camel's back had been a strong one to last so long. *'It may not work out with Gianni,'* she said. *'Don't close the door Dad, please.'*

It is the thought of Rachel being aware of Harriet's matchmaking attempts that sends a tremor of anxiety through Edward. He would have preferred there to be something concrete to report before Rachel was perplexed.

In the evening, Patrick calls about the forthcoming documentary. 'This section about guerrilla gardening,' he says. 'Might it be seen as putting unwelcome ideas in peoples' heads?'

'It's hardly a new idea,' says Edward. 'Richard Reynolds created a blog several years ago about illicit cultivations around London. It's still illegal, but Glasgow City Council, for example, has let it be known they will turn a blind eye. They haven't the resources to do similar and as long as the projects are safe and advantageous, they won't intervene. If we mention it, perhaps pressure will be put on other councils to follow suit. Or perhaps the activity should be decriminalised and a simple system of gaining permissions put in place.'

He then mails Marianne to tell her he is enjoying the book and that the Oakleigh scenes have reminded him of things he had forgotten. But he emphasises that there is still a long way to go before he finishes it.

When later he takes Meg out into the darkness of the night, he hears the owl, just as he and Marianne did when they walked back from Jessica's. He stops to listen. There is rain in the air and drizzle blows against his face.

He wants to hold her close again.

25

Prickly Holly

Holly casts an accusing glance at her mother. 'You've been to Edward's for a couple of weekends; he's been here; and not a word to me. Am I to put two and two together?' She paces the living room at Beechview Close having arrived fifteen minutes earlier.

'No. Not yet.' Marianne thought she would break the difficult news first before they sat down to Sunday lunch. It is not going well.

'What about Dad?'

'Your father died over a year ago.'

'It's not exactly a long time. When I come home, I still expect him to be here and it's a shock when he isn't. I feel his absence. It still upsets me.'

'Of course it does. That's how it was for me every day at first. I've had more days to adjust, that's all.' Marianne chooses her words carefully. Watching Holly is like staring at a film of herself, half her life ago. The way she moves, her gestures and expressions. It is unsettling. 'There is at present nothing untoward between myself and Edward. We're friends and we've had vague discussions around possibilities because we like each other very much.'

'Like?'

'Perhaps a little more than that. But surely if there *was* someone else in my life, you wouldn't object?'

Holly flushes. 'Are you in love with him?'

'Far too early to tell.'

'You were the one who said to me I'd know when it was the real thing. Is this the real thing?'

'I don't know.'

'If you don't know, it probably isn't. That's what you told me.'

'It's not so simple at my time of life, having lost someone as important as Dad.'

Marianne understands more about her feelings than she is letting on. She doesn't want to give too much away to her daughter. In truth, she is embarrassed, much as she was when she was a teenager and her mother probed about her relationships.

'It feels weird. Like you can just forget Dad and move on. If you really loved Dad, I don't see how you can. I've not been able to move on properly since Dylan.' Holly sits down on the edge of a chair, her knees tightly pressed together under a short, flared blue skirt, her hands clasped against her nose.

'You haven't met the right person, that's all. And Dylan was special. Remember, you are young and looking for someone to be with for the rest of what will hopefully be a long life; someone to provide a home, father children. You have reason to be choosy.'

'And you don't?'

'It's not the same. Choosy, yes, but different criteria. I have enough money and security. I'm past childbearing and my needs are different – especially looking into the future. There is something to be said for simple company and friendship.' As soon as these words are out of her mouth, she doubts them when applied to herself. They may be wise words, but her heart still wants to feel the beat of passion. Maybe it already does. But she can't tell Holly. She continues, 'As I'm retiring this year, I'll have more time to fill. Apart from that sticky patch ten years ago, your Dad and I were very happy. And he will always be my great love. No one can replace that. But Edward is kind and clever and we get on very well. Dad wasn't selfish. He wouldn't want me to be alone if there was an alternative. Especially someone like Edward.'

'I can't imagine not coming home – to here.'

'I intend to sell soon anyway. It's too full of reminders and it's too big for me.'

'What about me?' Holly's voice wavers and she sniffs. Her eyes begin to fill.

'Wherever I am, I'll make sure there's a room for you, but you have your own life now. In any case, we're rushing ahead. There is no "me and Edward", merely a possibility; something we are thinking about. I don't know if he wants a serious relationship with me. I don't think he knows either.'

Holly unclasps her hands, wipes her eyes with a tissue and sits back in the chair. 'I do like Edward. I can think of worse men. At least I know he wouldn't fleece you or drink your money away in some disreputable bar. I was sorry when he stopped lodging; when we stopped seeing him.'

For several years Marianne kept up the pretence that she was still in touch with Edward by email and that his leaving was to do with his job. As time went by, Holly and Johnny asked less and less frequently about how he was and what he was doing. As far as they were concerned, there had never been any parting of the ways.

Marianne says, 'It's been a very difficult year. I've been lonely – what with you away too. I haven't lived on my own since I was in my early twenties. Younger than you.'

'I come as often as I can.'

Marianne thinks Holly could come more often and that she could stay overnight like she used to do instead of making a round trip in a day. Since Johnny died it is as though she can't bear to stay in the house. 'You and Dad and my job took up my world. I didn't need much else so I didn't build many other local friendship networks. Most of my closest friends live elsewhere.'

'Sasha's in London,' says Holly. Sasha was Marianne's best friend at school.

'Sasha lives on the other side of the river. Last time I spoke to her, she said she was seeing Sam again. Her silence would suggest romance in the air.' Since divorcing her husband, Sasha had been out with a couple of high-profile figures in the legal world and also tried internet dating. It is interesting that she should eventually turn back to her first true love.

'So go to evening classes. Get out there,' says Holly.

'I expect I will in time, but it's no substitute for a meaningful relationship.'

'Auntie Taryn? Have you told her?'

'Taryn has some idea of what's going on. But no details. I'm not sure I know myself. Which is one of the reasons I didn't say anything to you earlier.'

Marianne wonders how she would have felt if one of her parents had taken up with someone else in midlife. Probably not happy. It was a less familiar circumstance for her generation than for subsequent ones, reconstituted families almost being the norm now, rather than the exception. Harriet's positive encouragement had caused her to hope that all the children would feel the same way.

'You should think carefully about change at your age,' says Holly.

'Holly, love, I'm fifty-five, not seventy. And I've waited for over a year, maintaining the status quo. I've not made any changes since Dad died. But now is the time to think of the future. I'm not sure if I want another relationship, but nor am I attracted by the prospect of spending the next fifteen years alone if there is an option. And I don't mean any old option, but an option that would make me happy.'

'And is Edward that option?'

'That remains to be seen. We're both hurting from what happened with Felicity and your Dad. Different reasons. He's less trusting and I'm still grieving. It might be enough to be friends, but what if one of us wants more and someone else comes into the picture? It would be easy to miss out and have regrets.' Images of Jessica float into her mind.

'Okay,' says Holly. 'I'll try to get my head round it.'

'Always supposing there is an "it".'

After a traditional roast chicken dinner, during which Marianne listens to Holly's news about a new boyfriend called Will who seems to have more potential than some, she presents her with a signed copy of *Lydia*. 'I know you know some of it is based on fact, but most of it is fiction. It's best you think of it that way should you decide to read it.'

'I don't think I will read it just yet. I'm a bit scared. I'll wait until you've had some feedback from other people. You don't mind, do you?'

'I understand completely.'

Holly leaves at five and Marianne is about to check her lessons are organised for the next day when the phone rings. Although Edward seldom phones her, she always hopes. But once again she is met with silence. Except it isn't quite silence. As she listens, she can hear the twittering of birds in the background.

Caged birds.

No one speaks. For over a minute Marianne listens to the twittering, trying to visualise the scene. A picture of a room comes into view: a room with a cage on a stand. A Hitchcockian thought occurs. She rests the phone on the table and goes to prepare supper. When she returns, whoever it was has hung up.

After she has eaten, she goes upstairs to the computer to mail Edward.

To: Edward Harvey
From: Marianne Hayward
Date: 13th May 2012, 19.33
Subject: Holly

Dear Edward,
Had a visit from Holly today. Thought I had better fill her in. When I visited you I told her I was seeing an old friend. She assumed someone from college. She is still very upset about Johnny so finds the thought of my 'seeing' anyone else very difficult.
Very busy at work with exam prep. It is weird knowing it is the last time I will be doing this.
Signing at the bookshop was interesting but fairly quiet. No queues! The marketing aspect is going to be trickier than I thought.
Have been getting a few nuisance calls in the past couple of weeks. Today I could hear birds twittering in the background. I remember seeing a cage with a scarf over it at Jessica's party. Could it be her? I know she resents me.
love,
Mari

She doesn't tell Edward about the hostile exchanges with Olivia at the party and in the post office. If he knew what had been said, he might have been more inclined to think there was a

194

connection. As it is, his reply appears to be an attempt to reassure.

To: Marianne Hayward
From: Edward Harvey
Date: 13th May 2012, 21.20
Subject: Re: Holly

Dear Mari,
Phone calls: Sorry to hear but I can't believe Jessica would be malicious. How would she know your number?
Signing: It's very early days.
Holly: Ditto
Have had a couple of chats with Patrick. Because of the drought and now all this rain, there's more urgency to push things forward with the filming.
Bookings have been made for the Scilly trip in early September. He would like to see us both next month. Are you free on Friday 8th June – end of half-term?
Missed you these past weekends …
love,
Edward x

To: Edward Harvey
From: Marianne Hayward
Date: 14th May 2012, 19.21
Subject: Re: Patrick

Dear Edward,
I can be free. Are you staying over as before? Would you like to stay into the weekend?
Phone numbers are probably quite easy to track down. I

have a large social networking presence – because of the book.
Missed you too – a little.
Mari x

She wonders if Taryn's rules would say she was being too eager, arranging her weekend around Edward. But with a long-distance relationship and this professional complication with Patrick, she considers that playing the unavailability card would be counter-productive.

To: Marianne Hayward
From: Edward Harvey
Date: 14th May 2012, 22.36
Subject: Re: Patrick

Would be pleased to stay over Thurs night but sadly have to return to Devon on Friday as James and Kate just announced coming down. Will phone you re trains.
If you continue to be troubled by calls, put a block on the number. Will explain when we speak.
Edward

She is disappointed he can't stay longer, but elated that they will meet again soon. She starts to think about what she will wear, what they might eat, what she will say, where they could go, what they might do on this one precious evening. Some of it is fantasy, the *doing* bit. She experiments again with the vision of him coming to her room at night, whispering the sweetest nothings on a voyage to the stars.

But the reality is that she is less likely to venture closer to him in her own house than at the Deer Orchard. The essence of Johnny is still in the brickwork and the furnishings, a benign force, but force enough for her to save her Edward passions for another day.

26

Patrick

'What's your thinking re the Education Pack so far?' says Patrick to Marianne.

Edward has made the introductions and they are sitting round the table in Patrick's spacious office. Marianne is wearing a smart navy dress with matching jacket. She told Edward it was her latest Parents' Evening attire. He said there was no need to dress up for Patrick. She said first impressions were important and she wanted Patrick to take her seriously. Also, as both of them would likely be wearing suits, she didn't want to look like someone Edward had dragged in off the street.

'At primary level, it's simple,' she says, handing Patrick some documents in a clear plastic wallet. 'Growing vegetables and learning how to prepare and cook them. Many schools are already doing this. The challenge will be to roll it out nationwide – and not all schools will have the facilities. Participating schools without much land will have to consider raised beds in playground areas. Much can be done with pots or even window boxes. There might also be the possibility of cultivating some common land – like the guerrilla gardeners do, but with permission. It may stretch the imagination of some teachers, but the profession is skilled in making do.'

Patrick says, 'If any nearby parents have a spare patch in their garden, they might be able to help.'

'Good idea,' says Marianne. 'I've also suggested a House system could be employed with vegetable names. Beetroot, Parsnip, Onion … They could have sweatshirts with symbols, paid for by parents with profits towards funding for seeds. Competitions along the lines of a village show with House points for prizes and treats for the winning House. There's lots of opportunity for creativity and experimentation. I wouldn't want to be too prescriptive.'

'Like it,' says Patrick, casting an eye over the first of the documents. 'Who will provide the expertise?'

'Parent volunteers, and if none is skilled the school might approach a local professional to steer them in the right direction. Some people might be willing to offer their services free of charge because of the publicity.'

'Or possibly local business sponsorship?' suggests Patrick. 'I can see much scope for enterprise.'

'At secondary level there is opportunity to develop theoretical knowledge and create awareness of more complex aspects,' says Marianne. 'A starting point might be to examine population fluctuations in the natural world. For example, research on owls tells us much about sustainability. When voles and mice are plentiful, owls raise many owlets. The increase in numbers depletes food resources so fewer owlets survive the following year.'

'This would extrapolate to human communities shut away from outside influence,' says Patrick. 'Much scope for biology and geography lessons.'

Marianne nods. 'We might ask the students questions about how we could deal with food shortages, rampant consumerism or with the ever-ageing population and lack of funds. Kids will come up with answers that we find distasteful. They are far enough away from being old to be ruthless in their suggestions.'

'Like a cull, you mean?'

'Possibly. Or something we haven't yet thought. If we don't do it, it will happen eventually by natural means.'

'A woman after my own mind,' says Patrick. 'Was saying

something similar to Ted the other week regarding deer in Scotland.'

'Enantiodromia,' says Marianne. 'The principle of equilibrium.'

'Is that Jung? Ted did mention that you have a background in psychology. We could spend much time in happy psychological discussion, Marianne. Sadly, I have another meeting in half an hour.' Patrick's whole attention is on her and Edward watches, interested.

Marianne continues, 'If you look at document three, you will see examples of cross-curricular opportunities, with input into most subjects: maths, finance, economics; certainly the population and climatology aspect of geography, if not land usage and soils; biology, of course. Also, creative writing in English language: poems, essays and such. And debating. I would like to see horticulture on the school curriculum, specifically teaching organics and sustainable methods and running alongside home economics. I believe both should be compulsory in Year Nine, with the option of a BTEC or some such at Key Stage 4.'

'Radical, but am already hearing whispers that the government wants to do away with GCSEs and bring back something along the lines of O levels.'

'Yet more changes for teachers to deal with – and I wouldn't know where to start to try to influence the educationalists.'

'I have connections there,' says Patrick. 'A dragon of a woman of a certain age called Pauline Winterford. How will you incorporate these thoughts into a workable package to go with our programme?'

'With lesson suggestions for each relevant subject. Document four outlines a couple of lesson plans that could be used or adapted in maths and biology. If you feel it's appropriate, this idea can be expanded across each relevant subject area. In the pack we could have photocopiable worksheets: gap-filling tasks, word searches, quizzes – the usual. I also have contacts – at my workplace – who could help.'

'Excellent,' says Patrick, flicking through the pages. 'I like this idea of climate monitoring for teaching graphical techniques and percentages.'

'It's not a new idea. Having been on the receiving end of several impractical initiatives over the years, I don't want to be responsible for creating yet another burden for teachers. I remember when IT first infiltrated the curriculum. We went on courses, re-wrote schemes, only to find the proposals unworkable in practise and abandoned after a year. I wouldn't want that to happen.'

'Exactly,' says Patrick. 'The people at Flying Owl are in communication with the DoE to see if we can get government funding. They won't be successful if they can't convince re value for money.'

'Teachers are more likely to buy into this, and to be enthusiastic, if we give them a chance to take ownership by developing their own ideas and devising resources. Also, if they understand the purpose and believe it is sustainable and worth the investment of their time.'

Patrick casts an eye over the paperwork she has given him. 'I like what I hear and see and shall copy this for Gillian Fylde. She will be in touch. We need to work quickly on this. Much will depend on whether the DoE decides to implement the initiatives in a number of schools on a trial basis.'

Marianne looks relieved.

'I'm also thinking you might be useful on Scilly to ensure the commentary ties in with the resource packs wherever possible. What do you think, Ted?'

Edward has been watching Marianne and listening intently, quietly impressed by her presentation skills. This is a side of her he hasn't seen before.

'What do you say, Marianne? Interested?'

'I might be,' says Marianne. 'I wondered if there could be a short film created specifically for use in schools. It could form the stimulus for another idea I'm working on for cross-curricular primary teaching.'

'Good idea. In which case, you must come. Persuade her, Ted. Always useful to have a woman on board.'

'Why exactly might that be?' says Marianne.

Edward detects flirtation on both sides.

After a pause, Patrick says, 'Useful arbitrators.' Then he winks at Edward.

'As long as I'm not cast as tea maker,' says Marianne.

She exchanges a glance with Edward.

'Wouldn't dare,' says Patrick.

Afterwards, Edward and Marianne go for a bite to eat at a coffee shop nearby.

Marianne seems almost as excited as she was on the night of the party.

He says, 'I think Patrick has taken a shine to you.'

'So *la-di-dah*,' says Marianne. 'Before I met you, I thought you might be like that.'

'Me? La-di-dah? Good grief! Are you disappointed?'

'Glad. He's very self-important. Difficult if crossed, I'll bet. But I like the sound of Scilly – if you wouldn't mind me tagging along. I'll give it serious thought.'

'I would be delighted.'

'Where is everyone staying?' she asks.

This could be tricky. 'I'm going back to the Parsonage because Pam and Julian are a fund of information and I'm already in touch with them about whom we should talk to. They will be able to line up some interviews before we arrive. There will be a minimalist team: camera, sound, director, Patrick, me, you – if you decide to come. The others are going to Lowertown Farm. You could stay there with them … or with me.' He searches her face.

Implications dance in the balmy evening air.

'Strings?'

'No strings. Unless you're ready for strings.'

'Am I being too cautious?'

'I had hoped …'

'Keep hoping,' says Marianne. 'I'm all over the place at the moment.'

He decides to say no more but to be pleased about hope and pleased about her considering Scilly. He has found this visit far too brief and tantalisingly unproductive with regard to moving their relationship forward. The night before, she had greeted him in much the same way as in the days when he was lodging and they had maintained the same respectful distance as on his previous visit. Nothing had been said about what happened after the party. Scilly would provide neutral territory and a perfect opportunity to establish intimacy and a way forward.

27

Strings Theory

Edward accompanies Marianne to Victoria station, where she leaves him with nothing more than the briefest of hugs and a kiss on the cheek. By the time she has walked half the length of the Orpington train, she is regretting her coolness and castigating herself for being an idiot. The previous evening, she hadn't wanted things to go too far and so was careful not to send what she thought were messages with sexual undertones. Consequently, it is hardly surprising his behaviour towards her was no more than it ever had been at Beechview Close.

After supper he had explained how she could put a block on the number of the nuisance caller. It is one of BT's add-on services and involves keying in a four digit number following the suspicious call. He still isn't convinced by her theory that it is Jessica.

'What can she possibly hope to achieve?' he said. 'You're hardly going to disappear on the basis of a few random calls.'

'It is malicious, though,' said Marianne. 'Twice I have been woken up in the dead of night.'

She finds a seat by a window, opposite the direction of travel. If there is a choice, she prefers to travel backwards because she read somewhere that if you hit anything, you will be forced into your seat rather than out.

She is playing by Taryn's rules and waiting for Edward to take the lead with clear-cut declarations of intent: an acknowledgement of strong feelings at the very least, or even better, love. She wants reassurance that this isn't going to be a fling. But she had wanted something to happen to move things forward, so when Scilly was raised and she said, *'Strings?'* she wanted him to say *'Let there be strings aplenty'* – or words to that effect. His answer, *'No strings unless you're ready'*, suggested he was prepared to proceed at her pace. *'I had hoped ...'* was ambiguous and not indicative of the nature of the relationship he desired. It could mean that he merely wished for a repeat of the night after the party, or for sex with no commitment, no talk about the future. She needs something tangible to make her put the guilt aside and take the risk. If he is ambivalent, it isn't worth it.

She replays the conversations that took place on his bed after the party. He seemed to be responding to her, following her, agreeing with her. But is she remembering right? Perhaps he was carried away by the moment and alcohol. If it hadn't been for Olivia in the post office, she might have been less reticent.

'You can never be more than a stepping stone.'

She is so different from Superwoman Felicity that the weight of comparison is making her anxious.

She knows Edward is not like Johnny either. Yet if the differences don't matter to her, then perhaps they don't matter to him. Edward most certainly isn't like Johnny when it comes to relationships. Johnny had always been decisive and sure of what he wanted; he had taken the lead from the start. Everything she knows about Edward suggests relationship naivety – especially after what Harriet has said. He is taking her at her word; that she needs time; that he shouldn't push too hard. Yes, she needs time. And she doesn't want to be pushed. But that doesn't mean she wants nothing. She wants wooing; some good old-fashioned wooing. If he showed love, hers might be allowed to flourish instead of being stifled in a crate in the cellar of her heart. But from what her friends and colleagues say, it is typical of midlife men to have forgotten the importance of romance. She was lucky that Johnny was a romantic and rarely had to be reminded, except during the Charmaine episode.

The commuter train disappears into the Sydenham tunnel and Marianne counts to a hundred until she sees the daylight again. She hates that tunnel. While in it, she senses the frustration and despair of a life with no immediate direction.

Taryn reckons restraint by the woman eventually provokes a response in the form of traditional gestures like flowers and other gifts. 'It's in their genes,' she said. 'Hold off from the nookie and they tax their brains to see how to win you over.'

Marianne remains unconvinced.

She has no sooner arrived home and turned on her computer, when she receives an email from Patrick.

To Marianne Hayward
From: Patrick Shrubsole
Date: 8th June 2012, 15.44
Subject: Sustainability

Marianne,
Good of you to pop by today. Delighted by your enthusiasm and impressed by your ideas. Have spoken to Gillian, outlined your proposals and faxed her copies. Am sure she will give green light. Have given her your email and phone number. She will call you regarding terms and contract details. You can trust her. You will essentially be signing over partial intellectual property rights. They will have responsibility of final production based on your ideas and materials, but she says you can input at each stage if you wish. She will

explain when you speak to her.

Have you seen on the news about the floods in
Aberystwyth?

Do come to Scilly. The more we link the programme with the
book and the Education Pack, the greater the impact. And I
like your idea of a separate short film for schools.

Best regards,

Patrick

To Marianne Hayward
From: Edward Harvey
Date: 8th June 2012, 18.01
Subject: Scilly

Dear Mari,

Thanks for your hospitality last night. Good to see
you again – but alas, too short. Please do come to
Scilly. Patrick has mailed me to say how impressed he
was. Asked about your marital status and how I come
to know you. Definitely think he fancies you! Would
welcome your company at the Parsonage but
wouldn't wish to deter you from coming if you would
prefer to be with the others (and Patrick!) at
Lowertown Farm.

James and Kate arriving tomorrow morning and say they
have news to share – which I will tell you about when I
know more.

love,

Edward

How can he think for one moment that she would rather be
with Patrick? Or is he teasing?

She calls Taryn.

Taryn says, 'It's a no-brainer. "Yes" to Scilly, "Yes" to Parsonage. By then you will have had more time to adjust to being without Johnny and more time to think about your future. He will have had time to convince you of serious intent.'

'He's being very cautious.'

'Has he mentioned the L word?'

'No.'

'How many bedrooms at the Parsonage?'

'One double, one single.'

'The rules would say you start off in the single room. Otherwise there's a danger of a holiday fling and you don't want that. Your being in close proximity should provoke a response. If something happens before then, you can always revise your plan.'

'Rules are not working very well at the moment. I did at least hope to make some progress this visit.'

'You are giving the wrong vibes. Rules say you must send signals; let him know you are receptive to overtures. Think of a gas oven: you want to be about Mark 3, simmering. I think you have switched off since the party.'

'During the three years Edward lodged with us, I was so careful not to flirt. This conditioning is very hard to break. The party was a performance. We are back in the real world now. My efforts are probably too oblique for him to interpret.'

To Patrick Shrubsole
From: Marianne Hayward
Date: 8th June 2012, 22.11
Subject: Re: Sustainability

Hi Patrick,
Thanks for this info. Gillian called and we are proceeding as you suggested.

Am pleased to take up offer of trip to Scilly and will discuss details with Edward. Let's hope weather better than it is at the moment!
Thank you.
Best wishes,
Marianne

To: Edward Harvey
From: Marianne Hayward
Date: 8th June 2012, 22.32
Subject: Re: Scilly

Dear Edward,
Will be pleased to come to Scilly with you. If what you say about Patrick is true, I'd feel safer at the Parsonage. I'm too old for him anyway!
love,
Mari

She doesn't mention strings. This is a conversation for nearer the time when she knows how she feels and if she has more confidence in longevity of the relationship.

Then she sends off a batch of emails to a dozen local libraries, offering to talk about how she came to write and publish *Lydia*. She also contacts a couple of local independent bookshops, asking if they might consider hosting a book signing event. She is beginning to realise that she needs to be more proactive in creating marketing opportunities.

To: Marianne Hayward
From: Edward Harvey
Date: 8th June 2012, 22.58
Subject: Re: Scilly

That's great news! Patrick thinks you are about forty-six.
I didn't tell him otherwise.
Edward

To: Edward Harvey
From: Marianne Hayward
Date: 8th June 2012, 23.05
Subject: Re: Scilly

Men are so useless when it comes to age! However,
would rather he underestimated than overestimated so
will take as compliment.
Mari

It has been a very productive day from several perspectives and she goes to bed in a positive and optimistic mood, mulling over romantic developments on sun-drenched islands.

28

Proposals

The following morning, Edward wakes at the Deer Orchard and his first thought is of Marianne coming to Scilly. He imagines gazing at the wide vistas with her by his side, perhaps holding hands, doing the young-love romance things that now seem so long ago. After a day filming, they might take a boat trip to watch the evening gig racing, then have a drink at the Turk's Head before returning as the darkness falls to stare into the vast blackness of the universe through unpolluted skies and then creep upstairs for some shared moments of closeness under the duvet. In his mind he moves things on from the night after the party; moves on from outside to inside, from top to below; moves on from Moota.

Soon after breakfast, James and Kate arrive in a red hatchback car. The previous night they had stayed over at a newly married friend of James's in Budleigh Salterton.

James is tall, tanned and angular, his long wavy hair in a ponytail. He would not have looked out of place in a 1970s commune. Kate floats beside him in a floral maxi dress, cardigan and sandals, brown hair in two plaits, girlish and bohemian. Both are now aged twenty-seven and there is an ease of maturity and coupledom about them as they walk towards the house with their overnight bags.

Edward is delighted to see them – the first time since their fleeting visit at New Year and many months since they had spent significant time together the previous summer. Hands are shaken, hugs exchanged. Edward is pleased that at least one of his children is settled in a relationship. They may not be married yet, but they are a perfect match. He loves Kate's enthusiasm and gung-ho approach to the outdoors. She is never defeated by weather. He is impressed by that.

It is starting to rain yet again and Kate mentions the inclement conditions that have leapt from drought to flood and her concerns for the fruit crop with the general lack of insects, the saturated blossom in April and May and now the wind.

'Good for our electricity production, though,' says Edward, nodding in the direction of the orchard and the towering structure with its white blades going lickety-split. 'Felicity was right about the turbine paying for itself and then some. We are just about beginning to reap the benefits.'

James says, 'The ones at Robin Rigg make ours look small.'

Inside they gather in the kitchen and make tea. Harriet rushes down from upstairs and beams greetings.

'I've booked a table for the four of us at the Retreat for one o'clock,' continues James. 'Kate and I have news to share. Not babies – before you jump to any conclusions. Work-related news.'

Edward is intrigued and also pleased that neither he nor Harriet has to bother to think about lunch. He found it difficult at first to accept his children making arrangements without his input, but since Felicity left and Harriet took over most of the day-to-day running of the home, he has begun to enjoy relinquishing some of the responsibility.

They sit round the breakfast bar.

James says, 'Rachel tells us you're having a midlife crisis and are in hot pursuit of another woman. Is this true or is she exaggerating?'

Edward is taken aback and looks sternly at Harriet.

She says, 'I know, I shouldn't have said anything but we

were talking on the phone a couple of days ago and Rach wanted more details about Marianne's visit. She said she was worried about you. I thought a few details might reassure her that you were okay.'

'That backfired,' says James. 'Rach is in meltdown. Expect her to vent her thoughts soon.'

'I asked you to wait,' says Edward to Harriet.

'So?' says James.

Edward chooses his words carefully, 'Warm pursuit, perhaps. Too old for "hot".'

Kate says, 'I think you should grab happiness when you can. Rachel would feel differently if she were settled. You are still the main man in her life – even though she doesn't see you often. She may be jealous of someone other than her mum, being of importance to you.'

'Delayed Electra complex,' says James. 'We both liked Marianne when we met her years ago. There are worse people you could shack up with.'

'Like Jessica,' says Harriet.

'We are nowhere near "shacking-up",' says Edward. 'Marianne has been a shade evasive since Harriet persuaded her to pretend to be my girlfriend at Jessica's party.'

'Is this for real?' says James.

Harriet folds her arms. 'Jessica needed a deterrent. She's being very persistent.'

James asks, 'Is this "Jessica" from down the road?'

Kate says, 'Not your type, surely?'

'She's a head-case,' says Harriet. 'But Dad likes her cooking.'

Edward glares again at Harriet.

'So how far did this girlfriend business go?' says James.

Edward thinks he might be blushing and is aware of Harriet's raised eyebrow. 'Marianne has been ignoring my suggestions that she comes down for another weekend and although I've just been to her place, I can assure you, it was all above board.'

Harriet says, 'I thought after Jessica's, one thing would lead to another.'

'You thought wrong,' says Edward. 'We have talked after a fashion, but you must remember her husband has only been dead a year.' He decides not to mention Scilly yet. He doesn't want that news filtering back to Rachel until he has had a chance to speak to her.

'Are you in love with her?' asks Kate.

'Yes,' says Edward, so shocked by the boldness of the question that he hasn't time to think of a more obtuse reply. Perhaps Kate feels she can probe where his children fear to go.

'Have you told her?' says Kate.

'No,' says Edward.

'Is she in love with you?'

'I don't know,' says Edward.

'See what I mean?' says Harriet. 'Hopeless.'

They all laugh and then Edward says he wants to stretch his legs. Kate asks if he would like some company and if he can wait while she puts on some jeans. While he waits for her, he says to James, 'About this news, is it something I should be pleased about?'

'That remains to be seen,' says James. 'But it's nothing for you to worry about.'

Soon Edward and Kate, attired in waterproof jackets, set off across the paddock with Meg. The rain has become more persistent and a cool breeze is gaining strength.

Kate says, 'I think it's fantastic to fall in love again. Don't be deterred by Rachel. Harriet clearly approves and James and I will be very happy for you if something comes of it.'

'Relationships at my age take much consideration, not least because of the other family members.' He is anxious about

James's comment regarding Rachel. He wouldn't be deterred by objections from his children, but he cares what they think and doesn't want to upset them if at all possible.

'My grandmother had an admirer after her husband died,' says Kate. 'They'd be in their sixties though. My mum and her brothers disapproved. Thought he was after her money. Constantly made sniping remarks both to her face and behind her back. They called him Penguin Bob because he walked like one.'

'Was he called Bob?'

'Oddly enough, no. He was called Fred. I don't know where the Bob came from. But when my mum was widowed, she said even though she wouldn't have wanted to get married again, she could see the advantages of a male companion. She said she was sorry to have been obstructive. If Rachel is awkward, refer her to me.'

'Always assuming there's anything to be awkward about.'

They climb over the stile and turn down the lane that borders the Molwings' farm. Edward asks Kate about their work at Robin Rigg and is aware that she answers hesitantly.

In the Retreat at lunchtime, it is only when they have eaten their starters that James breaks the news that Edward has been wondering about all morning.

'One of the reasons we are here this weekend – as well as seeing you – is that we both had interviews at Exeter uni yesterday. We didn't want you to know earlier in case nothing came of it, but we have every reason to believe that we have both been successful. In my case it's a full-time lecturing post in the biology department and for Kate, a part-time research assistant.'

'Congratulations,' says Edward, and glasses chink across the table. This is indeed exciting news because it means another child likely to settle close to home.

'We thought you'd be pleased about that bit,' says James.

'What's the catch?' asks Edward.

'We finish at Robin Rigg at the end of July so we'll probably have a holiday before starting the new jobs in September.'

'Come to Scilly for a few days. You'd be useful if we need extra help.'

'Something to consider,' says James, 'but a more pressing concern is sorting out where we're going to live.'

'Here of course, until you find somewhere.' Edward mentally installs James in his former bedroom along with Kate and hopes that by then, any visit from Marianne will not have need of the guest room. If so, there is still Christopher's room though it is small and still covered with football-related posters. 'If that's all you're concerned about, it's no problem.'

'It's not quite all. We have a proposition, but we don't know how it can be realised. We know you are thinking of moving from the Deer Orchard.'

Again Edward gives Harriet a stern look.

'Don't glare at me. You asked Rick to reinstate lawns with that in mind.'

'And then I asked him to forget about it.'

'For the time being,' says Harriet.

'Anyway,' continues James, 'you may not be going immediately, but you probably will in the future. Especially if something happens between you and Marianne. And we – Kate and I – were wondering if there's a way that we could take it over, buy you out, but in stages. Kate wants to do what Mum did. Not the restaurant, but she wants to produce and sell organic food – probably on a larger scale than mum; a broader range of animals: geese, pigs possibly, in addition to sheep, goats and chickens. And we're thinking of starting a family.'

'This is a lot to take in,' says Edward, shocked by the extent of the news.

James continues, 'We don't want to lose the Deer Orchard when you and Harriet leave. It's perfect for what we want. Kate's mum said she would help with some money, but we don't have the funds for a complete buy-out, although we should be able to get a fairly decent mortgage. And I know there's Yetti and Rachel and Chris to be taken into consideration.'

'Too right,' says Harriet, reverting to her awkward little-sister role. 'And will you stop calling me Yetti.'

'And I'm not dead yet,' says Edward.

'And you, of course. But if you sell up and move somewhere small, how are we all going to get together for family reunions? If we're here, then Christmas is sorted for the foreseeable.'

Edward has to admit that this is an attractive proposal. One of the reasons for his sluggishness in moving is because he can't bear to lose all that has been gained. 'It's worth thinking about, but your mother is still officially joint-owner. She said I could have it when she went to Italy; said she would take her share in the form of the proceeds from the Retreat and the rest of her inheritance. But we have nothing in writing. Not that she has reason to grumble because it was a fair split if you take into account the value of our respective pensions. Now the wind turbine is starting to generate income, I suppose she could argue she should have a share of that, but it's a separate issue from the house.'

'But do you like the idea?' says James. 'In principle.'

'If you give me some figures about the capital you can raise, I will consult Tim Chassey about contractual possibilities.' Tim is one of the lawyers who does work for the Killerton Estate and with whom Edward has had dealings on several occasions over the years. Indeed, it was Tim who dealt with Felicity's purchase and subsequent sale of the Retreat. 'And if Tim says it's workable, I'll get in touch with your mother.'

After lunch, Kate – who never drinks alcohol – drives them back home where they discover Jessica peering through the kitchen window. A few expletives run through Edward's mind.

She comes over to the car, carrying a tin in her arms. 'I saw you had family visiting and thought you might like a cake. It's a Victoria sponge, nothing too fancy.'

Edward wonders again what part of their previous conversations she has failed to understand.

'I did ask you not to give me any more food, Jessica,' he says, closing the car door and walking over to the house. 'I meant it. I don't feel it is fair in view of our misunderstanding.' If he was expecting her to retreat quietly, he was mistaken. She totters after him.

James, Kate and Harriet loiter tactfully by the car.

'I wanted to make it for you. Surely you wouldn't refuse a gift?'

Edward realises he has a problem which, if not addressed now, will continue. 'I don't wish to accept it, Jessica. It may seem ungracious, but I need you to understand that I don't want our acquaintance to be misconstrued. We have no pending relationship and continued acceptance of food would not be appropriate.' He turns away. 'If you'll excuse me.'

Jessica rushes at him, flinging the tin at him. 'Take it; take it!' Her eyes bulge wildly.

Edward pushes it away and as Jessica releases it, the tin falls to the ground.

Harriet intervenes. She runs forward, picks up the tin and thrusts it back at Jessica. 'Take your bloody cake and leave my dad alone. Get it into your stupid head he's involved with someone else and he doesn't want you.'

Edward pulls Harriet away.

Jessica shouts, 'You little cow!' and lunges towards her, unsteady on her heels, the cake tin dropping for the second time.

'Hey, hey!' says James, striding over and jumping between them. 'Steady on!'

'Harriet is only saying what I should have said,' says Edward. 'Please leave us alone.'

'Don't think you can pick me up and put me down just because of some London tart.' Jessica tosses her hair and steps back.

'I didn't "pick you up" or promise you anything at all,' says Edward, carefully. 'We had one meeting about wind turbines which you initiated. I was merely trying to help you out.'

'You took me for a meal!' she shouts, shaking off James.

'You coerced him into going,' says Harriet.

Edward says, 'I paid for the meal that you booked; as a thank-you for the food, not for any other reason.' He is rapidly realising that Harriet is correct. The woman is unhinged.

'Bastard,' mutters Jessica. 'You men are all the same.' Then she turns, picks up the cake tin and makes her way carefully down the gravel path.

'Interesting,' says James. 'Does having an added stalker mean we can negotiate more generous terms on the property?'

29

Stalking

*Stalk: pursue persistently and sometimes attack
(a person with whom one is obsessed).*

Collins Dictionary

Nineteen sixth-formers sit in twelve double desks, arranged in a horseshoe around the psychology room in an upper floor of North Kent College on the edge of Beckenham. Not a full complement: one off sick, one probably bunking off, one disappeared to the loo – or as Marianne suspiciously thinks, consulting her text messages without the threat of censure. They are a lower sixth group, an ethnically diverse mix, reluctantly returned to college after their AS exams and forced to begin the upper sixth specification when they would rather escape the dismal summer and be sunning themselves on a Spanish island beach or visiting relatives in Ghana or Nigeria, Latvia or Poland. Anything but more work; particularly work that is more challenging than the previous year.

'Why do we have to be here, Miss?' wails a disgruntled student with a hangdog face. The plea echoes round the room. Several haven't brought pens or folders.

'Because all around the country other students are beginning their courses and we wouldn't want you to be disadvantaged. Because beginning your A2s will help to inform you which one to drop next year.'

'I already know I'm going to drop psychology, Miss. Do I still have to come?'

'If you don't come and if for any reason your results are not as you would wish; if you change your mind, we will not have you back if you have not completed this introduction.'

They want to watch films and go on trips. The psychology department intends to familiarise them with the rigours of A2 so that the weak or undecided have sufficient evidence about whether they are capable of continuing the subject in September. The only concession is starting with a topic that should be of particular interest from the *Relationships* section of the specification.

Stalking.

Eventually the class settles.

'What is stalking behaviour?' Marianne asks. 'Discuss with the person sitting next to you. You have one minute.' She clicks the clock feature on the interactive whiteboard and watches as it begins counting down the seconds. Something about the time pressure seems to focus the students' attention and they immediately begin to argue among themselves and scribble down their thoughts.

Marianne overhears the word *EastEnders*.

When the minute is up, she asks each pair in turn for a comment. Their efforts are unsophisticated and centred around obsessive following behaviour. She gives them a dictionary definition and the students begin to make notes.

Marianne continues, 'Cupach and Spitzberg (2004) say there are eight categories of stalking.' She writes *hyper-intimacy* on the board. 'This is another way of saying "excessive courtship", like giving loads of presents or very extravagant gifts to someone with whom one hasn't a particularly significant relationship.'

'My mum does that,' says Alicia. 'She's always giving stuff to her boyfriends. It was an iPad last time.'

'Oh my days!' says Eric, from the other side of the class.

'What's her number?' There is a ripple of laughter.

Marianne generally tries not to make judgemental comments when her charges reveal personal information about their families. She moves swiftly on to the next listed item. 'What does *surveillance* mean?'

'Spying, keeping watch,' says Mary.

'Exactly. And *interactional contacts* would be simply trying to bring about communication opportunities.'

'So, Miss, if I, yeah, plan to bump into someone I like so I can say hello, and I knows they do RE at the same time as I do psychology, is that stalking?' asks Ryan.

'Yeah, I seen you,' says Eric. 'It's that Gloria, innit? You stalker, man!'

There is more laughter and Marianne remembers the times she conspired to meet Johnny when he was a sixth-former at Derwentbridge Grammar School and she was about fifteen, engineering meetings on the main staircase every Friday because she knew after the first lesson, he would be coming down from English when she was going up. If she scampered across the playground from her chemistry lesson, she usually timed it right and he always smiled at her, even though she was just a teenage kid in the fourth form and he was one of the coolest guys in the school. She takes a deep breath, the memories a powerful reminder of her loss. 'We've all done that. But if there's no sinister purpose, and no harm done, it's not really stalking.'

There is a pause while there are murmurings of other personal experiences.

'*Harassment, intimidation, coercion and threat* are self-explanatory and more serious. Coercion means forcing,' she adds. '*Aggression* is worse still and is more likely after the ending of an intimate relationship. The more intimate the relationship with someone, the greater the threat of actual harm, ranging from over fifty percent for ex-partners and suchlike to less than ten percent for strangers. Perhaps surprisingly, mentally sick stalkers are no more likely to be violent than other types.'

Debra says, 'I knows someone who had to move, yeah, because her ex used to spy on her to see who she was seeing. Then he get mad, shouting, making threats to her, saying she was a whore.'

'Lastly, *cyber-stalking,* involving unwelcome contacts via email or the net. This is a growing problem on social networking sites. Why do you think that might be?'

'So easy to find people and contact details,' says Alicia.

'Easy to send messages,' says Kobi. 'People can hide their identity.'

'Especially on Twitter, says Eric. 'And even if you don't follow someone, you can see the tweets they send.'

Marianne says, 'But does reading someone's tweets constitute stalking? People send tweets knowing this may happen. Reading doesn't mean intention to harm. However, if you repeatedly send hostile tweets to a person, or regularly mention a particular person in a defamatory way, that might constitute stalking. Some recent high-profile cases have led to police involvement. And you are traceable, whatever identity you assume.'

There are one or two worried looks among the students; some whispering in the back corner.

'Now I'd like you to make two columns and list who might be a stalker and who might be stalked. You've already mention celebrities, but who else?'

'Miss, I'm being stalked by someone in my history class,' says Jermaine. 'She keeps emailing and texting. She got my number from a friend. She try to talk to me in class and keep saying, "Hi" in the corridors. I don't want to know her; like she's weird. She don't take the hint. She even wait for me, yeah, to leave college so she can follow me.'

Marianne says, 'I think in a school or college situation we have to be careful to distinguish between normal behaviour that is harmless and that which becomes a nuisance or a threat. If you are worried, then you might discuss it with your tutor.'

'No, seriously?'

'Oh my days.'

While the class discuss, Marianne thinks again about Jessica; about her persistence despite Edward's apparent discouragement. She ticks a lot of the stalking boxes both in her behaviour towards Edward and – from what he says – in her loss profile of significant others: parents and two husbands. And the last husband looks to have been unfaithful, so in some ways she lost him twice. Then there's the nuisance phone calls. She wonders whether to be more forceful in highlighting her suspicions to Edward, or to wait and see if anything further happens.

She draws two columns on the whiteboard and asks the class to feed back their potential stalkers and stalkees. Most students have listed celebrities and exes as the main type of person to be stalked, but a few suggest that anyone can become the victim of an obsession, particularly those who are popular.

'High status individuals: alpha men and women,' says Marianne. 'Key characters in school, university or the workplace. And this gives a clue as to what type of person tends to stalk someone where there has been no previous relationship.'

'Losers,' says Eric.

Some of the students laugh.

'Perhaps Eric is on the right track,' says Marianne. 'Evidence suggests such stalking might be due to disturbed attachment in childhood because insecure attachment links with high fear of rejection and emotional instability. Research shows that many stalkers have had both attachment disruptions in childhood and lost someone in the months leading up to the stalking behaviour – either through marriage break-up or even losing a child in a custody dispute. This might cause preoccupied attachment: idealising another person and needing their acceptance for their own well-being. So what are the advantages to an insecurely attached person in forming an attachment to a celebrity or other unattainable figure?'

'It's not real, Miss, innit. It's never gonna happen, right. They can't ever dump you,' says Ryan.

Marianne says, 'This theory is particularly relevant for celebrity stalking, but what about exes and other random people? Why do people stalk them?'

'They're obsessed, innit,' says Eric.

'Yes, but why do they become obsessed? It's a little trickier to fathom,' says Marianne, sitting on the table at the front of the class. 'The Relational Goal Pursuit theory is one plausible explanation for these cases. We all have goals and these are structured in a hierarchy so that lower-order goals are necessary in order to achieve higher-order goals.' She moves her hands through an imaginary hierarchy by way of illustration. 'If a person links the lower-order goal of having a particular relationship, with a higher-order goal of happiness, then McIntosh (1976) believes this may begin the stalking process.'

Jermaine says, 'Does this mean my history class stalker thinks if she get me in a relationship, she will be happy?'

'Perhaps,' says Marianne. 'But this might be the case even if she wasn't a stalker and was just interested in you. The theory suggests that stalking happens when the goal is blocked and the person dwells on the distress of not achieving their goal. Intense negative feelings may occur, such as jealousy or anger. This is known as emotional flooding and because such feelings are unpleasant, the person is motivated to try to reduce this by trying even harder to attain their goal. This leads to excessive pursuit behaviour – chasing – and a tendency to misinterpret any rejection as encouraging. We all want what we can't have.'

Marianne sets a task in which the students have to find studies to support the theories discussed. After they collect text books off the shelves and settle into searching for information, she walks around answering questions, all the while a grain of fear germinating and taking root that Jessica Hennessy is not only her nuisance caller, but also stalking Edward. She decides to say nothing until there is more evidence. She doesn't want to alarm him unnecessarily.

30

Daughters

During the week after the cake incident, Edward keeps careful watch for any signs of Jessica picking her way up the gravel path with food offerings. James had wanted to go and visit her with view to reiterating Harriet's words about leaving Edward alone.

'I don't want any more unpleasantness if it can be helped,' said Edward, mildly irritated that his son thought him incapable of deterring her from pursuit. 'She is a neighbour after all.'

'Are you sure you didn't lead her on?' said James.

'Only if accepting the odd pie or stew can be interpreted in such a way. And I never should have gone to the restaurant. My rejection of her advances wasn't well handled. I was too ambiguous. At the time I thought it was the right thing to do. I didn't want to hurt her feelings.'

He is quietly pleased that James and Kate will be moving back to Broadclyst. Their plans for the Deer Orchard will make it much easier for him to leave, to downsize, to contemplate a fresh start. By the middle of the week he has spoken to his solicitor Tim Chassey and it seems there are several available options, all of which first require an untangling of Felicity's joint ownership agreement. Despite what he said to James, he has not been able to bring himself to contact her. There is no immediate rush and with his own situation being fluid, it might be better to wait until there is more certainty about his future before the inevitable confrontation. The knowledge that the idea is workable, is sufficient for James and Kate to make plans.

The weather remains stubbornly cool and wet with regular reports of flooding from different parts of the country. The evening news is filled with tales of rescue and ruined possessions, with pictures of water rising up living room walls or cascading down streets while displaced homeowners, tearful and anxious, praise the emergency services and the community spirit. Aerial shots from helicopters show the extent of the problem. In towns and villages, the streets are waterways with the odd boat ferrying supplies or extracting a determined resident who refuses to evacuate until there is no alternative. In the countryside, rivers expand onto fields and clusters of sheep or cows huddle on tiny patches of visible ground, entirely surrounded by murky water. Meanwhile, the environmentalists gather on *Newsnight* and weather presenters begin their forecasts with apologies and *don't blame me* expressions.

Edward continues to exchange emails with Marianne, hinting again that she might like to arrange another visit to the Deer Orchard. She says she is too busy with upper sixth exams and other college-related preparation. 'And I need my weekends for completing the Education Pack,' she adds. He decides not to issue any more invitations until she appears to have fewer commitments.

He asks Gemma to post her another pile of literature that he has discovered about education and sustainability. He gives Gemma an acknowledgement slip on which he has written: *To peruse if and when you have time. Edward x.*

'I'm afraid you'll have to give me her address again,' says Gemma, looking flustered. 'That piece of paper on which you wrote her details seems to have vanished into thin air. It's odd. You know I don't lose things. I meant to file it after addressing the last batch, but it disappeared. I couldn't find it anywhere and I went through everything on my desk.'

'Gemma, don't worry. It's probably caught up with

something else and will turn up eventually.' He checks his diary and scribbles Marianne's details on a memo pad.

Two days later Marianne texts to say thank you. She also writes that she hasn't had any more nuisance calls since putting a block on the phone.

Edward is relieved. If it was Jessica, he assumes she has given up the chase. She seems to be keeping a low profile, no more food having been brought to the Deer Orchard. At last the message appears to have sunk in that he is not interested in having a relationship with her.

When he returns home from work at the end of the week, he can hear raised voices from the kitchen long before he opens the door. One is Harriet's, sharp and aggressive; the other is Rachel's, calmly assertive.

He is always pleased to see Rachel and his heart fills. First daughter, sensitive and sweet; daddy's girl. He is lucky if he sees her three times a year since she moved from uni to employment in London, and he returned to Broadclyst on a permanent basis. He's always had a special bond with her, the image of Felicity with her long wavy hair. But she has a temperament like himself. She understands him like no one else on the planet.

He overhears: 'And you're just going to stand by and watch him bring another woman into *our* house?' This is Rachel. Not so sweet today. Perhaps she doesn't understand him as much as he thought.

He steps inside and the voices still. Harriet is leaning against the counter with a mug in her hand and Rachel appears to have been pacing the floor. He catches her looking distinctly cross. When she sees him her expression changes and she walks over to him, giving him a somewhat tentative hug which he returns.

'What a lovely surprise. To what do we owe this unexpected visit?'

'I've come to check up on you, Dad.'

'So why the arguing?'

'A few rumours on the Harvey grapevine. I want to know what's going on with you and Marianne Fanclub.'

For an instant he wonders if their night together has been discovered. He looks at Harriet.

'I've said nothing specific,' says Harriet. 'Other than I think you and Marianne would be good.'

'And I think it would be dire,' says Rachel. 'What will Mum think?'

'What your mother thinks is hardly relevant,' says Edward. 'But more to the point, there is no me and Marianne. But I'd like there to be.'

'And what about us?'

Edward takes off his jacket. Perhaps Kate is correct and she is huffy about the idea of taking second place to Marianne. He plays for time, going over to the kettle while the eyes of both daughters follow him, waiting for an answer.

'I see you at Christmas and possibly another couple of times a year. James even less – although that looks likely to change; Christopher, not at all since he went to Italy. You have chosen to live away from home, therefore it should be of little consequence to you whether or not I share my life with someone else.'

'And I would like Dad to find someone,' says Harriet, stoutly.

'Only so you can shack up with—.' Rachel stops short and looks away.

Harriet yells, 'You bitch, you promised!'

'What's this?' says Edward.

'Irrelevant,' says Harriet. 'I want to be independent, that's all. And I would prefer to leave you with someone to keep you company rather than being on your own – as long as it's the right someone and not the witch Jessica. Marianne is perfect for you. I can't see why Rachel would object.'

'This is our home. It doesn't seem right that another woman should be in it.'

'So Dad is supposed to stay on his own so you can come here for a few days a year? That's so selfish.'

'Irrespective of Marianne,' says Edward, 'I will probably move. Somewhere smaller. So the idea of the family home is not relevant.' He sits down at the table with a mug of tea. 'Did James also fill you in about coming back to Broadclyst? He and Kate may take over the Deer Orchard.' He is deliberately vague, not wanting to add further problems until James and Kate begin to put their plans into action.

Rachel appears to ignore the implications of her brother's involvement. 'Let's assume there is Marianne. What happens when you die?'

'Rachel!' says Edward.

'Ah, so this is about money, is it?' says Harriet.

Rachel sits down and flushes. 'It can't be ignored.'

Edward says, 'Do you think if I were to get together with anyone, I wouldn't ensure your interests were taken care of?'

'You might be carried away with love for some spendthrift manipulating hussy.'

Edward can't help but laugh. 'You think I lack judgement?'

'I hear loneliness does strange things to older people.'

Harriet says, 'Marianne isn't a spendthrift or a manipulator. We know her. She's trustworthy.'

'I keep telling you there is no me and Marianne. If there were, Harriet is right, she's no manipulator.'

Harriet says, 'But you'd like there to be a "you and Marianne". And so would she, I think. You're both being too cautious. And,' she adds, scowling at Rachel, 'we need to support this rather than finding yet more reasons for it not to happen.'

'So you'd take out a pre-nup, or something?' says Rachel, ignoring Harriet.

'Or something,' says Edward. 'If I were to be seriously involved with another woman – any other woman – I would protect your interests in the long term. There are various ways it can be done. Possibly by creating a trust fund for use during the lifetime of whoever it happens to be. And that's assuming I don't outlive her. If we're talking Marianne, she has her own money and only one daughter, so if anyone needs their interests protecting, it will be Holly.'

Rachel looks suitably chastened.

'What was that you were going to say about why Harriet wants me settled with someone?'

'It was nothing.'

'She was having a go at me, that's all,' says Harriet.

Edward isn't so sure.

'I'm meeting some friends in Exeter,' says Harriet, a little too quickly in Edward's opinion. She turns to Rachel. 'Give you a chance to catch up properly with Dad. Sort supper, perhaps? There's fish in the fridge.' Then she is off before she can be questioned further.

Rachel sits down opposite Edward, her mouth in a tight line.

Edward continues, 'Marianne has been a very good friend to me in the past – when I was in hospital and when I was lodging in Beckenham. She was a great support when your mother and I were struggling. I became very fond of her, but she had a husband with whom she was happy, I had your mother with whom I wanted to try to recapture the good times. When I returned to UD, Marianne and I drifted out of touch. It's what happens when life gets in the way. Then all my efforts to improve the situation with your mother failed and she left with Gianni.'

'Didn't see that coming,' says Rachel, mellowing slightly. 'He used to flirt with me.'

'Harriet suggested I get in touch with Marianne again. She found her on Twitter and only then did I discover Johnny died just over a year ago. All things then became possible – except we are both in our mid fifties with grown up kids and living two hundred miles apart. She has been down for a couple of weekends and we pretended she was my girlfriend to throw Jessica off her pursuit – not that it did, but that's another story. It was fun. I began thinking we might take things further … and I thought she was thinking that too. But suddenly she backed off and although we email, she keeps resisting my invitations to come to stay.'

'I can't take it all in,' says Rachel. 'You being close to another woman.'

'I understand your concerns. If anything should develop, the family will not be forgotten. That is the only assurance I can give.'

Then Rachel asks him about Jessica, having heard about the cake incident from James. 'I never thought you would have been so naive,' she says. 'Don't you understand women at all? If you give us the tiniest hope, we embellish; we create our own fantasy and believe it's real.'

That night, with two girls under the roof looking out for him, he is enveloped by a feeling of being ancient and it makes him sad. There seems to be so little time to do all the things he wants to do; to start afresh. He replays parts of the day's conversations, trying to think of the most diplomatic way of dealing with Rachel's concerns. And what was that sentence she cut short, the one that inflamed Harriet? He remembers: *shacking up*. He hasn't been aware of Harriet seeing anyone for some time but now his suspicions have been aroused, he doesn't like to be kept in the dark.

'Harriet,' says Edward, at breakfast the following morning

when they are alone. 'What was Rachel saying about you "shacking up" with someone? Is there anyone in your life I should know about? Is this why you want me to get together with Marianne?' He has one eye on some grilling bacon and is unprepared for the bombshell she is about to drop.

'I would be happier moving out if you were not on your own. I don't think you're very good at looking after yourself long term.'

'I wouldn't want you to feel obligated to stay here. The others have gone; you deserve your chance of independence.'

'It's Rick.' She blurts it out behind his back.

'Rick who?'

'Rick. Our Rick.'

Edward swings round on his heels. He's becoming used to the unpleasant visceral reactions to shock. 'Rick!' He can't believe what he is hearing. 'You are seeing Rick? Rick who's had almost every woman in Broadclyst, married or otherwise?'

'Don't exaggerate.'

'You know his reputation.'

'He's changed since he and I—'

'Him and you! My God, girl, wait till I see him. Are you completely insane? I mean how? When?'

'You know when I go to my Italian classes? Well … I don't go.'

'You underhand little madam. I thought better of you.'

'Stop talking to me as if I were a child.'

'He's old enough to be your father.'

'You always discourage us from using clichés.'

'He's not good enough for you, Harriet.'

'And what exactly is "good enough"? If you mean he didn't go to a private school like you and Mum, no, he didn't. But nor did we. And no, he didn't go to university. But that's because he didn't have the opportunities we have had, not because he's not intelligent.'

They are now facing each other across the central work station. The smell of burning bacon fills the air and the smoke alarm starts bleeping. Edward rushes to rescue his breakfast while Harriet wafts a damp dish cloth at the alarm.

Edward is not distracted for long. 'He has relatively low earning potential, as you know.'

'How can you be so materialistic? I thought better of *you*. That's Mum talking. You once said you would be happy living in a caravan if you had her and us.'

This was true. And in his heart, he still believes it – the caravan part. But his children only know the comfortable life. He isn't sure how any one of them might cope on a budget. 'Much of what he earns has come from me or your mum over the past ten years. Which is why you were so defensive about me downsizing the vegetable side of our arrangement, I suppose.'

'He makes me happy,' says Harriet.

'But for how long? He's fit enough now to keep up with you. But twenty years on?'

'You wouldn't be like this if he was Rod Stewart.'

'Because Rod Stewart isn't short of a bob or two.'

'Charles and Diana?'

'That didn't go too well, if I remember.'

'But no one objected to the age difference, which was huge.'

'Ditto financial security.'

'I can't believe you're being so money-driven. It's not like you, Dad. I have earning power too.'

'And when you have kids?'

'I don't want kids. We don't want kids.'

'Is this another of Rick's ideas?'

'At the moment we feel the same. Rick says, "it's better to be an old man's darling than a young man's slave". My experience of young men says give me Rick anytime. In any case, you can't stop us. But we'd rather have your blessing. I can't believe you're being like this when I have been so supportive of you and Marianne.' She starts to gulp away tears.

Edward has rarely seen Harriet cry. She is the tough one, the unemotional one, the one who confronts and won't back down. Then he remembers how touchingly compassionate she was when he was injured all those years ago. 'I only want what's best for you. I don't want you to make a big mistake.'

'Sometimes we have to take a chance. This is a considered chance, just like you and Marianne would be.' She starts to sob and flees upstairs.

Too much stress. He now understands how easy it would be to have a nervous breakdown. If only Felicity were here to help him deal with this. She was the one who said yes or no to the children when they were teenagers wanting extra freedom. Only rarely did she defer to him for adjudication. Mostly it wasn't necessary. But if anyone pushed boundaries it was Harriet, so this latest announcement is hardly a surprise. It is no use expecting Felicity to help now. No matter what she said, Harriet would not be influenced by a mother who had left with a significantly younger man. He might ask Marianne for some advice.

He settles at the table with his overcooked bacon sandwich. Now he has two unhappy daughters, an estranged wife, a stalker and a woman full of mystery, sometimes beckoning, sometimes pulling away, often confusing. All he wants is the quiet domestic life he once took for granted; a life that freed his mind to wander and wonder, to theorise, idealise and hypothesise about archaeological matters and the essence of being. Each time he believes he might be getting there, someone pulls the rug.

31

Messages

All is not well in Beckenham either.

Marianne comes home from work after a difficult day with her returning lower sixth students. She collects her post from behind the door: the usual collection of junk mail, a bank statement, an energy bill and another large brown envelope with a University of Devon stamp across the top.

More guff from Edward, she thinks, pleased rather than otherwise. Then the phone rings.

She puts the mail on the table in the hall and rushes to answer it. Nothing. She hangs up. She thought the block had solved the problem but perhaps the caller is using another phone. Most people still have a landline and a mobile. She assumed the block was most probably on the withheld landline number. She punches 1471, and it sounds like a mobile number. Of course, it could be someone else.

She goes through to the kitchen and puts the kettle on. The cat appears at her ankles. The phone rings again.

This time she doesn't say hello. Instead, she listens intently. She can hear the birds twittering. She closes her eyes.

Then a female voice says, 'She thinks she's so wonderful with her London ways.' It is as if the speaker is talking to someone else by their side. 'Thinks she's so clever; a teacher; psychology to boot. And an author too.'

Marianne catches her breath, wants to defend herself but knows she mustn't let on that she is listening.

The voice lowers, still seeming to be talking to someone

237

else. 'But clever isn't everything, is it?' Perhaps she is conversing with the birds.

Then staccato, low and determined. 'He's not stupid. It won't last.'

It is unmistakably Jessica.

Marianne hangs up and takes the unusual step of trying to reach Edward on his mobile, but is diverted to answerphone. She leaves a message, asking him to call as soon as possible. Her mind is working overtime, fretting.

It is over an hour later when he calls back with apologies about being in a meeting.

She tells him the details.

He says, 'Are you absolutely sure it's Jessica?'

'One hundred percent.'

'I could go and confront her. Tell her we know; tell her to stop, or else.'

'That might be what she wants,' says Marianne. 'She might be trying to lure you into a visit.'

'I doubt we've enough to interest the police. She hasn't made any threats.'

'Yet,' says Marianne. 'If you confront her, she might say you're the one making threats. I'd stay away. She might try to get you into trouble. Don't want to make things worse. If she calls again, I'll try to block this number too.'

Edward tells her not to worry.

Easier said …

She makes supper but struggles to eat it. She is unsettled and fidgety. When she goes upstairs to check *Lydia* sales figures on Amazon, she finds an email from Edward.

To: Marianne Hayward
From: Edward Harvey
Date: 18th June 2012, 18.23

Subject: News

Dear Mari,

Always lovely to talk to you despite the circumstances. I promise to keep away from Jessica. Feel free to call me anytime.

When I sent you the first batch of sustainability info, I scribbled your name and address on a piece of paper for Gemma. I think it might have been the same day that Jessica made an unexpected visit to see me at work. When I asked Gemma to send the second batch, she said she couldn't find your address, that the paper had gone missing. Gemma doesn't lose things. Now we know it's definitely Jessica making the calls, all I can think of is that she might have had access to it while she was waiting to see me. If she had your address, it would be easier for her to find your phone number. I'm sorry for the carelessness. Try not to worry.

Things very busy here workwise.

Forgot to mention Rachel made fleeting visit during which discovered Harriet has been involved with Rick for over a year. She goes to see him instead of her Italian evening classes!! Should have been suspicious as no attempt to practise language skills. They are apparently very serious. Wondering whether to speak to Felicity – except doubt it would do any good.

Is there any point in me saying anything to Rick?

Violence is not my style but can see why some resort to such in similar circumstances.

love,

Edward

For an instant she has an image of Edward and Rick scrapping by the greenhouse. She suspects that Edward would come off worst.

To: Edward Harvey
From: Marianne Hayward
Date: 18th June 2012, 18.53
Subject: Re: News

Dear Edward,
Not worrying about you is difficult. Jessica seems unstable. But you couldn't have anticipated her stealing my address, so please don't blame Gemma or yourself. She would have found my number via some other means if she was determined to do so.
Regarding Rick and Harriet: am not surprised. I did wonder, but didn't like to say in case I was wrong and caused you unnecessary concern. Whatever you say won't make any difference so if you can try to accept, it will be less painful in the long run. I don't mean to trivialise. I would feel the same if it were Holly. We think we know what's best for our children and if we were to choose their partner, we would choose safe and dependable over the riskier options. But risky options carry the excitement that is often needed to fuel love. That's why it's called a crazy thing; an illness.
Have had discussions with Holly about my visiting you. She is similarly anxious. So no time of life is easy when it comes to matters of the heart. Sometimes we have to take a risk. That is probably what Harriet is thinking.
love,
Mari

To: Marianne Hayward
From: Edward Harvey
Date: 19th June 2012, 18.23
Subject: Re: News

Dear Mari,
Thank you for wise words and caution against rash
response. Harriet has been keeping out of my way but I
will try to be more understanding.
Seems like your conversation with Holly might have
been similar to one I had with Rachel. Find odd that kids
are turning tables when it comes to 'advice'!
I hope your heart is sending same messages as mine!
love,
Edward

To: Edward Harvey
From: Marianne Hayward
Date: 23rd June 2012, 20.11
Subject: 50 Shades

Dear Edward,
I was book signing today in Wimbledon and there was a
pyramid of 50 Shades in the bookshop entrance. Many
customers never bothered to venture any further into
the store so I had few opportunities to tell anyone
about Lydia. The hype for 50 Shades is something else.
One woman said she liked the sound of my book, but
she was buying a present for a friend who wanted to
see what all the fuss was about with 50 Shades so she
felt obliged to buy her that. It is flying out of the shops
in ways once unimagined for the erotic genre. Sex sells. I
suppose I am jealous. Need to look for something

hypeworthy in my own writing!
Gosh! I mentioned the S word. The received wisdom is to be wary of such in cyberspace when dealing with a gentleman!! I would like to discuss it with you – the book, I mean – from a purely intellectual and literary standpoint of course …
love,
Marianne

Marianne wonders how Edward will respond to this. She is presenting him with an opportunity; dropping hints that it is safe to mention previously forbidden topics. If they are going to have a relationship, some barriers need to be broken down.

A further email from him sends her to Twitter where he has replied via direct message.

@marihay1 Perhaps I am a ★shade★ disappointed that you only wish to discuss this at a higher level! #50shades

Ah, he has taken the bait, albeit via the concise medium. Perhaps brevity was his intention and the 140 character limit gave him an excuse not to elaborate.

@Edward_Harvey1 LOL! I didn't have you down as a swinging from the light-fittings type!
@marihay1 I am a man of a certain age.
@Edward_Harvey1 Am shocked!
@marihay1 Am joking!
@Edward_Harvey1 Some say it's peeps of certain age due to flagging libidos indulge in sado-masochism as necessary prerequisite to arousal.
@marihay1 Not everyone of certain age needs 'prerequisite'!
@Edward_Harvey1 Sounds promising!

@marihay1 Perhaps that only true if love is lost.
@Edward_Harvey1 Now you are mentioning the L word!
@marihay1 I mention it to you without fear.
@Edward_Harvey1 Without fear of what?
@marihay1 Without fear that it will cause you difficulty or offence.

Marianne is unsure how best to respond to this and decides to sign out before she spoils this otherwise progressive exchange.

32

Harriet

When the direct messages stop, Edward wonders if he has overstepped that invisible boundary where propriety lies on one side and unseemliness on the other. It is hard to know with a woman in whose company he has spent so little time discussing anything that edges towards a lack of decorum. Privately he hopes that they might have such a discussion face to face and that it might lead to an exposure of their feelings, a laying of cards on the table in a way they haven't before. Whenever he tries since that fateful night of the party, she shuffles them into a pack and hands them back to him. Perhaps it is still too soon in her grieving process.

Harriet seems always to be going out when Edward tries to speak to her, and his exchanges with Rick have reverted to nods and grunts, Harriet no doubt having told him that the cat has escaped. It isn't until early Sunday morning that he corners her in the kitchen while she is eating cereal.

He remembers Marianne's words and opts for the softly-softly approach. 'I want to know how it happened. Why it happened.'

Harriet's look is defiant. 'I'm very serious about Rick. He is serious about me. Nothing you say will change that.'

'I'd like to try to understand.'

Harriet appears surprised by his tone. 'Do you fancy a walk? I don't want you staring at me. Give me a second to finish this.'

They take Meg with them, out into another changeable

morning with clouds scudding across grey-blue skies and inclement temperatures for the end of June. Because the fields are so wet, they keep to the road and head away frim the village in the direction of the New Inn.

Harriet takes a deep breath. 'When Mum left, you were upset. I didn't want to bother you with my emotions. You know what I'm like. I prefer not to show stuff – a bit like you. It was one Saturday morning when you were away giving a lecture. Rick was in the garden and I made him a cup of tea, like Mum used to do. He saw how upset I was and he gave me a hug. Just a friendly, comforting hug—'

'Opportunist,' says Edward, flicking the end of Meg's lead against his free hand.

'Dad! Wait till I've finished, please. I realised I wanted him to keep on hugging me. Rachel and I used to fancy him, but he was always chasing some glamorous woman. I couldn't imagine him wanting me. I told him how everything had gone wrong, how all my relationships ended in disaster and now Mum had gone and I would have to look after you. I said that I thought I'd be here forever, the typical old-fashioned spinster-teacher looking after an ageing parent while all the rest of the family are having their fun and then having kids.'

'Harriet, I've never expected you to look after me.'

'But you're so lost and useless on your own.'

'Thanks!'

'And I care what happens to you. You work so hard; your minds always off in the theoretical clouds. You're not good at making time for shopping and all the domestic stuff.'

Edward is now on an emotional brink himself. He knows all his children care about him, but Harriet is the one who shows it least, is less demonstrative, except for that one time when he came out of hospital after being attacked.

She continues, 'Rick said to me "But you're a beautiful girl;

245

a beautiful young woman. You have spirit and passion and you'll find someone to love you".'

Edward's throat tightens at her words – at Rick's words.

'I told him all the guys I go out with end up being losers and he said "If I were ten years younger", and I said, "What?" I made him tell me. And he said how much he admired me; how I made him laugh with my craziness; how much he enjoyed our conversations – about plants and stuff – when me and Rach used to help him in the greenhouse. I thought it was her he liked. Everyone likes Rach. But no, it was me. And I asked him to kiss me properly. He wouldn't. He said you'd go spare.'

'Too right,' says Edward. 'Spare is an understatement.'

'He said he didn't want to let you down after all you'd been through and all you and Mum had done for him. He said I was in an emotional state and I'd feel differently in a day or two; he didn't want to take advantage.'

'Some integrity at least,' says Edward, mellowing slightly.

'And that's how we left it, but I couldn't stop thinking about him; about what he said; about him thinking I was beautiful. And I went to his house one night instead of going to Italian. I half-expected him to be with another woman, but he let me in. I asked him again to kiss me, and this time he did. But that was all. That was all for weeks.'

'You kept going back?'

'Mostly we just talked. About his childhood and stuff. His dad died when he was fourteen and he became a bit of a rebel; had lots of rows with his mum; didn't bother with school. He went out with lots of girls. He said he never found the right one – until I grew up and came back from uni and he began to wonder. But he told himself not to go there and he didn't.'

'He encouraged you to keep going to his house.'

'I suppose I was lonely. You were too busy, Rachel was

away. My best friends from school had found jobs in other parts of the country. And we weren't doing anything much except talking. Rick thought I was going through a phase and he wanted to be sure I was serious; that we both felt the same.'

'And you're serious now?'

'Dad, he makes me so happy. The only problem is, because we're being secretive, we can't go anywhere or do normal things. But he wants us to be together and I want to be with him.'

Edward rubs his hand across his eyes and taps his forehead as if willing his brain to select the right words. 'Doing normal things may take the shine off the relationship. Secrecy brings its own excitement.'

'If that is the case, I would like the opportunity to find out.'

'That's when you'll discover he doesn't want to do the things that twenty-somethings do; when people think he's your father when they see you together.'

'Dad! I already don't do what most twenty-somethings do. Half the time I'm too tired after school. I did all the clubbing and stuff when I was a teenager and at college. That's how I know that Rick is what I want. I'm not naive.'

This is true. Harriet pushed boundaries and led what some of his friends called a 'wild life' while she was still at school. 'You may end up looking after an old man.'

'Which is not so different from if I stayed here and looked after you.'

And agan Edward sees the approach of his advancing years and the window between then and now shrinking like a puddle in the sun. 'I don't want you to stay to look after me. I want you to find someone nearer your own age with prospects.'

'I would rather have twenty years of happiness with someone I love who loves me, than forty or fifty years of mediocrity. And none of us knows what's round the corner. I may get sick first. And what about you and Marianne? If you were together now, how long before something happens to one of you? Does that mean you don't bother to snatch some time while you can? That's what I want you to do. Not because of me, but for you.'

'I'm trying, Harriet. Believe me, I'm trying. But Marianne has to be ready to move on.'

'You haven't told her exactly how you feel.'

'Because I don't want to scare her off.'

'There's probably a higher chance of Rick and me staying together than if I was with someone else; someone younger. Look at you and Mum. No one would have predicted you'd split up.'

Edward drops his shoulders, defeated. Harriet has presented a rational argument and perhaps his prejudices and pre-conceived ideas need to be addressed.

They have reached the New Inn, shining white through the damp air.

'I'm going back home now,' says Harriet. 'I have some school work to do.'

'I may be a while,' says Edward. 'I'll pick up a couple of croissants at the shop.'

He continues with Meg for a long walk, following the lane past Burrow Farm and then back towards the village, all the time thinking about how to deal with Rick. They have had a much better relationship since Felicity left. It is a pity to spoil it with a confrontation. Marianne is probably right. Again he wonders whether to call Felicity but that will surely drive a wedge between him and Harriet and serve no useful purpose.

He continues up Town Hill, across the main road and up through the churchyard to the field that goes down to Clyston Mill. There, he lets Meg off the lead and throws her a stick. She bounds after it, tail held high.

'Daft dog,' he says when she retrieves it, drops it at his feet, and as if her paws are on springs, she bounces in front of him, pleading with him to throw it again.

After a few more minutes of stick chasing, they return home via the post office, acquiring croissants and a paper.

Later, he phones Marianne to ask if she's had any more weird calls.

'One,' she says. 'A silent one and I blocked the sender.'

Then he updates her with what Harriet told him about Rick. 'It does sound very serious,' he says.

Marianne puts on her typically dispassionate psychologist's voice and tells him that he should release his negative thoughts; Harriet and Rick will pursue their relationship no matter what he says or does and it is therefore less stressful to be supportive. 'You can tell them you don't approve if you must, but even that will sour relations. People must be allowed to make their own choices – as I have been pointing out to Holly.'

'Re us?'

'Re us.'

'Have you thought any more about "us"?' asks Edward, at last venturing to raise the other difficult topic.

'Perhaps we might meet again after the end of term.'

It is a line that has an echo of familiarity, though he can't remember from when or where.

'That would be lovely,' he says. 'Will you come here?'

'I have a few reservations in case I bump into Jessica.'

'I'm sure we can keep out of her way.'

'Then perhaps I will.'

A new rush of hope.

At night in bed, he mulls over Harriet's words: *'You're so useless on your own'*. If all goes well, there may be an alternative.

33

Perhaps

There is much mileage in a 'perhaps'. It betrays uncertainty yet creates possibility. It may be added to a proposal to avoid over-eagerness; or as a flirty addition, a tease, a request for more input before the prize. It is a breath of hope wrapped in a cloak of mystery: sexy eyes over the rim of a wine glass, a fleeting glance over the shoulder, a glimpse of lace at the neckline. Perhaps is maybe; or maybe not. It tantalises and seduces and plays a waiting game.

Marianne expects Edward to respond to the suggestion of meeting with some specific dates and is surprised when he doesn't respond at all. She deduces that he is distracted by the Harriet and Rick business.

It is therefore with utter amazement that she opens the door to a knock soon after she arrives home from work the following Wednesday and finds Edward standing there in a khaki anorak looking a little damp and dishevelled from yet another shower. He carries a briefcase in one hand and a large bunch of yellow and pink tulips in the other.

'A sudden meeting with Flying Owl,' he says. 'Arranged late last night. I wasn't sure how much time it would take so I couldn't make any plans to come here. And I have to be at work early tomorrow. But I have an hour or so to spare before I need to catch a train home and I'd love a cup of tea.'

'What if I'd been out?'

'You would have come home to find a mysterious bunch of flowers on your doorstep. I took a chance. I wanted to surprise you.'

The flowers are a barrier to her giving him the biggest hug.

He offers them to her and she thanks him and takes them through to the kitchen, babbling her delight and surprise, placing them in water in the sink.

He follows her and removes his anorak. His hair is also slightly wet. 'This weather,' he says. 'Will we have a summer?' And then he wraps her in a tight embrace and she kisses his cheek.

He feels cold against her lips. 'I miss you,' she says. 'Will you stay for something to eat?'

'I'd love to but I haven't time. I need to be back at a reasonable hour.'

She makes mugs of tea and they go through to the living room, where she sits in Johnny's armchair and he relaxes into the sofa.

'Any more phone calls?' he asks.

'Not since I put a block on the second number.'

'Jessica's not been round with food since Harriet had a go at her. Indeed, I haven't seen her anywhere for a few days.'

They talk trivia and family issues, an invisible charge seeming to fly in both directions across the narrow chasm that separates them. Edward elaborates his concerns about Harriet and Rick, and tells her of Rachel's worries about him.

'She thinks I might be having a midlife crisis and says she's worried about her inheritance. But I think it's more to do with jealousy; another woman competing for my affections.'

'What woman might that be?' says Marianne. She is still in flirtatious mood.

He doesn't reply but gives her a knowing look.

Marianne says, 'Do you think you *are* having a midlife crisis?'

'If so, I've been having one for about eight years. If anything, I'm coming out of it; seeing a way to the future.'

Marianne wonders if this is an opening for one of Taryn's exploration rules. 'And where do you see yourself, say, in the next five years?' She says this unthreateningly, as if genuinely curious to know the answer.

He hesitates. 'In all seriousness, that might depend on you.'

There is a pause. There have been many such pauses in their dealings over the years. Pauses filled with the sound of alternatives that have the power to change lives one way or another.

'Holly has concerns,' she says. 'More to do with the idea of anyone replacing her dad. But she trusts you.'

'And you, Mari? What about you?'

'Felicity and Johnny were very different from either of us. With them we have each made a happy life for many years. I know we get on well; I know there is attraction. But is that enough? Are we too set in our ways to accommodate someone new? We need time together to understand our different ways. Not a weekend or a snatched moment like this. Proper time and a leap of faith. It will be easier when I have finished work.'

They are disturbed by a knock on the door.

'I think I know who this might be,' says Marianne, 'it being teatime.' She grimaces, more concerned for his feelings than her own.

Edward hears words being exchanged on the doorstep but before he has had time to think, Taryn breezes into the room in her teacher's gear: a plain black knee-length skirt and red fitted top with a fashionable draped neckline.

'The unpredictable life,' she says.

Edward stands to greet her and is surprised when she holds out her hand to be shaken. She doesn't even kiss him on the cheek, but keeps him at arm's length. He assumes this is to tell him loud and clear that he doesn't need to worry about her any more. She looks older; but then she would. And she is much less glossy magazine than before; more Sunday supplement. If anything, he prefers this more natural look.

Marianne offers tea but Taryn says water or juice will be fine. 'I won't stay more than five minutes. Strict instructions. I understand you're on a tight schedule,' she says to Edward.

Marianne disappears to the kitchen.

'Who would have thought we would meet again like this?' Taryn sits on the chair furthest away from Edward. 'I hope your intentions are honourable.'

He sits down again and gives an arch smile. 'You know they are.'

'And how would I know that, pray?'

'You know, Taryn, because you told me my thoughts before I even recognised them myself. Remember? Of course, if my home life had continued on a more secure footing, they would have remained under wraps.'

'I wouldn't want to see her suffer any more.'

Edward wonders if this is the same woman who single-handedly wrecked both their friendships with Marianne almost a decade earlier. 'And neither would I. She's the one pulling the strings. She seems to be able to look after herself. I wait patiently. Indeed, I wondered if you might have had some input.'

'And what makes you say that?'

'A few of her reactions have been unexpected. And don't forget, I know her quite well.'

'But this is a new situation. She is still grieving for Johnny and she struggles with loyalty and guilt. Can't imagine what it must be like to have been with one person for thirty years and then start again with someone new.'

'Indeed,' says Edward.

'But she's much livelier since you came back onto the

scene. I have both your interests at heart. I think it would work. Does that allay your suspicions?'

'Having a master schemer on my side can only be viewed as an advantage.' He gives her a lingering stare.

'In that case, may I advise you to wait actively?'

'I just did,' he says. 'My coming here today was a spur of the moment decision.'

'Promising,' says Taryn. 'But you will have to do more than that if you want to convince her that you're not in it for the short term.'

'Surely we cannot know exactly what we're in it for until we try?'

'Playing safe versus risk,' says Taryn. 'It's a question of probabilities of a successful outcome. What are the odds? Two to one, or ten to one? Are you a gambling man, Edward? I think not. The price is higher the older you get. The cost of failure may be huge – especially if you give up a secure life to start afresh somewhere new.'

'What odds would you give me and Marianne?'

'Favourable, on balance. But staking your future on another human being will always be a game of chance.'

Edward thinks this is something to mull over when he is on his own. 'Are *you* happy, Taryn?'

'I'm tickety-boo. Thanks to you I found a new way of being. My life is changed beyond recognition. As an educationalist, I know that much can be achieved with the right teacher, the right guidance. All people in our lives are teachers, but when it came to men, I had the wrong sort. From you I learnt that something else was possible; not so different from my evoking a love of Shakespeare in a twelve year old who has watched nothing but TV trash.' She pauses and then stares him in the eye. 'I would like to think you learned something from me too.'

'A dramatic analogy in more than one sense.' Edward privately acknowledges that he discovered much from her about the potential for midlife passion, but he decides not to comment.

'It is likely that our paths will cross again,' continues Taryn. 'I wouldn't wish you to be uncomfortable in my presence. I remember the night we shared. Do you?'

Edward raises an eyebrow, but doesn't answer.

'I will assume you do,' says Taryn. 'And soon after, I became the epitome of a modern housewife.'

'But you don't live with your partner.'

Marianne returns with Taryn's juice and another pot of tea for herself and Edward. She brings malt loaf, cake and biscuits too.

Taryn says, 'Neil has moved to a nearby street. We are less than five minutes' walk away from each other. We have space when we need it and company is a phone call away. We may combine resources when we retire. More people would do this if finances permitted and if it were more socially accepted. New roles for women require new attitudes to partnership that extend beyond couples cohabiting. There are many options available in later life, but few embrace the unusual for fear of ridicule. Why is it okay for a group of twenty-somethings to share a house, but not sixty-somethings? House-sharing for single and widowed men and women seems like an ideal antidote to loneliness. You could say this is behind the principle of sheltered accommodation, but it would be a completely different and much more positive experience to join forces with existing friends.'

'Another solution to the housing shortage,' says Edward.

Taryn is as good as her word and leaves after she has drunk her juice, nibbled a biscuit and told Edward and Marianne she will await developments with interest.

The room is so much emptier and quieter after she has gone.

'An interesting woman,' says Edward. 'I'm glad you two have patched things up.'

'She has changed. It took a while, but I trust her now.'

'So,' says Edward. 'Here we are alone again. So much I would like to say, but so little time.' He remembers what Taryn said about waiting actively and decides to be bold. 'I think about our night after the party. I think about you constantly.'

'And I you.' Her pupils have dilated and her breathing has quickened.

'You were saying something about a leap of faith. Might that be when we can spend a block of time together?' he asks. 'Perhaps on Scilly, if not before?'

'Perhaps.'

34

Meg

After his impromptu visit to London, Edward is optimistic about Marianne and clearer in his thinking about his problems with Rachel and Harriet. He has decided to say nothing to Rick and to proceed with the productivity side of the garden as normally as possible.

The preparations for the documentary and filming are occupying much of his spare time but all seems relatively calm, until he comes home from the university on Friday and is surprised not to be greeted at the door by Meg. He drops his case and calls for her, but there is no sound of trotting paws from any part of the house. This is most unusual. She always heads for the door as soon as she hears the car. Harriet is not yet home so she can't have taken her anywhere.

He turns cold. His mind spins with unpalatable thoughts as he rushes from room to room downstairs, calling, wondering, thinking the worst. She is not in any of her usual favoured places. He climbs the stairs two at a time and in his room on his bed she is lying motionless, her tongue lolling from her mouth, bluish tinged, a deathly shade. A trickle of blood escapes from her nose onto the duvet.

Time slows and does that weird thing when a multitude of thoughts that would take minutes to write or read, all clamour for attention simultaneously.

He strokes her. She is warm and he realises she is still breathing, a faint rattling sound. Her belly is swollen. He grabs the phone by the bed and the pop-up directory of emergency numbers which Felicity always kept close at hand in case there was an animal problem at night. He wonders if Meg has had a fit.

Thankfully the nearest vet's practice is holding an evening surgery. He speaks to one of the vets and she asks a few questions about symptoms. Then she asks if Meg had access to any toxic substances.

'So you think it might be poison?' asks Edward.

The vet tells him to bring her in as quickly as possible.

He carries her downstairs, her weight awkward in his arms. He speaks soothing words to her, while inside he is frantic. He has to put her down on the sofa to open the back door and then the car door, then return to collect her and slide her gently onto the back seat. He covers her with the tartan rug that he keeps in the boot. Every second is crucial; he knows he must make haste. Apart from her breathing, she makes no sound, she does not move; he feels the hope draining away that she can be saved.

He returns to lock the house, then leaps into the car and with wheels spinning on the gravel, he heads in the direction of the vet's. He remembers the speed cameras on the road but travels as fast as safety will allow.

He calls Harriet on his hands-free speakerphone. She is shocked and says she will come home as soon as she can. Meg had seemed fine when they both left in the morning. 'Could be the witch's revenge for the cake incident,' she adds.

'Steady on, Harriet, you can't make accusations like that. This is serious.'

'Exactly. And she's bonkers. You saw her go for me.'

Edward processes this possibility. It is an uncomfortable thought but true that Jessica's pursuit of him was veering on the obsessional. 'Don't for God's sake mention this to anyone else yet. We can't make such inflammatory accusations without a shred of evidence.'

'Her husband was in pest control,' says Harriet.

A shiver runs down Edward's spine. 'I'd forgotten about that. But we still can't be sure it's poison.'

Another chilling thought.

'Harriet!' His tone is urgent now, his mind on full alert. 'Don't leave school. If you're right, you may be a target too. Stay put until you hear from me. Promise me. I'm calling Rick. He'll come for you.'

His heart begins to pound as memories of his own encounter with danger explode into his consciousness like the bubbles of a geyser. He remembers the darkness, the flash of the blade, the pain, the fear. Perhaps he is over-reacting but now Harriet has put the thought in his head, it would be foolish to ignore it.

Rick says Meg was fine at lunchtime when he let her out. He knows what Harriet thinks about Jessica and echoes Edward's concern.

'I'll go fetch her, don't worry.'

The two-mile journey to the vet's seems to take an age. He fears Meg will have died by the time he arrives.

At the surgery, Edward is ushered immediately into a consulting room where he gently places Meg on the table. She is still breathing, just; long pauses between breaths. He feels a silky black ear, willing her to get better.

The vet with whom he had spoken on the phone is a woman called Natalie Bell. She starts checking Meg over, asking Edward more questions about any events leading up to her collapse.

'It does look as if she could have been poisoned. Obviously it would help us if we knew with what. The bleeding is indicative of a rat poison. We'll treat her with that in mind; there's no time to waste.' She turns to a nurse and asks for various things to be prepared, all the while examining Meg: her eyes, her mouth, her heartbeat, her temperature. She glances up at Edward. 'Check your house to see if there are any signs that she could have accessed any chemicals so we can rule them out. Call if you find anything. We'll do what we can, but be prepared.'

Edward knows what this means. *'Be prepared'* is what the vet said when Felicity lost a sheep, and when the first of the spaniels died. 'I know you'll do your best,' he says. 'I'll call when I've checked the house.'

Edward drives back home in a state of high anxiety. Poisoned? They were always so careful in shutting away anything that could cause harm to children or animals. And they have never used rat poison. He wonders about Rick and the garden, but as everything is organic, there is no use of chemical fertilisers or pesticides. Could Jessica be the only logical explanation, no matter how far-fetched?

He tries to get hold of Rick again on his mobile but is diverted to his answerphone. He leaves a message to call him as soon as possible.

Back at the house he goes through each room, checking cupboards are closed and that everything is where he expects it to be. Then he searches the outbuildings and finds nothing sinister. He calls the vet and is informed that Meg is very poorly, but hanging on. They have taken blood samples, but it will be a while before the toxicology report comes back. They are giving her a blood transfusion and vitamin K to aid clotting. They tell him to call again in the morning and they will ring him if there is any change for the worse.

He puts down the phone and is lost as to what to do. Normally, he would be off for a walk with Meg but to go on his own seems pointless. And to work would be impossible. He calls Marianne at home but receives no reply. He opens the fridge, looking for clues as to what Harriet planned to cook for supper. He finds a chicken and starts to peel some potatoes.

Soon Harriet returns with Rick. When she hears the details, she is visibly upset. After she has recovered from the shock and sat down with a coffee, she says, 'Why don't I go and ask Jessica straight?'

'You are going nowhere without me until this is sorted,' says Rick, hovering and looking uncomfortable and out of place in the kitchen.

Edward says, 'Because she'd deny it and if it has nothing to do with her, it is a terrible thing to suggest. I'll have a quiet word with Olivia.' He goes to pick up the landline.

'Hello, darling Ted. What can I do for you?'

'Olivia, have you seen Jessica lately?'

'Come to think of it, not for a week or so.'

'It is difficult for me to say this, but she's been paying me rather too much attention since we had that meal at the Retreat.'

'Aren't you the lucky one?'

'This is serious, Olivia. It's as if she's stalking me.'

Olivia laughs. 'Oh Ted, don't be silly.'

'I know you were matchmaking, but it would never have worked. I believe she was quite rude to Marianne at the party.' He didn't add that he thought Olivia had been rude too. 'Hear me out before you say anything else.' He tells her about the repeated references to a relationship in waiting; about the continued attempts to give him food, even when he asked her not to; about her coming to the university and about the cake incident. Then he tells her about Meg.

'This is Broadclyst, Ted. Not *Midsomer*. Couldn't the dog have picked up something when you were out walking?'

'She could, but I have no recollection of anything like that. She's not the type to pick things up or eat odd bits and pieces when we're out. Not like the spaniels.'

'Okay, Ted. I'll go and see her and have a diplomatic word to put your mind at rest.'

Edward wonders if diplomacy and Olivia belong together, but in the absence of a better plan, he thanks her. 'Can you do it now, Olivia? If she did do something, it's urgent we know what.'

Rick says he will do some work on the garden while waiting for news and Harriet says she will carry on preparing supper.

'Can I invite Rick to stay to eat, please?'

Edward agrees but with mixed feelings. He is still uncomfortable at the thought of Rick doing what he is no doubt doing with his daughter.

An hour later, Olivia appears up the drive in her little hatchback. Edward invites her into the kitchen, but Olivia says she would rather speak with Edward alone so he leads her through to the living room.

'I rang Jessica and she was a bit odd on the phone,' says Olivia, sitting on one of the sofas. 'So I've been to see her. The house was in quite a mess – not like her – and she was behaving very strangely. When she was speaking to me, it was as if she was talking to someone else standing next to me.'

Edward recalls Marianne telling him something similar when Jessica phoned her. *As if she was talking to someone else …*

Olivia says, 'She didn't look me in the eye and was very nervy and anxious. I haven't seen her like that since after her husband died when, understandably, she was in a state. I casually mentioned Meg was at the vet's and that you were very upset. Her response was unexpected. Last time I saw her you were a saint and now she said, "Well, he had it coming". I asked her what? She said, "Nothing". Then she said, "He's just like all the others". I asked her whether she had harmed Meg and she said something like, "Every man is a bastard". She really seemed unhinged. Then she sat down and we had a cup of tea and she started telling me about her violent husband. Anyway, in the course of this she said something that made me very uneasy. I can't remember her exact words, but the implication was that her husband had it coming too and she wasn't one to miss an opportunity. I said, "You don't mean you pushed him down the stairs?" And she said, "He was so drunk, it only needed the slightest touch to knock him off balance". Then she seemed to snap into the present and she laughed in a weird way and said, "Not that I did, but I could have". She added that I shouldn't take any notice, she was a little stressed and what was I saying about Edward's poor dog. I asked her again whether she had harmed Meg but she had regained control of herself and said it was ridiculous to think she would do such a thing.'

'I don't like the sound of this,' says Edward.

'I went home, called the police, told them what she said and that she seemed quite unwell. They said they would investigate my concerns. I expect they will go and talk to her. I mentioned about Meg and I think they thought I'd been watching too many crime dramas. They said they would let me know if there's anything to report.'

'I had better call them too,' says Edward.

'Yes, that will help. And I think you should be extra vigilant – just in case. Doors locked, watch your back. And tell Harriet to be careful. If she did do something to Meg, she's trying to hurt you indirectly via the things you care about.' Olivia pauses and looks at him intently. 'I can't believe I'm saying this. It's madness.'

'I was thinking the same, Olivia,' says Edward.

'I hope it's nothing but I promised Flick I'd look out for you. I think I might have been wrong about Jessica. I'm sorry.'

Edward is surprised that Felicity should have had any thoughts about his welfare when she was so wrapped up with Gianni and her departure to Siena.

As Olivia leaves, Edward promises to keep her informed of

any developments and joins Harriet in the kitchen. Rick has reappeared and is sitting by the table.

'Are you sure about this?' he says awkwardly.

'I'm sure,' says Edward. 'You've helped us; I'm grateful.'

'I'll take you to and from work,' says Rick to Harriet. 'I'll give your car the once over before you drive it again. As it's at school, I can do it when I take you in tomorrow.' He looks at Edward. 'Check your windows and smoke alarms. Garage your car when not in use. Keep the gates closed.'

'Are we over-dramatising?' says Edward.

'Better to be safe,' says Rick. 'Perhaps I might stay here overnight? I could sleep in Felicity's outside office like she did for a while. Keep an eye on things.'

Edward at first considers that this is a threat to his ability to protect his family, but safety is more important than pride and he gratefully consents.

'Stay in Chris's room,' says Edward. 'I'd rather you were in the house than outside if she does try something.'

'Why don't I stay in Chris's room,' suggests Harriet, 'and Rick in my room. If she *is* after me, she will get an unwelcome surprise.'

Edward agrees, then calls the police and tells them everything he thinks might be relevant, including Marianne's nuisance phone calls.

'We're making enquiries,' was all they would say.

By late evening there has been no word from the vet, so he hopes no news is good news. He doesn't like to think of Meg being in a cage at the surgery but knows there is no other option.

He is about to go to bed when he receives a call from Olivia.

'Jessica has disappeared,' she says.

35

Doubts

Marianne is asleep when she receives the late night call from Edward. Straight away she picks up on his anxiety as he delivers the bad news about Meg. She knows he will be devastated if anything happens to the dog and as for Jessica being the culprit, she would not be surprised. She worries for his safety, unable to bear the thought of him suffering. She knows since he was mugged, he has concerns about being attacked or hurt. He alluded to occasional nightmares. Still worse are fears that she might lose him. On top of her other losses, it would be too much.

Edward says, 'I'm calling so late because Olivia has just phoned to say Jessica has gone AWOL. I don't want to alarm you, but if she did take your address from Gemma's office … Could you possibly go to stay with Taryn? For a day or two till we know what's what? It's probably nothing. But just in case. I'd be happier. If you go to Taryn's she'd never find you.'

'I can't do anything tonight. It's too late. I'm sure I'll be okay.'

'I'd come up but I need to be here for Harriet and Meg.'

'Don't even think of it – I wouldn't want you to. I promise I'll contact Taryn tomorrow.'

After Edward's call she realises she is more concerned than she was admitting and she re-checks all her windows and doors. She spends a restless night with many awakenings, each sound causing her to listen intently for anything suspicious.

In the morning she is exhausted. She knows exactly how

Taryn will feel at the suggestion of sharing her space, even for a short time. But she calls her all the same.

'A surreal occurrence is underway,' says Marianne. She elaborates.

'A stalker – imagine that! How bizarre,' says Taryn. 'If this were *Morse*, the police would suggest using Edward as a lure – with cops strategically placed around his house to catch Jessica in the act. And if it were *Morse*, the cops would be at the front, while Jessica makes an entrance through a poorly secured back window. It would be night time with Edward in bed, sleeping soundly while Jessica ascends the stairs with a kitchen knife.'

'Stop it, Taryn. You're scaring me. Edward has already had one altercation with a knife.'

'Sorry, I forgot. How thoughtless of me. I'm a little manic today. I'm sure Edward will be fine and the dog too. Try not to worry and of course you can stay. It won't be for long, will it? Pop over with your bag after work. Perhaps Neil would come over and be bodyguard. He'd like that. He's got aspirations to save the world. I call it his Batman complex.'

When she hangs up, Marianne envisages Taryn jolted from her usual morning work preparations into hurtling around her flat on a cleaning mission. She doesn't like anything out of place when she has visitors.

Surely Jessica wouldn't come after her? She double checks her house security again before she leaves for college.

All day between lessons, she struggles to concentrate. As if life isn't difficult enough at the moment. She has only three weeks left before the holidays, during which she must sort through a massive accumulation of papers and files. She doesn't officially retire until the end of August and can see she will be spending the first part of the summer holiday in her office with a few bin liners.

★

'Tell me how things are going relationship-wise,' says Taryn, after a supper of seafood in a tomato sauce with home-made pasta. 'When I saw you last week, Edward seemed to be doing all the right things. An unexpected visit. Flowers.'

'Not much to tell,' says Marianne. 'I've been too busy with work. He says he doesn't want to pressure me. That's giving me a chance to work through my feelings; whether I want to take a chance with anyone, never mind him. I was thinking of going to see him after the end of term, but I've so much clearing up to do at college. And even if I do go, Harriet will be around. I believe Scilly will be the watershed if anything significant is going to happen.'

They are sitting at the glass dining table in Taryn's living room. Marianne arrived earlier, with a small case on wheels and many apologies for inconvenience caused.

Taryn says, 'Now that I've met him again and had a chance to talk to him, I've reviewed my advice. You need to be much flirtier. It's no good waiting for Scilly. If this is what you want you have to make your intentions clear.'

'I don't know what I want. I vacillate each day. There are vibes when I speak to him on the phone. I know he's interested, I know he cares. But I don't know how much, and I'm not convinced that his feelings for me are strong enough to compensate for me not being like Superwoman Felicity; in other words strong enough for him to want more than a kind of "friendship with benefits" with me, or even a fling.'

'Irrelevant,' says Taryn. 'Felicity, that is. She is history. And I don't know where you get this idea that it will be a fling. I believe he is deeply in love with you but perhaps a little apprehensive.'

In love … Marianne savours the thought for a few seconds. Is he? Is she? It was easy to fantasise when nothing was likely

267

to happen; easy to see him as being relationship material. She says, 'We both had happy marriages. I'm doubtful that either of us could live up to what we had before.'

'It won't be the same because you are older now. People's needs change. It could be that no one would live up to what either of you had before. That doesn't mean you shouldn't give it a chance.'

'But being alone has its advantages. I sleep much better. I can make X-shapes in bed without disturbing anyone.'

'There's no reason why you can't have separate bedrooms for when you need to sleep well. If Neil and I ever live together I will insist on it. It's a growing trend. Get together at the start of the night and then escape.'

'It's not only that. It's liberating being able to please myself. I don't have to worry about meals and being a domestic goddess.'

'Ah, so it's you who has the doubts.'

'Perhaps it is,' says Marianne. 'The more Edward talks of a future, the more I am unsure. Our differences might not be tolerable. We are both too old to remould ingrained habits to fit those of another.'

'Never too old,' says Taryn, 'if the rewards are worth it. Look at me. But this is exactly why Neil remains at another address for the time being. However, with Edward being in Broadclyst, you can't start worrying about living arrangements until the relationship has been moved forward.'

'We both know Edward was firmly set against compromise when Felicity started her eco-farm and restaurant.'

'You are the goal this time, and your life will change with retirement. He may retire from his current job too. You might find a different way together. Also Edward probably realises his mistakes. He may be more willing and able to compromise now.'

'We have a difference of opinion regarding division of labour on the domestic front,' says Marianne. 'This might be an obstacle that would eventually lead to discord. Johnny was very liberated; happy to cook and share in the domestic duties. Edward might be persuaded to iron his own work shirts, but I doubt this would extend to my dresses – particularly the frilly ones. And you know how much I hate ironing.'

'Give me a man who irons frilly dresses and I will be in domestic heaven,' says Taryn. 'As I said, the time to worry about this is when you start talking about living together, not before you've even had a shag. If he lives up to your expectations, you might be prepared to compromise on the ironing.'

Taryn clears the plates and disappears into the kitchen, returning with strawberries and ice cream in two glass bowls.

'You may have noticed I've put *Fifty Shades of Grey* on your bedside table. It's been doing the rounds at school. Regardless of its literary merit, it's causing a stir; legitimising eroticism. I think it may help to focus your mind on physical pleasures. Not that I'm suggesting anything quite so extreme. I don't think Edward would be too keen on extreme.'

'For which I'm thankful,' says Marianne.

'If you get on in the bedroom, the rest of your life will fall into place,' says Taryn.

'That wasn't the case with you and Marc.'

'Marc didn't love me. It was sex, not a relationship with emotional investment. I'll rephrase. In a love relationship, bedroom compatibility helps to smooth out other differences.'

'Edward is Leo and I am Capricorn. Our suns are squared. We view the world through different eyes. I prevaricate to the point of immobilisation while he generally grasps his opportunities.'

'In that case, you will balance each other perfectly,' says

Taryn. 'There are some areas where opposites are preferable.'

'We do have compatible moons and Mercurys,' adds Marianne. 'Emotional and intellectual understanding and harmony – which can't be bad. But I'm scared; simply scared. It requires such a leap into the unknown.'

'And if he gave up on you and turned his attentions elsewhere?'

'I'd be devastated.'

'Then you have your answer.'

'But Holly isn't too keen.'

'So? Again, irrelevant. Eventually Holly will be distracted by her own love affairs; her own life.'

Every problem envisaged by Marianne is countered by Taryn with common-sense reasoning, yet still she hears the voice of Olivia and dare not believe that Edward would want her for the long term.

36

Turbulence

It has been two days since Meg was taken ill and Edward drops in at the vet's on the way back from work. He has visited each morning and evening, his emotions stirred by the helplessness of this once vibrant animal. She has kept him sane since Felicity left.

This evening he finds her with eyes open and the faintest movement of her tail as she tries to wag a welcome. She is attached to a drip. He sits on the floor by the cage and strokes her, talking calmly to her, willing her to get better. Natalie, the vet, says there is small improvement but with the probability of at least some organ damage, it is still too early to be optimistic of recovery.

He tells Meg about his day; about the walk he had that morning that seemed purposeless without her; about wishing she were home to act as guard dog while Jessica's whereabouts are unknown. Each time he says goodbye, he wonders if it might be for the last time and he gives her a pat, saying, 'Thank you, old girl, for watching over me, for being such a good friend.'

And this time the tail moves a little and the dark brown eyes look mournful. He is sure she understands, if not the words, then the depth of his feeling and his pain.

At the Deer Orchard, Rick is temporarily housed in Christopher's room and Edward is unnerved by the sexual chemistry that crackles like static whenever Harriet and he are in close proximity. He is surprised he never noticed it before.

Perhaps they hid it well, or it dissipated into the ether because they were mostly outdoors when they were together on the premises. Or perhaps, like his failure to notice Felicity and Gianni, he saw what he wanted to see. Nothing.

Harriet's car appeared fine when Rick checked it and when not in use it is now garaged along with the Volvo. Sometimes he thinks they are being over-cautious, but Rick is adamant that until they know for certain that Jessica is not responsible for Meg's illness, it is essential to assume the worst and to take care. It is reassuring that he is showing such responsibility – not a characteristic Edward had previously attached to the person some had spoken of as the Lothario of Broadclyst.

'We know she's nuts, and nutters are unpredictable,' said Rick.

Edward would have been more politically correct in his use of language, but he agrees with the sentiment.

In the middle of the night, Edward is in a deep sleep when he wakes with a start. It takes a while to process the possibility that there might have been an unusual noise. The security light is on outside and the clock registers 02:07. He grabs his dressing gown and opens the bedroom door, his heart audible, pulsing in his ears. Christopher's door is open. Perhaps it was Rick going to the bathroom, but the bathroom door is ajar and there is no sound from within. He creeps downstairs in the darkness, mindful of the creaking floorboards. Again he wishes Meg were at home. She would be sure to bark if anything were amiss.

In the kitchen he jumps when he sees a figure crouched by the window. The prickle of sweat begins to bead on his forehead.

'Oh, it's you,' he says to Rick, relieved.

'Hush, get down,' says Rick. He is bare-chested but has had the foresight to put on his jeans.

Edward squats below the kitchen cabinets. 'What is it?'

Rick points up to the window above the sink. Against the glow from the security light, Edward can see cracks radiating outwards from a smash in the double glazing. They exchange glances.

Harriet appears in pyjamas and slippers and Rick gestures urgently for her to get on the floor. 'Harriet, get hold of a phone and stay out of sight. Call the police and tell them you've had an attempted break-in. Right?'

Harriet begins to object.

'No argument,' whispers Rick. 'Do it. Now.'

Harriet creeps away and Edward listens. All he can hear is the low whirr from the freezer.

After several minutes, Rick says, 'The plods will take ages from Exeter. Where's your torch? I'm going out.'

Edward finds the torch behind the breadbin, used by Felicity for checking the animals at night or on a winter's morning. They stand on the back doorstep while Rick shines the beam in an arc beyond the range of the security light, across the gravel to the vegetable garden and beyond.

Nothing.

But below the kitchen window is a large, sharp rock.

'We best leave it,' says Rick. 'Fingerprints.'

'Do you think someone was trying to get in?'

'Probably scare tactics. Put all the lights on. If you check the rest of the inside, I'll have a mosey round the outside.' Rick takes his leather jacket from behind the back door.

Edward feels unsuitably dressed in his dressing gown but goes from room to room inspecting the windows.

When Rick returns, he says the gates have been left open, but there is nothing else as far as he can see. They sit at the kitchen table waiting for the police to arrive, avoiding eye contact.

After a while Rick says, 'I will take care of Harriet. You

don't need to worry. I've never loved a woman before. She's changed my life.'

This is the chance for Edward to object, to threaten, to give a piece or two of his mind, but for Rick to say this shows courage and his helping them out has been a great support. Instead, he turns and says, 'She's not the easiest of my children. But you know that and you make her happy.'

The police come and go as dawn is breaking, taking particulars and saying they will send a forensics team later in the morning. They are vague about the progress of enquiries regarding Jessica. Edward returns to bed, hoping to catch a couple of hours sleep but it eludes him. In the morning he is ashen-faced and lethargic. This is when he would go for a walk with the dog to clear his head. He looks at Meg's lead hanging forlornly on its hook and goes outside to check the hens, his head pounding.

He calls Gemma to say he will be late and to cancel his morning lecture. After breakfast, two SOCOs – a man and a woman – ferret around the outside of the house looking for evidence and fingerprints. They believe the sharp rock may have come from the rose garden where there are other similar pieces, and after detailed examination find traces of a small footprint in the flowerbed from which to make a cast.

When they have gone, Edward goes to work leaving Rick in charge of the house. 'Ring me if anything is amiss,' he says.

All afternoon he is tired and unproductive, anxious about developments. He visits Conrad in his office and collapses in the easy chair squeezed between two filing cabinets. He explains what has happened.

Conrad is unusually serious. 'Could we be talking psychopath?'

'Rick and Harriet think so. I won't rest easy until she is apprehended.'

'Go home. We can manage here.'

Edward hates to take time off for anything other than essential business but today he has found it impossible to juggle the challenges of both home and work. It is on days like this that he thinks retirement would be a very pleasant prospect and he decides to take Conrad's advice.

He returns home via the vet's where there is again some small improvement in Meg's level of alertness.

At the Deer Orchard, he finds Olivia waiting for him in the kitchen.

'Jessica has been found in Hebden Bridge,' says Olivia. She looks tired and less lacquered than usual. 'It's where she and her first husband lived. She's in custody.'

'I wonder how she got up there,' says Edward. 'Especially if she was here last night chucking that rock at the window.'

'I asked that. Apparently she hired a car.'

'I didn't know she could drive.'

'Nor did I. At least you can breathe again.'

He does. Then he calls Marianne on her mobile but is diverted to answerphone. He hangs up, preferring to email the details.

To: Marianne Hayward
From: Edward Harvey
Date: 3rd July 2012, 18.23
Subject: News

Dear Mari,
Jessica found in Yorkshire and being questioned – not sure whether up there or down here. Police activity down the lane around her house. Expect they are doing a search.
Meg continues to make slow improvement and may be

coming home for the weekend. Not out of woods yet, but great if she can be back with us soon. Lost without a dog to walk – although she won't be able to walk, yet. Rick has made effort to assuage my fears re Harriet – makes it easier to communicate as not deliberately avoiding the issue. Given Harriet's support for 'Us', I was perhaps unreasonable to react as I did.
love,
Edward

To: Edward Harvey
From: Marianne Hayward
Date: 3rd July 2012, 19.15
Subject: Re: News

Dear Edward,
Glad to hear on all fronts.
In that case I will return home. Taryn will be pleased!
In haste,
Mari

To: Edward Harvey
From: Patrick Shrubsole
Date: 3rd July 2012, 20.03
Subject: Scilly

Ted,
Flying Owl is hoping to get Mathis Wackernagel (president of the Global Footprint Network) to present a piece to camera – but that can be added after we've been to Scilly.
Last Thursday caught out in hailstorm driving back from Leicester Uni. Size of golf balls. Car covered in dents as

if it's been to a panel beater. Smashed windscreen too. Looks like write off.

We need to finalise details for the trip next time we speak. Hope Marianne hasn't changed her mind. Is she staying with you at the Parsonage or will we have the pleasure of her company at Lowertown Farm?

Cheers,

Patrick

Edward wonders about Patrick and Marianne. He suspects motives that are not entirely professional. On the other hand, this may help to promote his own cause as he can act as the gallant protector of her honour. Except he has his own designs where that is concerned. He replies to Patrick, suggesting a meeting via Skype later in the evening.

To: Marianne Hayward
From: Edward Harvey
Date: 4th July 2012, 07.15
Subject: July

Hi Mari,

Jessica still banged up. No chance of bail with new enquiries underway. Toxicology report on Meg said a type of rat poison and given husband in pest control, it is highly likely this will match samples taken from house or outbuildings. The RSPCA is involved. Much writing and editing of documentary scripts and last night had a meeting via Skype with Patrick. Would like to think we might do same.

love,

Edward

To: Edward Harvey
From: Marianne Hayward
Date: 4th July 2012, 20.15
Subject: Re: July

Dear Edward,
Skype: I prefer invisibility of phone and email. No
pressure to look respectable!
As if the weather hasn't been bad enough, the
Countryfile forecast suggests something worse heading
your way.
love,
Mari

Rachel calls him.

'I've been thinking about everything,' she says. 'And I've
been so worried about you with all this Jessica stuff. I do like
Marianne and I'm sorry I was a cow. It's because I care. It's
not just the money thing, it's because I find it difficult
imagining you paying attention to another woman; making
someone who isn't family important in your life. I'm jealous.
I'm sorry, I can't help it. But I'm trying to get used to the
idea.'

'Nothing is happening, Rachel, as I said before. Marianne is
a theoretical partner, not an actual one.'

'She's probably scared.'

Edward considers the word carefully. '*Scared?*'

'It's a big step at your age.'

'It is. It feels huge. Not least the logistics.'

'Do you love her? Does she love you?

'That's what Kate asked. I think so, and I don't know.'

'You have to talk.'

'I don't want to frighten her away. And I don't know what

to say. Don't know how to do this dating thing. Your mother chased me. I didn't do anything except follow her lead.'

'Oh Dad,' Rachel says. 'Harriet is right, you are hopeless.'

The following morning, Harriet comes home from Rick's with a rumour of an exhumation in the churchyard overnight: Jessica's second husband, according to the early morning gossip. Persons in white decontamination gear have been seen.

Harriet says, 'There's tape across from the Red Lion to the field. The area is being patrolled by uniformed officers and there are newshounds with cameras lurking in Church Close and asking questions. I can't get my head round it. This is becoming more and more like something off television.'

Before he sets off for work, Edward calls Olivia to see if he can find out more. She says that Jessica is still under arrest and being assessed by a psychologist.

'I did hear there was some hoo-ha up at the churchyard,' she says. 'But I don't know any details. I feel a little awkward about it all. Because of you and split loyalties. But Jessica is a friend and she's clearly unwell. She doesn't have anyone else so they are keeping me informed. I suspect she will end up in hospital.'

When he returns in the evening, a news reporter from the local paper phones the Deer Orchard to ask for an interview about what happened to Meg. Clearly someone in the village has said something. Edward is curt and deliberately vague. 'We think she may have been poisoned but nothing is confirmed regarding with what, or how or by whom.' He refuses to be drawn about any connection with the goings on up at the church.

On his way home on Friday, Edward collects Meg from the vet, the final outcome still very much uncertain. It is pouring with rain again and he wraps her in a blanket to take her to the car.

'I have to say I am surprised she's pulled through so far,' says Natalie. 'Given the state she was in. She must be tough.'

She is very weak and thin but he will give her plenty of TLC over the weekend. She can stand, but barely walk. For a day or two he will have to carry her when she needs to go outside. Next week he will be dependent on Rick to check on her during the day.

Edward phones Marianne with an update. He says, 'Have you thought any more about coming to stay when you finish work?'

She says, 'I have so much clearing up to do at college. I'm not sure when I'll be free. I'm not being evasive, but if it happens, it will have to be a last minute thing.'

'Okay,' says Edward, disappointed.

To: Edward Harvey
From: Marianne Hayward
Date: 6th July 2012, 22.25
Subject: Weather

Dear Edward,
The man from the environment agency has just been on the news and referred to the latest weather issue as a 'major set of rains'. Is this new terminology that we are going to have to get used to? Last week it was massive hailstones in the Midlands and North East, today it looks as though it will be the same areas hit again with high potential for flooding. Also looks bad in your area. We may escape until Sunday.
love,
Mari

To: Marianne Hayward
From: Edward Harvey
Date: 6th July 2012, 23.14
Subject: Re: Weather

Dear Marianne,
Cagoules at the ready!
love,
Edward

To: Marianne Hayward
From: Edward Harvey
Date: 7th July 2012, 07.15
Subject: Re: Weather

Dear Mari,
Broadclyst is awash – or at least the road to Killerton is
flooded; and the Honiton road on both carriageways. It
could get worse as the River Clyst is on flood alert.
Phone lines may be affected but we are unlikely to be
flooded at home so don't worry if you don't hear from
me.
love,
Edward

To: Edward Harvey
From: Marianne Hayward
Date: 7th July 2012, 20.13
Subject: Re: Weather

Dear Edward,
Am concerned. TV pictures look awful across your
region. Ottery St Mary has a river running down the

road. What is happening to our planet? Are these summer floods the shape of things to come? Difficult to think of planning holidays. Food prices have already risen at alarming rate so if there are shortages and we have to rely on imports am scared about where this will lead. Makes the sustainability issue so relevant. Even more evidence that we need to act; to have strategies. Perhaps early retirement is not a sensible option just now. Too late to change mind!
love,
Mari

To: Marianne Hayward
From: Edward Harvey
Date: 8th July 2012, 07.15
Subject: Re: Weather

Dear Mari,
You are not 'retiring' per se. Your career as a writer has a better chance of success if you go sooner rather than later. When you feel as if you've given all you can in a job, then it is time to consider options. Meg is now able to accompany me outside under self-propulsion. We go as far as the paddock and back – very slowly. Progress, but whether she will ever regain any of her former vigour we don't know. I've also been warned that organ failure could kick in too. Had thought of making another attempt to persuade you to come down for weekend but would hate to think of you marooned in Broadclyst.
love,
Edward

To: Edward Harvey
From: Marianne Hayward
Date: 8th July 2012, 09.25
Subject: Re: Weather

Dear Edward,
Can think of worse things than being marooned with
you!
love,
Mari

To: Marianne Hayward
From: Edward Harvey
Date: 8th July 2012, 20.25
Subject: Re: Weather

Dear Mari,
Shall I arrange to have you helicoptered in?!
Flooding worse today.
love,
Edward

To: Edward Harvey
From: Marianne Hayward
Date: 8th July 2012, 21.32
Subject: Re: Weather

Watching out for the Sikorsky!!
Marianne x

Edward has a fleeting fantastical thought about helicopters and
being with Marianne, completely surrounded by water like in
a medieval castle. Then the fantasy evolves into open fires with

burning logs, the floor covered in plush rugs on which to lie. Clothes are shed along with inhibitions and all the barriers that are currently in their way. Ever since the party he has nurtured the love until he can hardly bear to be away from her. If her courage should fail on Scilly, he must prepare for a life without her; a life alone.

37

The Alternative

Marianne thinks the exchanges about the flood and the helicopter have stretched the limits of Edward's flirting repertoire. Afterwards, he resumes cautious and measured dialogue by mail and phone, mostly focused on their respective work for the documentary series.

Term finishes officially at college although she pops back most mornings during the first week of the holiday to clear her desk and shelves. At first she finds it difficult throwing things away, years of accumulated notes bursting out of folder upon folder. She reasons that if she were to return to teaching or tutoring, she would have to update her knowledge and now that she has her new writing career, the probability of doing this is small. She doesn't want to add more clutter to her house if she is going to downsize so it is logical to load the papers into a recycling bag. As she goes through her ring binders, sorting the pages into what to keep, what to throw away and what to pass on to the HoD, she remembers the effort that went into their creation, the hours of cross-referencing from two or three text books, the endless revisions of worksheets on the computer and the life that she had with Johnny while she was teaching in her prime. She mourns the years that have gone, never to be reclaimed and wobbles under the weight of her decision to retire.

A week later, Marianne is in central London in Gillian Fylde's office at Flying Owl, talking through amendments to the Education Pack.

Gillian is a woman in her early forties with an ash blonde, low maintenance, short blunt bob and fringe of the sort favoured by headteachers. It transpires that she began her working life in a school.

'I am intrigued by this initiative in the Primary materials,' she says, finding the appropriate page amid the pile on her desk. *'Rejecting Aspirational Fashion,'* she reads. 'You say, "We need to make it trendy to be untrendy and to adapt, mend and recycle clothes instead of always buying new".'

'Consumerism is one of the chief enemies of sustainability,' says Marianne. 'And children must be educated in this view when they begin to show interest. It will be too late by secondary school.'

'Without media and celebrity support, this has no chance of catching on,' says Gillian. 'However, I take your point that we need to reduce consumerism and that clothes are the area where there is currently most resistance. My boss says there might be potential for a series on environmental issues to be created for children. He's talking to a couple of producers and I've given him copies of your draft packs so they can see what we're doing thus far.'

'The sticking point is sex,' says Marianne, noting Gillian's startled expression. 'I mean relationships. The last two decades have seen a shift towards *more* fashion consumerism, not less, with men joining women in their quest to buy clothes for appearance rather than functionality.'

'This is hardly relevant on a children's channel,' says Gillian.

'Pre-teens may not realise that the underlying purpose of fashion is to attract a mate, but the media has sexualised tweenagers in the past few years such that they are almost as interested in fashion and make-up as adolescents. I would like to see a reversal of that trend and it's more likely to happen if the media message for all age groups is one of less consumerism.'

'Businesses will try to fight back, otherwise they risk going bust.'

'Businesses will need to adapt and evolve. If we are to consume less, it is essential. It won't be popular, but ultimately there will be no choice. I am not suggesting that we lose interest in clothes, but that we need to embrace classics and longevity rather than disposable fashion. This might mean paying more for the original garment for it to last more than a couple of seasons. If we could turn the focus towards accessorising, it would be more economical and would place less stress on raw materials. The water consumption in textile production is phenomenal. If men and women believe their dating strategies are enhanced by these new behaviours and attitudes, then they will adopt them.'

'In which case, we have to get a few of the younger celebrities to endorse it. I'll put out a few feelers and see who's already banging the environmental drum. They may be persuadable.'

Marianne keeps Edward informed of progress, mostly by email and text. Since the floods, he has made no further suggestion that she visit Broadclyst, even though the weather has improved. She deduces that he is waiting for her to make the next move but with the onset of the London Olympics and distracted by equestrian events and the tennis, she is disinclined to leave the city.

To: Edward Harvey
From: Marianne Hayward
Date: 27th July 2012, 22.27
Subject: Re: Olympics

Hi Edward,
Andy Murray has won Gold!
Am super-excited by the way the Olympics have lifted everyone's mood. Great to have so much good news on TV instead of all the doom.

How is Meg?
love,
Mari

To: Marianne Hayward
From: Edward Harvey
Date: 28th July 2012, 18.31
Subject: Request

Dear Mari,
Agreed.
Meg is a little better but still can't walk far or fast. Mostly
we stay on home territory. Yesterday we ventured as far
as the Molwings' lane. She seemed to want to go further.
Then suddenly she sat down and I had to carry her
home. So sad to see. Have started going further afield
without her otherwise will become unfit.
Patrick has offered me last minute ticket for closing
ceremony. Wish I could invite you too. This will mean trip
to London mid August. Wondering if you would like me to
visit? We could discuss Scilly preparations – and stuff.
love,
Edward

And stuff …

To: Edward Harvey
From: Marianne Hayward
Date: 29th July 2012, 19.47
Subject: Re: Request

Dear Edward,
Stuff might be thwarted as Holly here for long weekend

Friday–Monday. Don't want to put her off as it is the first time in ages that she has said she will stay over. Think she wants to have chats before Scilly! But that doesn't mean you can't come. Indeed, I'd like you and Holly to meet again.
Mari x

To: Marianne Hayward
From: Edward Harvey
Date: 29th July 2012, 23.11
Subject: Re: Request

Dear Mari,
How about I come Saturday afternoon until Sunday morning? I could take you both out for a meal on Saturday evening? I will be out of the way late morning Sunday as am meeting Patrick to discuss planning. He says he can put me up Sunday night after the ceremony and I need to return to Exeter Monday morning as am giving talk to history branch of local U3A in the afternoon.
love,
Edward x

Marianne is excited at the thought of another encounter which with Holly's presence in the house, removes any anxiety about strings or escalating intimacy. Scilly is only weeks away and it will be a turning point one way or another. Either she takes the plunge, or she doesn't. If she doesn't, she might as well say goodbye to a future with this most delightful and extraordinary man.

Without the day-to-day whirl of bells, meetings and lessons, she can think more easily about the future. She asks her regular set of workpeople to give her quotes for various home improvements that need to be done ahead of putting the house on the market. Two rooms need decorating and she wants the old carpet in the hall replaced by a laminate floor. She has ignored major refurbishments since Johnny died, unable to face the upheaval of workmen on her own.

When Holly arrives, she embraces Marianne and says, 'I have felt far away and useless while you have been going through this Jessica thing. And I haven't been very understanding, have I? About Edward. I've been selfish and blinkered. I'm sorry. It makes me sad to think of you here without Dad and I don't want you to be lonely any more.'

With Holly's permission, it is another obstacle removed.

It has been almost two months since Edward has seen Marianne and as he waits on the doorstep in Beechview Close, he is hoping that she will give some indication, however subtle, of there being progress in their relationship.

But it is Holly who answers the door. She shrieks his name and rushes at him with the abandonment of a five year old, almost knocking him over. His own children never welcome him with such enthusiasm. This is a type of greeting he only experienced from Meg.

She plants a kiss on his scarred cheek and gives him a big hug before he has had time to drop his bag and briefcase. 'When Mum said you were coming, I was so excited. It's been ages. We so missed you when you left; Dad, especially.'

Dad, especially. Not Marianne. She must've hidden it well. But then she was used to hiding her feelings from him so it must be one of her traits.

Edward absorbs details: tall and attractive, more woman than the girl she was when he was lodging; still the same long dark hair now in random waves, the modern untidy look. She wears a long blue dress and sandals, her mother's casual summer style.

'I was sorry to hear about Felicity. Can't believe it. Mum said the chef is loads younger.'

'Holly!' says Marianne, hovering in the background, awaiting her turn.

Edward parks his bags in the hall and fleetingly places his arm round Marianne's back. He is cautious about displaying affection in front of Holly. Marianne catches his eye, then goes to make tea while Holly ushers him into the living room.

'Mum tells me you're going to Scilly together. I'm cool about it now, but it was a shock at first. Another man; it takes some getting used to.'

Edward sits on the sofa, considering what to say. 'It isn't quite like that, Holly. I would like us to have a relationship of the sort you imply, but she's probably told you we're being very cautious. Plenty of time to think about the risks. Would have been much easier if we lived in the same area and could go on dates.'

'Mum misses Dad a lot and I can't be here much because of work and my new relationship with Will. I don't want her to be lonely. But I don't want her to be hurt. You're not divorced yet, are you?'

'No, but only because Felicity and I have avoided communicating since she left. The time will come.'

'If you need any legal advice.' Holly laughs.

'Of course, although a degree of impartiality might be advisable.'

'How is your family adjusting to the idea?'

'Harriet is very supportive, ditto James. Rachel is anxious and Chris probably doesn't know yet – because there isn't anything to know. Now your mum has finished teaching there's more chance of spending time together – although with the floods and now the Olympics, we haven't managed to meet until now. Scilly will be a defining time. Afterwards, if she comes to stay at the Deer Orchard, she can spend more time there; bring her writing.'

In meeting Holly again, Edward is even more aware of the enormity of starting a serious relationship with Marianne. He would be taking on the equivalent of a step-daughter too, perhaps slotting into some of the roles filled by her father. And there are four of his children for Marianne to acquire and with whom to forge relationships. No wonder she is sometimes overwhelmed at the prospect. Of course their mother is still alive, but Marianne would still be by his side to advise, not least because Felicity is in Italy.

In the evening, the three of them go to Cinnamon Culture, a superior Indian restaurant in Sundridge Park between Beckenham and Chislehurst. Edward knows that Marianne and Holly favour Chinese, but Marianne is keen to try this restaurant as she has read rave reviews on Twitter via the #BeckBromFL and thinks its authentic Indian menu will be more to her taste than the typical takeaway.

The restaurant was once a pub and has a spacious dining room with high ceilings and two long rows of tables covered with crisp white tablecloths.

All three of them have the starter of jumbo prawns in a delicious herby marinade. They discuss Holly's career and then her relatively new relationship with Will.

'He is the closest thing to a Dylan,' she says. 'Of course, there will never be another Dylan because he was young and some of those crazy traits mellow as you get older. But I can imagine Dylan evolving into someone like Will. He's not as good-looking, but he's kind and thoughtful and very persistent. I'm warming to him.'

'I haven't met him yet,' says Marianne.

'I didn't want to dump him on you unless I felt it was going somewhere. Now I think it might, we can arrange a meeting. After you've been to Scilly, perhaps.'

Holly asks Edward about his children's relationships. 'If I remember, James was with Kate, and Rachel and Harriet weren't serious about anyone.'

He thinks it is perhaps best not to mention the Harriet and Rick situation. If Marianne tells her, that is a different matter. 'Kate is eminently suitable. Indeed, they want to buy me out of the Deer Orchard.'

'Have you told me this?' says Marianne.

'Probably not,' says Edward, taking a sip from his glass of water. 'Waiting to see what can be done, finance-wise.'

Through main courses of lamb biryani (Marianne), chicken tikka (Holly) and wild boar vindaloo (Edward), they discuss Edward's hopes for the documentary series and Marianne tells Holly about her involvement in the creation of the Education Pack. The food is lovely, the ambience buzzing but not intrusive and Edward is pleased to find conversation flowing easily between the three of them.

They return to Beechview Close for a cup of tea and at ten o'clock Holly announces she is retiring to bed to catch up on some reading.

'I'm making a tactful retreat,' she says. 'I remember what it was like when I had boyfriends over and the parents wouldn't leave us alone. Dad used to disappear and then keep coming back on the pretext of having forgotten something. So embarrassing. I won't do that.'

Marianne blushes and closes her eyes. After Holly has gone, she remarks that to be chaperoned by your own daughter is weird and she supposes Edward felt the same about Harriet's presence at the Deer Orchard.

'It seems a very long time since that delightful night,' says Edward.

'With each passing week I find it easier to imagine us together without feeling guilty. And I don't want to feel the slightest trace of guilt. You don't deserve that. When the time comes, I want you to know that I am with you and only you, with no regrets or anxiety.'

But he doesn't want to take liberties; not with Holly upstairs and Marianne sure to stop him. The promise for the future is ever clearer, ever more inviting. It won't be long now.

Surely.

38

The Waiting Game

The following morning Marianne drives Edward to Beckenham Junction. He kisses her on the cheek, says, 'It's been lovely, as always,' and as she watches him stride under the station's archway entrance and through the ticket hall she knows that it is decision time. After what didn't happen the night before, she recognises a different mood: her guilt has all but gone and in its place a certainty that she would like to move things forward. Holly's cautious approval helps. And time is slowly healing, gradually lessening the grief.

She wonders about the love issue; wonders how much it matters at this time of life. Does he love her? She thinks he does but is unsure whether he is *in* love – or lust – or whether it is a deeper, more all-consuming and enduring variety. It would be useful to know, yet generally it is only the poets who put their complex emotional feelings into words.

Taryn's rules suggest she should wait until he says so.

'And you mustn't say it to him first,' said Taryn. 'On no account. No matter what. Only then will you be sure of his commitment.'

To: Edward Harvey
From: Marianne Hayward
Date: 12th August 2012, 10.14
Subject: Visit

Dear Edward,
Let me know what it's like at the ceremony. Details, not a cursory overview!

Thank you for being.
love,
Mari x

To: Marianne Hayward
From: Edward Harvey
Date: 14th August 2012, 20.12
Subject: Re: Visit

Dear Mari,
Thank you for everything ...
Was lovely to see Holly again too. She has grown up so
much but still retains her youthful charm.
When we arrived at the Olympic Park, we were struck
by the wild flowers, even though they were fading
slightly – such a good idea using so many native species. I
thought of our sustainability project and how the insects
would benefit if every landscaping development took
this into account. There was also an inspired use of
water which helped soften some of the more angular
and functional buildings.
Acoustics were amazing for such a large space, but
despite its size there was an intimacy – much as must
have been felt in Greek and Roman theatres and
amphitheatres. It was an incredible spectacle in terms
of people – with athletes from a host of nations
supporting each other and a positive atmosphere in the
crowd too.
A longish trek to the nearest tube station, but made
easier by the humour and joie de vivre of the volunteers
– all still lining the route home after the show.
Overnight stop at Patrick's riverside flat was
revealing: a pristine sterile space devoid of any

clutter; a typical bachelor pad with a modern arty
feel. It was a bit awkward but at least he has a spare
room.
Must dash.
love,
Edward

To: Edward Harvey
From: Marianne Hayward
Date: 14th August 2012, 21.04
Subject: Re: Visit

Dear Edward,
Sounds like it was wonderful! The mood did come
through on TV – up to a point. Was the timing of your
sending your email deliberate?
love,
Mari

To: Marianne Hayward
From: Edward Harvey
Date: 15th August 2012, 22.39
Subject: Re: Visit

Dear Mari
Time was pure coincidence. Yes, it was wonderful. The
memories will stay with me for a long time.
We must speak again soon.
love,
Edward

She reflects on their email relationship, now spanning
twelve years if you don't count the missing five. When she

wants to tell him something she finds email the best medium, even now. She knows the phone will distract him from whatever he is doing. Email can be dealt with at a convenient time, or even ignored. Taryn says even emails should be rationed but Marianne has always written to him straight away when something of interest enters her sphere.

To: Edward Harvey
From: Marianne Hayward
Date: 17th August 2012, 20.04
Subject: Population Issues

Dear Edward,
They're banging on in the news about building more homes to cope with the UK's burgeoning population – now at 62 million, and that's only those we know about.
As usual no mention of trying to halt the people explosion. Your documentary is ever more relevant.
Looking forward to Scilly!
love,
Mari

To: Marianne Hayward
From: Edward Harvey
Date: 22nd August 2012, 21.08
Subject: Re: Population Issues

Dear Mari,
Today is Earth Overshoot Day. According to the Global Footprint Network, we have spent our natural resource

budget for the year. This means we are now in ecological deficit.
love,
Edward

She then receives a call to discuss final arrangements for Scilly. The phone conversation is short and to the point. He rarely chats on the phone. Marianne suspects it is how he manages to do so much. But he ends by saying, 'I'm looking forward to spending time with you again,' and she echoes the words back at him.

To: Edward Harvey
From: Marianne Hayward
Date: 24th August 2012, 11.21
Subject: Richard III

Dear Edward,
Fascinated by the search for Richard III's remains in Leicester car park. God help the poor chap if they find him. His poor bones will be given the third degree. And then what? As I've said before, cremation is the answer. But as an archaeologist, I imagine you have a different take on the matter.
love,
Mari x

To: Marianne Hayward
From: Edward Harvey
Date: 24th August 2012, 22.22
Subject: Re: Richard III

Dear Mari,

Quite so re archaeology! It will be most unexpected and exciting if they do find him. Most of these searches end in disappointment.

James and Kate have arrived with a vanload of stuff and moved into James's old room. May be temporary – will have to see how it works and what all our future plans are. House feels full again. Harriet and Rick have gone public. He wants her to move in with him but am pleased she's not rushing. This means, I'm afraid, that you will be relegated to Chris's old room for the night before Scilly departure. Hopefully this will not be necessary when we return!! Sorry, being presumptuous

...

love,

Edward x

To: Edward Harvey
From: Marianne Hayward
Date: 27th August 2012, 10.24
Subject: Food Crisis

Dear Edward,

After Scilly, who knows?!! We may drive each other crazy after ten days together. It happens!

Almost every day this week there has been a news crisis story over food. First fish shortages and then another reminder about bees. Today we hear that the plum harvest is poor and that prices are rising. The maize crop has been devastated worldwide and in UK cereal yield is down. It was reported that the UN say food prices may rise 70% by the middle of the century. Not only due to adverse weather, but increasing global population also cited, but not elaborated or linked to any ideas of control. If we don't impose control, then as in the natural world there will be starvation and survival of the fittest.

It is interesting that when African countries were hit by years of drought and war, we used to say that the world had plenty of food to feed everybody and that distribution was at fault. Now it is no longer so certain.

There is talk of people needing to change what they eat; to become less reliant on expensive meats and to follow a more vegetarian-based diet. Some are even talking about insects being a staple food!

And now the ice caps are melting faster than anticipated. What are we going to do? The sooner the programme airs the better. At least it will get people talking.

love,

Mari x

To: Marianne Hayward
From: Edward Harvey
Date: 27th August 2012, 19.55
Subject: Re: Food Crisis

Dear Mari,

You sound so like Patrick! Not that I disagree.

I know you won't drive me crazy. You keep forgetting that we have virtually lived together for almost half of three years. I know lodging is not the same, but if anything, having a closer relationship will be easier.

Our local news reports apple crops failing in West Country. In Somerset they believe yield is down 90% – due to bees lying dormant during the cold blossom time and therefore insufficient pollination. This means reliance on imports and higher prices.

Looking forward to your arrival on Wednesday.

love,

Edward x

Wednesday, Broadclyst; Thursday, Scilly. The beginning of a dream or the beginning of the end.

39

St Agnes

'Paradise,' says Marianne to Edward as they walk up the path from the St Agnes quay.

'What a sky,' says Edward.

It is an uninterrupted blue and there is warmth in the air. It seems that their week on the island will be a window of something bordering on an Indian summer relative to the unsettled weather during most of the previous few months. The vegetation is still green but the faded heads of the agapanthus betray the end of the season. They exchange a few comments about previous visits, but mostly they are lost in thought, appreciating the scenery.

At the Parsonage they are welcomed at the door by Pam Beresford-Smith, full of smiles and introductory questions about the flight from Exeter to St Mary's.

Edward has been a visitor with Felicity and several times since. And Marianne has been twice with Johnny. Pam is aware of both their circumstances, but Edward apparently said only that they were friends. They follow her up the small dark staircase to the bijou flat overlooking the lush garden. In the living room with its galley kitchen in the corner, she peers at them as if unsure how to react.

'There are beds made up in both the rooms,' she says, without any hint of judgement. 'We have turned the bunk room into a single room since you were last here. More suitable for most of our visitors.'

After Pam returns downstairs, Marianne looks at their cases

and bags expectantly waiting on the green carpet. The butterflies in her stomach begin to flap their wings. Somebody is going to have to say something.

Marianne swallows. 'Despite the fact that you stayed in our house for three years, and I have since been to yours and you to mine, this seems strangely intimate.'

'It's because we are alone, properly alone. No ghosts.'

'No Johnny, no Harriet, no Holly,' says Marianne. She decides to take charge and err on the side of caution. 'I'll sleep in the little room. I'm quite happy in a single bed.'

'Oh,' says Edward, frowning.

'What do you mean, "Oh"?' says Marianne, somewhat sharply. She immediately regrets her tone.

'You don't have to.'

'Meaning?'

'Meaning … When you said you'd stay here with me, I hoped …'

'Don't you think that's a bit previous?' says Marianne. She remembers what Taryn said; that if sex comes before love, you can never go back to doing it in a different order.

'I thought—'

'You thought wrong. I can't suddenly sleep with you just because we're here. I don't want to be used as a stepping stone between Felicity and your next great love.'

'Used? Stepping stone? Is that what you think of me?' says Edward.

Marianne realises her poor choice of words but is unsure how to retract. 'No, I didn't mean that.'

But he appears not to hear her. His expression has changed from relaxed and happy to tense and stern. 'You've made your position clear. Forgive me. I didn't think you were a tease. I've misinterpreted …' And his words trail away as he grabs his jacket and heads back down the stairs.

He is gone before Marianne can speak again. He has never raised his voice to her before and is clearly frustrated by her mixed messages. She didn't intend to sound so reticent, but the words came out all wrong. The compact space and the double bed had scared her: the thought of such intimacy, the disrobing, the expectation of what would follow. She chokes back tears. How has this happened without warning? Here she is in the place of her dreams with the man of her dreams – because there is no denying that he has been for a very long time – and in the space of five minutes, she has destroyed the brightening flames with a bucket of ice cold water.

She sits down on the little green sofa, her eyes stinging, her stomach clenching. She knows she has upset him. What should she do? How can she repair the damage without taking risks?

Minutes later, a phone rings. Not her phone, but Edward's. It is on the table in the window, behind a brown paper bag of apples that they brought up from the shop. She hesitates then answers it, struggling to find the right button on an unfamiliar keypad.

It is Harriet.

'Your Dad's gone for a walk and he left his phone. I'm not sure where he is or when he'll be back.' Her voice cracks with emotion. She is close to tears.

'That doesn't sound like Dad. What's happened? Are you all right, Marianne? You sound weird.'

'We had a misunderstanding.'

'And there was me thinking this would be the place and time when you two got together, properly.'

'Which is clearly what he thought too.'

'And you didn't?'

'I did. But I panicked. I wanted to take it one step at a time. And it came out all wrong. I keep having doubts because of something Olivia said.'

'What in God's name has that witch got to do with it?'

'In the shop after the party, she told me I didn't measure up to your mum. She implied that all I would ever be was a fling.'

'Oh good grief! And you believed her? Surely you know better than that after everything you and Dad have talked about? And he's walked off? Do you like him as much as I think you do?'

'Yes.'

'Go and find him. Tell him what you've told me. Tell him!' And she hangs up.

Marianne stares at the phone for a while, confused. Then she grabs her cagoule, the sunny weather no insurance against the possibility of a shower, particularly this year.

She locks the door out of London habit, steps softly down the stairs, puts on her shoes and heads outside, up the dampened leaf-strewn path, through the Parsonage trees and hydrangea bushes to the roadway. She pauses, glancing left and right. Instinct makes her turn left up the hill. At the junction with the main road, by the red telephone box, she sees Pam coming up from the shop with a bag of groceries.

'You haven't seen Edward, have you?'

'Lost him already?' Pam grins. 'I think I saw him heading up towards the lighthouse a few minutes ago.'

Marianne considers the options. On an island only a mile square, one would think it would be easy to find someone. She thinks she knows where he would go. It would be where she would run for solace. She heads up past the lighthouse and beyond the line of coastguard cottages where she cuts through a gate and down the hill to the rock formation called the Nag's Head. The turquoise sea and granite piles fill her view with breathtaking splendour. At the Nag's Head she touches the stone as if for luck, turns right and follows the path to the Troy Town maze.

Edward is sitting on the mound of tufted grass next to the

most recent incarnation of the maze. His almost euphoric mood as they crossed by boat from St Mary's to St Agnes has quickly been extinguished.

He is furious with himself for sounding presumptuous about the sleeping arrangements. He hadn't meant to. He had been carried away by things that had been said in the long weeks before. And then when she implied that he might use her as a stepping stone … That hurt him badly and all the anticipation collapsed in seconds into a disordered mess.

Too much has been left unsaid. He tries to remember their conversations. He is sure that he hasn't misinterpreted her genuine feeling for him beyond the friendly, and equally certain that she hinted at the possibility of intimacy while on Scilly. Yet she retreated the day after the party. There was no mistake about that. And she avoided further visits to Broadclyst despite his invitations.

He is not used to taking the initiative in relationships. Felicity chased him and she was the first. Taryn chased him. Even Jessica chased him in her own gauche and inappropriate manner. He is more skilled in running away – an art in itself. Marianne's withdrawal from him, he saw as guilt; something she would recover from in time. He has since been waiting for her to indicate her readiness. And she did say that Scilly might be the time. Or is his mind playing tricks?

This is the closest they have been to an argument since their renewal of friendship. When he thinks of what she has been through with Johnny dying, it saddens him that she has misinterpreted his motives.

He hears the sound of shoes on the path behind him and looks up. He is relieved to see her.

'Harriet called,' she says, joining him on the ground. 'You left your phone and I've upset you.'

'I don't know where I am with you. I thought we had

something special after the party and I imagined that in time you would feel like taking it further. Everything you've said … I'm sorry if I've expected too much.' He stares out to sea, to the Bishop Rock lighthouse rising in the distance. He does not meet her eyes.

'We do have something special.'

She tells him about the conversation with Olivia in the post office.

'And she's right,' she continues. 'I cook, but I'm useless at catering. I'm a dreamer who needs plenty of space. I can barely organise myself, let alone you. I'm not and never can be like Felicity. To have a fling with you might be glorious. But what happens after? It's so easy to let down my defences and to flirt. But then I remember.'

There is a pause while Edward registers what she is saying. In the distance, gulls swoop over the Western Rocks. His shoulders drop and he turns towards her.

'You think I'm after a fling? I have never intended to give that impression. Do you think that I would risk hurting you; or me? Everything we've talked about – the future, the children. I thought you knew. I know there are no guarantees, but my intentions are serious, not frivolous.' He takes hold of her hand and with his other hand he very gently brushes her wind-blown hair away from her face.

'Mari,' he says. 'You know that I love you, don't you? It's because you're *not* like Felicity that I do.'

Marianne's eyes register surprise then joy.

He continues, 'Felicity's attributes were everything I needed when I started out, when we had the kids. I don't need someone running my life any more. I know you, Marianne. I lived with you and Johnny for nearly three years. I know what you can do and what you can't. I know your moods. I couldn't bear to hurt you again with a mere fling.'

'You love me?' says Marianne.

'Of course I do. How could you possibly think otherwise?'

'Because you never said.'

'I thought you would assume, as I assumed.' He takes a chance. 'You do, don't you?'

She pauses and meets his eyes. 'Yes. And I'm sorry I doubted you. Sorry for what I said.'

'I'm sorry you had to endure the spite of Olivia.'

'When we were talking about possibilities, it felt far away. Now here we are on St Agnes; you and me alone in the flat and faced with the question of bedrooms. I didn't mean to say what I said. The wrong words came out in the wrong tone.'

He pulls her to her feet. When he was young, a declaration of love had been easier because it didn't carry the weight of expectation of a future. Felicity had been the first to stir the passions and he had been swept along with her enthusiasm in a rush of sexual energy and hormones. Now the fire burns with more gentle flickering flames. He understands the challenges of partnership. His words have not been said lightly.

'Look at that view,' he says, waving towards the jagged outlines of many small rocky islands, and beyond to the Bishop Rock lighthouse, rising in the mists four miles away. 'What better place to ask you to take a chance with an ageing archaeologist. I know you are uncertain. I know because you send mixed messages in your emails, texts and phone calls. And I do understand. But sometimes that leap of faith that we mentioned needs to be made and we are unlikely to have another opportunity such as this.' And he faces her and touches her cheek.

Marianne's green eyes sparkle in the sun. 'I trust you,' she says, briefly laying her head on his shoulder.

It's all she needs to say and he puts his arm around her and they breathe the salty air and gaze across the beginnings of the wide Atlantic to an ocean of unseen delights.

Patrick and the rest of the documentary team are due to arrive the following day for their week at Lowertown Farm. Edward considers himself the Advance Party, and after walking with Marianne back to the Parsonage via a late lunch sandwich at the Coastguards café, he leaves her to plan an evening meal while he consults Pam and her husband Julian about prospective interviewees on St Agnes and St Mary's.

He is clearly in work mode when he returns and over a simple supper of spaghetti bolognaise, he relays what he has discovered and how he expects the next few days to pan out.

'Pam and Julian have already earmarked several people to be interviewed regarding their roles in the day-to-day working of the islands,' he says. 'Farming is obviously an area to cover, but waste disposal is of particular interest, both sewage and domestic rubbish. We will also explore education, health care and building maintenance.'

'We take so much for granted on the mainland,' says Marianne.

'At the core is population management and housing development, those from the older generation primed to tell stories passed on by their ancestors who suffered hardship in the 1800s.'

Afterwards, they walk down to the Turk's Head for a drink. The question of sleeping arrangements that night hasn't been raised again but Edward is aware that Marianne has unpacked her things in the single bedroom.

When the darkness begins to fall and they return to the flat under a blue-grey sky, Marianne says, 'I'm glad you said what you said about Felicity. It makes a difference; in a good way.'

He takes her hand as they pick their way carefully along the uneven stretch of path, wondering what this good-way difference might be and reminding himself that he might need to take the lead.

In the flat, he makes tea for them both. 'Just to demonstrate that being tea-lady is not the purpose for inviting you.'

Marianne sits at the table, staring out into the night, reporting on the lighthouse beams and other flashing markers as they become visible.

In between her sporadic comments, the silence in the room is audible.

Edward sits on the sofa, making notes for the following day. After half an hour he puts his papers to one side and says, 'Are you going to sit there forever? Come sit by me.' He holds out his hand and she leaves her chair and slips down beside him. 'Closer.' She moves until her body touches his and he puts his arm around her shoulders and turns her gently towards him. And then he kisses her softly on the mouth, long and slow and lingering. She follows his lead, she closes her eyes.

For half an hour or so they talk about their feelings for each other, interspersed with kisses, giggling like teenagers, awkward in the confined space of the two-seater sofa. Edward harks back to the night after the party, dropping hints that he would like to take things further.

'You've been very patient since then,' says Marianne. 'Since our conversation earlier, I'm a pushover.'

He takes the hint.

She is wearing a strappy dress with buttons up the front and a wool cardigan. As she melts into his space he undoes a couple of the buttons and then a third. There's a lot to be said for buttons and zips.

When she doesn't object, he slides his hand beneath. He wishes she would touch him more. She has yet to venture anywhere under his clothes, even the night after the party. He would like her to make explorations.

As if reading his mind, she undoes a few of his shirt buttons and sneaks her hand inside.

'I thought you might have a hairy chest,' she says. 'From the time I saw you in hospital, there were hints.'

'I hope you're not averse,' says Edward. 'I am too old to embrace the trend for waxing.'

'I'm not in the least averse,' says Marianne, feeling her way around. 'It's not excessive. In fact I find it rather sexy. I expect it helps to keep you warm in winter; reduce the need for vests.'

'You do say the funniest things,' says Edward, kissing her again, moving his mouth onto her neck and then, tentatively at first, her breast.

She lays her cheek against his hair and makes a contented sound.

He thinks that it was many years ago when he last felt so accepted by Felicity. And his night with Taryn doesn't count. It never did. But he doesn't want to take too many liberties without permission. He moves away, kisses her nose and interlocks his fingers with her own.

They talk some more about their time together while Johnny was alive, the pain of separation, Marianne's struggle to open her heart again.

After some minutes, she says, 'Shall we continue in bed? The fresh air has made me sleepy.'

'In my bed? Both of us? Together?'

'I think so. I would like to lie with you, if that's okay. And then, who knows.'

She goes to clean her teeth and shower while he watches the weather forecast. His attention wavers, anticipation building of what may follow.

Minutes later, she reappears in the doorway, wrapped in a green towel, her hair piled on top of her head with damp tendrils falling over her face. 'Finished,' she says, tiptoeing into the little bedroom, giving him little chance to enjoy the view.

In the bathroom, under the shower, he lets the water bounce and splash over his hair and body, revelling in its freshness, the scent of the soap, the gathering steam in the air.

When he emerges, dry and naked, he finds her in bed and slips under the duvet beside her. She turns her back on him and he moulds himself to her shape, enjoying the silky feel of her nightdress against his skin. He places his hand around her waist, wondering if this is all it will be.

'We can carry on where we left off, if you like,' says Marianne.

'I like,' says Edward, nuzzling her neck.

He knew Felicity's needs, and their lovemaking had followed a similar script for years. Then there was feisty Taryn who led the way like a woman of the night.

Felicity always told him to start at the top. She said that while most men prefer to have their most erogenous zone targeted as quickly as possible, women prefer the circuitous route – and the more circuitous, the better. Peripheral touching, she said, was the way to open the gates of desire. Although he is perhaps not typical of men, he hopes Marianne is like most women in this respect and he kisses her neck and shoulder before making exploratory caresses of safe areas.

He traces a line across her back, noting the contours; a flatter shoulder blade than Felicity's; smoother, less-weathered skin, smaller, but more resilient breasts. He eases a strap gently down to her elbow, releasing softness, playing, stroking. She makes appreciative noises. How good it is to touch again and to know the touch is appreciated.

'You are in great shape,' he says, meaning it, considering she is fifty-five. He hopes to reassure her.

'Too kind,' she says. 'And I could say the same about you.'

After a while she flips around to face him and he kisses her on the mouth, still unfamiliar, learning a new way as a teenager might. He is out of practice, but then as far as he knows, so is she. She returns the favour, and it is some time before she moves her hand elsewhere and makes him sigh. He can be in no doubt about her intentions.

'So how would you feel about my taking you to Carlisle?' he says, marvelling at his bravado. Something about the euphemism makes it easier to say.

'And back?' says Marianne.

'Of course,' says Edward.

'I feel it might be most delightful, sir,' says Marianne, coquettishly.

It is as if she is someone else, confident of her sexuality, of her ability to please. He cannot equate this woman in his bed with the sometimes bashful Marianne.

The route to and from Carlisle turns out to have many unexpected diversions and when Edward finally sinks back on his pillows, it is with a deeply contented sigh.

They lie for a while without speaking, her arm across him.

Eventually she says, 'I've been here before, in dreams.'

He wonders if she means sleep dreams or fantasies, and if there is a difference, and if it matters. All the years of family angst and wanting the impossible seem to have led him here, to this moment.

'It's been a long time since I've had a night such as this,' he says. 'Years. Decades, even. All the more precious because I am older now and know such nights are rare. When I was young I thought it would always be this way. In recent times, I never thought I would feel like this ever again.'

'Nor I,' says Marianne. 'That was simply lovely.'

Her hair is tousled in a way he has never seen before, and she seems vulnerable and childlike, so different from the woman who had brought him to such peaks of pleasure only minutes earlier.

His heart slows to its normal rhythm and he is suffused with peacefulness, happiness and hope. He kisses her again, says goodnight, believes her to be as contented as he is and turns out the light; a busy day to come, a week of magic dancing in the air.

40

Filming

The television programme is to be called *From Scilly to the World*. The book will have an added subtitle: *An Extrapolation from the History of the Islands to the Growing Global Population Crisis.* Yes, it is a mouthful but it is merely an explanation and not something that will be in large enough font to distract.

With the potential of world TV rights, Edward is already considering the implications on his future and whether it is time to leave the University of Devon for the second time in order to focus on his writing career and – as Marianne suggested – occasional lectures at Stancliffe and elsewhere. It is probable that once the TV programme is ready for airing, there will be marketing opportunities via broadcasting media. If he is tied up at UD, these will be hijacked by Patrick. Edward would very much like to increase his own public profile, not least because any platform will have a knock-on effect on his other book sales and perhaps lead to further work in television.

Also, if Marianne is going to feature in his future life, greater flexibility will allow more freedom to do things together – especially now she has taken early retirement to concentrate on marketing *Lydia* and working on the sequel. He has known since lodging at Beechview Close that she is not the archetype of domesticity and he would like to have the time to be more supportive on the home front.

He has a vision of them writing in separate rooms in some as yet unrealised house, reading each other's work, offering advice, a *frissant* in their exchanges, perhaps the occasional sexual indulgence in the afternoon – something that he doesn't remember doing since before the children were born.

The previous night has left him in a state of unparalleled contentment and in the morning, after watching the sleeping Marianne and the unaccustomed stillness of her profile, he rises early and walks to the Nag's Head and back, all before eight. He is in the process of making a few phone calls when she surfaces.

'I always suspected you were a lark,' she says, popping her head round the living room door before disappearing into the bathroom.

When she emerges, he says, 'How would you fancy a few nights on Tresco at the Island Hotel after we leave here next week? A proper mini-break with no work distractions? They have a vacancy in one of their Sea Garden Cottages – and we can eat at the restaurant or the pub so you – sorry, "we" – don't have to cook. I've checked about moving the flight home and that's okay too.'

'Extravagant – but it would be fantastic.'

'It will give us a chance to talk about things before I become sucked into the preoccupations at the beginning of term.'

Things … There is so much to discuss and so little time before she will be back in Beckenham again. This opportunity must not be wasted. The complexities of reorganising a life – two lives – are almost too big to face but they have to start considering the options. He wonders how people have the courage to take midlife risks with others whom they meet via the internet and never in person until one relationship is abandoned in favour of starting again. Such risk-taking which often ends in disaster. He supposes he and Marianne are cautious. He never used to be cautious. He remembers how Felicity blew into his life like a whirlwind and he followed where she led. But in those days the only risk was to himself.

There were no children to consider. And there was no property, no security. The difference now is the wealth of accumulated past stacked up on one side of the scales, against uncertainty on the other; the same for both of them. Conversations will help to narrow the odds that Taryn referred to when he met her at Marianne's.

Patrick and the film crew turn up at lunchtime on the catamaran *Spirit of St Agnes,* having docked earlier at St Mary's on the *Scillonian*. Edward strolls down to the quay to greet them, their baggage going by trailer across the centre of the island and down to Lowertown Farm.

There are three additional members of the team. The director is a dumpy woman called Geraldine Plover who reminds Edward of a potato. She is of indeterminate age, with hair and nails that clearly spend time in salons. She doesn't look the type to enjoy the outdoors. Nick Nightingale, tall and balding, is the cameraman, with an impressive list of credits including several major wildlife documentaries, and Jack McIntyre – 'JackMac' – is the sound engineer, also in charge of anything lighting-related and Twitter publicity. Patrick will be leading the presenting – no doubt posing in scenic places as was his wont during his previous TV appearances. Later he will add voice-overs.

Edward suggests they have lunch at the Turk's Head before he escorts them round to their accommodation to settle in and have a strategy meeting.

Geraldine says, 'I didn't realise everything would be so far apart. We must have some meals at the farm or we will waste too much time walking back and forth.'

Edward notices she has a slight lisp. 'Far? It's minutes at a brisk pace. Nowhere is far on St Agnes.' He hopes she isn't going to be awkward.

★

Meanwhile, Marianne has again been left to prepare the evening meal. She is happy to take on a domestic role while they are on St Agnes and even relishes the challenge of sourcing ingredients. Chicken breasts from the shop are always versatile and if she finds some tomatoes, courgettes and potatoes from the trolley outside the farm near the lighthouse, she can put everything in the oven with some red onions and olive oil, Jamie Oliver style. She had the foresight to bring a few sachets of herbs, including oregano.

All the while she drifts about her business with tranquillity of mind, savouring the night before as a confirmation of everything she had dreamed. She hopes the filming will not get in the way of further such pleasures, but even if it does, with the prospect of extra days in Tresco, she is more content than she has been since Johnny died.

On the way back from the shop, she meets Pam who tells her that there is gathering excitement on the island now that the film crew has arrived.

Marianne says, 'Edward tells me that they will probably interview you about the water situation. And also the way you manage your fruit trees.'

'We were concerned earlier in the year,' says Pam. 'We are totally reliant on rainfall here. Our bore hole at the Parsonage has never let us down yet, but during the drought in March we were quite worried. A dry summer and who knows what might have happened. Then the rains came in abundance. Crisis averted. Not that we wanted or needed so much rain.'

Back at the Parsonage flat, and after an egg sandwich lunch made with wholemeal bread from the St Martin's bakery, Marianne's mobile rings. She expects it to be Edward and is surprised to hear Patrick's voice.

319

'May we borrow you down at the farm? The team would like your input on the education side. See how best we can incorporate the ideas into the film.'

The film to which he refers is a short piece of about fifteen to twenty minutes, separate from the documentary series and intended to be shown to children and teachers to help to inspire. Different voice-overs will be done for different age groups, posing questions with a range of complexity.

Patrick Shrubsole is not a person to refuse or delay and Marianne grabs her bag and trots down the stairs.

Lowertown Farm is further down the hill below the Parsonage, nestling in the dip before the flat plain of the cricket pitch and freshwater pool. In a few minutes she arrives and is shown into a white-painted kitchen with a huge rectangular pine table at which the team has gathered.

Patrick introduces her as Edward's friend and the principal author of the education materials. He then takes his seat at the head of the table and Marianne wonders what Geraldine will think of his assuming so much control. She sits down between Edward and Nick, opposite Geraldine and Jack.

Patrick asks her to outline one or two ideas from the pack that could link directly to Scilly.

She says, 'St Agnes is perfect for children to understand about finite resources because it's a small island. Yes, it has neighbours, but it's twenty-eight miles from the support of the mainland. A land-based community of similar size wouldn't have the same impact.'

She is aware of Edward sitting back, watching her intently. Ever since she met him and discovered his success, she has thought, *if Edward can do it, so can I*, and it gives her confidence when public speaking. Of course, their temperaments are different, but she is no longer as fazed as she used to be by new situations.

'When Edward and I were at school we had an amazing teacher, Mr Jenks, who created a fictional island of two countries, each with different resources. We pupils were given occupations and cheque books and in English lessons we traded with each other and with the class above us. I was too young to understand fully what was going on, but I remember it well and I believe this basic idea can be used to teach the concept of sustainability.' She looks at Patrick and he nods encouragingly.

'Primary children could invent their own island having perhaps seen some film footage of St Agnes. The only requirement is that they keep to the small size and limited resources. They could decide what occupations are needed to sustain the community, and this is where the film could inspire by dropping visual hints. For example, the hens in the field down the lane leading to Wingletang Down.'

Nick Nightingale says, 'In which case we probably need a montage of scenes showing what individuals in the community do to keep the island running.'

'Exactly,' says Marianne. 'And the teacher could represent the person with whom they communicate for trading with a neighbouring island.'

'Or different classes could take on different islands,' offers Geraldine, 'with distinct characteristics so a variety of trade could occur between them. Rather like your experience at school.'

'I'll add the suggestion to the Primary resources,' says Marianne. 'I have proposed that teachers could present the children with problems – like someone wanting to build a new house. So if you can bear this in mind when filming, it would be good. The lack of space makes it easy to see how quickly life could become untenable if properties were allowed to spring up willy-nilly.'

Marianne then stops talking and answers a few questions.

'I'd like to make use of this sunny afternoon,' says Patrick. 'We'll interview Ted down by the maze. Stunning backdrop of the Bishop, the Western Rocks and round to the Camper Dizzle rocks on Castella Down. I'll do a couple of pieces by the Nag's Head and the Punch Bowl. I'd rather like to pan across Wingletang Down; huge area covered in gorse and boulders; useless for cultivation but good for rabbits.'

Geraldine says, 'So to summarise: our two main areas of focus are firstly, how does St Agnes self-sustain as far as possible and secondly, how does it create the funds to buy in goods and services it can't produce itself? This is where the flower farming and the tourism are relevant.'

'I have someone lined up to take aerial shots for us,' adds Patrick. 'Best way to show how small the island is; how little land is available for crops and animals. This will be useful for both the documentary and the education piece.'

Marianne says she will leave them to it and Patrick escorts her to the door.

'That was top drawer,' he says. 'You are quite a find. I'm pleased Ted has someone in his life again – but if you want a little more excitement, you have my details.' He winks. 'I didn't know you and Ted were at school together. You don't look old enough.'

She ignores the compliment. *Such a rogue,* she thinks, and takes a circuitous route back to the Parsonage around the cricket pitch and by the pool. She reflects on her delivery of information at the farm and is pleased by the way it flowed, despite her lack of time to prepare. Then past the Turk's Head and back up the hill, she muses on what she might like to do with Edward when they are alone again that night.

41

Heaven

On a bright sunny day under a cloudless blue sky stretching from one horizon to the other, the island of Tresco is another heavenly dreamland in which to escape from the modern world of bustle and noise.

Edward and Marianne have transferred by boat from St Agnes and are now installed in a one-bedroom cottage which is part of the latest incarnation of the Island Hotel, changed significantly since Edward's last visit in 2004. The cottages can be rented by the night and are set up for self-catering although visitors may eat if they wish at the new Ruin Beach café by the shore.

They are in the café having lunch beside tranquil waters. Marianne is looking forward to some quality time away from documentary distractions. Patrick and the film crew have been dispatched to the mainland leaving her and Edward free to explore their new-found intimacy.

'We must use this time to talk about the future,' says Edward, over open crab sandwiches and salad. 'I'd like to think we can find a way to spend more time together when we get back home.'

More time ... Marianne agrees but is unsure of how far or how fast he wants to move things forward. She doesn't want to presume too much despite everything they've shared. She knows what men can be like about commitment. Taryn said, and Taryn knows about such things. Of course, Edward, being unusual, may not follow the trend. After all, from what he said, he committed to Felicity without any hesitation. She lobs the ball back to him. 'What do you suggest?'

'We *can* wait,' he says. 'But if we wait, what do we do? Snatched weekends and uni holidays?' It is as if he is equally unsure of her reaction; wanting to test the water first.

'It is odd making life-changing plans together so soon,' says Marianne.

'I've been thinking about this for weeks,' says Edward. 'I know I would prefer not to waste any more time living our lives as separately as they have been. We are too old to wait.'

'So if we take the plunge, what do you propose?'

'I was wondering if you would consider a merger of a sort.'

Not the most romantic of suggestions, she thinks. She gives him one of her open-eyed looks, inviting more.

'There are several areas to consider: house, children, money, jobs.'

'This sounds like a business proposal.'

Edward laughs. 'The practicalities can't be ignored. We need to thrash out possibilities, problems and how to overcome them. The most pressing issue is one of accommodation – because that affects everything else. If we stay as we are, then I don't see how we will find time for each other.'

'Why do you want us to be more together?' Marianne wants him to add romance, love and even sex to his list.

'Is that not obvious?' He reaches across the table and touches her arm. Their eyes meet and lock for a few seconds.

Already Marianne has been surprised at Edward's ability to be romantic if the right buttons are pushed. But it is as if she has to make it an agenda item on one of his lists and once it is there, he attends to it with the same zealous enthusiasm with which he approaches all his work. He notes the issue, considers how it can best be achieved and then acts. It could be a random hug or a kiss or a compliment, even a small gift – a picked wild flower, the last strawberry. Marianne finds it endearing, even if lacking spontaneity.

She has also been surprised by his transformation in the bedroom. Once his working day is over and he is given the slightest encouragement, he becomes extraordinarily passionate. Marianne has realised that the years of rejection by Felicity have sapped his confidence in making the first move, so this past week she has exercised her flirting repertoire to flag her interest. Despite being busy and tired, there were several early nights and long and leisurely love-making sessions which left them both feeling that midlife sex has its advantages.

Edward continues, 'If I sell half the Deer Orchard to James and Kate, and if you follow through your plan to sell Beechview Close, we could combine resources.'

'We could,' says Marianne. 'I've been thinking of selling Beechview Close for a while. Too many memories and too big. I could buy a flat. Two bedrooms so there's somewhere for Holly to stay – and more security if I'm spending time away. It would give us a London base which would be useful as far as our writing projects are concerned; also if your TV work expands. And it means I can keep in touch with my friends.' She pauses and scans the view of the nearby islands and their fading summer brightness. 'I'd like to invest some of the proceeds to supplement my pension – because of the years I worked part-time when Holly was young and also recently. Some of the shortfall has been compensated for by Johnny dying while still in service, but with the state of the economy and the cost of food, I would prefer not to be stretched financially. I would be able to put the rest into a property for both of us.'

'If you have your flat and I still keep half of the Deer Orchard, we both have an insurance policy. I'm not suggesting that we need it, but it might persuade you to take the plunge sooner rather than later. There's no reason why you can't continue to spend time in London while we set up home in Broadclyst – or wherever.'

'I can't believe we're saying this. I'm scared it isn't real. That you are going to tell me you've made a mistake; that it's too fast.'

'I'm very sure,' says Edward. 'I've been alone longer than you. Much longer if we're talking "connection". And I used to be envious of the closeness you had with Johnny. I'm not sure Flick and I were ever that close after the kids were born. I was always busy. Always working, writing, lecturing. Looking back, it's easy to see why she was disgruntled. It didn't matter when the kids were young and occupied all her time but I think she must've been lonely sometimes when I was away.'

They consider the options; the relative merits of Broadclyst and Beckenham; the possibility of somewhere new.

'Since Johnny died, I've been bereft on my own. Holly doesn't visit often enough for it to matter where I am. If James and Kate and Harriet are going to be in Broadclyst, it's logical for you to be there too.'

'For "us",' Edward corrects.

'I'm scared of saying "us" in case it causes a jinx. It's been a while since things went smoothly. You know I still miss Johnny and that my grieving for him is not over. But it doesn't mean I care less for you. I care differently, though. Perhaps more "in love" because it's new. Less old love because less time.'

'Don't over-analyse,' says Edward. 'I know it's what you do, but don't worry about what I think. It will take years before you recover from losing Johnny. We're both damaged from our experiences in different ways. But if we wait until we're healed, we may be too old to enjoy what we can enjoy now. And I think we can each help the other through the healing process. Best to look forward, not back. I'm happy that you've agreed to walk the path with me.'

'That's a lovely thing to say,' says Marianne.

Over the next two days, in between walks and cycle rides, restaurant meals and romantic interludes, they continue to talk about the practicalities of merging their lives.

Gradually the options are narrowed and Edward can see a future with them setting up a home together in Broadclyst or nearby and Marianne buying a flat in Beckenham, initially for her to live in and for them both to use eventually.

When he joins her on the second afternoon in the Jacuzzi after a dip in the indoor pool, she says, 'In among your list of things we need to discuss, have you considered the question of division of labour on the domestic front? I know you are usually too busy to play much of a role, but I don't want to be a housekeeper just because my new writing career is based in the home. It isn't my way.'

'We shall have dishwashers in both homes and a cleaner. And if you hate ironing so much, then I promise I will do my own shirts or buy in the services of someone in the village.'

'I remember when Johnny and I decided to get married, there wasn't the same anxiety.'

'Youth and thousands of years of procreation programming,' says Edward. 'Felicity more or less arrived without much discussion at all – as far as I can remember. Then a couple of years later she told me we needed to start a family and being married was therefore a wise move.'

'And now these children present an added complication,' says Marianne.

'Harriet will probably move in with Rick. James and Kate will be fine about us and I've no worries about them being happy and successful at whatever they do. Rachel and Holly are the ones with more clear-cut anxieties.'

'That's probably because they're not certain about their own futures. I'm hoping something comes of Holly and Will.'

'Some sort of legal document might be necessary to ensure the interests of the children are taken care of should anything happen to either of us.'

'Like a pre-nup. Without the wedding,' adds Marianne hastily.

Edward is silent for a while. This was what Rachel had suggested. 'If anything happens to either of us, we would need to know that we are not going to lose our homes. I know we don't want to think such things, but it's better to be safe.'

'So some sort of trust fund could be set up, perhaps?'

'I'll talk to our solicitor.' As soon as he says it, he realises he has said *our,* meaning him and Felicity. Marianne appears not to notice but he must be careful. 'With your pension, you are self-sufficient. The surplus from your house sale can be invested as you suggested to generate more income or to be used as capital for funding projects like your writing. We are lucky to have options. So many people are trapped in unhappy situations because they can't afford to escape.'

After the Jacuzzi and a cycle ride to the Abbey Gardens, after dinner and another walk, they retire to their sumptuous bed.

'I think I am completely sexed out,' says Edward.

'A hug will be just fine,' says Marianne.

Felicity told him the importance of hugs when they were first together. At the time he hadn't appreciated it but when she distanced herself from him, it was the hugs he missed as much as the sex. Marianne turns away from him and he moulds to her shape through her nightdress. He has ceased to wear his pyjamas, enjoying the direct feel of skin or satin. He holds her close, no need for words. So many months of waiting; so many years of fantasies.

Now this. And he drifts into an untroubled sleep.

On the final morning after breakfast, they sit on rocks in a cove facing the island of St Martin's and the smaller uninhabited island of Teän.

'I've had the most amazing time,' says Marianne. 'On St Agnes and here. When we return to the real world, that's when it may be more difficult.'

It has been years since Edward felt so physically satisfied and emotionally fulfilled and he is satiated in a way that only equates to a distant pre-children memory. On their first night on Tresco, Marianne surprised him with her adventurousness, emerging from the shower with a mischievous expression that he hadn't seen since the party. It was as if she had metamorphosed into another person and he watched transfixed as she stepped across the floor and began to strip in front of him. First she removed her earrings and necklace, then she asked him to unbutton her dress, a delicious request which no one had ever asked of him before. She let the dress fall at her feet, gazing at him provocatively before joining him in bed in white satin underwear.

He remembers having a conversation with his Australian friend Glen Rushworth about what women wore in bed. Glen was of the view that the less the better, or a t-shirt at most. 'So when she takes it off there's nothing else to get in the way.' The preference for lace and underwear he viewed as more of a British than Australian peccadillo.

Now he watches her sitting demurely on her chosen rock, a long skirt hiding her ankles, and he marvels that she is able to transform into a siren in the bedroom. She is a cuttlefish of changing colours and it isn't something he expected. It is a bonus. Perhaps it was being friends with Taryn for so many years; or perhaps it was Johnny. Either way, he is reaping the benefits.

'Marry me,' says Edward. 'Be in no doubt as to where I would like this to go. As soon as I'm divorced, of course.'

42

Falling

'Dad, we have a problem,' says Harriet, as soon as Edward is within speaking distance as she waits by her car in the pick-up area at Exeter airport.

Marianne detects a meaningful glance and is gripped by anxiety.

'Mum has turned up.'

'What? When?' says Edward.

'Day before yesterday,' says Harriet.

'That's all we need. Trust her, now of all times. I suppose she's come for the rest of her things?'

'More complicated than that,' says Harriet, 'but I'll leave her to explain. There's other stuff too.'

Marianne registers the consternation in Harriet's voice; the words that are not being spoken are more significant than those that are. They hang in the air with the menace of a hovering buzzard as the luggage is bundled into the car. She says, 'It probably wouldn't be wise for me to show up with you.'

Edward frowns and looks at Harriet. 'Have you or James told your mother I was away with Marianne?'

'No. I said you were on Scilly. Nothing more. You've been so often these past few years, it's hardly a surprise.'

Marianne says, 'I need to find somewhere to stay overnight and I'll return to London tomorrow.'

'No,' says Edward.

'It is the only way. You don't want to be explaining about

me in my presence. In any case, if Felicity has things she needs to discuss with you, I would feel awkward.'

'Are you sure?' says Edward. 'I can't apologise enough.'

'How about Heath Gardens B and B?' says Harriet. 'It's nearby and it's comfortable. They may be able to fit you in short notice at this time of year.'

'Or a hotel in Exeter near the station?' says Marianne. 'I can go home first thing without bothering anyone for lifts.' Already her paradise world is crumbling and she feels sick.

'I would rather have you stay in Broadclyst,' says Edward. 'It isn't right that you should be elsewhere.'

In the car, he makes a phone call and secures a booking at Heath Gardens. There is an ominous silence as Harriet drives them to Broadclyst and twenty minutes later Marianne is deposited in a traditional yellow-ochre cottage with a thatched roof.

'I'll be back to take you for a bite to eat when I see what's what,' says Edward, kissing her on the cheek.

After he has left her, she cannot help feeling alone and abandoned, even though it is only a relatively short walk down the nearby lane to the Deer Orchard.

She sets about unpacking essentials. The room is on the ground floor by the front door. It is lovely and cosy, painted cream, with a plush carpet, a double bed and two chairs either side of a table in front of a window with views over the road to the crop fields beyond. In any other circumstances she would have been very happy to be in such a place.

When they arrive back at the Deer Orchard, Edward is about to get out of the car when Harriet stops him.

'There's something else, Dad.'

She pauses for an instant and Edward knows what's coming.

'It's Meg. She died. I'm so sorry. We found her yesterday

morning. She was okay the night before. But you knew how she was struggling. There was nothing we could have done.'

He had a feeling, one of those wispy thoughts that never form into something tangible. A blankness envelopes him and he closes his eyes. He is tired from travelling, stressed by leaving Marianne, thrown into confusion by Felicity's reappearance and now this, so very sad. His throat hurts with the effort of controlling his emotions.

'What have you done with her?'

'She's in the orchard beyond the olive tree. James buried her and we laid some flowers, said a few words.'

'Thank you,' he says. 'I'll take a look shortly, but first I have to face your mother.'

He takes his bags from the car to the house. In the hallway he sees an alarming number of packing crates and cases.

'Mum's in the greenhouse with Kate,' says Harriet, scuttling upstairs to her room.

There will never be a good time to speak to his estranged wife. He strides across the garden and finds both women examining the pots of winter veg seedlings that Rick is nurturing.

'Ted!' says Felicity, grinning like a long lost friend and holding out her arms to him.

She is sun-bronzed to a degree he has never seen and her hair has golden streaks amid a rich brown colour.

No doubt dyed because of her toy boy, he thinks.

She wears jeans and a red top with a plunging neckline. Her lips are shiny and her perfume wafts towards him, an evocative reminder of the past. He detects a calculated strategy, no longer so naive where women are concerned. He does not return her greeting and folds his arms when she steps towards him. Kate makes a diplomatic retreat.

Initial exchanges are hostile.

'Harriet says you're back,' says Edward. 'For how long do you intend to stay?'

'I've come back,' says Felicity, 'as your wife. We are still married. This is still our house.' She emphasizes the *wife* the *we* and the *our*; words of connection; of possession. She must know she is on shaky ground, but she was always bold.

He is taken aback at this unexpected announcement. 'Only in theory. In real terms we are no longer married and when you left, you said all this was mine. There's been hardly a word from you in over a year.'

'Things change, Ted. The future is never predictable. You, of all people should know that.' She absently feels the compost on the tops of the seedlings, checking their moisture levels out of habit.

Edward wonders whether she is referring to the time when he was mugged, or to something else. 'What happened to lover-boy?'

'He lacks ambition. He's quite content to carry on his parents' place in exactly the same way as they had been doing. They put pressure on him and he capitulated. And being together full-time hasn't worked out. His language skills; my language skills. He reverted to Italian much more when we were there. His default setting. We couldn't communicate at a deeper level.'

'And you didn't realise this before you went away?'

'Midlife does things to you. Crazy things. I thought once we were there, I would pick up the language more easily. And I did, but it's not the same. And there was an ex-girlfriend paying him a little too much attention for my liking. Perhaps that's the real reason.'

'You made it clear you no longer loved me.'

'But you never said that you didn't love me,' says Felicity. 'I pretended you didn't because it made me feel less guilty. I thought we might try again. I know I haven't been the wife you wanted for the past ten years, but now my menopause is over and I've satisfied my large-scale career ambitions, I can do the restaurant thing on a smaller scale and can refocus my attention on you and the family.'

'I think not,' says Edward.

'Everything is possible, Ted. Most things are still in place here. All I need is a venue. I could locate in a different village this time. There's a little place this side of Exeter, near Pinhoe, that's up for sale. I've thought about it carefully and am sure of what I want. I never really stopped caring about you; I was carried away by romance. Gianni flattered me.'

Edward hesitates. She is the mother of his children. He cares, but he doesn't care enough. Her sudden departure with Gianni hurt him and insulted him. It was then that any remaining romantic feelings slipped away like baby turtles into a vast blue ocean to make a new life elsewhere. And Marianne is no Gianni; no whim, no unknown quantity. 'Have you forgotten the last five years we were together? It wasn't much of a marriage. Had it occurred to you that I may have moved on too?'

'Oh Ted!' Felicity smiles disarmingly. 'You take ages to make relationship decisions. If I hadn't come along when you were at uni, you'd still be sitting in a fusty garret writing archaeology books.'

Edward is annoyed. 'I don't love you any more, Flick. My feelings had been dying for years before you left. I fought to keep them alive as best I could but, in truth, I stopped loving you long before you went off with Gianni. Now I feel nothing that would offer hope.' He realises this is largely true.

'We are married and I know you have principles.'

'And those principles are telling me to let go.'

'In a few years' time we'll probably have grand-kids. Don't you think it will be a lot less complicated if we are together?'

'Probably, but you should have thought of that before you left us. I don't want to spend any more of what's left of my life in a loveless situation, creating a pretence for as-yet theoretical grand-kids. If I don't start afresh now, it will be too late.'

'Do you have someone in mind, Ted?' She laughs as if this is an impossibility, then walks past him, back to the house. 'We'll talk some more when you've recovered from the shock. I can understand why you're hacked-off, but when you stop and think, you'll see it makes sense. When you get to our age, practicalities should inform decisions.'

Edward follows her. 'You can't stay. You can't move back in as if nothing has happened.'

'I already have, more or less. I know my rights.'

'Where have you been sleeping?'

'In our room of course.'

And before Edward has time to object further, she is marching ahead of him, yet again railroading, steamrollering, whatever you would like to call it, just as she has always done. He will have to stand up to her, but given his lack of success in the past, he isn't sure what to do.

'You will have to move into Chris's room,' he says, following her into the kitchen where Harriet has reappeared to start making supper. 'Harriet, find some clean bedding for your mother.' Then he goes upstairs ahead of Felicity and begins ejecting any signs of her from his bedroom, gathering up an armful of clothes and handing them to her as she protests on the landing.

He says, 'Very underhand turning up without a word while I was away. Reminds me of when you had the wind turbine installed. I suppose one of the kids told you?' He picks her nightdress off his bed and flings it at her.

'Rachel mentioned it in passing. I thought it would be easier to talk with me here than over the phone.'

'What else did she tell you?'

'Nothing. Other than she thought if I was going to come home, it would be better not to delay. Why? Is there something I don't know?'

'Later, Felicity.' He sweeps the creams and lotions and make-up from the dressing table straight into one of her open cases which he zips and places firmly outside the room.

She says, 'You are so over-reacting. You'll give yourself a heart attack if you carry on like this.'

'For once, Felicity, you need to hear what I'm saying. Our marriage is over.'

Felicity stands with the pile of clothes in her arms, looking perplexed. 'I suppose Harriet told you about Meg?'

'She did.'

'I expect you're shocked and upset. So am I. But you know how poorly she was. We did the best for her but yesterday morning we couldn't wake her. She'd gone. Slipped away in the night.' She places the pile of clothes on the landing floor and comes into the room.

Edward sinks onto his bed and puts his head in his hands. 'I can't take it all in.'

Felicity's voice softens. 'I'm sure she would have waited for you if she could. I know she was special to you, and you to her.' She sits beside him and puts an arm around his shoulder. 'I loved her too, you know. She was a lovely dog.'

He doesn't look up. He cannot give in to Felicity's play of gentleness. It is an act he no longer trusts and he leaps from her embrace, brushing her aside, heading down the stairs to the kitchen, where Harriet is hanging about looking uncertain with a pile of bed linen.

'What's happening?' she says.

'Your mother will not be staying long,' says Edward. 'Take that lot upstairs.'

337

He wonders if James and Kate are hiding in their room and overheard everything. Too bad if they did. They are both old enough to understand that relationships are rarely straightforward. And Felicity doesn't even know about Marianne yet. No doubt she will go beserk.

He heads for the orchard, his mind awash with unsavoury thoughts. He remembers seeing a programme about consciousness a few years earlier during which Professor Susan Greenfield explained that all our different strands of thought were neurones in our brain grouping together in separate 'parties', the loudest being the one we attended to at any given moment. This, she said, was consciousness. When we think about something different or change our mind about an issue, it is merely another group of neurones making their presence felt. He remembers being impressed by the analogy. If this is so, he has at least three almost equally loud parties all competing for attention: Felicity, Meg and Marianne. He is overwhelmed. Perhaps his brain will shut down completely.

Beyond the olive tree is a newly created mound. *Poor old Meg,* he thinks, hunkering down, running his hand over the roughly replaced sods of grass. He apologises for going away, for leaving her, knowing he had no choice, but guilty that his absence created stress that possibly tipped her over the edge. He closes his eyes, desperate not to lose control lest Felicity thinks she is the cause of his grief. He stays for several minutes before wandering slowly back to the house, his head down.

He has almost reached the gravel when for the third time in the day his heart jumps. It is a woman with short blonde hair carrying something covered in a checked cloth.

Jessica.

'I heard you were home,' she shouts.

He freezes, wondering in seconds what she is doing loose in the village. Another set of neurones begin to socialise. He assesses the distance between where he is standing and the back door.

'I've come to apologise. This is a peace offering,' says Jessica.

'I don't want your pies, or your apologies. You killed my dog.' He moves to side-step her, heading for the house. 'You – killed – my – dog.' As he says the words again, the truth sinks in.

Jessica follows him. 'Did she die? I didn't realise. Please hear me,' she pleads. 'I've had a few problems. I wasn't very well. I stopped taking my medication. I thought I was okay, that I could do without. I didn't mean to do so much harm. It was a mistake. I'm very sorry. I've been in hospital. I'm better now.'

'I thought you were being held on suspicion of murdering your husband,' says Edward, walking faster.

'A misunderstanding. I'm on bail. It will be sorted.'

'It won't be "sorted",' says Edward, turning. 'Whatever did or did not happen with your husband, you still poisoned my dog. The RSPCA is dealing with it.'

Jessica appears not to hear him. 'I've brought you a cheque to cover the cost of the window.'

He takes it. 'And the phone calls to Marianne? I know it was you.'

'Tell her I'm sorry.'

Edward stares into her bug eyes, wondering why he didn't notice the hints of madness when first they met. 'You must leave me alone now, Jessica. Completely alone. I'm sorry you're ill, but you've done too much harm.'

As he reaches the door, Felicity steps outside and confronts Jessica. 'You've got a nerve turning up here after what you've done. Are you mad? Stalking my husband, poisoning Meg … I thought you were a friend of mine.' She takes a step forward and slaps Jessica hard across the face.

Jessica gasps and touches her cheek. She looks alarmed. 'It's not me he's seeing. It's some woman from London called Marianne.'

Felicity looks first at Jessica and then at Edward. 'Marianne? Fanclub Marianne? What's she got to do with anything?' She pauses for a moment and then begins to nod. 'Oh, I see. I knew there must be something. Now you're the one with a secret lover. You didn't waste much time.'

'Come inside, Felicity,' says Edward, ushering her into the kitchen. He shuts the back door on Jessica, his mind all over the place, knowing he will have to explain everything, when he would rather have waited until later in the evening.

'So,' says Felicity, turning on him in the middle of the kitchen. 'Marianne?'

'I was on my own for nine months. You never gave me any reason to suppose you would be back.' And he sits down at the table, defeated.

Meanwhile, Marianne stands looking out of the window of her room at Heath Gardens, drinking a mug of tea and watching a hen strut across the small lawn in front of the house. It is black, with speckled red-brown plumage on its neck and breast. It looks at her quizzically, head on one side, and then marches off towards the perimeter wall and starts pecking under two bright yellow dahlias.

Across the road and over the hedge there is what looks like a field of onions. And at the top of a slope, on the horizon, the unmistakable shape of the red sandstone sail-less windmill that can be seen from the back of the Deer Orchard. The top part of Felicity's wind turbine is also in view although the house is out of sight in a dip.

For a few delightful days, Marianne believed that this village of Broadclyst would hold her future. She imagined upping sticks from Beckenham to live here with Edward among the thatch and the yellow-ochre limewash. She was beginning to get used to the idea that there was an alternative to being alone, but now all their discussions are falling away like the leaves of autumn. Delight has turned to dust. The holiday feeling has evaporated and it seems a lifetime since the conversation on the beach.

Marry me … After Edward's indirect proposal, Marianne stared out to sea, watching boats bobbing on the waves and thinking about her response. The old-fashioned advice was to refuse three times. 'Are you asking?'

'I'm asking.'

'I will.'

A pushover. She should have resisted at least until they came back to the mainland.

Panic settles in her soul. She needs her home, her friends and Holly, but she is trapped with nothing but her wild imagination and her fears. She can 'what if' until she is exhausted. She knows she shouldn't. But old conditioning resurfaces under stress.

What if he's seduced by her beauty again?

What if he chooses family familiarity over risk?

I am not Felicity.

I am not good enough.

What if he loves her again?

This is the old Marianne; the menopausal Marianne; the Marianne subdued by the Cow-Charmaine.

She has no power. If anyone has rights and power it is Felicity. She might come and shout those rights at Marianne. '*Leave my husband alone.*' *My* husband. So possessive.

'*He doesn't belong to you or anyone. He never did. He can make up his own mind now, he owes you nothing.*'

'*You snake-in-the-grass. Worming your way into his pants because your husband's dead. You're nothing but a cheap slut. My Ted won't give you house room when the lust wears off. Lust! That's all it is. He's sex-starved. Been frustrated for years. Poor Ted. My fault, I admit. I hold up my hands. He was so loyal. But I'm back now and I can be a siren too. I've learned a few tricks from my Italian lover; I've read* 50 Shades of Grey. *And I know Ted in the trouser department better than you ever will. We've had four kids; loads of sex at our prime time. You can never have that.'*

Marianne searches in her case and finds her old journal. She intended to write while on the islands but she couldn't concentrate. While her emotions are high, she should try to fill some pages with her thoughts. Something positive may come from the pain. Potential novel-writing material. Potential for the sequel to *Lydia*.

Later, Edward returns to Heath Gardens to take Marianne for some supper. He is completely exhausted and emotionally drained. She invites him into her room.

He says, 'Nothing has changed between us. Please trust me. Felicity wants to come home, but I no longer want to be with her. This is a blip.'

'You're still married.'

'Only in name. I love *you*.'

'I want to believe you.' She sinks onto the bed.

The question of undoing a marriage, however dysfunctional and no matter what he said to Felicity, goes against the grain. When it was Felicity's decision, he had no control over the situation. Now he is the one being challenged to loosen the knot, he is troubled. Her softness over Meg had reminded him of times so very long ago when they had been happy. A tiny remnant of something lost had revealed itself. He is trying to ignore it.

'I am so very tired,' says Edward, falling to his knees in

front of Marianne. 'The last couple of hours have been hell. Not only dealing with Felicity, but Jessica turned up with a pie and told her about you before I had a chance. And Meg died while we were away.' He lays his head in her lap and clings to her as a child might and she strokes his hair while he breathes her essence and feels her warmth. Since arriving home, he has been trying to keep his emotions in check and now they ooze out of him and into the folds of Marianne's dress. It is a measure of his trust.

He stays like this for some time, releasing the preceding hours of tension until his body feels capable of normal functioning. Then he drives them both down to the New Inn where they sit across a table in the restaurant area, barely speaking.

'Don't shut me out,' says Marianne. 'I want to know; I don't want to guess. You know what I'm like, I'll imagine all sorts.'

'Remember Tresco and everything we said,' says Edward. 'Nothing will change. This is a delay. An inconvenience.'

But his certainty of words is not matched by certainty within. Felicity is a powerful force; a woman who always seems to have her way.

In the late evening, when Edward and Felicity sit in uncomfortable silence in the living room and James and Kate have gone to visit their friends in Budleigh Salterton, Harriet comes in with a tray on which are mugs of tea and a plate of biscuits. She sits down, eyes her parents, takes a deep breath and launches.

'You know I love you, Mum, but I think you've a bloody cheek coming back like this and expecting to move in here as if nothing's happened. It's not fair on Dad. Don't kid yourself that you two are somehow going to sort out your differences.

They're too ingrained. You were leading separate lives long before you ran off with Gianni. Dad needs a chance at happiness now.'

'Aren't we Miss Hoity-Toity-Holier-than-Thou all of a sudden? Since when did you become the expert on marriage guidance?' Felicity stiffens in her chair. She takes a biscuit and dunks it in her tea.

'Harriet, this isn't necessary,' says Edward.

'Yes it is. You are pussyfooting around, Dad, and you cannot afford to prevaricate when another person's feelings are at stake.'

'Huh, Marianne, I suppose. What about my feelings?' says Felicity.

Harriet ignores the comment. 'I'm not a child any more. My interests are for both of you separately, not just staying together for the sake of the kids. Mum, you took a chance and blew it. Now it's Dad's turn. It's taken him a while to readjust. He was totally shocked when you left. He may have stopped loving you, but he was resigned to you spending the rest of your lives being miserable together—'

'That's a horrible thing to say.'

'Harriet, please!' says Edward. But there is no stopping her.

'I like Marianne. So do James and Kate. Rach will too when she gets to know her. And Chris. She's good for Dad at this time in his life. And they've not been rash or foolish. They've waited until now to make a commitment – and now you've blown back in and upset everyone.'

'A commitment! You've made a commitment?' More scowling at Edward. Then she turns back to Harriet. 'Your dad and I are still married. She knows that.'

'In name only. She's had a dreadful time with her husband dying. It's taken a lot to get her to take a chance with Dad. I know because I had to persuade her that he was worth it. That he really cares about her, that he wouldn't let her down.'

'This is news to me,' says Edward, shrugging.

'She believed she was living in Mum's shadow. That she couldn't match up. Ha! Ironic! Olivia the witch tried to convince her that she wasn't good enough for Dad because she isn't like you. Such a joke.'

Harriet pauses and Felicity is silenced. Edward is amazed by his daughter's passion. So often he finds her reserved and distant, but in times of crisis, she demonstrates her love in overt and powerful ways.

When Harriet has gone to bed, Edward says to Felicity, 'You will have to go as soon as possible.'

'Where, exactly? We are joint owners of this property.'

Edward wishes he had sought legal advice when Felicity left. He takes a chance. 'If we go the legal route, it will cost a lot of money and even if our assets are split in half, it wouldn't amount to significantly more for either of us than if we each stick to our original agreement. Except if I remember, it wasn't an agreement. You went, and told me I could have the house. In a court of law, I am the wronged party. You chose to leave. I doubt there would be much sympathy for you.'

'This Marianne must be something special,' says Felicity. 'But I suppose now her husband's dead, she wants company.'

'Wrap it however you want, Flick, but we are going to make a new life together.'

'If she comes to live here, she will regret it.'

'Bloody hell, Flick. Is that a threat?'

'I still have many friends in the village.'

'Don't be so sure. They weren't too impressed when you absconded.'

Felicity gives a harsh laugh. 'Ever the dramatic choice of words.'

The following morning, Edward goes to pick up Marianne from the guest house to take her to the station. She looks tired and is edgy when he greets her. He detects anxiety and suspects she hasn't slept very well. His heart reacts and he hugs her tightly.

They drive to the station and he gives a censored version of the previous night's events with Felicity.

'It's all in the open now,' he says. 'And I'm sorry you can't stay longer as we planned.'

'It has been a most magical time on Scilly,' says Marianne, 'and for that I thank you.'

It is with heavy heart that he waves her off on the train. It wasn't meant to be like this. They were supposed to enjoy a few more days and discuss plans with James and Kate and Harriet. The majestic balloon in which they soared above the islands of Scilly has crash-landed in a tree. And he knows Felicity will not give up easily.

43

New Beginnings

To: Edward Harvey
From: Marianne Hayward
Date: 14th September 2012, 15.18
Subject: Future

Dear Edward,
Today I watched a young woman cross the road in front of
my car at the traffic lights near Waitrose. She was
somebody's daughter, somebody's Harriet or Rachel or
Holly. She was pretty, slim and petite, wearing a short black
coat, tied against the cold; thick tights, black boots and a
black hat; effortless autumn chic. Her brown hair was
straight and glossy, blowing in the breeze as she hastened
into the town, nose down and determined. She would be
twenty-something and she seemed to have it all.
In those few seconds I wondered at her life; imagined
she was cohabiting and madly in love with a good-
looking young man who adored her; that she was
working for a large and important company in a job with
prospects. She had two parents, both alive, living in the
country but not too far away, and she had a wide circle
of friends with whom to socialise. I envied her because I
had given her the perfect life.
But I was aware I didn't want to go back to when I was
young, because no matter how much fun, the future scared
me. There were always decisions to be made and pressures

to choose wisely. And I didn't really want to be her now, because even though I had imagined her life full of treats and pleasures, I might have been wrong. And even if true, she had no idea of the challenges that lie in her future.

We people of a certain age may recognise our possible future as one of retirement and slowing down; of losses of people who are dear to us; of increasing aches and pains and probabilities stacking up against health and general well-being. But we can still dream of something better or different; still hope for surprises.

Meeting you for the third time has been such a joyous interlude after my few years of sorrows. It is as if you saved me yet again. I dared to dream while we were on Scilly. I dared to love you in the romantic sense, the girlish sense and the madly-deeply passionate sense. After Johnny died, I never believed I could feel that thrill again. But you must do what is right for you. You made no promises that cannot be undone. Do not feel any pressure from me when you decide. You are free and we can still be friends. I'd like that. To be friends was always what I wanted from the start. These past few weeks have been an unexpected bonus, a treat, a present which I will always treasure.

I really do love you, Edward, and in loving you I set you free from any obligation.

Marianne

To: Marianne Hayward
From: Edward Harvey
Date: 14th September 2012, 19.39
Subject: Re: Future

My dear Marianne,
I thought to phone you – and I will later – but a letter

348

such as yours deserves a considered response in kind, written from the heart.

You are my life now. If I stay with Felicity, we will lead an unfulfilled future of disagreements and disillusionment. She no longer loves me and has said as much. She stopped loving me long before she left; long before I finally gave up on her. It is purely for practical reasons that she wants to come home, and what kind of life does that promise? We would never find our way back to physical intimacy. It would be as it was before she left: hostility with no compensation. Am hoping to have a few more years of health and enjoyment before the inevitable decline. Am hoping for some of the dreams of which you write.

If you'll have me, I want to try to make our relationship work. It has been so long since I loved and was loved back and on Scilly I came properly alive for the first time in years. Harriet approves. Indeed, she told me that she believes both Felicity and I will ultimately be happier if we lead our own lives – as we have been doing for long enough. I don't want to be without you.

All my love,

Edward x

To be happy for a while is as much as he dares hope and he resolves to grasp this new opportunity much as a burnished conker bursts from out of its prickly shell.

Later, he calls her as promised, to reassure again and catch up further. 'I'm beginning to enjoy our chats on the phone,' he says. 'I miss you more than ever. Now I know what it is to be with you properly. It's difficult to find the words. If I were a songwriter, I would write you a song.'

'I appreciate the thought,' says Marianne. 'I feel the same. It's the dizzying stage. I expect it will pass.'

He laughs and tells her he has had to go straight back to meetings at work and is incredibly busy ahead of the students arriving. 'But the big news is that I've decided to resign with effect from the start of the Spring term. I know it's an awkward time to leave, but with so much to organise on the home front and opportunities that may ensue from the documentary, it's the only way. I will offer to fill gaps in a part-time capacity until the end of the academic year. But come January, I will be free to focus fully on all the changes we discussed on Scilly.'

'Such good news,' says Marianne, excitedly. 'I can't believe this is really going to happen.'

'Felicity thinks I'm having a midlife crisis and it will pass. She says I'm acting out of character; taking risks.'

'Not all midlife changes should be seen as crises,' says Marianne. 'Evolution and adaptation is good. Look at me and the writing. You've been unsettled in your job for a while. It's time to move on.'

'That's what I tell her. But she always has to be right, always has to have the last word. Also, I am not taking a risk with you. I have known you nearly all my life.'

Not so happy with the news is Gemma. She is at her desk behind her computer when he tells her and she is visibly upset. She takes a tissue from her bag and dabs her eyes. 'I hope you'll come back and see us sometimes.'

'You'll probably see me often until the end of the year,' says Edward.

'I've enjoyed working for you,' says Gemma. 'It wasn't the same when you were in London. I hope you'll forgive me saying, but I've always had a soft spot for you. When your wife left, I hoped … I wished …' But her voice trails away and she shakes her head as she appears to realise that whatever her wishes, they can never come to fruition.

'Your hard work and zeal have made me look more efficient than I am and I thank you,' says Edward, embarrassed.

To: Marianne Hayward
From: Edward Harvey
Date: 19th September 2012, 22.39
Subject: Re: Future

Dear Mari,
It appears that the untangling of our assets is going to be more complicated than envisaged, not least because Felicity's plans to open a new restaurant mean she has vested interest in the produce from the Deer Orchard. With Kate's ideas to expand the animal and vegetable production side over the next few years, Felicity doesn't want to miss out on what she sees as her rightful share. She is also after some of the proceeds from the wind turbine and says she won't leave the house until she has written agreement on all that she believes is her entitlement. I don't want to bore you with details but I have decided that legal help will ensure I don't lose out, arguing that Felicity's restaurant profits might also be considered part of the joint pot if they are actualised as a result of free produce.
The wrangling looks like it may go on for some time, but at least there are more immediate moves to sign over part of the Deer Orchard to James and Kate with view to releasing some capital for me.
love,
Edward x

Then Rachel visits and despite being instrumental in the timing of her mother's return, and against Edward's expectations, sides with Harriet in her belief that it would be fruitless to try to repair the marriage. Not that he has any intention now he has recovered from the shock.

Another piece of good news to share with Marianne and he reaches for the phone, not wanting to delay.

'Rachel said Felicity was selfish and controlling. That she walked out on three kids who although not exactly children any more, still needed help and support while making their way in the world. Felicity was silenced until Harriet broke the news about Rick. Then World War Three began. She said I should have sacked him.'

Marianne listens, sympathises, empathises and offers support should Harriet want to speak to her.

Edward continues, 'Kate said to me, "Don't you dare sack Rick, at least not until we've developed a more self-managing system with less digging". Then she and Felicity argued about who would be giving him orders now I was taking a back seat. Kate said, "This will be our home, Felicity. You and I can't both be telling Rick what to do. I want greater focus on crop rotation and companion planting. I'll seek your advice, but as I'll be paying him, I'm the one who will give him instructions". You have to admire her spirit. It's what I should have done, a long time ago; stood up to Flick instead of opting for the quiet life.'

'What's done is done,' says Marianne. 'The future calls. We must look forward, not back. We could all do things differently with hindsight.'

Later, Edward overhears Kate pacifying Felicity by suggesting she take charge of the added-value products for the markets.

'You will have all the facilities at your new restaurant,' says Kate. 'And all the know-how. If we can agree on a price for the fresh produce, the profits on the added-value items will be all yours.'

He continues to be impressed by the diplomacy of his virtual daughter-in-law.

To: Marianne Hayward
From: Edward Harvey
Date: 21st September 2012, 23.04
Subject: Re: Future

Dear Mari,

Felicity is now committed to buying the vacant premises she saw in the neighbouring village of Pinhoe and is busy planning the refurbishment of the kitchens, the dining area and the upstairs flat. Chris is apparently talking of returning to work as chef once she has the restaurant ready to run. At least she won't be in Broadclyst. She's also put a stop to Jessica visiting. I never did explain exactly what happened on the day we came back from Scilly. Felicity told her where to stick her pies in no uncertain terms. And she hit her. The latest news from Olivia is that Jessica has been re-arrested and charged with the murder of her second husband. There are also rumours about the first, but no details. At least that gets her out of the way. It's like a bad dream.

Harriet moves in with Rick tomorrow. Felicity keeps trying to deter her with warnings of his reputation. Strangely enough, I find myself siding with Harriet. Rick has changed and I'm optimistic. Indeed, since Kate began discussing her expansive plans for the Deer Orchard, Rick expects his employment prospects to increase and even extend to animal management when the livestock is re-introduced.

The documentary is currently being edited and polished and is expected to air soon after Christmas, so there

may be some midweek stopovers in London. I am
almost ready to give you the latest draft of the book.
I will visit soon and stay the weekend if that's okay.
I can't wait to see you again.
love,
Edward x

Meanwhile, Marianne is lost without the ritual of returning to work. She looks at her empty diary and sets about filling it, not wishing to brood endlessly on matters far away, over which she has no control. She phones Taryn to arrange a game of tennis before the winter sets in.

'I knew you were meant for each other,' says Taryn. 'For each other's second chance. Imagine that!'

Then Marianne plans a couple of dinner dates with ex-colleagues to ensure they don't lose touch, a pre-Christmas book signing in a local shop and a couple more library talks in Bromley. She still has a long way to go in spreading the word about *Lydia*. There is also much communication with Gillian Fylde about the Education Pack.

Edward phones and asks if she heard the news report that the Arctic ice cap has shrunk this summer more than ever and that the glaciers are melting at an alarming rate.

'The experts believe it is due to man-made global warming,' he says. 'Rising sea levels will potentially threaten existence of low lying islands. Those in the Pacific and Indian oceans are at risk, but what about our own Scillies?'

It's good to hear his voice, even if it is to tell her about a news report. While he elaborates, she checks out the story online and is similarly alarmed. 'Your programme has the potential to turn outmoded attitudes towards environmentalism upside down. The new generations need to learn new ways of living.'

'So much to do, so little time,' he says. 'As soon as Felicity moves out, you must come to stay again, but for now it's probably best I come to you. As things stand, I can manage weekends on the fifth and twenty-sixth and possibly the odd weeknight between, when I'm meeting Flying Owl.'

'That would be lovely,' says Marianne. 'And I have news too. My offer for the flat in Coppercone Lane has been accepted.'

'Are you sure you want to be so close to Taryn?'

'It's a lovely street and an easy walk to Beckenham Junction. Perfect for use when we're in town and Taryn will keep an eye on it when we're elsewhere.'

'Have you considered any further where elsewhere might be?' says Edward.

For a moment she hesitates. Part of her would like a fresh start in somewhere new to both of them and far away from Felicity. But the most practical option is for Edward to be close to some of his children. Forging new friendships post-retirement is tricky and she will find it easier if there are already some contacts in their chosen area.

'Would you still prefer to be in Broadclyst?' she says. 'I'd be perfectly happy there, despite Felicity.'

He expresses delight. 'And as soon as both of us have finance available, and you are able to visit down here, we will look for somewhere,' says Edward.

'Perhaps we should have a dog,' says Marianne. 'Someone for you to walk and to keep me company when you're away.'

'I'd like that,' he says. 'Another Border collie would be just the thing, if you agree. I appreciate the way they think. Kate and James intend to have one for when they get their sheep. They would look after ours when we're in London.'

'We could try to find siblings,' suggests Marianne.

'I expect Felicity to be moving out in December, so we

could have our first Christmas together down here.'

'Christmas in Broadclyst,' says Marianne. 'How delightful.' And she imagines an old-fashioned village scene of carol singers, mince pies and neighbourliness; of trees decorated with tinsel, baubles and fairy lights; of frost-covered fields and open log fires in cosy pubs. It will be far removed from the previous year when she was so miserable and insular, she couldn't wait for the holiday season to pass so she could get back to the normality of work.

'I hope you haven't changed your mind about marrying me,' says Edward. 'When my divorce comes through.'

'Of course not, but I don't want fuss,' says Marianne. 'We'll leave the fuss for the children, if and when they want fuss.'

Later in the evening, Holly calls and tells Marianne she is bringing Will to meet her. *This can only mean one thing!*

The old Marianne would have been overwhelmed by so much emotion. She would have analysed and weighed-up and beaten every pro and con until they were squeezed of life-force. But she is tougher now. After years of anxieties, decades of being a martyr to her chattering brain, she releases all her doubts and fears, hands over her trust to Edward and the fates and believes in the end, all will be sorted.

Epilogue

It is over a decade since Edward opened an email from Marianne Hayward via Friends Reunited, the consequences of which neither he nor she could ever have realised at the time. He remembers it because it was on the eve of a party in November 2001; one simple communication that has ultimately altered their life paths in far-reaching ways.

On a chilly damp evening, the twenty-sixth of October, they go to see *The Rivals* at the Ashcroft Theatre in Fairfield Halls in Croydon. It is a performance by a young and inventive group of actors called *Creative Cows* who are based near Exeter and are already known to Edward. Their company name derives from the fact that they rehearse on a farm.

Six players double up the parts, the ladies wearing long cage skirts with bloomers clearly visible underneath, the gentlemen with colourful jackets that can be easily swapped for something plain. The setting is spartan, simple and charming, scene changes indicated by music while the actors carry white-painted chairs, as if in a dance, to different positions on the stage.

Edward and Marianne sit in row L. When Marianne bought the tickets, she told him it was symbolic.

As the opening scene unfolds, he knows she is remembering …
Lydia and Lucy … aged eleven.

It has been forty-four years since they played their roles on the tiny stage at Brocklebank Hall – sweet young children, uncut rocks, unknown lives ahead, perhaps retrospectively, the tiniest clues of the teacher and the archaeologist in the making.

Now when Lydia and Lucy speak their opening lines, Edward reaches over and takes hold of Marianne's hand. Their eyes meet. Their story has come full circle, from inauspicious beginnings when they barely exchanged a friendly word, to an intertwining of hearts and minds and lives.

Meeting Lydia

"Edward Harvey. Even thinking his name made her tingle with half-remembered childlike giddiness. Edward Harvey, the only one from Brocklebank to whom she might write if she found him."

Marianne Hayward, teacher of psychology and compulsive analyser of the human condition, is in a midlife turmoil. After twenty years of happy marriage, she comes home one day to find her charming husband in the kitchen talking to the glamorous Charmaine. All her childhood insecurities resurface from a time when she was bullied at a boys' prep school. She becomes jealous and possessive and the arguments begin.

Teenage daughter Holly persuades her to join Friends Reunited which results in both fearful and nostalgic memories of prep school as Marianne wonders what has become of the bullies. But there was one boy in her class who was never horrible to her: the clever and enigmatic Edward Harvey, on whom she developed her first crush. Perhaps the answer to all her problems lies in finding Edward again …

Meeting Lydia is a book about childhood bullying, midlife crises, obsession, jealousy and the ever-growing trend of internet relationships. It is the prequel to *A Meeting of a Different Kind* and the first part of a trilogy, the third part being *The Alone Alternative*.

Paperback: 9781848767126   *Ebook: 9781848768574*

A Meeting of a Different Kind

"Taryn thinks about Mr Perfect Edward Harvey and the news that he will be visiting London over the next few weeks. Marianne keeps saying he isn't the philandering type; Taryn doesn't believe a word of it. There isn't a man alive who doesn't have the potential to philander, given the right material to philander with ...'

When archaeologist Edward Harvey's wife Felicity inherits almost a million, she gives up her job, buys a restaurant and, as a devotee of Hugh Fernley-Whittingstall, starts turning their home into a small eco-farm. Edward is not happy, not least because she seems to be losing interest in him.

Taryn is a borderline manic-depressive, a scheming minx, a seductress and user of men. When her best-friend Marianne says Edward is not the philandering type, Taryn sees a challenge and concocts a devious plan to meet him at the British Museum – a meeting that will have far reaching and destructive consequences on both their lives.

Set in Broadclyst and Beckenham, with a chapter on the Isles of Scilly, *A Meeting of a Different Kind* is the stand-alone sequel to *Meeting Lydia*, continuing the story from the perspectives of two very different characters. Like its prequel, it will appeal to fans of adult fiction, especially those interested in the psychology of relationships.

Paperback: 9781780883250   *Ebook: 9781780887739*